PRAISE FOR ASHFALL

The book is well written and its protagonists are well-drawn, particularly the non_____ mechanically inclin_____ is a riveting tale of survival

—**Publishers Weekly**

Mullin's debut novel is carefully researched and vividly imagined, a post-apocalyptic backdrop for an intense tale with adventure, graphic violence, and two young teenagers learning to love. A sure hit for older readers who like intense action, a believable narrator, and a dystopia that could actually happen.

—**Horn Book**

Readers will be propelled along to find what happens to Alex, the environment, and his love life while also asking what they would do in a similar disaster. First time author Mullin has a winner here!

—**Library Media Connection, starred review**

ASHFALL by Mike Mullin is an amazing debut novel and seems to have captured the hearts and minds of review___ ___ ___ ___ pages and unable to stop reading, will predict this is going to be very popular with young adult readers. Fans of **Gone** in particular will be demanding this is available on the day of the October release since the buzz is out there.

—**Diane Chen, School Library Journal Practically Paradise blog**

I found it hard to stop reading ASHFALL. Common sense told me to quit at midnight, but I soon turned the light on again and read two more hours.

—**Carol Chittenden, Owner, Eight Cousins Children's Books**

Mike Mullin's ASHFALL glows and throbs with everyday life and the business of survival in a dystopic future, after an unthinkable disaster.

—**Richard Peck, Newbery Medal-winning author of A Year Down Yonder and Three Quarters Dead**

The scariest apocalypse is one that could really happen. Mike Mullin's ASHFALL is way too real for comfort: you'll live the panic and despair and know that all of this could really happen. It will be a long time before you get the taste of volcanic ash out of your mouth. This isn't fantasy, this is real.

—Michael Grant, New York Times bestselling author of *Gone, Lies, Hunger,* and *Plague*

Mike Mullin catapults readers into a surreal, cataclysmic world that will hold them until the last page. If you aren't exhausted by the end of the first thirty pages, you may want to check your pulse. ASHFALL is the perfect book for reluctant teen readers who 'can never find anything good to read.'

—Dave Richardson, The Blue Marble Children's Bookstore, International Reading Association's READING TODAY book reviewer, and Cincinnati State College children's literature professor

*This is riveting. Fans of post-apocalyptic thrillers like **The Hunger Games** will love ASHFALL.*

—Cinda Williams Chima, *New York Times* bestselling author of *The Exiled Queen* and *The Warrior Heir*

I loved every minute of it, I really did. I read a lot of teen survival stuff, it's kind of my thing. And this one does it just right—the way I wish more books would do it. It is very realistic. These are characters I can root for. And there is so much texture, so much background. This world is completely realized. . . . I cannot recommend this book highly enough.

—Karen's Reviews, Goodreads.com (#1 ranked reviewer), and fiction manager, Barnes & Noble/Union Square (NYC)

One word: Wow. I was blown away by this book. ASHFALL sucked me in and wouldn't let go until it was three a.m. and I fell asleep. I fell in love with this fine literary work. And what a cliffhanger! I cannot wait for the sequel. This book is on its way to stardom.

—Flamingnet.com, Top Choice Award, 10 out of 10 Rating, 13-year-old Reviewer

Because of Mullin's great writing I could smell the sulfur in the air, hear the ear deafening blast, feel the ash and snow crunch beneath my feet.

—Bending the Spine blog

Ashfall truly is a harrowing read.

—Bibliosaurus Text blog

The little details were all there, and while they may not all have been strictly necessary, they all come together to add depth and richness to the story that set it apart from many other post-apocalyptic books I've read in the past.
—**Bibliotropic blog**

I devoured this book, reading the mammoth 466 pages in just a couple of days. I could not put it down! Mullin's writing style is reminiscent of Rick Riordan's.
—**Bound and Determined to Find a Good Read blog**

I laughed, I cried, I fell in love with this fine literary work.
—**Flamingnet.com Top Choice Award**

One of the most intense books I read this year.
—**Fragments of Fiction blog**

This is not a boy book or a girl book. It will appeal to both.
—**Goddess Librarian blog**

Ashfall è un bellissimo libro, ben scritto e coinvolgente.
—**Sonia's Reviews**

Some parts are so heart-wrenching, I gasped out loud and put my hand over my mouth.
—**Mrs. Readerpants blog**

This book is going to have you running in the opposite direction like a bat out of Hell.
—**Watercolor Moods blog**

It's the mix of action, science, thrills, romance, and the nitty-gritty details that make this book so gripping and good.
—**Our Time in Juvie blog**

Hands down the best debut I've read all year, dare I say best book I've read all year, and definitely in my top ten books EVER!!
—**The Reading Nook blog**

I loved every second, even the sad and painful parts.
—**Sizzling Reads blog**

Mike Mullin's Ashfall is a book I will be recommending to all martial artists.
—**Brian Myers, Third Degree Black Belt and Certified Instructor.**

The book is great. I love it.
—**We Fancy Books blog**

I was captivated by this book from the start, and I think everyone should read it.

—**Reads with Wreckless Abandon blog**

Mike Mullin to the list of authors who have kept me up way too late reading their novels.

—**bookdads.com**

This book will make you want to both cry and cheer, and definitely makes you want to hug everyone you love. It's fantastic, and I cannot wait until the sequel.

—**thekams.wordpress.com**

My hat goes off to you, Mr. Mullins! You have written an end of the world as we know it story, but infused it with hope. Hope in love. Hope in humanity. Survival is key, but who we choose to surround ourselves with and how and what we do to survive should be the most important parts of the journey.

—**galleysmith.com**

It was a very refreshing take on the genre and I look forward to the next book!

—**Laura McCoy, Goodreads**

A thriller that will suck in even the most reluctant teen reader.

—**goodschools.org**

ASHFALL

By Mike Mullin

Tanglewood • Terre Haute, IN

Cover photograph by Ana Correal
Design by Amy Alick Perich

Tanglewood Publishing, Inc.
4400 Hulman Street
Terre Haute, IN 47803
www.tanglewoodbooks.com

Printed by Maple-Vail Press, York, PA, USA
10 9 8 7 6 5 4 3

ISBN 978-1-933718-74-3

Library of Congress Cataloging-in-Publication Data

Mullin, Mike.
    Ashfall / Mike Mullin.
        p. cm.
    Includes bibliographical references.
    Summary: After the eruption of the Yellowstone supervolcano destroys his city and its surroundings, fifteen-year-old Alex must journey from Cedar Falls, Iowa, to Illinois to find his parents and sister, trying to survive in a transformed landscape and a new society in which all the old rules of living have vanished.
    ISBN 978-1-933718-55-2
    [1. Volcanoes--Fiction. 2. Survival--Fiction. 3. Science fiction.] I. Title.
    PZ7.M9196As 2011
    [Fic]--dc22
                                        2011007133

For Margaret,
my Darla

Chapter 1

*Civilization exists by
geological consent, subject to
change without notice.*
—Will Durant

I was home alone on that Friday evening. Those who survived know exactly which Friday I mean. Everyone remembers where they were and what they were doing, in the same way my parents remembered 9/11, but more so. Together we lost the old world, slipping from that cocoon of mechanized comfort into the hellish land we inhabit now. The pre-Friday world of school, cell phones, and refrigerators dissolved into this post-Friday world of ash, darkness, and hunger.

But that Friday was pretty normal at first. I argued with Mom again after school. That was normal, too;

we fought constantly. The topics were legion: my poor study habits, my video games, my underwear on the bathroom floor—whatever. I remember a lot of those arguments. That Friday they only fueled my rage. Now they're little jewels of memory I hoard, hard and sharp under my skin. Now I'd sell my right arm to a cannibal to argue with Mom again.

Our last argument was over Warren, Illinois. My uncle and his family lived there, on a tiny farm near Apple River Canyon State Park. Mom had decided we'd visit their farm that weekend. When she announced this malodorous plan, over dinner on Wednesday, my bratty little sister, Rebecca, almost bounced out of her chair in delight. Dad responded with his usual benign lack of interest, mumbling something like, "Sounds nice, honey." I said I would not be going, sparking an argument that continued right up until they left without me on that Friday afternoon.

The last thing Mom said to me was, "Alex, why do you have to fight me on absolutely everything?" She looked worn and tired standing beside the minivan door, but then she smiled a little and held out her arms like she wanted a hug. If I'd known I might never get to argue with her again, maybe I would have replied. Maybe I would have hugged her instead of turning away.

Cedar Falls, Iowa, wasn't much, but it might as well have been New York City compared to Warren. Besides, I had my computer, my bike, and my friends in Cedar Falls. My uncle's farm just had goats. Stinky goats. The males smell as bad as anything short of a skunk, and I'll take skunk at a distance over goat up close any day.

So I was happy to wave goodbye to Mom, Dad, and the brat, but a bit surprised I'd won the argument. I'd been home alone before—I was almost sixteen, after all. But a whole weekend, that was new. It was a little disappointing to be left without some kind of warning, an admonition against wild parties and booze. Mom knew my social life too well, I guess. A couple of geeks and a board game I might manage; a great party with hot girls and beer would have been beyond me, sadly.

After I watched my family drive off, I went upstairs. The afternoon sun blazed through my bedroom window, so I yanked the curtains shut. Aside from the bed and dresser, my bedroom held a huge maple bookcase and desk that my dad had built a few years ago. I didn't have a television, which was another subject Mom and I fought about, but at least I had a good computer. The bookcase was filled with computer games, history books, and sci-fi novels in about equal proportions. Odd reading choices maybe, but I just thought of it as past and future history.

I'd decorated my floor with dirty clothes and my walls with posters, but only one thing in the room really mattered to me. In a wood-and-glass case above my desk, I displayed all my taekwondo belts: a rainbow of ten of them starting with white, yellow, and orange and ending in brown, red, and black. I'd been taking classes off and on since I was five. I didn't work at it until sixth grade, which I remember as the year of the bully. I'm not sure if it was my growth spurt, which stopped at a depressingly average size, or finally getting serious about martial arts, but nobody hassles me anymore. I suppose by now those belts are burnt or buried in ash—most likely both.

Anyway, I turned on my computer and stared at the cover of my trigonometry textbook while I waited for the computer to boot up. I used to think that teachers who gave homework on weekends should be forced to grade papers for an eternity in hell. Now that I have a sense of what hell might be like, I don't think grading papers forever would be that bad. As soon as Windows started, I pushed the trig book aside and loaded up *World of Warcraft.* I figured there'd be enough time to do my homework Sunday night.

None of my friends were online, so I flew my character to the Storm Peaks to work on daily quests and farm some gold. *WoW* used to hold my interest the way little else could. The daily quests were just challenging enough to keep my mind occupied, despite the fact that I'd done them dozens of times. Even gold farming, by far the most boring activity, brought the satisfaction of earning coin, making my character more powerful, achieving something. Every now and then I had to remind myself that it was all only ones and zeros in a computer in Los Angeles, or I might have gotten truly addicted. I wonder if anyone will ever play *World of Warcraft* again.

Three hours later and over 1,000 gold richer, I got the first hint that this would not be a normal Friday evening. There was a rumble, almost too low to hear, and the house shook a little. An earthquake, maybe, although we never have earthquakes in Iowa.

The power went out. I stood to open the curtains. I thought there might be enough light to read by, at least for a while.

Then it happened.

I heard a cracking noise, like the sound the hackberry tree in our backyard had made when Dad cut it down last year, but louder: a forest of hackberries, breaking together. The floor tilted, and I fell across the suddenly angled room, arms and legs flailing. I screamed but couldn't hear myself over the noise: a boom and then a whistling sound—incoming artillery from a war movie, but played in reverse. My back hit the wall on the far side of the room, and the desk slid across the floor toward me. I wrapped myself into a ball, hands over the back of my neck, praying my desk wouldn't crush me. It rolled, painfully clipped my right shoulder, and came to rest above me, forming a small triangular space between the floor and wall. I heard another crash, and everything shook violently for a second.

I'd seen those stupid movies where the hero gets tossed around like a rag doll and then springs up, unhurt and ready to fight off the bad guys. If I were the star in one of those, I suppose I would have jumped up, thrown the desk aside, and leapt to battle whatever malevolent god had struck my house. I hate to disappoint, but I just lay there, curled in a ball, shaking in pure terror. It was too dark under the desk to see anything beyond my quivering knees. Nor could I hear—the noise of those few violent seconds had left my ears ringing loudly enough to drown

out a marching band if one had been passing by. Plaster
dust choked the air, and I fought back a sneeze.

I lay in that triangular cave for a minute, maybe longer.
My body mostly quit shaking, and the ringing in my ears
began to fade. I poked my right shoulder gingerly; it felt
swollen, and touching it hurt. I could move the arm a little,
so I figured it wasn't broken. I might have lain there longer
checking my injuries, but I smelled something burning.

That whiff of smoke was enough to transform my sit-
here-trembling terror into get-the-hell-out-of-here terror.
There was enough room under the desk to unball myself,
but I couldn't stretch out. Ahead I felt a few hollow spaces
amidst a pile of loose books. I'd landed wedged against my
bookcase. I shoved it experimentally with my good arm—
it wasn't going anywhere.

The burning smell intensified. I slapped my left hand
against the desk above me and pushed upward. I'd moved
that heavy desk around by myself before, no problem. But
now, when I really needed to move it, nothing . . . it wouldn't
shift even a fraction of an inch.

That left trying to escape in the direction my feet pointed. But I couldn't straighten my legs—they bumped against
something just past the edge of the desk. I planted my feet
on the obstacle and pushed. It shifted a little. Encouraged, I
stretched my good arm through the shelves, placing my
hand against the back of the bookcase. And snatched it away
in shock—the wall behind the bookcase was warm. Not hot
enough to burn, but warm enough to give me an ugly mental picture of my fate if I couldn't escape—and soon.

I hadn't felt particularly claustrophobic at first. The violence of being thrown across the room left no time to feel anything but scared. Now, with the air heating up, terror rose from my gut. Trapped. Burned alive. Imagining my future got me hyperventilating. I inhaled a lungful of dust and choked, coughing.

Calm down, Alex, I told myself. I took two quick breaths in through my nose and puffed them out through my mouth—recovery breathing, like I'd use after a hard round of sparring in taekwondo. I could do this.

I slammed my hand back against the wall, locked my elbow, and shoved with my feet—hard. The obstacle shifted slightly. I bellowed and bore down on it, trying to snap my knees straight. There's a reason martial artists yell when we break boards—it makes us stronger. Something gave then; I felt it shift and heard the loud thunk of wood striking wood. Debris fell on my ankles—maybe chunks of plaster and insulation from the ceiling. A little kicking freed my legs, stirring up more dry, itchy dust.

I forced my way backward into the new hole. There were twelve, maybe sixteen inches of space before I hit something solid again. The air was getting hotter. Sweat trickled sideways off my face. I couldn't dislodge the blockage, so I bent at the waist, contorting my body around the desk into an L shape.

I kept shoving my body backward into the gap between a fallen ceiling joist and my desk, pushing myself upward along the tilted floor. A lurid orange light flickered down into the new space. When I'd wormed my way fully alongside the joist, I jammed my head and shoulders up through the broken ceiling into what used to be the unfinished attic above my room.

A wall of heat slammed into me, like opening the oven with my face too close. Long tendrils of flame licked into the attic above my sister's collapsed bedroom, cat tongues washing the rafters and underside of the roof decking with fire. Smoke billowed up and pooled under the peak of the roof. The front part of the attic had collapsed, joists leaning downward at crazy angles. What little I could see of the back of the attic looked okay. An almost perfectly round hole had been punched in the roof above my sister's bedroom. I glimpsed a coin of deep blue sky through the flames eating at the edges of the hole.

I dragged myself up the steeply angled joists, trying to reach the back of the attic. My palms were slippery with sweat, and my right shoulder screamed in pain. But I got it done, crawling upward with the heat at my back urging me on.

The rear of the attic looked normal—aside from the thick smoke and dust. I crawled across the joists, pushing through the loose insulation to reach the boxes of holiday decorations my mother had stored next to the pull-down staircase.

I struggled to open the staircase—it was meant to be pulled open with a cord from the hallway below. I crawled onto it to see if my weight would force it down. The springs resisted at first, but then the hatch picked up speed and popped open with a bang. It was all I could do to hold on and avoid tumbling into the hallway below. It bruised my knees pretty good, too. I flipped the folded segments of the stair open so I could step down to the second floor.

Keeping my head low to avoid the worst of the smoke, I scuttled down the hallway to the staircase. This part of the house seemed undamaged. When I reached the first floor, I heard banging and shouting from the backyard. I ran to the back door and glanced through the window. Our neighbor from across the street, Darren, was outside. I twisted the lock and threw the door open.

"Thank God," Darren said. "Are you okay, Alex?"

I took a few steps into the yard and stood with my hands on my knees, gulping the fresh air. It tasted sweet after the smoke-drenched dust I'd been breathing.

"You look like three-day-old dog crap. You okay?" Darren repeated.

I looked down at myself. Three-day-old dog crap was way too kind. Sweat had drenched my T-shirt and jeans, mixing with plaster dust, insulation, and smoke to form a vile gray-white sludge that coated my body. Somewhere along the way, I'd cut my palm without even feeling it. A smear of blood stained the knee of my jeans where my hand had just rested.

I glanced around; all the neighbors' houses seemed fine. Even the back of my house looked okay. Something sounded wrong, though. The ringing in my ears had mostly faded, but it still took a moment to figure it out: It was completely silent. There were no bird or insect noises. Not even crickets.

Just then Joe, Darren's husband, ran up behind him, carrying a three-foot wrecking bar. "Glad to see you're out. I was going to break the door down."

"Thanks. You guys call the fire department?"

"No—"

I gave him my best "what the hell?" look and extended both my palms.

"We tried—our house phone is dead, not even a dial tone. Cell says 'no service,' but that can't be; it's usually five bars here."

I thought about that for two, maybe three seconds and took off running.

Chapter 2

Darren and Joe yelled something behind me. I ignored them and made tracks as best I could. My bruised knees weren't helping, neither was my right shoulder. I probably looked kind of funny trying to sprint with my left arm pumping and my right cradled against my side.

Still, I made good time toward the fire station. Partway there, I realized I was being stupid. I'd taken off impulsively, needing to *do* something— anything—instead of jawing with Darren while my house burned down. I should have asked Darren and Joe to drive me or stopped to grab my bike from the garage. But by the time I'd thought through it, I was almost at the fire station.

I noticed a couple of weird things along the way. The traffic light I passed was out. That made the run faster—cars were stopping at the intersection and inching ahead, so I could dart through easily. I didn't see house lights on anywhere; it was early evening and fairly bright outside, but usually there were at least a few lights shining from somewhere. And in the distance to my left, four thin columns of smoke rose against the deep blue sky.

A generator growled at the side of the fire station as I ran up. The overhead door was open. I ran through and dodged around the truck. Three guys in fire pants and light blue T-shirts with "Cedar Falls Fire Department" on the back huddled around a radio. A woman dressed the same way sat in the cab of the ladder truck.

"Piece of crap equipment purchasing sticks us with," I heard one of them say as I approached.

"Hey kid, we're—" The guy broke off mid-sentence when he got a good look at me. Then he sniffed. "Burnt chicken on a stick, you've been in a fire. Y'ought to be at the hospital."

I was gasping, out of breath from the run. "I'm okay. . . . Neighbors been trying to call . . . "

"Yeah, piece of junk ain't working." The guy holding the radio mike slammed it down.

"My house is on fire."

"Where?"

"Six blocks away." I gave him my address.

A guy only slightly smaller than the fire truck beside him said, "We're not supposed to go out without telling dispatch—how we gonna get backup?"

"Screw that, Tiny. Kid's house is on fire. Load it up!"

They all grabbed helmets and fire coats off hooks on the wall. In seconds, I was sandwiched between Tiny and another guy in the back of the cab. I could just see the firefighter at the wheel over the mound of equipment separating the two rows of seats. She flicked a switch overhead, starting the sirens blaring, then threw the truck into gear. It roared down the short driveway and narrowly missed a car that failed to stop.

I glanced at Tiny once during the drive back to my house. His eyes were scrunched shut, and he was muttering some kind of prayer under his breath. The firefighter at the wheel laughed maniacally as she hurled the huge truck back and forth across the lanes, into oncoming traffic, and even halfway onto a sidewalk once. She swiveled in her seat to look at me, taking her eyes off the road completely. "Anyone else at home, kid?"

"No," I answered, hoping to keep the conversation short.

"Any pets?"

"No."

The ride couldn't have lasted more than a minute, but it felt longer. Between the crazy driving and Tiny's muttered prayer, I wished I'd run back home instead. The truck slammed to a stop in front of my house, and before I could get my stomach settled and even think about moving, the cab was empty. Both doors hung open. I groaned and slid toward the driver's side. Everything hurt: both knees, my right shoulder, the muscles in my calves and thighs: my eyes stung, my throat felt raw and, to top it all off, my head had started to ache.

Two huge steps led down from the cab. I stumbled on the first one and almost fell out of the truck backward. I caught myself on the grab bar mounted to the side of the truck. When I reached the ground, I kept one hand on the bar, holding myself upright.

The house was wrecked. It looked like a giant fist had descended from the heavens, punching a round hole in the roof above my sister's room and collapsing the front of the house. Flames shot into the sky above the hole and licked up the roof. Ugly brown smoke billowed out everywhere.

Thank God my sister wasn't home. If she'd been in her room, she'd be dead now. An hour ago I'd been looking forward to an entire weekend without her. Now I wanted nothing more than to see her again—soon, I hoped. Mom would burn rubber all the way back from my uncle's place in Illinois as soon as she heard about the fire. It was only a two-hour drive. I gripped the bar on the fire truck more tightly and tried to swallow, but my mouth was parched.

The firefighter wrestled a hose toward the front of the house. Tiny hunched over the hydrant across the street, using a huge wrench to connect another hose to it. Darren and Joe were standing in our next-door neighbor's yard, so I stumbled over to them. From there I could see the side of my house. One of the firefighters opened the dining room window from the inside and smoke surged out.

"You okay?" Darren asked.

"Not really." I collapsed into the cool grass and watched my house burn.

"We should take you to the hospital."

"No, I'm okay. Can I borrow your cell? Mine's in there. Melted, I guess." I wanted, needed, to call Mom. To know she was on her way back and would soon be here taking care of things. Taking care of me.

"Still no service on mine, sorry."

"Maybe it's only our carrier," Joe said. "I'll see if anyone else has service." He walked across the street toward a knot of people who'd gathered there, rubbernecking.

I lay back in the grass and closed my eyes. Even from the neighbor's yard, I felt the heat of the fire washing over my body in waves. I smelled smoke, too, but that might have been from my clothing.

A few minutes later, I heard Joe's voice again. "Nobody's got cell service. Verizon, Sprint, T-Mobile, AT&T—all down. Nobody's got power or landlines, either."

I opened my eyes. "I thought landlines weren't supposed to go down. I mean, when our power's out, the old house phone still works. Just not the cordless phones."

"That's the way it's supposed to be. But nobody's telephones work."

"Huh."

"You know what happened to your house? Looks like something fell on the roof."

"I dunno. Power went out, and then wham, the whole house fell on me."

"Meteor, you think? Or a piece of an airplane, maybe?"

"Would that make the power and phones go down?"

"No . . . shouldn't."

"And there are other fires. At least four, judging by the smoke."

Joe peered at the sky. "Yeah. Looks like they're a ways off. In Waterloo, maybe."

I tried to sit up. The motion triggered a coughing spasm—dry, hacking coughs, every one of them setting off a sharp pain in my head. By the time my coughing fit passed, the headache was threatening to blow off the top of my head.

"You want some water?" Joe asked.

"Yeah," I wheezed.

"We should take you to the hospital," Darren said again, as Joe trotted back across the street toward their house.

I closed my eyes again, which helped the headache some. The water Joe brought me helped more. I chugged the first bottle and sipped the second. Joe left again—said he was going to find batteries for their radio. Darren stood beside me, and we watched the firefighters work.

They'd strung two hoses through a window at the side of the house. All four of the firefighters were inside now, doing who-knew-what. The hoses twitched and jumped as water blasted through them. Pretty soon the flames shooting out the roof died down. I heard sizzling noises, and the smoke pouring out the windows turned from an angry brown to white as the fire surrendered.

Two firefighters climbed out a window. One jogged to the truck and got two long, T-shaped metal pry-bars. The other guy walked over to me.

"Are you okay? Having any trouble breathing?" he asked.

"I'm okay."

"Good. Look, normally we'd call a paramedic and the Red Cross truck to get you some help, but we can't even raise dispatch. You got anyone you can stay with?"

"He can stay with us," Darren said. "Till we can get hold of his family, anyway."

"That okay with you, kid?"

"Yeah, fine." I'd have preferred to see Mom's minivan roaring up the street, but Joe and Darren were okay. They'd lived across the street from us forever.

"The fire's pretty much dead. We're going to aerate some walls and do a little salvage work. Make sure you stay out of the house—it's not stable."

"Okay. What started it?"

"I don't know. Dispatch will send an investigator out when we reach them."

"Thanks." I wished he knew more about what was happening, but it didn't seem polite to say so.

"Come on," Darren said. "Let's get you cleaned up."

I struggled to my feet and plodded across the street alongside Darren. The sun had gone down; there was a hint of orange in the west, but otherwise the sky was a gloomy gray. No lights had come on. About halfway across Darren's yard, I stopped and stared at the white steam still

spewing from my partly collapsed home. I put my hands on
my knees and looked at the grass. A numb exhaustion had
seeped into every pore of my body, turning my muscles
liquid, attacking my bones with random aches. I felt like I'd
been sparring with a guy twice my size for an hour.

Darren rested his hand on my shoulder. "It'll be all
right, Alex. The phones will probably be back up tomorrow, and we'll get your folks and the insurance company
on the line. A year from now, the house will be as good as
new, and you'll be cracking jokes about this."

I nodded wearily and straightened up, Darren's hand
still a comfortable weight on my shoulder.

Then the explosions started.

Chapter 3

The sound hit me physically, like an unexpected gust of wind trying to throw me off my feet. Two windows in the house next door bowed inward under the pressure and shattered. Darren stumbled from the force, and I caught him with my left hand.

I used to watch lightning storms with my sister. We'd see the lightning and start counting: one Mississippi, two Mississippi . . . If we got to five, the lightning was a mile away. Ten, two miles. This noise was like when we'd see the lightning, count one—and wham, the thunder would roll over us— the kind of thunder that would make my sister run inside screaming.

But unlike thunder, this didn't stop. It went on and on, machine-gun style, as if Zeus had loaded his bolts into an M60 with an inexhaustible ammo crate. But there was no lightning, only thunder. I glanced around. The firefighters were running for their truck and the knot of rubberneckers had scattered. The sky was clear. I could barely make out a couple of columns of smoke in the distance, but those had been there for more than an hour. Nothing obvious was wrong except for the godawful noise.

My hands were clamped over my ears. I had no memory of putting them there. The ground thumped against the soles of my sneakers. Darren grabbed my elbow, and we ran for his front door.

Inside, the noise was only slightly less horrendous. The oak floor in Darren's entryway trembled under my feet. A fine waterfall of white plaster dust rained from a crack in the ceiling. Joe ran up carrying two stereo headsets and a roll of toilet paper. A third headset was clamped over his ears. He pantomimed tearing off bits of toilet paper and stuffing them in his ears. Quick thinking, that. Joe was definitely the brains of the couple.

I jammed a wad of toilet paper into each ear and slapped a headset on. The thunderous noise faded to an almost tolerable roar. But I heard a new sound: my ears ringing, like that annoying high-pitched whine a defibrillator makes when a patient is flatlining on TV.

We probably looked silly, standing there with the black cords dangling from the headsets, but nobody was laughing. I shouted at Joe, "Should we go to the basement?" But I couldn't even hear myself talking over the noise.

Joe's lips moved, but I had no idea what he was saying. Darren was shouting something, too, but the noise of the explosions drowned out all of us. Joe grabbed me and Darren and towed us toward the back of the house. We ran through their master bedroom—it was the fanciest bedroom I'd ever seen, but with the auditory assault we were enduring, I wasn't about to stop and gawk.

The master bathroom was equally impressive, at least what I could see of it by the dim light filtering in from the bedroom. Pink marble floor, huge Jacuzzi tub, walk-in shower, bidet— the works. But best of all, it was an interior room, placed right in the center of the first floor. So it was quiet, sort of. When Joe closed the door, the noise diminished appreciably. Of course, that plunged us into total darkness. Joe reopened the door long enough to dig a D-cell Maglite from under one of the sinks.

I held my hands out at my sides and screamed, "Now what?" but I don't think they could hear me. I couldn't hear myself.

Joe yelled something and pointed the flashlight at the tub. Darren and I didn't respond, so after a moment Joe stepped into the tub, knelt, and covered the back of his neck with his hands.

That made sense. The tub itself was plastic, but it was set into a heavy marble platform. If the house fell, it might protect us. Maybe we'd be better off outside, in the open, but the explosive noise was barely tolerable even now, in an interior room. Joe stood up, and I stepped into the tub beside him.

Joe shined the flashlight on Darren's face. It was red and he was shouting—I saw his mouth working, but his eyes were wide and unfocused. His arms windmilled in wild gestures. Joe stepped out of the tub and hugged him, almost getting clocked by one of his fists in the process. Darren tried to pull away, but Joe held tighter, stroking Darren's back with one hand, trying to calm him.

The beam from the flashlight lurched around the room as Joe moved, giving the whole scene a surreal, herky-jerky quality. He coaxed Darren into the tub, and all three of us knelt. It was a big Jacuzzi, maybe twice the size of the shower/tub combo I was used to, but we were still packed tightly in there. I put my head down on my knees and laced my fingers over the back of my neck. Someone's elbow was digging into my side.

Then, we waited. Waited for the noise to end. Waited for the house to fall on our heads. Waited for something, anything, to change.

My thoughts roiled. What was causing the horren-dous noise? Would Joe's house collapse like mine had? For that matter, what had hit my house? I couldn't answer any of the questions, but that didn't keep me from returning to them over and over again, like poking a sore tooth with my tongue.

I wasn't a religious guy. Mom was into that stuff, but I had won that fight two years ago. Except for Christmas and Easter, I hadn't been inside St. John's Lutheran since my confirmation. Before then, I had gone pretty much every Sunday, sometimes voluntarily.

When I was eleven or twelve, we had this real old guy as a Sunday school teacher. Mom said he'd been in some war: Iraq, Vietnam . . . I forget. Anyway, almost every class he'd say, "There are no atheists in foxholes, kids." At the time, it was just weird. What did we know about either atheists or foxholes? Nothing. But I sort of understood it now.

So I prayed. Nobody could hear me over the noise—I couldn't even hear myself—but I guess it didn't matter. It was probably better that Joe and Darren couldn't hear me, because it didn't come out too well. "Dear God, please keep my little sister safe. I don't know what these explosions are, but don't let them hurt my family. They're probably in Warren, but I guess you know for sure. I swear I'll do whatever the hell you want. Go to St. John's every Sunday, try to be nice to my mother, whatever. Do what you want to me. Just please keep Rebecca, Mom, and Dad—" Thinking about my family got me crying. I hoped prayer counted without the amen and all at the end. I was pretty sure it did.

I don't know how long I knelt at the bottom of that tub. Long enough for my tears to dry and my neck to cramp.

I stretched out, kicking someone. Joe lifted the flashlight, and by its light we rearranged ourselves so we were lying in the tub instead of kneeling. We were still packed in there way too tightly. Someone's knee dug into my thigh. I tried to rearrange myself but just got an elbow in my shoulder instead.

Then we waited some more. Two hours? Three? I had no way of knowing. The noise didn't abate at all. What could make a noise that loud for that long? Thinking about it made me feel small and very, very scared. The smell of fear filled my nostrils—a rancid combination of smoke and stale sweat. The flashlight started to dim, and Joe shut it off—to save the batteries, I figured.

Sometime later, someone kicked me in the chest. Then I felt a shoe on top of my hand and jerked it away quickly to avoid getting stepped on. Joe snapped on the flashlight. Darren was standing up, feeling for the edge of the tub. He stepped out gingerly. Joe shrugged and followed him.

I got out of the tub, too. The sweaty plaster dust from my house had dried on my arms and face, making me itch. I twisted the handle on one of the sinks. The water came on, which surprised me. Nothing else was working; why should that have been any different? I washed my arms and face as best I could in the darkness. I realized I was thirsty again and gulped water from my cupped hands.

While I was cleaning up, Joe had left the room. Darren was sitting on the edge of the tub, staring at his hands folded in his lap. Now Joe returned, carrying an armload of pillows, blankets, and comforters. He spread a comforter in the bottom of the Jacuzzi, added a pillow and a folded blanket, and gestured with the Maglite for me to get back in. I pulled off my filthy sneakers.

I climbed into the Jacuzzi and lay down, fully dressed. I felt bad about dirtying their comforter with my nasty clothes, but who knew what might happen later. If something else bizarre went down and I had to run, I sure didn't want to do it butt naked. I lay on my left side in the Jacuzzi, one pillow under my head, the other clamped on top over the headphones and the toilet paper. The head-phones dug into my temples, but that was a minor annoy-ance. I could still hear both the explosions outside and the ringing in my ears.

It's hard to fall asleep when Zeus is machine-gunning thunder at you. It's hard to stay awake after an evening spent surviving a house fire. It took a couple more hours, but eventually sleep won, and I drifted off despite the ungodly noise and vibration. Everything would be better tomorrow. I thought: a new day, a new dawn would have to be better than this.

I was wrong. There was no dawn the next day.

Chapter 4

I woke up and groaned. Everything hurt. My back ached from lying curled in the tub. My right shoulder had frozen up overnight. The muscles in my legs and bruises on my knees screamed with pain. My head throbbed, and my mouth tasted of ash and fungus. I rolled onto my back, throwing the pillow off the top of my head.

Losing the pillow was like turning up the volume on the radio four notches—if the radio happened to be playing a thrash band with five drummers. That damn noise. It was still every bit as loud as it had been the night before. I checked the toilet paper in my ears, making sure it was still securely jammed in. The headset had dislodged when I rolled over, so I put it back on, which helped a little.

I had no idea what time it was, but I felt like I'd slept for six, maybe eight hours. So the explosions, thunder, or whatever they were had gone on at least that long? What could make a noise like that? Everything I could think of—bombs, thunder, sonic booms—would have ended hours ago. It was warm in the bathroom, but my hands and feet still felt cold and numb. I stayed in the bottom of the tub for a while, trembling and trying to get my breathing under control.

But lying around in the bottom of a Jacuzzi wasn't going to answer any of my questions. I pushed myself out of the tub and fumbled in the darkness for my shoes. Putting on shoes one-handed in darkness so complete that I couldn't see the laces or my hands was a bit of a trick. I gave up on tying them—my right arm wouldn't cooperate with the left. I jammed the laces down into the shoes so I wouldn't trip.

I needed to take a leak. But Darren and Joe had sacked out between me and the toilet last night. I had no idea if they were still there, and I really didn't want to kick them in the dark. After all, I was a houseguest. Sort of a weird houseguest—a fire refugee, sleeping in their bathtub—but still. I figured I could hold it for a while.

I had a general memory of where the door was—a few steps diagonally from the head of the bathtub. I stretched out my left arm and shuffled in that direction. Of course I found it by jamming my middle finger painfully against the knob. I slipped into the master bedroom and closed the door behind me.

Blackness. It was so dark I couldn't see my hand held in front of my face. I'd expected the bathroom to be dark since it was an interior room. But last night I'd been able to see fine in the bedroom—the three huge windows let in plenty of light. Even if it was still nighttime, I should have been able to see *something*. The darkest overcast night I'd ever been in hadn't been this black.

I'd been in darkness like this only once before. About five years ago, Dad took me and my sister into a cave on some land one of his friends owned. Mom flatly refused to go. I didn't like the narrow entrance or the tight crawlways that followed, but I endured it without complaining; I couldn't let my sister show me up, after all. I even got through the belly crawl okay, pulling myself along by my fingers, trying not to think about the tons of rock pressed against my back.

We stopped in a small but pleasant room at the back of the cave to eat lunch. After we finished, Dad suggested we turn out all our lights to see what total darkness was like. I couldn't see anything, not even my fingers in front of my eyeballs. As we sat there, it got more and more claustrophobic, like a cold, black blanket wrapped around my face, smothering me.

I grabbed for my flashlight, only to feel it slip from my sweating hands and clatter to the cave floor. I groped for it but couldn't find it. Next thing I knew, I was screaming

in my high-pitched, ten-year-old voice, "Turn it on! Turn
on the light! Turn it on!"

Now, the darkness was exactly like the cold black blanket that had smothered me at the back of the cave. I stifled
a sudden urge to yell, "Turn it on!" The only flashlight
was back in the bathroom with Joe and Darren. And Dad
was over a hundred miles away.

I stumbled forward, found the bed by banging my shin
into the metal bed frame, and sat down. Putting a dirty butt-
print on the bed probably wasn't the nicest thing to do, but
it couldn't be helped. The world had tilted under me—I had
to sit down or fall down, and I had enough bruises already.

The gears in my brain ground over the possibilities,
trying yet again to make sense of what was happening.
Nuclear strike? Asteroids? The mother of all storms?
Nothing could account for everything that had happened:
the thunderous noise, the flaming hole punched in the roof
of my house, the dead phones, this uncanny darkness.

A beam of light shining from the bathroom cut through
the room. Darren appeared in the doorway; I could see his
face in the backwash from the flashlight. The light poked
around the bedroom a bit and came to rest on me.

Darren said something. I couldn't hear him over the
noise, but I could sort of see his lips. Maybe, "Are you
okay?"

I shrugged in response. Then I stood up and pantomimed taking the flashlight and going to the bathroom.
Darren nodded and handed it over. As I walked into the
bathroom, Joe passed me on his way out.

I used the toilet and washed my hands at the closer of the two sinks. The water still worked, but the pressure seemed to have dropped since yesterday.

Back in the master bedroom, I handed the flashlight to Darren and mouthed "Thanks" at him. He and Joe walked to a window on the other side of the room and pointed the flashlight at the glass.

The beam died not far outside, snuffed out by a thick rain of light gray dust falling slowly, in a dense sheet that blacked out all light. Little drifts of dust clung to the muntins dividing the window panes. I tapped the glass, and a bunch of the stuff sloughed off and drifted down, joining the main flow raining down unceasingly.

Darren took two steps backward and collapsed onto the bed. The flashlight in his hand trembled as he sat there, staring at his feet. Joe sat beside him and put an arm around his shoulder. I could see Darren's shoulders shaking—the cord dangling from his headphones wavered—so I turned away to give them some privacy.

I stared out the window, trying to figure out what the falling stuff was. It was light gray, like ash from an old fire, but a lot finer—sort of like that powder for athlete's foot. I leaned closer to the window, trying to get a better look. What I got instead was a smell—the stench of rotten eggs.

Someone tapped my shoulder. I turned, and Joe gestured for me to follow. The three of us trooped out of the room using the flashlight to find our way. When we got to the entryway, Darren shined the flashlight on the front door. It was closed and presumably locked, but a two-inch drift of ash had blown under it. I reached down and touched the stuff—nothing happened, so I picked some up between two fingers. It was fine and powdery but also gritty and sharp, like powdered sugar but with the texture of sand. Slicker than sand, though. It reeked with the same sulfur smell I'd noticed at the window.

Joe was wearing a wristwatch. I held out my own wrist and tapped it. He nodded and pushed a button on the side of the watch, lighting the display. It read 9:47.

Joe led us into the kitchen and passed out Pop-Tarts for breakfast. We had no way to toast them, of course, but I was so hungry it didn't matter. He pulled a half-full gallon of milk from the dark fridge. The milk was still cool, even after a night without power. We drank most of it.

The flashlight dimmed further while we were eating breakfast. Joe used it to retrieve a candle and matches from a kitchen drawer along with a pad of scratch paper and a pen. He carried everything back to the table. While Joe lit the candle and shut off the flashlight, I snatched the pen and scribbled, "What's happening?"

Joe read my note and added his own below it. "Volcano. The big one. Yesterday, while you guys were watching the fire, I heard about it on the radio." Joe passed the tablet around. I had to hold the note near the candle and hunch over to read it.

Darren took the tablet and wrote, "So that stuff outside is ash? From the volcano?"

I wrote, "Volcano? In Iowa?"

"No. The supervolcano at Yellowstone," Joe wrote back.

"But that's what—one thousand miles from here?" Darren wrote.

Joe took the tablet back and wrote for a long time. Darren tried to pull it away once, but Joe swatted his hand. "About nine hundred. The volcano had already gone off yesterday when Alex's house was burning. You remember the big earthquake in Wyoming a few weeks ago? The radio said that was either a precursor or trigger for the eruption. The little tremor we felt yesterday was the start of the explosion. I don't know what hit Alex's house. My guess is that it was a chunk of rock blasted off the eruption at supersonic speed. Then about an hour and a half later, the sound of the explosion finally got here. The ash would be carried our way on the jet stream and take eight or nine hours to arrive."

"Should we go check on the neighbors?" Darren wrote.

"Radio said to stay indoors during the ashfall. If you have to go out, you're supposed to cover your mouth and nose."

"What about my family?" I scrawled.

"They're in Warren with your uncle, right?" Joe wrote.

"Supposed to be. How'd you know?"

"Your mother told us you'd be home alone this weekend," Joe wrote. "She asked us to keep an eye out for you."

Typical Mom. Of course she'd figure out a way to spy on me—although now I was happy she had. "Warren is 140 miles east of here, even farther from Yellowstone. It could be better there, right?"

"Yes," Joe wrote. "There will be less noise and ash the farther you are from the volcano. There could be a heavy ashfall here but almost none in Warren."

I hoped Joe was right. I hoped my family was in Warren. They should have made it—they'd left three hours before everything had started. I didn't remember them talking about stopping for dinner on the way, but I couldn't really know.

"How long is this noise going to last?" Darren jotted.

"The news didn't even warn it was on the way, let alone say how long it would last."

"What about the darkness?"

"Anything from a few days to a couple weeks. They didn't know exactly how big the eruption was."

We traded notes for another hour or so, rehashing the same information. Joe had already told us pretty much everything he knew. We'd burned more than half the candle and completely filled the scratch pad by then. Joe wrote, "I'm going to blow out the candle, to save it. Relight it if you need anything."

The next few hours were, well, how to describe it? Ask someone to lock you in a box with no light, nobody to talk to, and then have them beat on it with a tree limb to make a hideous booming sound. Do that for hours, and if you're still not bat-shit crazy, you'll know how we felt. Before that day, I had no idea that it was possible to be insane with both terror and boredom at the same time. I'm not normally a touchy-feely kind of guy, but the three of us held hands most of that time.

Lunch was a huge relief, if only because it gave us something different to do. Joe squeezed my hand once and let go. I saw a couple little flashes of light, him using the light of his watch to find stuff. A few minutes later he was back, pressing food into my hand: a few slices of salami, a hunk of Swiss cheese, and two slices of bread. We finished off the milk as well, passing it around and drinking straight from the jug. Glasses would have been too much of a pain without light to pour by.

After lunch, more terrified boredom. Nothing to do but endlessly ponder: Is my family alive? Would I survive? I sat and thought for uncounted hours. Then something changed.

There was silence.

Chapter 5

The silence was an enormous relief—sort of like coming out of that cave into the sunlight when I was ten. I peeled the headphones off my ears and pulled out the toilet paper plugs. They were stuck; it hurt to remove them.

I heard someone—Joe maybe—say, "Can you hear me?" His voice was hollow, as if he were down a well.

"Yeah," I said.

"Can you hear me?" he said again, a little louder.

Finally I caught on. I shouted, "Yeah!"

"Good," he shouted. "I think my ears were damaged by all that noise."

"Yeah, mine too," I yelled back.

"How you feel?"

"Not good," I yelled.

"Darren?" Joe yelled.

Darren looked up, but didn't reply.

"You okay?"

Nothing.

"Darren! You okay? What's wrong?" Joe lit the candle.

Darren's face was scarlet. He stared sightlessly at a point about halfway between Joe and me. Joe reached out and put a hand on Darren's shoulder. Darren batted Joe's hand away and turned on him, screaming, "What's wrong? I feel like I've been thrown into the gorilla cage at the zoo, and they've been using my head as a goddamn volleyball!"

I felt pretty much the same way. Plus I was worried about my family. But screaming wouldn't help anything.

Joe stood up, walked behind Darren's chair, and started rubbing his shoulders. Darren seemed to deflate, collapsing with his head down on the kitchen table. Joe stood behind him, trying to comfort him.

Finally Darren looked up from the table and muttered something I couldn't hear.

"It's okay," Joe yelled. "I'm going to see if there's anything on the radio." He picked up the candle and used it to find a clunky old boombox on the counter. He carried the radio to the kitchen table and blew out the candle, plunging us again into total darkness.

After a while I heard a soft hiss of static waxing and waning as Joe dialed through the stations. I imagined he had the volume cranked up to the max so we could hear anything at all, but still the static sounded faint and hollow. We bent forward, pressing our heads together close to the radio, and listened to static for about an hour.

Every now and then, I could hear a roll of thunder coming from outside—not the painful continuous booms we'd been suffering through, only a natural clap of thunder sounding soft and echoey in my messed-up ears. The sulfur stench was stronger. I could smell it everywhere now, not just near the windows and doors.

"I've been through AM and FM three times each. There's nothing!" Joe shouted.

"Why?" I yelled.

"I don't know. I was getting all the usual stations on it yesterday. Maybe the ash somehow interferes with radio reception."

Darren flipped open his cell phone. The bluish light from the screen illuminated his face, hanging ghost-like in the gloom. "Cell phone still doesn't work."

Joe held down the button on his watch and used its faint light to stumble to the house phone. "It's dead, too," he yelled.

"How long is everything going to be down?" Darren asked.

"I don't know." Joe shook his head slowly.

"Why's the water work?" I shouted. "Everything else is down, why should that be any different?"

"Good point," Joe yelled. He lit the candle and we went upstairs, cleared the bedding out of the Jacuzzi and filled it with water. The water trickled slowly out of the spigot. It smelled funny, too, a bit like rotten eggs. I tried a sip— it didn't taste too bad.

After that, we got an armload of towels and walked around the house by candlelight, jamming them under the doors and along the windowsills. It didn't help, though— the rotten egg smell kept getting worse.

As the afternoon and evening wore on, the thunder outside got louder. I didn't know if the storm was getting worse or if my ears were getting better; the latter, I hoped. Joe wanted to cook some of the stuff in the freezer for dinner, but the gas cooktop wouldn't light. He sniffed it and said there was no gas, although I didn't see how he could tell—I couldn't smell anything but sulfur. So we ate bread again, this time with some lettuce and fresh peaches. Darren wanted salami and cheese, but Joe overruled him. He said we needed to save the food that would keep the longest.

As we were finishing dinner, I said, "Thanks for taking me in and feeding me and all. I really appreciate—"

"Don't be silly," Darren said. "That's what neighbors are for."

"Well, thanks. You guys are great neighbors. At least that's what Mom always—" Thinking about Mom got me choked up, and I had to stop. We sat in silence then, waiting for nighttime, although we could have gone to bed whenever—it was still pitch black and had been all day.

Then the explosions started again.

Chapter 6

Boom-boom-boom-boom-boom! The continuous thumping roar hurt my ears and drowned out the normal thunder. Joe flicked on the Maglite and used it to find a box of tissues on the kitchen counter: Puffs with lotion. Slimy, but they felt better than toilet paper while I was jamming some into my ears. Darren pressed the headphones into my hands, and I slapped them over my ears.

We sat in the kitchen, going crazy with both worry and boredom. The fear rested on my stomach like a dull weight, pressing down and making me queasy. I didn't want to go to bed and try to sleep through another night of that horrid noise, and Darren and Joe must have felt the same way, because neither of them made any move to leave.

At least I knew what it was now. That made the current round of explosions a little better than yesterday's, when the boredom and terror were compounded by wild speculation. This, I figured, must be the noise of some kind of secondary eruption. There was still plenty of reason to be scared, of course. My house had been hit by something thrown off by the eruption. What if Darren and Joe's house got hit, too? We weren't even taking cover in the bathtub like last night. Besides, the noise itself was terrifying without even thinking about the awesome eruption it represented—powerful enough to hurt my ears from nine hundred miles away.

I endured hour after hour of nothing: nothing to see but blackness, nothing to hear but machine-gunned explosions, nothing to do. Nothing to smell but—well, okay, there was something to smell: sulfur and yesterday's sweat. My breathing slowed, and the fear gave way to numb, wary boredom. The noise lasted for a little over three-and-a-half hours by Darren's watch. And then, mercifully, the explosions stopped again.

I yanked off the headphones and pulled the Puffs out of my ears. I heard a normal thunderclap as if from a storm. It sounded puny and hollow after the aural bombardment we'd just endured.

Joe lit the candle and, by its light, led me to the guest room upstairs. There was another box of Puffs on the nightstand, so I set my headphones beside it, within easy reach. Joe turned down the covers and left the lit candle and a book of matches on the bedside table.

I kicked off my shoes and climbed into the bed fully dressed in the same disgusting jeans and T-shirt I'd been wearing for two days now. I blew out the candle, rolled onto my left side, and fell asleep the instant my head settled on the pillow.

* * *

The next day started out pretty much the same. It was still pitch black. Ash still fell in a thick blanket past the windows. We could still hear normal, storm-like thunder. It sounded maybe a little louder, which I took as a hopeful sign that my ears might be improving. The storm had been going on for a day and two nights now. Perhaps it was related somehow to the volcano. The other weird thing about the thunder was that I hadn't seen any lightning, and there was no rain, at least not that I could see by candlelight through the windows.

When I turned on the kitchen faucet, hoping to wash up, nothing came out. Hot, cold—neither worked. I checked the downstairs bathroom; there was no water there, either. So we'd have to drink from the bathtub now. And the toilets were only going to flush one more time. That was a problem—it was going to get stinky in a hurry.

Joe served more lettuce for breakfast. He wanted to finish all the perishables. Darren grumbled about it some—I didn't like a salad for breakfast any better than he did, but I figured

Joe was making sense. Complaining wouldn't improve anything. Besides, I was a guest—they didn't have to share.

After breakfast Joe took me to the master bedroom and got some clean clothes out of his closet for me. They didn't fit very well. Darren and Joe are both a bit taller than I am and a lot heavier. Not fat, exactly, but big enough that Joe's jeans bunched uncomfortably around my waist and his T-shirt was like a maternity blouse. Still, it beat my filthy clothing.

Late that morning we noticed something new. There was an occasional flash of lightning visible in the windows through the ashfall. It was always accompanied by an immediate clap of thunder—the lightning was close.

As the day wore on, it got steadily brighter. At first, we could only see during the lightning flashes. But by late afternoon, it wasn't pitch-black anymore. Oh, it was still dark, but I could see my fingers if I stood by a window and waggled them near my eye. It was like a moonless, overcast night—about like the darkest night I'd ever experienced until two days ago. But it beat the cave-like blackness I'd woken up to that morning.

Joe played with the Maglite for a while, swapping D-cells to it from the boombox until it had a pretty strong beam. He tried the boombox again too, quickly scanning all the channels. Nothing. He shut it down to save the batteries.

It started to rain. Fat black raindrops splattered on the windows and washed streaks in the fine dust that clung to the panes. It was strange; I would have thought the rain would wash the ash out of the sky, but it didn't work like that. The rain fell, and the ash kept coming down, at about the same rate and density as before. It didn't even clump up like ash from a fire.

The rain had been falling for a couple hours, and we were thinking about dinner, when we heard a cracking sound and then a huge crash from outside. Joe grabbed the Maglite and ran for the front door. Darren and I followed him.

The ash had blown up over the front porch, covering it in a layer a couple inches deep. It was dry under the porch roof, so our feet stirred up the stuff. It rose in little clouds around us. I took a deep breath, which was a mistake, earning me a mouthful of sulfurous grit. It tasted nasty and set off a fit of hacking coughs. I tried to breathe shallowly and through my nose after that.

A concrete stairway led to the yard from the porch—four steps, I remembered. The bottom two were now buried in ash. Joe took a tentative step into the ash. His foot sank a few inches and pulled free only with a visible effort. I followed him, and we slogged around to the side of the house in the direction the noise had come from, while Darren waited on the porch.

Walking in the wet ash was like walking in thick, wet concrete. My sneakers kept trying to pull off my feet. Scrunching up my toes helped some.

The side of the house was a mess: a confused tangle of wood, asphalt shingles, and metal guttering. The ash, heavy with water, had pulled down the old-fashioned, built-in gutters, taking the soffit and the edge of the roof as well. As we gawked, a load of wet ash landed with a splat amid the wreckage.

We couldn't see the roof very well, even in the powerful beam of the Maglite. What if more of the roof fell while we were standing there? I took a couple steps backward. Then another worry occurred to me: How long would the house itself be able to withstand the weight of the ash and water on the roof?

Joe shrugged and plodded back to the front door. As we were closing the door behind us, we heard a crack and crash from the other side of the house. I assumed the gutters on that side had just fallen.

Ash clung to us everywhere. Joe and I beat at it, knocking clumps of wet ash onto the entryway floor. It was hopeless, though; the stuff was so fine it clung to our clothes and skin despite our efforts.

The ash looked almost white in the dim light, giving us a ghostly aspect. Maybe we *were* ghosts of a sort, spirits from the world that had died when the volcano erupted. Now we haunted a changed land. Would there be any place for us in this new, post-volcanic world?

Chapter 7

It was brighter the next morning. Still dark—the ash continued to fall—but at least we could walk around the house without crashing into stuff.

Joe and I dragged the propane grill into the kitchen from the back deck. We wet rags before we went out and tied them around our mouth and nose, like old-time bandits. That kept most of the grit out of our mouths and lungs. The grill was buried in a foot and a half of heavy, wet ash. I cleaned off the top of the grill while Joe tried to pull it free. Even when both of us heaved, the legs wouldn't come up. Joe fought through the ash to his detached garage

and returned with a shovel. I volunteered to dig—it took
about ten minutes to free the grill.

Miraculously, the grill worked. The smoke wasn't going
to do their kitchen ceiling any good, but neither Joe nor
Darren seemed to care. Their house was pretty much
wrecked, anyway. I'd noticed water running down one of
the guest room walls that morning, presumably from holes
ripped in the roof when the built-in gutters had fallen.

We ate steaks for lunch, Black Angus filet mignon. They
tasted heavenly after a day and a half of salads for breakfast,
lunch, and dinner. Joe told me to eat as many as I wanted
since they were all going to spoil anyway. I ate three.

That afternoon I was napping off the huge lunch in an
easy chair in the living room when somebody started
banging on the front door. They were whaling on it, too—
the noise was almost louder than the thunder, loud enough
to wake me up.

I stood and tried to shake the postnap loginess out of
my brain. Joe went to get the door. Something made me
suddenly nervous. Who would be out in the ash? And
why? Whoever it was kept hitting the door, slamming
something into it so hard that I wondered if it would
break. I suppressed a sudden desire to move away—hide in
the back of the living room or go upstairs, maybe. Instead,
I moved to the living room doorway where I could watch
Joe in the foyer.

"Don't answer," Darren said. I nodded.

"Why not?" Joe replied. "It's probably just the neighbors.
We ought to be banding together, helping each other out."

"You don't know that. It sounds like they're trying to break down the door." Darren retreated past me into the living room.

"If they weren't knocking that loudly, we wouldn't be able to hear them over the thunder." Joe peered into the glass peephole set into the door. "I can't see anything. Too dark." He unlocked the deadbolt and twisted the knob.

The door flew all the way open, pushed violently from outside. Joe stumbled backward as the door struck him. Three guys burst through. They were so coated in ash that it was impossible even to tell what color their hair or skin was. The lead guy was carrying a baseball bat. I shrank back into the living room, hoping they wouldn't notice me. My heart lurched, starting a hammering thump in my chest. I thought about running, following Darren toward the far side of the living room, but I would have had to cross the large open doorway between the living room and foyer. They'd have seen me for sure.

The second guy had a length of heavy tow chain, and the last one carried a tire iron. Baseball Bat advanced on Joe, waving his weapon wildly and yelling, "Where's the stuff? What you got? OCs? Boo? Ice? Tell me, old man!"

Joe held out both his hands, palms up. How he managed to react calmly was beyond me. I was shaking with a mixture of fear and adrenaline. I sent silent, useless orders to my body: Calm down. My breathing was ragged, so I focused on that. Two quick breaths in through the nose, two quick breaths out through the mouth. That helped some. Darren turned and ran toward the master bedroom.

"Stop that peckerwood!" Baseball Bat ordered.

Chain ran toward Darren, with Tire Iron right behind him. They were running right past me. I froze, unsure what to do. Chain ran by. He was swinging his weapon—he passed so close I heard the links clinking even over the roar of my labored breathing.

On impulse, I kicked out—a low, sweeping roundkick. Chain was already past me, but I kicked Tire Iron right in the shins, taking him down. His weapon clunked as it hit the wood floor. He yelled and reached for the tire iron.

I just stood there and watched him grab the tire iron and push himself onto his knees. I knew I should follow up on my kick, but I hadn't been in a real fight since sixth grade. And those didn't count as real fights, anyway—they were just stupid schoolyard stuff. Nothing like this.

Tire Iron started to stand, staring at me murderously. If I didn't do something—now—he'd cave in my skull. I stepped toward him and hit the side of his neck with a palm-heel strike. It's supposed to stun an opponent by interrupting the blood supply through the jugular, but I never figured I'd have to use it for real. It worked beautifully. The steel bar clattered to the floor, and Tire Iron followed it, falling sideways with a heavy thump.

I stood over him for a second, panting and trembling, and then looked around. Chain was at the back of the living room, chasing Darren, who had disappeared into the master bedroom.

I glanced at Joe in time to see Baseball Bat take a swing at his head, but I was too far away to help. Joe had the presence of mind to step toward Baseball Bat instead of away, so he got clubbed by the guy's hands instead of taking the murderous hit of the bat's business end. Still, Joe went down. I screamed, taking a step toward him.

Baseball Bat raised his weapon over his head and moved to meet me. Instinctively, I crouched in a sparring stance, hands up by my chin. My thoughts raced. What could I do? If he chopped down with the bat, maybe I'd sidestep and go for a wrist grab and joint lock.

I heard a noise like a pair of M80 firecrackers behind me. Blam-Blam! Something fell, tinkling to the floor with a noise like ice dropping into a glass. Baseball Bat lowered his weapon and took a step backward, so I risked a glance behind me.

Darren was stalking through the living room, a big chrome pistol clutched in front of him in a two-handed grip. Chain lay beside the sofa; blood gushed from his ruined skull and soaked the rug. My nostrils filled with the copper tang of blood blended with a faint fecal stink. I fought back vomit.

Darren got close enough to see Joe, motionless on the floor of the entryway. Darren screamed—an inhuman, animal yowl. Baseball Bat turned and took a step toward the door. He reached for the doorknob. Blam-Blam! Darren shot him in the back of the head. His face exploded. I heard a thunk as part of it hit the door and then a dull thump as Baseball Bat's body slumped to the floor. A dark stain marred the door, like someone had hurled a blood-filled water balloon against it.

Tire Iron moaned and pushed himself up on one arm. Darren screamed again.

I shouted, "Darren, take it—"

"Yearrrgh!" Darren pushed the pistol against Tire Iron's temple. Blam-Blam! His head pretty much burst, showering my legs with blood and bits of hair and skull and brain. The scent of blood and shit was overpowering now.

Joe groaned loudly and rolled over. Darren's gaze twitched from corpse to corpse, rage disfiguring his face.

I ran for the front door.

Chapter 8

The door snagged on Baseball Bat's body, but there was enough space for me to slip through. Behind me I heard Joe call out weakly, "Alex . . ." I didn't care. Didn't care what he had to say. Didn't care where I was going, either. I had to get away. Had to leave that horrible, gore-splattered foyer. Had to clear the stench of blood from my nostrils—if that was even possible.

Running through the ashfall wasn't easy. Water and ash scoured my face. With every step, my feet sank into the gooey mess. It was less like running than doing a fast, high-step march. I couldn't see very far, and I wasn't really looking around, but the street seemed deserted. There were no moving vehicles, only half-buried parked cars. No sign of any people. No noise except the thunder. Very little light other than the occasional flash of lightning.

I made it only two blocks before I got too winded to keep going. I'd lost my shoes somewhere, sucked off by the wet-concrete-like ash. I rested my hands on my knees and stood there a minute, panting. The image of Tire Iron's head exploding invaded my brain. I vomited. The steaks tasted a whole lot worse coming up than they had going down.

I didn't know if it was running or spewing, but something got me thinking straight again. I needed water, food, and some kind of protection from the ash. Shoes, too. Running around like a madman would get me killed in a hurry. But I couldn't go back to Darren's house. I doubted I could ever look at him again without seeing that rage-contorted face. And just thinking about returning to his gore-drenched foyer—no way.

But I had to go somewhere. I dragged myself slowly back down the road toward my house. The ash had permeated my socks and was abrading my skin. Every step hurt the sides of my feet where my skin was soft and thin. The ash caked the inside of my mouth and got into my eyes, making them water and causing me to blink constantly.

The front of my house had collapsed further under the weight of the ash. My room and my sister's were pretty much pancaked. The gutters had ripped off the house, but we had modern aluminum gutters, unlike Darren's, so it hadn't done much damage. The back part of the house looked okay. I found a window the firefighters had left open and climbed in.

The inside wasn't too bad. A lot of ash had blown in through the open windows, but so long as I didn't walk in it and stir it up, it didn't bother me. I checked the faucet in the kitchen sink. It sighed when I opened it, air rushing into empty pipes. No water. I got a warm Coke out of the fridge and used the first swig to rinse my mouth. That got me coughing. When I pulled my arm away from my mouth it was spotted with bloody flecks. That scared me; coughing up blood couldn't be good. But what could I do about it? I finished off the Coke, slugged down another, and devoured two apples.

I needed to pee. The downstairs bathroom and the one my sister and I shared were in the wrecked part of the house, so I went up the back staircase to the master bath. As I was getting ready to do my business, I thought of something. Grody though it was, I might need the toilet water. The water in the tank would be clean, right? And one of my friends had this cat, George, that always drank from the toilet—it hadn't killed him. I went downstairs and peed out an open window into the ash.

Back upstairs in my parents' bedroom, I stripped off the now repulsive clothing Joe had lent me and threw it in the trash. Ash clung to the inside of my underwear. My clothes were all burned or buried at the front of the house, but Dad's stuff fit me okay. Way too loose in the waist, but otherwise not bad. It was getting cold, which worried me. I thought for a moment and figured out it was the last day of August. The volcano must be messing with the weather somehow. How cold would it get? I had no way to answer that question, so I ignored it for the moment. I put on one of Dad's long-sleeved shirts over a T-shirt.

I slept in my parents' bed that night, fully clothed. Under the oppressive smell of sulfur, I caught a hint of my mom—a faint whiff of the Light Blue perfume we bought her every year for Mother's Day.

Lately I'd been so consumed with fighting with Mom that it never occurred to me what my life might be like without her. Without Dad's benevolent disinterest. Without the brat, my sister. Who would I be, if they were all gone?

I clenched my eyes shut and refused to cry. Would I see them again? Yes, I decided. If they were alive, I would find my family. There was no way they could come home to get me. Nothing short of a bulldozer would be able to move in all that ash. And if the gang that had invaded Joe and Darren's house was any indication, Cedar Falls would only get more dangerous. Tomorrow, I'd set out for Warren to find my family. The journey might be impossible, but I had to try. I had to find my mother. With that resolution, I drifted off to sleep.

I slept badly. Sweat-soaked nightmares featuring Tire Iron woke me a few times. Baseball Bat invaded my dreams, too. Morning announced itself with a shift in the darkness, from pitch black to merely dark and gloomy. I rolled over and went back to sleep, the first solid sleep I'd had in days.

A coughing fit woke me for good. No blood this time, thank God. I needed water, so I got up and found a cup in the bathroom. I took the lid off the toilet tank and scooped out some water. It smelled okay. I sipped it. It tasted fine, sweet even. I drank that cup and dipped myself another.

I brushed my teeth with my dad's toothbrush and rinsed my mouth with a tiny sip of water. My freshly brushed teeth felt heavenly. Maybe it was the normalcy of getting up and brushing my teeth, or maybe it was just having one part of my body clean, but I felt much better.

Breakfast was wilted lettuce and two more apples.

After breakfast, I searched for supplies. If I planned to honor the promise I'd made the night before, to find my family, then I needed to get prepared.

My backpack was buried in my room with everything else. But I needed a way to carry supplies, so I dug through my dad's closet. Way in the back, I found an old knapsack from back when he used to hike and ski. I wished it were bigger, but it would have to do.

I got one extra change of clothes out of my dad's closet, but I couldn't afford the space in the backpack for any more clothing than that. I did take two T-shirts though—I might need the cloth to make breathing masks. I also snagged a pair of Dad's work boots. They fit okay if I wore two pairs of socks.

We had six bottles of water in the fridge—I packed them all. Then I threw in all the food that would fit: cans of soup, pineapple, and baked beans, as well as all the cheese and ham from the fridge. I found an old, manual can

opener in the back of the knife drawer. I dug a few packages of peanut-butter crackers out of a cabinet and packed
those, too. It didn't seem like very much food. If it took
longer than a week to get to Warren, I'd be in trouble.

I tossed in a spoon, three books of matches, and a
couple of candles. I figured I'd want a knife, both to use as
a weapon and to eat with. I thought about the butcher
knives, but they seemed like they'd be too clumsy. I
grabbed Mom's favorite knife instead, a five-inch mini-
chef's knife that she kept honed to a wicked edge. I tested
it on one of the T-shirts, cutting a strip about the right
size to cover my mouth and nose.

I didn't want the knife in my backpack—too slow to get
at. So I took off my belt and cut a horizontal slit in the
leather. That worked okay as a makeshift sheath; it kept the
knife at my hip with the blade angled away from my body.

In the mudroom, I got the biggest rain poncho I could
find, one of my dad's. It had a hood and enough extra
girth to cover both me and my pack. I also grabbed the
spare garage key Mom kept there on a hook. All my keys
were gone, another casualty of my collapsed room.

Then I trekked back upstairs. I scooped water out of
the toilet tank and drank until I felt I might be sick. I wet
down my cut T-shirt bandanna and tied it around my face.
I was ready to go.

I got as far as the back door on the first try. The door
itself pulled open fine, but there was ash piled at least a
foot and a half deep against the storm door. I couldn't
force it open. I gave the screen door a frustrated kick and

then closed the back door and locked it. (As I turned away, I realized there was no point to locking the door, but whatever.) I climbed out a window instead.

Slogging to our detached garage through the ash was painfully slow. I sank three or four inches with every step and had to struggle to wrench my feet free. If I had to cover the 140 miles to Warren like this, it might take a year, not a week.

The pedestrian door to our garage opened inward, thankfully. When I pushed it open, the ash flowed in, so I couldn't close the door behind me. I saw a folded plastic dropcloth on a shelf and thought about using it as a makeshift tent. Of course it wouldn't fit in my pack. I moved some stuff to outer pockets and took out a couple cans of food to make room.

My bicycle was leaning against the garage wall next to my sister's. I wheeled it out into the ash-covered backyard. I mounted and put my feet to the pedals—I was on my way to Warren!

Chapter 9

I didn't even make it out of the backyard.

As soon as I stood on the bike, both tires sank into the muddy ash. It was slick, and within a few feet I was stuck. The back wheel just spun and carved a trough. I stepped off the bike, wrenched it free, and tried again. Same result. It was hopeless. I could make better time hiking, not that hiking would get me to Warren this year.

I pulled the bike free again and wheeled it back into the garage. Even that short trip had left it coated in nasty white-gray goop.

I shrugged off my pack and sat on the garage

floor to think. There had to be a better way to travel. I hadn't seen any cars moving—they'd probably get stuck instantly. Plus, I wondered what the ash would do to a car's engine. Nothing good. Walking was horrid because with every step my feet were swallowed by the stuff, and biking didn't work because the wheels sank and couldn't get traction due to the surprising slipperiness of the ash. It was sort of like a deep snowfall. Snowshoes might have worked if we'd had any. Maybe a couple of boards strapped to my feet? Or skis . . . ?

When I was little, my dad had been an exercise nut. He'd run in the summer and ski cross-country when there was enough snow. Then he hurt his knee and got kind of pudgy. But his skis might still be in the garage somewhere.

I hunted for a couple of minutes and found them, stacked out of sight on a shelf above my head. I dragged everything down to the floor of the garage. Two skis, a pair of boots, two poles, and a pair of ski goggles. Everything was covered in dust, but that was okay. It'd get a lot dustier the moment I stepped outside.

I took off my boots, tied them to the outside of my pack, and slid into the ski boots. I put on the ski goggles and everything turned pink. Typical Dad: Even his ski goggles were rose-colored. At least they'd keep the ash out of my eyes.

I carried the skis and poles outside. The poles stood upright when planted in the muck at least as well as they would have in snow. The skis barely sank at all when I stood on them to snap the boots in place. That was encouraging—maybe this would work.

I'd only skied cross-country twice, on family vacations when Dad had rented skis for all of us. But I sort of remembered how. The skis didn't glide over the wet ash the way they would have in snow, but the ash was slippery enough that I managed a decent pace by shuffling forward.

I headed northwest, toward my taekwondo dojang, Cedar Falls Taekwondo Academy. It was out of my way—I needed to go east to get to Warren. But I never brought my training weapons home; they stayed at the school. After what had happened at Darren's house, I'd have felt a lot safer with something more than a short knife at my side. I planned to pick up my competition sword and *ssahng jeol bongs* (nunchucks, but I prefer the Korean words). Competition swords are dull but made of metal. Maybe I could sharpen mine somehow.

The roads were a chaos of crashed and abandoned cars. All of them had a foot or more of ash blanketing their roofs and hoods. In some places, so many cars were jammed across the road that I had trouble finding a path among them. Everyone must have gone crazy trying to escape Cedar Falls while I was holed up with Joe and Darren. It didn't look like anyone had made it very far.

In other places, there were no cars at all. I didn't see anything moving. Of course, I couldn't see very far in the gloom and falling ash. The houses along the road were visible only briefly now and then during lightning flashes. Once, I thought I saw movement on a porch but couldn't be sure.

The skiing was tough. I'd only gone a couple of blocks when my legs started to burn. Sliding the skis forward was easier than pulling my feet out of the goop, but it used a different set of muscles than walking or taekwondo.

My right shoulder wasn't happy, either. It had gotten steadily better during the rest at Darren and Joe's house, but the repetitive planting and pushing of my ski pole was aggravating the injury. I tried to do all my pushing with my left arm and rest the right, at least for now.

I paused, leaning against the trunk of a car that had wrapped its front end around a telephone pole. The car's back windows were intact and opaque, caked with ash. I got a bottle of water out of the side pocket of my pack and sipped about half of it.

When I started out again, I saw the front of the car. The windshield and driver's window had broken with the force of the crash. A guy (or girl, it was impossible to tell) sat in there, head leaning lifelessly against the steering wheel. Ash had blown into the car, mummifying him. I turned away quickly, feeling a little ill, even though really there was nothing particularly scary about the corpse. I couldn't smell anything but sulfur or see any blood. Compared to the scene in Darren's foyer, the car wreck was downright peaceful. But after that, I avoided looking into the wrecked cars.

When I reached the newer section of town, I found a particularly bad stretch of crashed cars. It forced me to take to the yards, skiing beside the houses. They were ranch-style homes here: one-story houses with low-sloping roofs. At least every other roof had collapsed. On one house, the collapsing roof had taken the walls with it.

Nothing was left but part of the back wall and a lonely chimney.

I wasn't making very good time. I used to ride my bike to taekwondo; it took less than fifteen minutes if I rode hard. I don't know exactly how long it took me, skiing through the ash. Two hours, minimum. The slow pace was disheartening. At this rate, how long would it take me to get to Warren? Could I make it before my food ran out and I starved to death?

Across from the dojang was a restaurant I ate at sometimes, The Pita Pit. The skiing had left me hungry enough to eat two gyro specials and chase them with a two-liter Coke. I would have, too, if The Pita Pit had been more than a freestanding sign with a completely collapsed building behind it.

Amazingly, the strip mall that held the Cedar Falls Taekwondo Academy still stood. A pickup truck had rammed the front of the school, breaking most of the plate-glass windows. It had stopped with the cab inside the building and the bed on the sidewalk.

I unsnapped my boots from the skis. The mechanism had fouled with ash, and it took some work to scrape it clear. I walked through the window alongside the truck, carrying my skis in one hand and poles in the other. I tried to walk quietly, listening and looking around—it occurred to me that the occupants of the truck might still be there.

I didn't see or hear anything. The truck was empty. I leaned my skis and poles against the front bumper and looked around.

The school was one big practice area with a padded floor plus an office and restrooms off to the side. I could see the front part of the school okay. The back and the office were shrouded in darkness.

I dug a candle out of my pack and lit it. Exploring by candlelight, I found that the place had been looted. The office was a shambles. Master Parker's sword collection was gone. Someone had pulled the drawers out of the desks and file cabinets and dumped the contents, searching for God knows what. All the water bottles were missing from the mini-fridge.

I walked to the rear of the training room. That had been ransacked as well. Every one of the school's edged weapons was gone, and the other stuff was scattered all over, as if someone had gone though it in a hurry, throwing aside everything they hadn't wanted. I'd had a bag with my personal weapons on a rack at the back of the room. The rack was overturned, my bag gone.

I kicked the rack, feeling suddenly furious. What was it with Cedar Falls? People here had always been nice enough. But somehow the volcano had turned them into looters. Was everyone crazy now? We should have been sticking together and helping each other, not wrecking stuff.

I picked through the detritus on the practice floor. Most of it was junk that I hurled aside. Wooden practice swords. Soft foam *bahng mahng ees*, or short sticks. A set of padded *ssahng jeol bongs*, or nunchucks. Great to practice with, useless in a real fight. In the candlelight, I saw a dark gleam from the corner of the room and went to check it out. A long hardwood pole nestled against the edge of the mat. Master Parker's personal *jahng bong*, or bö staff. I wondered if she'd mind if I borrowed it. Under normal circumstances, yes, she would mind. Under normal circumstances, I wouldn't even ask.

It was a beautiful weapon. Six feet long, an inch and a quarter thick at the middle, and tapered to one inch at each end. Stained a deep chocolate color. The varnish was worn at the middle of the staff from hundreds, maybe thousands, of hours of practice. I carried it to the pickup truck where I'd left my skis and poles

I blew out the candle and sat on the front bumper to eat. I decided to have a can of pineapple for lunch on the theory that I'd get rid of some of the heavy stuff in my pack. I was still hungry when I finished but knew I needed to conserve food. I sucked down all the juice then tossed the empty can through the broken plate-glass window into the ash. With the ash and shards of plate glass everywhere, littering just didn't seem to matter.

Three of my water bottles were empty now, so I relit the candle and went to check the restrooms. The toilet tank in the girls' room was full. The water smelled fine and tasted okay, so I drank as much as I could and refilled my water bottles.

Judging time was tricky in the dim light. I thought about sacking out in the dojang. I was sore and hungry but not sleepy. I knocked as much of the ash off my makeshift bandanna as I could, wetted it down, and tied it around my face.

The bö staff was a problem. I couldn't figure out any way to attach it to my pack, yet still keep it easy to grab in a hurry. Finally, I decided to leave one of my ski poles behind and use the staff instead. Planting the end into the ash over and over wasn't going to do it any good, but I had little choice.

I pushed my skis east along First Street. Four blocks later, I turned south onto Division Street, which would take me past Cedar Falls High. I wanted to see if any of my friends were there. It didn't seem likely—the building would probably be deserted. Surely school was canceled on account of the volcano.

Actually, the school was packed.

Chapter 10

As I approached my school, I saw a group of four people wearing backpacks, trudging toward the athletic entrance. I couldn't tell who they were—they were covered in ash and had their backs to me—so I hung back and watched. They must have been dead tired; none of them so much as glanced around.

As I got closer to the building, I could make out a few figures on the roof. They were tossing shovelsful of ash over the edge.

The group ahead of me disappeared through the double doors that led to the school's ticket office and basketball courts. I stopped, trying to decide whether to follow them or not.

I waited a few minutes. Nothing changed. The people on the roof were still shoveling ash. The fact that they were clearing the roof, trying to keep the ash from collapsing it, seemed like a good sign. Perhaps there were more people here working together to fight the ash. It was worth checking out. I skied to the doors, cracked one open, and peeked in.

The light in the short hallway was bright enough to hurt my eyes, which were adjusted to the dimness outside. A kerosene lantern hung from the ceiling. At the far edge of the light, somebody who looked a bit like Mr. Kloptsky, the principal, sat slumped in a folding chair. Next to him was a wiry old guy with a shotgun across his lap and a big guy I sort of recognized, although I couldn't remember his name—a senior on the football team, I thought. He had an aluminum baseball bat between his knees. A couple of brooms leaned against the wall near the doors.

"Either move on or come in. You're letting the ash in." Definitely Mr. Kloptsky. I'd recognize that growl anywhere.

I closed the door, bent down, and popped the bindings on my skis. I reopened the door and stepped through, carrying my skis, pole, and staff awkwardly in both hands.

The guy with the shotgun walked up, eyeing me. He had the gun ready but pointed at the floor. "Bob'll get some of that ash off ya. Stand still."

The football player leaned his baseball bat against the wall and grabbed a broom. He proceeded to try to beat me senseless with it, scouring my clothing, backpack, and skis with the bristles. Wet ash fell off me in clumps.

When he finished, he started sweeping up the considerable pile of ash he'd knocked off me. The guy with the shotgun said, "Go on, Kloptsky'll talk to ya now."

I walked down the short hall to where Mr. Kloptsky sat hunched in his chair. He gestured at the empty metal folding chair beside him, and I sat down.

"You look familiar," he said.

"Yeah. I go to school here. Went, I guess. I'm Alex Halprin."

"Freshman last year. Mrs. Sutton's homeroom, right?"

"Yeah." Damn, I was impressed. Eleven hundred students, and he remembered one quiet freshman?

"Where are your folks?"

"Warren, Illinois, I hope."

"You can stay here. You'll have to work, though. Every able-bodied person is doing something. I'll assign you to a team in the morning. Food scavenging, roof clearing, or security, maybe."

Oh, I was tempted. Finally I'd found some people organizing, working to overcome the ash instead of just looting. Maybe I'd be safe here. But last night I'd made a promise to myself: I was going to find my family. "Actually, I was only looking for a place to sleep. I'll move on in the morning—I'm headed for Warren."

"Better you wait for help. We don't have any communication across Cedar Falls or Waterloo yet. Who knows what's going on farther east."

"I need to find my family."

"Suit yourself. Lord knows I've already got more mouths than I can feed here." His voice dropped to a whisper. "You have any food with you?"

"Yeah. You want some?"

"If you're trying to get to Illinois, you'll need it," he said, still whispering. "I'd advise you not to let on that you've got food. We ran out yesterday. We don't keep much in the cafeteria on weekends. We're scavenging what we can, but it's not enough. School has its own water tank, thank God. And there are plenty of cots and blankets— we're a Red Cross disaster site. But they planned on trucking in food during an emergency."

"Um, thanks."

"Cots are set up in the gym. Take any empty spot you like."

"Thanks."

I carried my junk into the gym. It was packed with row upon row of folding cots arrayed with the head of each almost touching the foot of the next. Narrow aisles separated each row. Maybe two-thirds of the cots were occupied. There were hundreds of people in there, not all of them students. Another kerosene lantern hung from one of the basketball goals, throwing long shadows toward the corners of the gym.

There was a cluster of empty cots in one of the dark areas along a wall. I picked a cot at random and shoved my skis, ski pole, and staff underneath. I was ravenous but didn't want anyone to see me eating, so I settled for drinking a bottle of water. Toilet water from the girls' restroom at the dojang, but who could be picky now?

I put the empty water bottle away, shoved my pack under the cot, and stripped down to my T-shirt and boxers. It felt great to get out of my filthy clothing and crawl into a bed.

My arms and legs ached. I'd only been skiing for a day, hadn't even left Cedar Falls yet, but I was exhausted. Could I make it all the way to Warren? Despite that worry, I felt hopeful. If people were organizing to survive the ashfall here, maybe they'd be organizing in Warren, too. Maybe my family would be okay.

The cot was small, with a tiny pillow and scratchy blanket. People were moving around, messing with their gear or talking to their neighbors. A bunch of them were coughing, great hacking fits brought on by the ash. A mother tried to shush a crying baby, and across the gym two kids argued. I was so tired that none of it mattered. I fell asleep inside five minutes.

Baseball Bat, Tire Iron, and Chain returned to my dreams. Baseball Bat wound up and swung at my head. I couldn't move, couldn't scream. As he was about to connect, his head exploded. When he fell, he opened up a whole new vista behind him, in that weird way dreams sometimes work. Mom, Dad, and Rebecca were there, eating Chicken McNuggets. I was in a clown costume, but they didn't recognize me. Every time I told them who I was, they laughed.

I woke up, panting quietly and staring into the darkness overhead. Someone had turned the lantern way down. I felt something bump my back through the canvas cot. I turned my head and saw a dim form kneeling beside me, reaching under my cot with one arm. I snaked my arms out from under the blanket and grabbed for it. I got a fistful of hair with my right hand and yanked it backward and up. That told me about where the guy's throat should be, so I went for a chokehold with my left forearm.

The whole thing was over in less than two seconds. I craned my head to get a look at the side of his face.

Her face. It was a girl, maybe eight or nine years old. I let go of her hair—my right shoulder ached, anyway. I kept my left forearm locked around her neck. She had pulled two packages of peanut-butter crackers out of my pack. They slipped out of her hands and fell to the floor.

What was wrong with me? I'd been shocked to see Cedar Falls degenerate into looting and violence, but here I was with my forearm crushing a little girl's throat, a little girl who only wanted something to eat. Was I any better than the looters?

I reached down and felt around the floor. I found both packages of crackers by touch. I scooped them up, put them back in her hand, and curled her fingers around them.

"If you tell anyone where you got these, I'll find you and break your neck." I tugged my forearm a little tighter against her throat to emphasize the point. I felt horrible. It was wrong, nasty even, to threaten her. But I couldn't think of any alternative. I didn't want everyone to help themselves to my food. She nodded, at least as much as she could with my arm crushed against her larynx.

I let her go, and she shot off into the gloom, both hands clutched around the crackers. The top of my pack was open under the cot, stuff falling out. I put it back together and set it on the cot next to me.

I lay awake for several hours with one arm thrown over my pack, hugging it and thinking. Would anyone survive if food was already so scarce that kids were going hungry? Then I thought about what might have happened if I'd tightened my arm a bit more around her throat, and I felt sick. Mostly, I thought about a little girl who had learned to steal just to get something to eat.

Chapter 11

When I awoke the next morning, about half the refugees in the gym were already up. They tried to move quietly and talked in whispers out of consideration for the sleepers. But more than a hundred people trying to be quiet made a heck of a lot of noise.

I sat up on the edge of the cot and groaned when my feet touched the floor. All that skiing yesterday had done nothing good for the muscles in my calves and thighs. So I staggered off the cot and forced myself through some martial arts stretches in my boxers. After I'd gotten my legs loosened up, I spent some time stretching my right arm and shoulder. It was feeling a lot better, although it still hurt to push my arm above my head.

By the time I finished stretching, I felt okay, so I started doing telephone-booth forms. An ordinary form is a series of kicks, punches, and stances that requires a pretty big space to perform. So to practice in a smaller area, I had to modify the moves. If the form called for a step forward, front kick, step forward, knife-hand strike, I'd step backward for the second move instead, covering and recovering the same small patch of ground.

People nearby were looking at me funny, so I called it quits after two forms and pulled on the same dirty jeans and long-sleeved shirt I'd been wearing yesterday. I put on my dad's hiking boots and threw my backpack over my shoulder, but I wasn't sure what to do with the skiing gear. I waited until nobody seemed to be paying attention and hid the stuff under the blanket on my cot. Hopefully it'd be okay.

The next order of business: a toilet. I knew where the closest boys' restroom was, but when I got there, partway down a pitch-black hallway, it was locked. I returned to the gym and asked the first guy I saw where we were supposed to pee. He pointed me toward the home locker room.

There was another camp lantern hanging in the locker room, turned about as low as possible while still giving off light. The urinals and stalls were blocked with yellow out-of-order tape. Somebody had dragged two Porta-Potties into the shower room, right in the middle near the floor drain. There were two lines, each four or five people deep, both men and women waiting for the facilities.

I got in line to wait my turn behind a young girl. I wondered if she was the same one who'd raided my pack last night. If she was, should I apologize or scold her for trying to steal from me? There were no marks on her neck, so I decided she must not have been the same girl.

The Porta-Potty reeked: a truly foul mix of feces, urine, and sulfur. I assumed they'd run out of that blue stuff they put at the bottom to keep it smelling decent. I took one breath while I was inside. I'd have skipped even that, but the idea of passing out in the Porta-Potty was even more disgusting than the smell.

While standing in the Porta-Potty, food was the last thing on my mind. But the moment I got out of the locker room, my hunger returned, gnawing at my gut. So I made my way down one of the dark hallways leading away from the gym. I navigated by feel, running my hand along the banks of lockers.

About halfway down the hall, I stopped at a door, which, if memory served, should have led to a classroom. The door was unlocked, so I opened it and stepped carefully inside. It was as dark in there as it had been in the hall. I sidestepped a couple feet, slid off my pack, and sat with my back to the wall.

I groped around in my pack and found a brick of cheese and two water bottles. I ate all the cheese and drank both bottles of water. What kind of guy eats his private stash of food when he knows there are hundreds of hungry people nearby? A guy like me, I guessed. Yeah, I felt bad about it. But I didn't think my meager stash would have made much of a difference to all the people in that gym. And I knew I'd need the food to get to Warren. I'd probably need more than I had. I reloaded my pack and ran my hands over the floor to make sure nothing had fallen out.

Back in the gym I asked a kid where to get water. He pointed me toward the visitors' locker room. There was another lantern hanging in there and two guys sitting on folding chairs. I asked them about water, and they led me to the showers. One of the showerheads had been replaced with a hose. I gave them my empty water bottles, and they refilled all of them from the hose, working carefully, spilling nothing.

I was a little surprised to see that the plumbing worked. But I figured it was like Mr. Kloptsky had told me yesterday—the school had its own water tank. It must have been high enough to feed the locker room by gravity. I hoped they had enough water to last until they got some help.

When I got back to the gymnasium, the lantern had been fully turned up and almost everyone was awake. I checked my skiing gear—it was still safely tucked under the blanket on my cot. I wandered around the gym for a bit, looking for anyone I knew.

I found Spork. Ian, really, but we called him Spork in honor of the utensil his dad had packed with his lunches in junior high. His mom was in the military. It seemed like every other year she was off in some Middle Eastern country. Afghanistan right now, I thought.

"Yo, Spork," I called.

"Yo, Mighty Mite," he replied, walking over to me. I hated that nickname. I mean, come on, I'm not *that* small. Sort of average-sized. Although I guess Mighty Mite beat Spork.

"So, is this messed up or what?"

"No, this is FUBAR. In the classic military definition. Effed up beyond—"

"Yeah, I know—all recognition."

"Recall, or remote possibility of rescue. So what you doing here? I think I'm on roof clearing duty today—want to see if we can get assigned to work together, man?"

"Roof clearing?"

"Yeah, Kloptsky thinks the roof'll collapse if we don't shovel it off."

"Huh. Bet he's right. The Pita Pit's flattened. Lots of houses on the way here were, too."

A girl I knew walked up while I was talking. Laura. A lot of kids called her Ingalls because of her name and the old-fashioned long skirts she always wore. I didn't because, well, she was cute. Even here she wore a long denim skirt streaked with ash.

"Yo, Ingalls," Spork said. "What duty did you pull? I'm on roof clearing."

She scowled at Spork and glanced my way. "Hey, Alex. Good to see you made it here okay."

"Yeah," I replied. "Good to see you're okay, too. You stuck shoveling roofs or something?"

"No, I'm getting out of here. My whole church is leaving today. You want to come?"

"Sure." I figured I'd see which way they were going. Maybe they'd head east, and I could tag along and get closer to Warren.

"So what're you doing, Ingalls? Driving the church bus out of here?" Spork smirked at her. We both knew there was no way anything short of a bulldozer could drive through all the wet, slippery ash. I was also a little puzzled about how her church planned to leave.

"No," she said. "Come on, Alex."

"I gotta get my stuff. I'll meet you at the door, okay?" I trotted to my cot and grabbed my gear. I put on the ski boots, tied the hiking boots to my pack, and carried everything else.

Laura and Spork were standing just inside the doors. They'd already wrapped their faces in damp rags. I dribbled a little water on one of my torn-up T-shirts and wrapped it around my mouth and nose.

"Thought you were shoveling off the roof," I said to Spork.

"So I'll be late. Won't be the first time Kloptsky has yelled at me. And I want to see how you guys are getting out of here."

I shrugged. "Okay."

It was a little brighter that morning. The ash was still falling, but I could see farther today. The rain had quit, but the ash was wet and slushy from yesterday. Oddly enough, the lightning and thunder continued unabated, even without any rain.

I slowed my skiing to a crawl so as not to outpace Laura and Spork. While they struggled with every step, wrenching their feet free of the muck and plodding forward, I skimmed the surface. It wasn't easy, though. My muscles protested, particularly after all the abuse they'd endured over the last few days. But watching Laura and Spork made me aware of how much the skis were helping.

Laura's church was only fifteen or sixteen blocks from the high school, but it took what seemed like hours to get there. The church was a yellow brick building dominated by a big square bell tower at the front. Metal letters bolted onto the brick beside the entrance proclaimed REDEEMER BAPTIST. Ash had collected in tall peaks atop the letters, giving them a Gothic look. I thought I saw some movement in the bell tower above us.

It was impossible to tell where the church's lawn, parking lot, and driveway began or ended. It was all one ashy plain. A couple of scraggly trees were bent under the weight of the ash, coated so thoroughly that not a speck of green was visible. Four cars and the church bus were parked to the side where the parking lot must have been. All of them were buried under more than a foot of ash.

Laura led us to the side door of the church, protected by a steep-roofed porte-cochère. I unclipped my boots from my skis and leaned the skis against the wall inside the doors. Spork was trying to bang the dust off his clothing and boots, but Laura told him to forget about it, since everyone would be leaving the building soon, anyway.

Someone had left a single candle burning in the sanctuary. By its light, I could see the church was modern, with a bright red carpet and oak pews. There was a path of near-white ash tracked on the carpet, which we followed to the back of the sanctuary and up a staircase to the small balcony.

Another, steeper staircase led upward from the balcony. It turned on itself in a square pattern, following the walls of the bell tower. I was surprised not to see any ropes dangling in the middle to ring the bells. Maybe they did that electronically or omitted the bells altogether. There were windows set into the walls, but the day outside was so dim that not much light leaked into the tower. I held the handrail and took the stairs slowly. It would be a long fall if I tripped in the darkness.

We went up five or six flights and stopped at a hatch set into the ceiling. Laura pushed the hatch open, and the three of us emerged onto an open area under the roof of the bell tower.

It was maybe sixteen feet on a side, but it felt small and crowded. At least twenty people were jammed together up there. All four walls of the bell tower were open to the elements; we were protected from a long fall by only a low brick railing. Ash swirled over the railings, forming drifts inside.

A guy in a minister's robe was preaching; everyone else faced him, listening. Laura slid through the crowd to someone I took to be her mom.

"Yo, Mrs. Wilder," Spork said.

"Our last name is Johnston, you idiot," Laura whispered.

"Be quiet and listen to Reverend Rowan," Mrs. Johnston whispered sternly.

So I did. He had a powerful head of preaching going: gesturing and sweating and shouting. He was saying something about a fourth seal when I started paying attention. "Behold! A pale horse. Pale because he's coated in this ash, my brothers and sisters. And his name that sat upon the horse was Death, and Hell followed with him. This," the reverend made a sweeping gesture, "is a foretaste of Hell; this is the ash that precedes the flood of fire and brimstone. A fourth of the earth shall be given over to famine and pestilence. This fourth, our fourth, where we lived. For this ash is the pestilence that will bring famine. If you are not summoned, if Jesus does not call you to His home, you will surely die. Our Lord told us this was coming. In the book of Matthew, He said, 'The sun shall be darkened and the moon will not give its light. Therefore you must also be ready; for the Son of man is coming at an hour you do not expect.' Pray with me now, pray with me, brothers and sisters, for Jesus to carry us up to sit at His right hand."

"So this is how you're leaving?" I asked Laura.

"Yes, Jesus is going to carry us to his home," Mrs. Johnston responded.

"So, if you're going to get carried up to heaven, can I have your stuff?" Spork said. He reached for Mrs. Johnston's purse and flipped up the flap. "Got anything good?"

My face got hot. Although I sort of saw Spork's point: If they were being summoned to heaven, they wouldn't need purses or their contents.

"Get out of there, you miserable child." Mrs. Johnston pulled on her purse strap, yanking it away from him and spilling junk on the ashy floor. A cell phone, a make-up case—and two Snickers bars. Spork pounced on the Snickers.

A couple people nearby were eyeing Spork angrily. The preacher shouted, "Peace, brothers and sisters, let us pray."

Mrs. Johnston swung her purse at Spork, but he was too quick. Clutching the candy bars, he sprinted down the stairs as one of the parishioners tried to grab him. I followed Spork.

We leaped down the stairs two or three at a time for the first two flights. I almost fell and had to grab the handrail and stop for a second. I couldn't hear anyone following us. They'd probably decided Jesus was more likely to take them to his home if they forgave the juvenile delinquents in their midst. I yelled at Spork, getting him to stop, and we walked down the rest of the staircase together.

"That was nuts." I tried to put some disapproval into my voice. I thought the parishioners in the bell tower were wrong, but that didn't excuse stealing from them. I think God helps those who help themselves. Yeah, I know it's not in the Bible, but it still makes sense. If the folks at Redeemer Baptist were going to be carried to heaven, God could have found them fine while they scavenged food and worked to survive. At least that was what I figured.

"Maybe it was nuts, but I got two candy bars out of it. You want one?"

"Sure." I was so hungry that I certainly wasn't above eating stolen food. I chewed my Snickers slowly, trying to make it last.

"Those skis work pretty slick. Where are you trying to go on them anyway?"

"East. Warren, Illinois. That's where my folks are, I think."

"I hope you make it, Mighty Mite."

"Yeah, me too. What're you going to do?"

"My dad and I are staying at the high school. We'll be okay there, maybe."

"Good luck." I reached out to shake his hand.

He surprised me by pulling me into a hug. "You too, Alex. I have a feeling we're going to need it."

Skiing away from Spork was one of the hardest things I'd ever done. But I needed to head east—I wouldn't find my family in Cedar Falls. A sense of dread and loneliness settled over me. I couldn't shake the feeling that I'd never see Spork, Laura, Darren and Joe, or anyone else from Cedar Falls again.

Chapter 12

I followed Main Street north to the First Street bridge. Most of the old downtown buildings along Main had collapsed. Their thick masonry walls still stood, but the roofs had fallen and the windows were shattered.

There was a semi twisted across the First Street bridge, blocking it, so I continued north on Main across Cedar River into Waterloo. I turned right, east, on Lincoln, figuring I'd skirt between Waterloo and the airport. I needed to get to Highway 20, but I also wanted to get out of town as fast as possible. If I went straight to 20, I'd have to pass through most of Waterloo. Maybe the people there would be fine, organizing and helping each other survive. Or maybe there'd be more looters. My palms got sweaty at the thought of meeting more people like Tire Iron and Baseball Bat. I didn't see any reason to risk it.

I passed under Highway 27. Enough ash had blown under the bridge that I didn't have to take off my skis—I was able to keep sliding along. A little farther on, Lincoln became West Airport Highway. There were lots of commercial and industrial buildings along the road there, mostly newish metal buildings with flat roofs. Every one of them had been crushed by the ash.

The road was deserted. I knew the airport was somewhere north of me, but I couldn't see it. On a normal day, I might hear a plane passing overhead or taxiing on the runway. That day, there was no sign of activity. The only noise was occasional thunder.

After a couple hours, the commercial buildings petered out, so I knew I was in the boonies. The corn was also a big clue. Cedar Falls and Waterloo form an island amid a sea of corn. In early September, it stands higher than my head. Now, though, the ash had flattened it. The only way I could tell I was passing a cornfield was the few hardy stalks still standing upright, coated in gray ash, leaves broken under the weight. Every now and then a metal seed sign protruded a foot or so above the ash bed. I passed an occasional field completely covered in ash, an unremittingly flat, gray expanse. Soybeans, maybe.

I might have been skiing on the surface of the moon for all the activity there was. I passed four or five farmhouses but saw nothing moving. Everything I normally saw in the Iowa countryside was missing: There were no people, no cars, no cows—not even a solitary turkey vulture circling in the sky.

The weird, rainless thunder and lightning continued. My eyes had adjusted to the darkness, so every time a series of lightning bolts lit up the landscape, it hurt. The thunder seemed strangely muted. Maybe the falling ash muffled it somehow, or maybe my ears hadn't fully recovered from the first enormous explosions.

Despite the ash, the road was easy to follow. It was raised, with deep ditches on each side. I skied along the crown of the road, where the centerline was buried under its blanket of ash.

I'd been skiing for four or five hours when I saw a thin line of trees looming in the dark about thirty feet ahead. They'd been beaten down by the ash. Most of the leaves were gone, and there were scars on the trunks where entire branches had ripped away. What was left was coated with gray-white ash. A small creek, only three or four feet wide, coursed along the line of trees. It had cut a channel through the ash, forming little cliffs almost two feet high on either side of the creek bed.

I unclipped my skis, slid my pack off my back, and leaned against a tree to eat. Lunch was a can of Dinty Moore beef stew, cold of course. Disgusting, normally, but I was so hungry I barely noticed. I drank a bottle of water with my stew.

The creek was so choked with ash that I couldn't see any water. But the ash was flowing, so there must have been water there, and I was worried about running out. I worked my way down to the water's edge, slipped in the ash and nearly went swimming. I found a sapling and held onto its trunk while I dipped my bottle into the sludge.

In my bottle, the water was grey-brown and opaque. It looked utterly undrinkable. I sniffed—it reeked of sulfur. I touched my tongue to it experimentally and immediately spit it out. The rotten-egg taste was overpowering, plus the water left a grainy texture on my tongue. I dumped out the sludge, packed the empty bottle, and resolved to drink less.

By late afternoon, the ash had pretty much dried out. Pushing the skis through it got tougher—they ground against the ash instead of sliding. I unclipped my boots and tried walking. In some places, the ash had dried into a fairly compact surface that wasn't too bad to hike on. In others, ash was blowing and collecting in drifts. There, my feet sank quickly in the fine, dusty ash, and pulling them free was difficult. I put the skis back on.

The scrap of T-shirt tied around my mouth and nose kept drying out. When it got dry, the tiny ash particles came through it, coating the inside of my mouth with nasty-tasting sludge and bringing on coughing fits. I remembered coughing blood at my house after breathing ash, and so I used more of my precious water to keep my breathing rag damp.

When the dark day started to fade to full night, I began looking for a place to sleep. Before the eruption, when I'd driven around Iowa with my parents, there was almost always a farmhouse in sight. Skiing through the darkness of the ashfall, I felt as if it were as deserted as Death Valley. I grew more and more worried about finding a place to sleep that night.

At full dark, I gave up looking for shelter and skied off the road into a cornfield. I don't know why I left the road; there hadn't been any traffic. I could have slept safely on the centerline. I shrugged off my pack.

A solitary stalk of corn coated in ash stood next to me. I broke off an ear, peeled back the husk, and tried to bite it. The kernels were small and hard. I almost broke a tooth gnawing a couple off the cob. I couldn't chew them, so I swallowed them whole instead. I tossed the rest of the ear away. I guessed this corn wasn't the kind meant for people. Growing up in Iowa, maybe I should have known more about corn. But while there was a lot of corn in Iowa, there were also lots of people who didn't know anything about it, like me.

For dinner, I ate chicken soup, cold and straight from the can. Tendrils of grease floated in the soup. They felt slimy sliding down my throat, but I was hungry enough that I didn't care. I drank another bottle of water, too. At this rate, I'd run out in the morning. At least my pack was getting lighter.

I slept wrapped in my plastic tarp with my pack as a pillow. It wasn't a particularly comfortable bed, but the day of skiing had worn me out, and I fell asleep quickly.

I dreamed about Laura. The first dream was just weird, not particularly embarrassing. (The embarrassing one was stupid. Black lace under that long denim skirt? I doubted it.)

In the first dream, some guy was hauling Laura up into the sky by one hand, through the ashfall. He was nobody I'd ever seen before: a short black guy with a strange expression on his face. Looking at him in my dream, I felt calm and peaceful for the first time in days.

So he was towing Laura up into the sky, and she reached into her purse and started pulling out Snickers bars and tossing them down to me. She was throwing them gently, like she was tossing me a gift, but I couldn't catch them and they kept hitting me: little missiles raining down and thwacking me on the head. Actually, thinking about them again, the first dream totally sucked. The second one was much better.

Chapter 13

I felt awful the next morning. My breathing cloth had dried out in the night, so I woke with a nasty cough. The inside of my mouth was caked with ash. I pulled the rag off my face and inspected it for blood. I didn't see any, which was a huge relief, although it was really too dark to be sure. I rewet my breathing rag and used a little more water to rinse my mouth. I drank the rest of the bottle. One bottle left. I *had* to find water today.

A thin layer of ash had settled on everything overnight. Ash had worked its way into my eyelids, armpits, and even my crotch. It rubbed as I moved, abrasive and gritty. I itched in at least a dozen places, because of dry skin or maybe something to do with the ash itself. I thought about changing clothes—I hadn't worn the fresh shirt and underwear in my pack. But changing my clothing in an ash-covered field during an ashfall probably wouldn't help much.

The ashfall seemed less intense than the day before. Lightning regularly cracked the sky, but the intervals were longer, and judging by the thunder, it was usually farther off.

I'd been skiing an hour or so when the road came to a T. I turned right, figuring if I went south I'd hit Highway 20 sooner or later. But I didn't see 20, and mostly I needed to go east, so I turned left as soon as I reached another intersection.

By lunchtime, I was getting desperate to find water. I'd crossed two tiny creeks, but the water was fouled with ash. I wet my breathing rag again, using the tiniest amount of water I could, and then drank two swigs. I had half a bottle left.

A couple hours after lunch, I saw a farmstead alongside the road on my left and turned toward it. The farm consisted of three buildings: a two-story white house with a steep roof, a large barn with a little red paint visible under its coating of ash, and a low, flat-roofed shed that had mostly collapsed.

The place looked deserted. But that was true of every farm I'd seen so far. The only hint of a driveway was a mailbox sticking out of the ash about a foot and a half.

There was a chain-link fence around the house, but the ash was so deep that only a foot of it protruded. I sidestepped over the fence and slid to the door.

Ash had drifted across the small front porch and lay deep enough against the screen door that I couldn't pull it open. I banged on it and yelled. No answer. I skied around the house to a side door. It was locked. More banging and yelling accomplished nothing. I left the yard, stepping over the chain-link fence and skied to the barn. Its doors were padlocked shut.

Perhaps I should have broken into that house—there might have been water there. But I couldn't bring myself to do it. For one thing, it didn't feel right to mess up someone's house even though I needed the water. For another, I was worried about what I might find inside. There must have been a reason that place was vacant—what if the owners *were* inside the house, dead or something?

A few hours later, I was cussing myself as an idiot for not breaking into that house. My water was gone. I'd used the last bit of it to wet my breathing rag over an hour before. It was starting to dry, letting nasty dust through the weave and into my mouth and lungs. If that farmhouse had reappeared in front of me at that moment, I would have rammed my staff through a window and climbed right in.

Not long after I'd had that thought, I saw another farmstead to my right, looming in the darkness. I picked up my pace and headed straight for it.

As I approached, I could tell that this farm was occupied or had been recently. The first clue was a smell—

wood smoke and a hint of meat under the omnipresent stench of sulfur. The farmstead consisted of five buildings: a house and barn nearly identical to the last place and three outbuildings, two of them collapsed.

There were footprints leading from a tiny, steep-roofed outbuilding to the back door of the farmhouse. The prints had to be fresh because they were already filling with ash and would soon be completely covered. Somebody had shoveled off the back porch. There were mounds of ash around it, but only a light dusting on the floor.

I unclipped my skis and hobbled across the porch with an awkward, sliding gait. My legs had frozen in ski mode. I pushed the doorbell and then rolled my eyes in irritation at myself—of course the doorbell wouldn't work. I rapped my knuckles against the door trim instead.

Nobody came. Maybe they couldn't hear my tapping over the thunder. I opened the screen door and beat on the entry door. Nothing. I tried again, whaling on it this time.

The door pulled inward in a rush, and I saw the long, black, double barrel of a shotgun pointing right at my nuts. My nuts knew where that shotgun was pointing, too; I could feel them trying to climb up into my body for protection. All my muscles tensed and my eyes widened, adrenaline coursing through my system.

The shotgun was held by a tall, rail-thin guy with a scraggly white beard, weathered face, and short white hair. The most amazing thing about him, though, was how clean he was. His face, hands, and bare feet were scrubbed. The jeans and flannel shirt he wore had not a speck of ash on them. Water—there had to be water here. Nobody could be that clean without it.

My first impulse on seeing the gun was to run and hope he didn't feel like wasting a shell on my puny back. But now I knew there was water here. I'd certainly die if I didn't find water somewhere, and soon. Was it more painful to die of thirst or a shotgun blast? I wasn't sure. I stood my ground.

He gestured at me with the shotgun. "Move along, boy." His voice growled like an engine that rarely saw oil.

I lifted my hands in front of me, palms outward, and backed up a step. A bad move if I had to fight; it took me out of range for a crescent kick. But kicking a gun is a stupid move, only worth trying if there's no other option. It takes a lot less time to pull a trigger than to launch a kick. "I'm only looking for water, sir."

"No water for you here. Move along."

A woman appeared in the doorway behind him. She pulled a dishrag out of her apron strings and whapped the man upside the head with it. "Elroy! We've got plenty of water. Can't you see this is just a poor waif of a boy?"

"Don't know him. Don't know who might be with him."

"Anyone with you, child?" she asked in a kindly tone.

"No, ma'am."

"Come on in then." She bustled around Elroy, pushing the barrel of the shotgun aside with her body. I was relieved to see it pointing at the wall, instead of at me. Maybe I could have fought then. But the woman seemed friendly enough; perhaps she'd fill my empty water bottles.

She herded Elroy backward through the mudroom and toward the kitchen beyond. She turned toward me. "Well, come on."

I stepped slowly through the doorway, my hands still raised. Inside there was a small entryway that held a huge freezer, a boot scraper, and a neat row of shoes and boots.

"My, but you're filthy with that ash." She handed me a whisk broom. "Brush yourself off with this, son. Now how do you like your steak?"

"My steak?"

"Why, yes. You get cleaned up, and I'm going to throw another steak on the fire for you. We were fixing to eat."

"No, I couldn't impose. If you'd fill my water bottles, I'll get out of your—"

"Nonsense. Why, if either of my sons were out in this, I'd sure want someone to take them in and give them a good meal. Not that they'd be out wandering alone, mind, they're grown men and have families to look after. So how do you like your steak?"

"Medium rare please, ma'am." My mouth tried to water at the mere thought of a steak, but it was too parched. Just then I remembered the last time I'd had steak, at Darren and Joe's house, and felt vaguely sick.

"I'll do my best. I haven't had to cook over a wood fire since I was a girl, and then we had a proper stove. I do wish we still had one, instead of that useless electric range. This business of squatting by the fireplace is hard on my old knees. Oh, where are my manners? My name's Edna. Edna Barslow."

"Alex." I started to reach my hand out, saw how filthy it was, and thought better of it. "Nice to meet you, Mrs. Barslow."

"Edna is fine, dear. Now leave your pack and boots in the mudroom and brush off as much of that ash as you can. I don't hold with ash in my kitchen."

"Yes, ma'am. I have some clean clothes in my pack, too."

"I'll close the kitchen door then, to give you some privacy to change. Come on through when you're ready."

I stripped off everything and left it in as neat a pile as I could manage on the mudroom floor. I kept an eye on the door while I changed. Mrs. Barslow seemed nice enough, but I was keenly aware that there was also a guy with a shotgun on the far side of that door.

The clothes in my pack weren't exactly clean, since the dust had seemed to find its way everywhere, but they were a huge improvement over the stiff, ash-caked clothing I'd removed. I attacked my hair and face with the whisk broom, which hurt some but brought a satisfying cloud of ash cascading off my head.

When I stepped into the kitchen, Elroy was sitting at the head of the table with the shotgun across his knees. Behind him I could see into a large living room with a fireplace. Edna was crouched by the fire. The aroma was so lovely, it made me dizzy.

"Edna put a pail of water in the bathroom for you to wash up, boy. It's behind you."

"Thank you." I glanced behind me and saw another door next to the one I'd come through. I sidled through it, keeping a wary eye on Elroy. In the bathroom, a sink held a sponge and galvanized metal pail. I picked up the pail and sniffed the water. It smelled fine, so I drank about half of it straight from the pail and used the rest to wash.

When I returned to the kitchen, Edna was setting a platter of steaks and a Dutch oven loaded with carrots and potatoes on the table. As we sat down, she asked, "Are you going to put that ridiculous gun away, Elroy?"

"Nope."

She stared at him a moment. "Will you bless this food then?"

"Yep." They folded their hands and bowed their heads. I noticed Elroy was still looking at me out of the corner of his eye. Suspicious bastard—although I was watching him, too. I imitated Elroy's pose as he said, "Dear Lord, bless this food to the use of our bodies that we may persevere in this time of trial and emerge stronger and wiser. Amen."

"Amen," Edna said, so I threw in one, too.

Edna talked during dinner. Elroy mumbled "yep" and "nope" now and then but otherwise didn't say much. Me, I just ate. I wasn't going to ask for seconds, but I sure didn't turn them down when Edna offered. I didn't turn down thirds or fourths, either. She offered coffee, but I convinced her I'd prefer water. I ate and drank until I was stuffed and sleepy and on the edge of getting sick.

I shook my head when Edna offered fifths and pushed my plate away. I felt a little woozy, so I laid my head on the table to rest, just for a minute.

I woke to Edna shaking my shoulder. She helped me to my feet and led me to the couch in the living room. It was hot in there, the remnants of the cooking fire glowing in the hearth. I sank into the couch, and Edna draped an afghan over me. I fell back to sleep instantly.

* * *

It was still fully dark when I woke again. Someone was shaking me. Elroy—I could see his face in the light of the candle he carried. I sat up on the couch and stretched.

Elroy spoke in a hushed voice. "Kid, I'm sorry about this."

I came more fully awake. "Sorry about what?"

"Edna's convinced we've got to keep you here, take care of you—"

"No, I can't stay—I've got to find my folks."

"That's a relief, then. Get up and let's get you on out of here."

I stood and followed Elroy to the fireplace. A line had been strung in front of it, and all the clothes I'd been wearing yesterday were hanging there. "What—"

"Edna, she stayed up last night and washed your things in the bathtub. They dry enough to pack?"

"Yeah, I think so. Thanks." I took my clothing off the line and folded it roughly. Then I followed Elroy's candle to the mudroom.

"I filled your water bottles last night. Here's a few extras." He handed me a plastic grocery sack with six twenty-ounce Diet Coke bottles filled with water. I'd eaten enough food over the last two days that the Diet Coke bottles would fit in my pack, though just barely.

"I should say goodbye to Edna."

"Naw, you do that and there'll be a weepy scene. You look kind of like one of our sons did when he was younger."

"Well, thank her for me. Thank you for everything— the meal last night, a place to sleep, the water. I really—"

"Now don't be getting maudlin. Just get on out of here before Edna wakes up and tries to convince you to stay."

"How is it that you've got water?" I asked as I finished tying my pack shut.

"First thing I did when we lost electric and the ashfall started was rig up a hand pump for the well. That was before my shop collapsed. So long as the hand pump works, Edna and I'll be fine for water. Food, I don't know. This goes on a couple months, we'll have trouble feeding two mouths, let alone three."

I nodded. "Thanks, Elroy." I shouldered my pack and tied a rag around my face. Then I stuck out my hand.

The last thing he said to me was, "You take care, now."

It was still too dark to see outside. I sat down, leaning against a porch pillar, and waited for the sun to come up. It never did, of course. Instead, there was a little brightening on the eastern horizon of the black, monotone sky. I snapped my boots into my skis and left the farm, sliding toward the light.

Chapter 14

About midday I happened across another farmhouse. As I skied up to the yard, a window opened, and I saw the barrel of a rifle poke out. I decided not to push my luck.

I avoided the rest of the farmhouses I saw. That was easy to do; I just stayed on the road.

That afternoon, it started to rain. It was getting colder—way too cold for early September. I stopped and got my poncho out of my pack, which helped some. With the rain, the thunder and lightning increased. The thunder had never completely gone away, just faded to an occasional clap in the background. Now it returned with a vengeance, although after that horrible night in the Jacuzzi back at Joe and Darren's, even loud thunder sounded puny.

The blessing of the storm was that it got easier to push the skis forward. They slid better on wet ash than dry. The curse was the cold water splashing my jeans and seeping through the hood of my poncho. Even working as hard as I was, I began to shiver. A wet night in the open might get me a bad case of hypothermia, flu, or worse.

About an hour after I'd started looking for shelter, I spotted a car. It was buried to the tops of its wheels, and ash was mounded nearly two feet deep on top of it. It was an odd place for a car, stuck in the center of the road without any buildings in sight. I wondered what had caused this car to be left here—had the driver fled the ashfall and only made it this far before getting stuck? Or had they run out of gas? More important, were the owners of the car still inside?

I brushed ash off the rear passenger-side window and tried to peer in. It was too dark to see anything. I pulled on the handle. The door was unlocked but would only open about two inches due to the ash. I still couldn't see anything through the door, so I sniffed instead. It smelled okay: the omnipresent sulfur stench and a hint of stale French fries.

It took me a while to dig away enough ash to open the door. As I dug, I thought about the corpse I'd seen in the wrecked car in Cedar Falls. I hoped this car would be empty.

It was. Inside, it was dry, dark, and felt somehow safe. I stripped off my wet clothing and spread it over the front seat, hoping it would dry overnight. It was too cold to sleep in my underwear, so I put on the clothing from my pack. It hadn't dried completely in front of the fire last night and felt clammy, but it was far better than the stuff I'd removed.

Despite my mostly dry clothing, I was cold. I got the plastic tarp out of my pack and used it like a blanket. That helped a little. I thought about how much worse off I'd be sleeping outside and sent a silent thank you to whoever had abandoned this car. Eventually, I drifted to sleep.

* * *

It was still storming the next day. I packed the tarp and the damp clothes from the front seat, pulled on my pack and poncho, and slid out into the rain. There didn't seem to be much ash coming down, but the storm kept everything dark, anyway.

It was a miserable day spent slogging through that slushy ash. The land was hillier here. Going down was fun—on gentle slopes moving forward was easy. On steeper slopes, I could glide to the bottom without doing any work at all. Going up was murder. On the gentlest slopes I could push my skis uphill in a straight line, as if I were on flat land. But sometimes I had to walk with the ski tips outspread in a huge V, which was brutally hard, or keep the skis parallel to the hill and sidestep up, which was excruciatingly slow.

I had trouble finding a decent place to sleep that night. I passed a couple of farmhouses, but after yesterday's experience, I'd started imagining guns in all their windows. Late that evening, when I was beginning to worry about being forced to sleep outside, I came across a slope that had been planted in pine trees—big ones, twenty or thirty feet high, not little Christmas evergreens. The pine boughs had gotten loaded down with so much ash that nearly every one of the trees had been pulled over or broken. The few trees still upright were stripped of their branches, lonely flagpoles without a nation to claim them.

I picked a large tree that had broken off four or five feet up the trunk and crawled under it. There was a hollow space there—the trunk was still attached to the stump where it had broken, so it formed the ridgepole for a natural lean-to, with pine boughs and the thick ash layer forming the roof. There was a sharp, welcome odor of pine resin almost strong enough to cover the pervasive stench of sulfur.

I settled into the space, trying not to stir up the ash. My pack became a pillow and my plastic tarp a blanket. If anything, it was an even better bed than the car last night. I wondered who I should thank for this shelter? I drifted to sleep thinking about how far I'd come and trying to guess how much farther I had to travel to reach Warren and, hopefully, my family.

* * *

The next day, my fifth on the road, started out pretty well. I'd only been skiing a couple of hours when the storm abated. The end of the cold rain came as such a relief that it took a while before I noticed the thunder and lightning were mostly gone, too. There was an occasional crack of far-off thunder, but nothing like what I'd been hearing for the last week. The ashfall was sparser. It was still hazy and dark, but more like twilight right after the streetlights pop on than dead night. All in all, the changes were very encouraging, and I made good time that morning.

What brought me crashing back to reality was the food situation. I ate my last rations for lunch, a cold can of Van Camp's Pork and Beans. Thanks to all the extra bottles Elroy had given me, I had enough water for another day, maybe two if I was careful.

Late in the afternoon, I came to an intersection: U.S. 20 and Highway 13, the sign read. There was a gas station near the corner—I recognized the sign. When my sister was little, we used to stop here every time we went to Warren. She had to pee thirty minutes into any trip, like clockwork. That thought was depressing: It had taken me six days to travel only about a quarter of the distance to Warren. On the other hand, I was glad to find U.S. 20; at least I now knew exactly where I was.

The freestanding metal roof had fallen and twisted, taking out two of the pumps. It lay there like the wing of a crashed airplane. I smelled gas as I slid past the pumps.

The station itself had collapsed. The cinderblock wall at the rear still stood, but the rest of the station was a tangled ruin of steel girders, glass, and blue plastic. I hunted through the front of the store, looking for something to eat, but there was too much ash and wreckage in the way.

I walked around to the back. Where the cinderblock wall stood, it had created a triangular space by holding up one end of the steel roof beams. I crawled inside, but there wasn't enough light to see anything, so I backed out to get a candle and matches from my pack.

I wasted half a candle and at least an hour crawling through the wreckage. My haul was four Starbursts and a handful of Skittles. The candy was shockingly bright against the gray ash. It was a pitifully small amount of food—not even a full meal. It seemed to me that there should be more food— after all, gas station convenience stores were full of stuff to eat. Maybe it had already been looted before it collapsed.

I rubbed the Skittles clean on the inside of my shirt and ate them and the Starbursts. Mom would have told me not to spoil my dinner with candy. I wished I had a dinner to spoil. Or a mom to tell me.

What little light there was had begun to fail. I pulled my pack into the gas station next to the cinderblock wall and curled up in the wreckage to sleep.

In the morning, I woke to the sound of breaking glass.

Chapter 15

I crawled to the edge of my hidey-hole and peeked out. Someone was rummaging through the front part of the gas station, picking up chunks of debris and tossing them aside. I slunk backward into the wreckage and packed up quickly, wincing every time I made a sound.

When I emerged from the hole, I crouched behind a twisted metal roof panel, hoping to watch for a while without being seen. A man and a woman were going through the rubble at the front of the store, sifting ash and moving bits of the wreckage. Behind them two kids, one maybe four or five, the other a bit older, sat on a warped piece of plywood. A rope was tied to the upturned edge of the board, turning it into an improvised sled. A pair of duffel bags rested on the board beside the kids.

I tried to clip into my skis and get ready to move without exposing myself. But it was almost impossible to put skis on while crouching.

"Hello?" the guy called. "Someone there?"

I stood up. "Hi."

The guy looked at me. Then I saw his eyes scan right and left. "You alone?"

"Yeah." I said, although the question made me wonder why he wanted to know. The woman kept poking through the rubble, ignoring us.

"You find any food here?"

"Only a handful of candy."

"You got any food?"

"No."

"You don't look hungry," he said, starting to slog through the ash toward me.

My heart drooped in my chest. I was hungry, tired, and sore from all the skiing. The last thing I wanted was a confrontation with this guy. I sidestepped on my skis, making sure I had a clear path to push forward or back. I stared at the guy, but said nothing.

"My family and I, we were on our way to Nebraska when it hit. We only had some snacks with us. We've had barely any food for a week."

"That's rough." I tried to sound sympathetic, but I kept my eyes wide and took a stronger grip on my staff. He was coming on strong, moving toward me as fast as the ash and wreckage would allow.

"That's a full backpack you're wearing. There's food in there. I can smell it."

"I don't have any food."

"Leave him alone, Darryl. He's only a kid!" the woman yelled.

I wished people would quit calling me a kid, although if it convinced Darryl to back off, I'd take it.

"Shut up, Mabel. We need food."

I thought about trying to run. I wasn't sure I could get my skis turned and get moving fast enough to get away. Then I considered the mechanics of fighting on skis while holding a staff and ski pole. Not good. I jammed the ski pole upward through my belt and hoped it would stay put.

Darryl was getting close—too close. I took the staff in a two-handed grip, like a six-foot baseball bat, and started whirling it over my head. Master Parker would have scolded me if she'd seen my form—you're supposed to step into each swing, so your body spins with the staff—but I'd like to see her do it right while wearing skis.

Darryl was either dumb, desperate, or both. He kept coming. The end of the staff was probably going a hundred miles an hour. If I hit him with it square, he wouldn't get up—ever. One of the kids on the makeshift sled started crying.

I swung the staff into the piece of corrugated roofing I'd been hiding behind. Smack! The metal made an echoey, booming sound, like reverb on an electric guitar.

Darryl stopped.

"I don't have any food," I bellowed. "Leave me alone!"

"Darryl T. Jenkins, get your butt back here right this instant and help me search," Mabel screeched.

I slid slowly backward on the skis and whirled the staff over my head again.

Darryl glared at me, a hateful stare. Then he slowly turned toward Mabel. I spun and pushed off, skiing as fast as I could to put some distance between us. When I looked back at the family, Darryl and Mabel were bickering as they searched the rubble. Both kids were crying.

Chapter 16

I followed U.S. 20 east. Last night I hadn't noticed any sign of other people along the road. Today, I saw several sets of tracks: prints from boots, tennis shoes, and signs of stuff being dragged, like the improvised sled Darryl had. All of them were headed east.

I couldn't tell if there were more people on the road, or if the reduced ashfall was just covering their tracks more slowly. I hadn't seen many houses along the backcountry roads, but there were none at all on U.S. 20. Clearly the prints weren't being left by locals.

I hadn't been skiing long when I topped a rise and saw a knot of five people ahead of me going east.

They moved painfully slowly, pulling their feet out of the ash with effort, earning each step. Two of them dragged suitcases.

I thought about Darryl and decided I didn't want to meet five adults who might share his attitude toward the contents of my pack. I skied about twenty feet back the way I'd come, enough to put the ridgeline between me and the group ahead. Then I turned off the road and took to the countryside, heading roughly southeast.

I worried a little about leaving Highway 20. My family always took 20 to get to Warren; I didn't know any other route. I wished I had a map, but I hadn't been able to find any in the wrecked filling station. Perhaps I could head east on some other road and then cut back to 20 when I got closer to Illinois. The day was dim, but brighter than any since the volcano's eruption. Very little ash fell and no rain at all.

Lunch was part of a bottle of water, and I felt lucky to have that. At the rate it was disappearing, I wouldn't even have water for lunch tomorrow.

I found it harder and harder to keep my skis moving, as though hunger were a companion riding behind me, weighing me down. I tried to think about something other than food—Laura, Spork, or my family—but my mind kept returning unbidden to waffles, DQ Blizzards, and the gyros at The Pita Pit.

About a year ago, Mom had brought a brochure for Action Against Hunger home from church. It was full of pictures—African kids with forlorn faces, swollen bellies, and skeletal limbs. St. John's was planning a fundraiser: Everyone would fast for twenty-four hours and donate all the money we would have spent on food to ACF. (I didn't understand why the brochure called the charity Action Against Hunger and abbreviated it ACF, but it did.)

So for a couple of days, Mom nagged me about doing it. I was in my no-religion phase, as Mom called it, and didn't really want to get sucked back into St. John's, but eventually I relented and said fine, I'll fast for two days. Then Mom was all, fasting for two days isn't safe, blah, blah, blah, and I pointed out that it took the kids in the brochure a lot more than two days without food to get the potbellies and Skeletor arms. Anyway, we had a huge fight about it, the upshot of which was that I didn't eat for two days. The first day my whole family fasted. The second, I just refused to eat and shrugged off Mom's threat to have me hooked up to an IV.

Going without food for two days was hard. I probably couldn't have done it if Mom hadn't been nagging me about the IV and constantly offering me stuff to eat. But not eating when there's a full refrigerator downstairs is a totally different experience than not eating because you have no food and no idea where your next meal will come from. Hunger of choice is a painful luxury; hunger of necessity is terrifying torture.

Early that afternoon, I was losing my battle to stop daydreaming about food when I saw a little flicker of light off to the right, just at the edge of visibility. It wasn't lightning—too orange and too persistent. But it was something different, something that might take my mind off food for a bit, so I skied toward it.

As I got closer, I saw another farmstead. The barn and both outbuildings were down, squashed flat, but there were two metal grain silos standing. The house was mostly intact, but some kind of porch or addition had been crushed. The mangled ends of a few rafters protruded from the wreckage.

There had been a stand of trees around the house, perhaps planted as a windbreak. Most of the trees were down, and the few still standing looked like ghost trees, coated with light gray ash. A campfire flickered, visible through the branches of a huge fallen tree. I glimpsed a figure silhouetted by the firelight. I skied up to the fallen tree and peered through its limbs.

A guy was sitting on a log between me and the fire. He was a big guy, that's about all I could tell with him backlit by the fire. He appeared to be alone. A haunch of meat was roasting over the fire. My mouth juiced up instantly at the smell. Sweet and fatty—pork, maybe.

I skied around the fallen tree to get a better look, moving as slowly and quietly as I could. When I cleared the edge of the brush, the guy looked straight at me and said, "You there. Want to give me a hand?"

I should have turned and skied out of there as fast as I could. This guy was big. NFL linebacker big. None of his clothing fit—his jeans missed the top of his boots by at least four inches, and the cuffs of his flannel shirt wouldn't button over his bulging forearms. His pasty white skin was tinged gray by a layer of ash. He had propped a broken mirror in front of him with a stick; it looked like a chunk of one of those big mirrors some people have in their closets. Beside him lay a wide leather belt, a bar of soap, and a hand-ax, its blade gleaming in the firelight. He had a bucket between his knees.

I stood there staring awhile. My brain and my stomach were arguing. Something rang warning bells in my head—his undersized clothing, outsized body, or maybe the hand-ax. I knew I should turn and ski away, but the smell of that meat made my stomach rumble in anticipation. The guy said, "It's okay, I just need a hand shaving. I'll pay you with some meat."

That tore it. I'd had nothing but a handful of candy to eat since yesterday. The aroma wafting off the meat was intoxicating. My stomach declared victory, and I slid the ski pole into my belt and skied slowly toward him, staff ready.

"You here alone?" he asked.

"Um . . ." I said, trying to decide whether to lie.

"Guess so. It's okay. I only need someone to hold this mirror."

As I got closer, I saw a couple more chunks of broken mirror lying flat in the ash. The back half of the guy's head was covered in half-inch stubble. The front half was shaved bald. A few drops of blood had run down the side of his head from a nick.

"Folks call me Target," he said. "What's your name?"

"Target?"

"Yeah, like the store."

"Alex."

"Pleased to meet you, Alex."

"Same here . . . Target." Now I was beside him.

He reached down and picked up the biggest shard of mirror from the ground. "I need you to hold this behind my head so I can see to shave back there, okay?"

"Sure." I unclipped my boots from my skis and took the piece of mirror from him. I held it behind his head so he could see it in the mirror propped in front of him, like they used to do at Great Clips when they wanted to show me the back.

He stropped the edge of his hand-ax on the leather belt for a minute. Then he grabbed the bar of soap and dipped it in the bucket. The splash made me want to scream: *perfectly good drinking water and you're spoiling it with soap?* He soaped up the back of his head and started shaving, using the blade on his ax.

He was scary-good with that ax. He held it up near the blade and ran it quickly and smoothly over his scalp. Soap and hair clung to the blade, and he cleared it off every now and then with a flick of his thumb.

Occasionally he directed me to move the mirror, a little to the right or tilted up a bit. He nicked his head twice. Both times he made no sound, just went on as if nothing had happened while the blood mixed with soap on his scalp. As he shaved, a design emerged from the stubble on the back of his head, a bull's-eye. It was crudely inked there, like prison tattoos I'd seen on TV.

"Guess you know why they call me Target now."

"Yeah."

"Anyone coming for me, best they aim right there. 'Cause if I can see them coming, they ain't going to take me down. No way."

I couldn't think of anything safe to say. The guy sounded seriously paranoid. Who would be "coming for him" and why? I hoped I could get some meat and move on soon.

Target finished shaving and rinsed his head, washing away the blood and soap. I set down the chunk of mirror. The aroma of the sizzling meat drew my attention. It was a big chunk of flesh, hacked crudely out of the haunch of some animal. I could see splintered ends of yellow-white bone sticking out both ends of it. I must have been staring at it, because Target finished rinsing his head and turned to me.

"I promised you some meat, didn't I?" He rotated the spit and propped a stick against it to keep it from rolling back. The top edge was charred black. He cut a long strip off it with his hand-ax, set it on a smashed-flat tin can, and handed it to me.

I bit into it too soon and burned my mouth. It was charred on one side and bloody on the other, but nonetheless the most delicious cut of meat I could recall eating. It tasted like pork, but not quite. Maybe it was from a wild pig—I had never eaten one, so I wasn't sure what that tasted like.

I was about to ask him what it was when Target said, "I'm getting a crew together. Some guys I know will join, if I can find them."

"Crew?" I mumbled past the meat in my mouth.

"Yeah, get a few guys together—watch each other's backs—we'll own this messed up place."

"I guess so." I was trying to be polite, not agreeing to join. But he misunderstood me.

"Cool, you're in." He thrust out his hand and elbow like he wanted me to clasp arms with him.

"I've got to keep heading east. I'm trying to find my family."

"You're Target's family now."

Target's family? "Thanks but—"

"Are you dissing me? Nobody disses Target. Ask anyone from Anamosa, if you're in Target's crew, you're golden. You diss Target's crew, there's blood on the floor. That's how it is."

"Anamosa?" I crammed the rest of the meat in my mouth, chewing fast. He was sounding more and more like a lunatic.

"State prison. What'd you think it was, a ballet school?"

"I gotta get going." I fumbled around behind me to find my staff, wondering how fast I could get clipped into my skis and get out of there.

"You know, I was going to make you first in my new crew, seeing as how I haven't found my guys yet. But you're too scrawny to be on Target's crew anyway. Maybe I'll just mess you up some." He stood up, and I jumped to my feet, holding my staff ready between us. He had over a foot of height on me, not to mention at least one hundred pounds of muscled flesh.

"I've gotta go." I tried to slow my overly rapid breathing and took a step backward.

"Aw, come on. Take it easy. I was just screwing with you." He reached out his right hand as if to shake.

I started to take another step backward and his hand moved, quick as a snake, and grabbed my staff. I managed to hold onto it, but God, the guy was strong. He whipped the staff to the right, spinning me around. I continued the motion and managed to twist my staff free. The hand-ax appeared in his left hand. He swung it overhand, chopping at my neck. I threw my right arm up to block and caught him on the wrist. That saved my neck, but the momentum of his blow was such that it slid down off my elbow, and the blade thunked into my right side just below my armpit.

It didn't hurt at all—not at first. There was a grinding vibration as the ax scraped my ribs. He raised it for another blow. The blade dripped red, and the coppery stink of my blood filled the air.

I stabbed the tip of my staff forward in a desperate strike. I'd practiced it thousands of times in forms and on Bob, the training dummy, but I had never figured I'd have to use it for real. I lunged, stepping with my right foot. I aimed for his eye, guiding the blow with my right hand, thrusting with my left.

The result was spectacularly disgusting. His eye pretty much exploded. Blood and some kind of fluid streamed down the side of his face. He staggered back a few steps, toward the fire.

"You mother—!" he screamed and started to step forward, raising the ax again. "I'll chop your—"

I reversed the staff into a low strike that knocked his

legs out from under him. He fell backward into the fire.

Target screamed and screamed in an eerie falsetto. He leaped out of the fire and ran about twenty feet, which only served to fan the flames licking his clothing. Then he got smart and dropped and rolled in the ash.

I thought about chasing him. But I'd either have to beat him to death, which didn't appeal to me at all, or . . . do what? I didn't even want to get close to him. Just the sight of the blood dripping from his eye made stomach acid rise in my throat. So I shouldered my backpack, causing a flash of pain to sear up my right side. Then I clipped into my skis and hauled ass.

During the fight, the wound hadn't hurt at all. Now it throbbed, sending pulses of flaming agony across my chest. Every time I twisted my torso, I had to bite back a scream. Blood poured down my right side, trickled past my belt, and made hot streaks down my leg.

I glanced backward. Target pushed through the ash, following me, burst eye, fire-blackened clothing and all. He saw me looking at him and yelled something about what he planned to do to the stump of my neck once he'd removed my head.

The homestead had been built at the top of a large, gentle ridge. I pointed my skis down the slope toward a line of dead trees in the valley below.

The slope was just steep enough to allow my skis to slide over the ash. I picked up speed and quickly left Target in the dust. As I slipped into the trees at the bottom of the slope, I faintly heard him yelling behind me,

"I'll find you, Alex. I'll roast your heart. I'll crack your nuts and . . ." I found a stream amid the trees, and the noise of rushing water drowned his shouted threats.

Taking off my pack made my eyes water, it hurt so bad. I pulled my shirt up to look at the wound. A huge flap of flesh hung loose from the gouge. Blood welled from it, hot and wet along my side. I took a breathing rag out of my pack and pressed it against my side. Now I was crying. I couldn't help it, it hurt that much. I tied a T-shirt over the breathing rag and around my torso as tightly as I could. It seemed to help—blood was still flowing from the wound, but more slowly.

I hung my pack off my left shoulder and squeezed my right arm through the strap, scrunching my eyes closed against the pain. Slowly, I worked my way across the stream, sliding my butt along a fallen log, and staggered up the bank on the far side. I had to put some distance between me and Target and find a place to hole up and rest. I wished I'd had the foresight to bring some Neosporin and an Ace bandage from home. If the wound got infected, I'd die for sure.

When I emerged from the trees on the other side of the stream, I glanced around. No particular direction suggested itself, so I struggled up the hill, keeping the brightest part of the sky to my back; heading east, I hoped.

Minutes blurred into hours in a long, gray nightmare. Slowly up one low hill: step, breathe, step, breathe. Resting as I slid down the back side. Another halting sidestep up the next hill. Each time I crested a hill, I looked around,

hoping for a good place to stop. Each time, I saw nothing
but ash-covered slopes and a few scraggly trees. I got
more and more tired, until nothing but the flaming pain in
my side kept me awake. I was thirsty, too; I drank all the
water I had left, but five minutes later, I wanted more.

The ease of gliding downhill got me moving off the
ridge-tops. The hope of finding shelter convinced me to
push laboriously up from the valleys. Each uphill slog was
slower than the last. As my legs dragged, my heart beat
faster until I could feel it palpitating in my chest. My arms
and legs were numb. After a while I was barely aware of
them at all, as if they were merely mechanical attachments
I could manipulate but not feel.

I traversed four, maybe five hills this way. As I
approached the crest of the latest hill, I thought it impossible to continue for even one more slope. I'd have to find
the best shelter I could, nestled against a tree in one of the
valleys, perhaps. Once I found shelter, I'd rest and wait—
to heal or die.

When I topped the ridge, I saw a farmstead ahead,
only a mile or two off at the crest of another hill. I started the long, easy downhill glide toward it and tried to
psych myself to battle one more uphill slope. I could make
it. I would make it.

The homestead was small and simple, just a house and
a steep-roofed barn. About half the trees around it were
down, but both buildings were intact. I worried about
being chased off by the owners. Maybe I could hide in
their barn unnoticed for a while.

My breathing mask had been dry for hours now. The ashfall was light and thin, but every movement kicked more of the fine dust into the air. I had to stop every few steps to rest and cough, great hacking spasms that brought up nothing but flecks of blood—my throat was so dry.

As I approached the barn, I heard a strange noise—a loud grinding, like two rocks rubbing together. I swayed on my feet, almost falling. I caught myself on the back of the barn and leaned against it for a few minutes, trying to catch my breath. The grinding noise continued uninterrupted.

I gathered my strength and slowly skied around the barn. There was a massive set of sliding doors on tracks facing the house. Someone had shoveled the ash away from the doors and thrown them wide, letting light into the barn.

The scene inside the barn was odd. A bicycle without its wheels had been bolted to a huge wooden workbench. A girl stood on the bike, kicking the pedals downward with her feet, sweating with effort. She looked to be my age, more or less. The back wheel of the bike had been replaced with a large gear, which connected to another gear and a belt that turned a cone-shaped chunk of concrete. An older woman was leaning over the concrete cone, pouring something into a hole in the center of it.

Neither of them gave any sign of having noticed me. I pushed my skis forward, down the little slope where the ash had been shoveled away from the barn doors. My skis caught on the barn's dirt floor, throwing me forward. I was too tired and weak to catch myself. My head thumped against the dirt. And everything went black.

Chapter 17

I woke to someone shaking me. I supposed it was a
gentle shaking, but I had a headache so gnarly that
it felt as if my brains were being beaten to liquid
against the inside of my skull.

"Sit up," a girl's voice said.

I cracked my eyelids and reached out, trying to
find my staff. I grabbed the girl's thigh instead.
She removed my hand. "Take it easy, you're in bad
shape. But I need you to sit up."

I let my hand drop and looked around, moving
my head slowly. I was on a couch in front of a fireplace. A big fire had been set—I could feel it on the

side of my face and arm, but I was still freezing, like being outside without enough clothing on a sunny winter day. Someone had spread a heavy wool blanket over my otherwise naked body. I couldn't remember getting undressed.

The girl stood above me. A strange angel, my addle-pated brain thought. Surely angels didn't wear T-shirts and overalls. And I'd never heard of an angel perspiring, let alone sweating as profusely as this girl was.

I slowly lifted my upper body, trying not to jostle my aching head. She jammed a pillow behind me, propping me partly upright. She held an oversized coffee mug to my lips. I freed one hand from the blanket and took the mug, drinking deeply. Warm water, but I was so thirsty that pure ambrosia wouldn't have tasted better.

The water brought on a coughing fit. Every rasping cough triggered a bolt of pain between my temples. When I pulled my arm away from my mouth it was spotted with globs of gray sludge and flecks of blood.

The girl took away the mug of water. She returned with a rag that I used to clean my lips and arm. When I finished, she put four dull-red pills in my hand. "What are they?" I asked.

"Just ibuprofen."

I took the pills and drank another mug of water. The older woman came into the room then, carrying a small bottle of Jim Beam. She poured a shot of it into the mug.

"Mom!" the girl protested. "We need that. As a disinfectant, not a drink."

"I know, Darla, but he's got to be hurting. This will take the edge off." She held the mug to my lips.

"I already gave him four Advil. Do we have to waste *all* our medical supplies on this kid?"

I took a sip of the bourbon and spluttered it back out. It tasted horrid.

"I'll hold your nose," the woman said. "Drink it all at once."

It burned my throat on the way down, and when she let go of my nose, the fumes burnt my nostrils, too. I had to side with Darla—bourbon made a better disinfectant than beverage—although I wasn't thrilled to learn that she considered using medical supplies on me a waste.

I started coughing again. The woman held out a rag, and I used it to wipe my mouth and arm. "Thanks. I appreciate—"

"Don't you mention it," the woman said. "I'm Gloria Edmunds, by the way."

"Alex."

Darla had been doing something by the fire. Now she returned and began stripping the blanket off me. I grabbed it before she could pull it away from my groin, to preserve my modesty.

"Let go. There's nothing there I haven't seen. Who do you think undressed you, anyway? And honestly, I've seen better equipment on goats."

"Darla!" Mrs. Edmunds said. "Keep a civil tongue with our guest."

"Some guest. He's using our medicine, drinking our water, and will be eating our food soon, no doubt. Why'd he have to find our barn?"

"Because the good Lord led him there, that's why, young

lady. And you'll treat him exactly as you'd want to be treated if you fell over in someone's barn, halfway bled out."

"Yes, Mother," Darla said. "But I'm not dumb enough to go wandering around in this crap," she added, muttering.

I let go of the blanket. Darla pulled it off me and set it aside. My equipment definitely wasn't looking very impressive. I guess bleeding all over northeastern Iowa hadn't done much for my manhood. The cut at my side had mostly crusted over. A little blood seeped slowly from one edge.

"Roll up on your left side, so I can get at that wound. What happened, anyway?" Darla said.

"Hand-ax," I replied.

"Christ, that was clumsy."

I decided not to try to explain it right then. I was too tired. It took all my strength to watch Darla and her mom. They set out a bowl of water, a pile of mostly ash-free rags, a pocketknife, a sewing needle, and some heavy black thread on the end table by my head.

"This is going to hurt," Darla said. "Try not to move."

"Uh, do you know what you're doing?"

She shrugged. "I got a prize in the 4-H junior veterinary program."

"Isn't that for animals?"

"Yeah, so? We're all animals."

"You'll be fine, hon," Mrs. Edmunds said. "Darla has better hands than mine for fine work. Uncle Arthur came to visit me early."

"What?" I asked, confused.

Darla leaned close and hissed in my ear, "Arthritis, dumbass. Now lie still."

It was fine while she washed the outside of the wound with water. It hurt, but I could cope. When she started washing it with bourbon, I clenched my teeth and felt tears leak from my eyes. When she pried the flap of flesh open with her pocketknife, I screamed and passed out.

Chapter 18

When I awoke, I was desperate for both water and a place to pee. Odd that my body both craved water and needed to void it at the same time.

I lifted my head to look around. A mistake, because it triggered a jackhammer headache that was worse, if possible, than the one I'd had before I passed out. I closed my eyes and rested my head, waiting for the pain to subside.

After the headache had died down some, I reopened my eyes. There was still a small fire going—either I hadn't been unconscious long or someone had been feeding it. I pushed the blanket off my torso and looked down. I was still naked. The clean area around my wound formed a big oval of pink skin on my otherwise gray, ash-stained body. An Ace bandage was wrapped tightly a few times around my chest, holding a folded white cloth against my side.

Gingerly I slid my fingers under the cloth. I wanted to get a look at the wound. I pulled it up as gently as I could, but it was stuck. It hurt like crazy to pull the cloth free. The Ace bandage stretched just enough for me to take a look underneath.

There was a huge cut on my side, about the same size and shape as a horseshoe. Darla had closed it with a row of neat stitches, at least thirty of them—I didn't have the strength to count.

I badly needed to pee. I had no idea where I was, where the bathroom was, or whether the toilet worked. I thought about peeing out the front door, but I didn't know where that was either.

I swung my bare feet off the couch and sat up. A bad idea. I must have still been short on blood, because what little I had rushed out of my head. The world started spinning around me, and I toppled forward onto the wood floor. Pain spiked in my side and head, and I let out a short, involuntary yell.

Darla swept into the room a few seconds later. I was curled up on the floor in front of the couch, trying to summon enough strength to get up. She wore a T-shirt that came almost to her knees.

"What the hell—are you trying to wake up everyone in the house?" she said.

"No. Just looking for the bathroom. If you could point it out?"

"Christ. Let me find something we can use for a bedpan."

Okay. I didn't like that idea one bit. It was getting a bit embarrassing, exposing myself to this girl every time I saw her, especially since she found my "equipment" so unimpressive and didn't mind telling me so. I certainly didn't want to pee in front of her. Nonetheless, she had already left. I heard the clank of metal pans coming from an adjoining room. If I hadn't already woken her mother, that racket was sure to.

She returned holding a bread pan.

"Really," I said, "if you could show me where the bath-room—"

"Can you even stand up?"

I pushed my head and shoulders up off the floor, pre-paring to try.

"Never mind! I don't want you ripping all the stitches out of your side. I worked damn hard on those." She grabbed me by my left arm and hoisted me onto the couch.

I lay back, grateful to rest my pounding head. "Thanks for sewing me up. The stitches look good."

"Why were you poking at them, anyway? I put the bandage on you for a reason, dumbass."

"I just wanted to see them." The insults she was dish-ing out were annoying, but I was grateful, anyway. She had probably saved my life with those stitches.

"Hmm. Well, they turned out okay. I've never actually done that before, but I've watched doctors stitch me up

twice. Wish I had curved needles like they used on me—
would have made it a lot easier."

"You should be a doctor."

"Maybe. Don't tell Mom we used her second-best
bread pan for this, okay?" She put the bread pan on the
couch next to me and stared expectantly. "So you need to
pee or what?"

"Yeah. Could you, like, turn your back or something?"

She rolled her eyes. "Whatever, sure." She stepped to
the hearth and added a log to the fire.

I pulled the pan to my groin, lined up my soldier and . . .
nothing. It's hard to pee when a girl's in the room—even
if her back was turned. And on top of that, I was worried
about whether I could get it in the pan without splashing.
I knew "performance anxiety" wasn't exactly the right
term, but something like that was going on. Or not going
at all, rather.

Darla had finished feeding the fire. "Are you ever going
to do it?"

"Yeah, I need to, but I can't. Not with you standing
there."

She let out an exaggerated sigh and strolled toward
the kitchen. "Yell when you're done."

It took a minute, but I finally got it done. Sweet relief.
I didn't splash, either. Well, not enough that anyone would
notice. "Finished!" I called out.

Darla returned and took the bedpan from me. I pulled
up the blanket. Despite the fire, I was cold. "Any chance I
could get some water?"

"Yeah. Sorry, I should have thought of that. You need to drink a ton. Blood loss—your right boot was completely full when I pulled it off you. You lost some more while I was stitching you up. I'll be right back."

When she returned, she was carrying two thirty-two-ounce plastic cups, like the ones I used to get at fast food restaurants. She handed me one. "Drink this. I'll put the other one beside the couch."

"Thanks," I said.

"Don't yell again unless it's something important. Mom needs her sleep," Darla said. Then she disappeared.

Chapter 19

I woke to a smell: something delicious wafting out of the kitchen. I retrieved the cup of water from the floor and drank it all. I lay back down, thinking about calling out and asking for food. Before I could act on the thought, I fell asleep again.

The next time I woke, it wasn't a sound or smell calling me from sleep. It was the imminent explosion of my bladder. My back hurt, too; I'd obviously been on that couch a long time.

I heard someone moving in the kitchen, so I called out, "Hello?"

Mrs. Edmunds came through the doorway. "My,

I thought you were going to sleep through another day and night. You must be hungry."

"Yeah. But, um, where's the bathroom?" I sat up, holding the blanket to my chest. "I think my eyeballs are yellow." I must have wobbled a bit, because she rushed over and grabbed my left arm.

"Sure you're up for a walk?" She peered at my face.

I nodded.

"Okay, I guess there is something sloshing around in there." Holding my left arm, she helped me stand. My head felt as if it might blow off my shoulders at the slightest breeze, but no way did I want to undergo the humiliating bedpan procedure again. I wrapped my left arm over her shoulder and held the blanket around myself with my right hand. Together we hobbled to the kitchen and from there into a bathroom.

There was no toilet. A sink stood just inside the door, and a shower/tub combo was tucked against the far wall. Between them, where the toilet should have been, someone had run a plastic pipe out of the floor. A big red funnel, the type normally used for gasoline, was affixed vertically to the end of the pipe at about knee level.

"Darla rigged it up. She calls it a squat tube. Although I guess you won't have to squat."

"It goes outside?"

"It connects to the septic system, like the toilet did. Now, it's only for number ones. Number twos we're burying over where the garden was, at the edge of the yard."

"Okay."

"I'll leave this door cracked in case you need any help," she said as she left.

I leaned against the wall, supporting my weight with one hand and aiming with the other, and peed into the funnel. When I finished, I twisted the knob on the sink, but nothing came out. What an idiot, I thought. Of course the water didn't work. And of course what water they had would be too precious for hand washing.

I was wrong. Mrs. Edmunds had laid a hand towel and a bowl of water on the kitchen table. I washed my hands as best I could one at a time, using the other to clutch the blanket around my body.

The kitchen was dim. There was light filtering in through the windows, so it must have been daytime, but it was an ugly yellow-gray half-light. Even in the poor light, I could see the water in the bowl darken as I washed.

Mrs. Edmunds walked into the kitchen carrying a pile of clothing. "Your clothes need some mending. These might be a little big on you; they were my husband's."

"Oh, is he—"

"Dead."

"Sorry. . . ."

She shrugged. "Three years, five months ago. He was cleaning out a cattle grate."

I didn't see how that could have led to his death, but it didn't seem polite to ask. I took the pile of clothes in one hand, hugged it to my chest, and hobbled to the living room to get dressed.

When I returned to the kitchen the stove was on. The

blue flame of the burner was shockingly bright in the dimness. Mrs. Edmunds was spooning some kind of thin yellow batter into a frying pan. It smelled heavenly.

"The gas works here?" I said.

"We're on propane," Mrs. Edmunds replied. "As long as the tank holds out, we'll be able to use the stove. Then I guess we'll have to switch to the fireplace for cooking."

"Where's Darla?"

"Out working. Digging corn, taking care of her rabbits, maybe cutting firewood . . . I don't know. I'd be helping, but she thought one of us should stay with you."

"Huh. I thought she didn't want me around."

"She said you'd ruin all her hard work stitching you up if you woke up and nobody was here."

"I know it's a pain, having me here. I really appreciate—"

"Don't mind Darla. I know she has a tongue so rough it could strip rust off a harrow disk at twenty yards, but she likes you fine. She's just scared. We both are. But the good Lord brought you to my barn door for a reason, and my job is not to ask why. Now eat up." Mrs. Edmunds flipped four small yellow pancakes out of the griddle onto a plate.

The pancakes were delicious. Yellow and crumbly, they tasted of cornbread and bacon. But then again, I was so hungry that anything probably would have tasted amazing. After three or four bites, I noticed a bit of a gritty texture and a hint of sulfur: ash, getting into everything. Between mouthfuls I said, "These are delicious, thank you."

"Oh, you'll get sick of it soon enough. It's only corn pone. That's mostly all we eat now. Corn pone for breakfast, lunch, and dinner."

"I could eat these all day."

"Well then, I'll fry another batch."

"Thanks."

Mrs. Edmunds' teeth gleamed in the half-light. She reached into a cupboard and pulled down a mason jar. "Don't tell Darla," she said as she poured a trickle of honey over the remaining two pancakes on my plate. "She wants us to save the honey—for what, I don't know."

I took another bite. Heavenly.

Two plates of corn pone and two glasses of water later, I was tired again. I limped to the couch and collapsed.

***

When I next opened my eyes, it was fully dark outside. Someone had fed the fire—there was enough flickering light to see by, and my side was uncomfortably warm. Darla was bending over me unbuttoning the shirt I was wearing, her dad's shirt.

I said something like, "Wha? Uh." Never mind full sentences, even polysyllabic words were beyond me when I was half asleep.

"Lie still. I'm going to check your bandage," she said.

She pulled the shirt open, slid the Ace bandage away from the wound, and lifted the white cloth. The wound was an angry horseshoe of crusty red scabs. I didn't see any pus or much swelling, which was a relief.

Darla began washing it using a bowl of water and hand towel. As she scrubbed the scabs, it hurt. When she finished that and washed the area around the wound, it felt good. Too good. By the time she finished, I had a hard-on so intense it hurt. It was pretty obvious, too, even in her dad's loose jeans. The heat in my face at that moment had nothing to do with the fire.

It didn't make sense. Darla hadn't said three kind words to me since I'd arrived. But my body obviously didn't care.

Darla put a fresh cloth over the stitches and pulled the Ace bandage back into place. She stood and glanced down. As she stalked out, I heard her mutter, "Boys." I curled up on my left side and tried to think about anything but the way her hands had felt against my side.

Sleep was a long time coming.

Chapter 20

I woke up in time for breakfast the next morning. Darla, Mrs. Edmunds, and I sat down together to eat corn pone. Darla ate mechanically, forcing down her food with a grimace. It tasted wonderful to me.

As we finished breakfast, Darla announced, "I'm going to spend the day digging corn. You going to care for the invalid, Mom?"

"You could take a day off," Mrs. Edmunds said. "How many sacks of cornmeal do we have now? Four or five—"

"Six," Darla said.

"It's enough. Rest for a day."

"How do you know it's enough? How long will it be before we can grow anything? Before any help comes from outside? A year? Three? How long will the corn keep, buried in that ash?"

"I'll help." It seemed like a perfect opportunity to try to pay back some of their generosity. I'd be dead now if they had rolled me back out into the ash instead of taking me in and stitching up my side. "I don't know exactly what you mean by digging corn, but I'm feeling better—"

"Yeah, so we're going to drag the invalid out to the field where he'll rip my stitches open and have to be dragged—"

"Darla! He's a guest, not 'the invalid.' And normally I don't hold with putting guests to work, but things are a little different now. Some exercise probably won't hurt him, so long as he doesn't overdo it." Mrs. Edmunds stared at me expectantly.

"No, ma'am, I won't overdo it."

"That settles it, then, we'll all go dig."

Soon I found myself carrying three empty feed sacks up a nearby hill. Darla and her mom each carried a shovel. The day was brighter than any I'd seen—nothing approaching normal, though. The sky looked sort of like a faded yellow twilight; not a hint of blue or cloud was visible, only a stifling blanket of yellow haze. No ash fell, but every time the wind gusted, it kicked up great plumes of the stuff. All three of us wore wet dishtowels around our faces.

It was so cold outside that I could see my breath in the air. I'd lost track of the date, but it must still have been September. Definitely way too cold for September in Iowa, whatever the date was. How cold would it get? And if winter was starting in September, how long would it last?

At the top of the ridge a huge rectangle was marked out with four bamboo poles. "That's the spot we've already dug," Darla said. "We'll work from this edge, throwing the ash into the marked area."

"We're digging for corn?" I asked.

Darla gave me that look I used to get from teachers when I asked a stupid question. "Yeah, you'll see." She started digging beside one of the bamboo poles, scooping up the ash and tossing it aside. Her mom moved about ten feet off and began digging as well.

Plumes of ash trailed in the wind as they worked. Darla shoveled maniacally, ramming in her spade and hurling each scoop away. Her mom kept up a measured pace, without any wasted effort. Soon they were both sweating and coated with clumps of white-gray ash. I stood watching them for a few minutes, at a loss for what to do. They'd only brought two shovels.

Darla motioned me over. She'd cleared most of the ash from a thin strip of ground. Stalks of corn, squashed under the ashfall, were visible here and there. They were a kind of sickly looking yellow, like grass that's been covered with something for a while. The ash layer was only five or six inches deep.

"Why's the ash so thin here?" I asked Darla. "It was almost two feet deep in Cedar Falls."

"Top of the ridge. Wind's been blowing it away like snow. It's about twelve inches on the lee sides of the hills, deeper in the valleys."

"Huh."

"Okay, so here's what you do. Come behind me and Mom and pull up each stalk of corn, like this." She grabbed a stalk and pulled it free of the remaining ash. She stripped the ears of corn off the stalk and tossed them into a feed sack. "Easy, right?"

"Yeah, no problem."

"Make sure you don't miss any ears. Too much damn work unburying them."

So I spent the day stooped over, picking corn. I tried shoveling for a while, spelling Mrs. Edmunds—Darla flatly refused to give up her shovel—but it put too much strain on my side. I couldn't shovel nearly as fast as Mrs. Edmunds, let alone match Darla's frenetic pace. It was frustrating being so weak, unable to contribute my fair share of work. I've never been the biggest guy or the strongest, but I've always made up for it with effort. Yeah, I might have blown off stuff Mom forced me to do, but if I'm into something, like taekwondo or *WoW*, I work like crazy at it.

We dragged three sacks of corn to the barn at lunchtime. Mrs. Edmunds made cornmeal mush for lunch—for variety, she said, laughing. And after lunch we did it all again, shoveling ash and picking corn until I was so stiff and sore that I could barely move.

By late afternoon we'd filled three more feed stacks. After we took them to the barn, Mrs. Edmunds returned to the house. Darla walked through an interior doorway, to a part of the barn I hadn't been in yet. I hesitated a moment, unsure which way to go, then followed Darla.

Chapter 21

Darla led me into a room filled with rabbit hutches, wire-mesh cages suspended from the ceiling by wires. The cages were linked together in two long rows, with eight cages per row. Two or three rabbits lay in most of the cages, just one in a few of them: maybe twenty or twenty-five rabbits in all.

I'd get teased mercilessly if any of the guys at Cedar Falls High heard me say this, but they were cute. Floppy gray ears and gray noses topped their white bodies. They were big, too, at least twice the size of the rabbits I used to see in pet shops.

Darla moved along the row of cages, pulling water bottles out of the little rings of wire that held them suspended beside each cage. I helped her gather up the bottles and then held them as she refilled them, pouring water out of a five-gallon bucket.

"They're all sick," Darla said.

"They look okay to me. Kind of cute, actually."

Darla glared at me. "They're meat rabbits."

"Oh."

"Look at this." She reached into a cage and pulled a rabbit out of a stainless steel bowl. It had been flopped across the bowl, panting a little. "They started running a temperature and drinking way more water not long after the ashfall. I put extra water bowls in their pens, but they just lie there in the water."

"Um—"

"I guess it's not a big deal; we'd have to butcher them soon anyway. I'm almost out of rabbit feed, and I can't get the dumb bunnies to eat corn."

"Weird."

"Can't say I blame them much, I'm getting sick of corn, too."

"So if you're going to kill them all anyway, what's the problem?"

"It's just . . . I don't know what it is." She spoke in a softer voice than I'd yet heard her use. "It must be something related to the ashfall . . . . What if it gets us, too?"

I couldn't think of anything to say. The same thought had occurred to me, that the ashfall might be killing me, especially every time I coughed up blood. But I didn't want to tell Darla that. I didn't want to admit to her that I was afraid.

"This guy, I named him Buck." Darla looked at me. "You get it? Buck and he's a buck. . . ."

I must have had a blank look on my face. I had no clue what she was talking about. And I was still wondering if the ashfall was somehow poisoning us.

"City people," she said, scowling. "Hold him for me, would you? No, by his haunches, upside down. Hold him tight, okay?"

I held the rabbit as she directed me, upside down in front of me. He waved his front legs feebly. Darla grabbed his head and pulled down sharply, twisting it. There was a soft pop, and he went limp in my hands. I was so startled, I dropped him.

Darla picked up the dead rabbit and said, "Bring the water, would you?"

I followed her into the main room of the barn, carrying the five-gallon bucket. A plastic double-bowl sink was built against one wall, with a couple loops of twine dangling from a beam above one of the basins. Darla slipped the dead rabbit's back legs into the twine loops so it hung upside down over the sink. Then she pulled a four-inch knife out of a block on the workbench beside the sink and began sharpening it on a rectangular stone.

I put down the bucket and watched. I wasn't exactly sure what she was doing, but I had an idea it wouldn't be entirely pleasant.

Darla reached up and ran her knife around each of the rabbit's hind legs, right below where the strings held it suspended above the sink. Then she cut a slit along its inner thighs on each side. She grabbed the skin and peeled it down the hind legs, turning it inside out as she went.

It wasn't nearly as gross as I imagined it would be. For one thing, there wasn't much blood. The skin peeled smoothly off the legs, although I could see Darla was pulling hard on it. Beneath it I saw the rabbit's muscles, pink and gleaming in the dim light.

It was uncomfortable to watch. I wondered what I would look like, dangling by my legs, skin slowly peeled back from the ankles down. I told Darla, "I'm going to go see if your mother needs any help."

She looked over her shoulder at me. "Grossed you out, huh?" She smiled—in victory, I imagined.

"Uh, no, it's not—"

"So you're a vegan or something?"

"No, I like meat."

"You just don't want to see where it comes from?"

"I know where it comes from: nice plastic-wrapped containers in the supermarket. . . ." I smirked and then shut up so I didn't sound like a wimp.

Darla was quiet for a few seconds. "Not anymore."

"Yeah. Look, you're right. I should learn how to do this."

"Fine. Watch, then." She made a couple quick cuts around the tail and pulled on the skin, tugging it down over the rabbit's hindquarters.

"I'll learn it better if you let me try."

Darla shrugged and handed me the knife. "Cut straight down the middle of the belly, from the tail to the neck. Try not to cut too deep. We only want to slit the skin now. We'll gut it next."

I tried sliding the knife gently over the skin. I wasn't cutting anything. Darla put one hand over mine and pushed down, forcing the knife firmly into the skin right below the tail. Together we drew the knife downward, and the pelt opened up like a bathrobe, exposing the pink muscle beneath.

"Okay, now grab the skin and pull down. Hard."

I did, and the skin peeled off the carcass like a sock, all the way down to the rabbit's forelegs.

"This part is kind of difficult; let me have the knife." Darla cut the rabbit's front paws off with a pair of garden shears and tugged the skin off its forelegs. Then she pulled the skin down over the rabbit's head, making tiny cuts here and there with the knife as she went. In less than a minute we had one very naked-looking rabbit carcass and an inside-out skin.

"What now?"

"Now we have to gut it." Darla made a deeper cut down the belly of the rabbit and pulled the muscle aside, exposing a gray, wormy mass of intestines and organs. She reached into the rabbit and pulled out its guts with her hand. It was so disgusting I had to look away.

"I'm going to pull out the liver, kidneys, and heart now," Darla said. "Pour a little water over them, would you? They're good eating."

I sloshed water over her hands while she pulled the dark red organs out of the rabbit's chest. She dropped them into one of two buckets in the other basin of the sink. The second bucket held the nasty, gray, spaghetti-like intestines.

I kept pouring water for her as she washed the inside of the carcass. She jammed her finger through the hole where its tail had been. "To clean out any last bit of lower intestine," she said.

Once Darla was satisfied that the carcass was clean, she taught me how to butcher it. She deftly cut off each piece of meat, naming it as she did: hindquarters, loins, etc. Pretty soon we'd filled the clean bucket with rabbit meat, ready for cooking.

"Will you take the meat in to Mom? I want to try tanning this skin. We might need it."

"Okay." I picked up the bucket of meat and shuffled out of the barn. It was getting more difficult to see as real twilight replaced the fake yellow version we suffered with during the day.

I found Mrs. Edmunds in the living room feeding the fire. "Darla asked me to bring you this rabbit meat," I said, holding up the bucket.

"Lovely, it'll be so nice to have some meat for a change. But I didn't think she was planning to butcher any of them for a while."

"It was sick. She didn't seem too happy about it."

"Oh dear. The Lord provides—maybe we were meant to eat rabbit tonight."

"You don't suppose it could hurt us, could it? Eating meat from a sick rabbit?"

"We're not sure why the rabbits are sick. Probably not if we cook it really well. I guess we'll find out. Tell Darla I need at least an hour to let it stew. Two would be better."

"Okay." I handed the bucket to Mrs. Edmunds and left the house. I figured it might be hard to find my way back to the barn since it was getting so dark, but it turned out to be easy. Darla had flung the big sliding door fully open and lit a makeshift torch on the end of a bamboo pole. She was visible from clear across the farmyard, bent over a bench near the sink, working on something.

As I approached, I called out, "Your mom says an hour or two on the rabbit stew she's making."

"Good," Darla replied. "That should be enough time to take care of this pelt. Would you bury the stuff in the offal bucket? Over where we put our crap."

I glanced into the bucket. The intestines had been covered with a mass of jumbled rabbit bones. On top of it all was the rabbit's skull. It had been violently crushed and wrenched apart, so it sat in two halves, like a discarded eggshell.

"Yipes, what happened to that?"

"What?"

"The skull."

"Oh, I smashed it with a hammer and scooped the brains out with a spoon."

"You what?"

"We need the brains to tan its pelt. I'll show you when you get back."

Dismissed, I picked up the offal bucket and a shovel. What kind of girl cuddles with a cute rabbit she named Buck one minute and the next smashes its skull with a hammer to scoop out its brains? I shivered—and only partly because of the cold night air.

I stumbled around in the dark, looking for the latrine area. I thought I had found it—it was impossible to be sure with everything covered in a featureless blanket of ash and no light except the faraway glint of the torch through the barn door. I buried the rabbit's remains in a shallow hole and rejoined Darla in the barn.

She had tied the pelt into a small frame built of lumber; two-by-twos, she said. A dozen or so small cords, shoelaces maybe, stretched the pelt tightly in the center of the frame. Darla was scraping the skin with a rounded piece of metal.

"The brains are in there," Darla said, gesturing at a bowl on the workbench beside her. "Pour a little water in with them—we want about half brains and half water. Then stir it up really well. It should look about like a strawberry milkshake when you're done."

"What?" Something about brains and milkshakes didn't compute. Had I wandered into a bad zombie movie?

"We need a brain-and-water mixture about like a strawberry milkshake," Darla repeated, talking very slowly, as if she were explaining to a preschooler.

"Why?"

"We're supposed to use the mixture to tan the skin. After I get it scraped, we'll rub the brains on it."

"That's kind of disgusting."

"I guess. But it's the traditional way to tan hides. There's some kind of oil in the brain that soaks into the pelt and keeps it soft."

"You do this a lot?"

"Nope, first time. Thought about trying it before, but never found the time. Some of the rabbit breeders I know do some tanning, and I've read up on it."

I poured a little water in the bowl with the brains. They were gray, with little red streaks here and there. Blood vessels, I guessed. I found a spoon in the sink and used it to mash them up. It took a bit of stirring to get the mixture to the texture Darla wanted. When I finished, it looked almost exactly like a strawberry milkshake. Not that I was going to take a sip or anything.

Darla worked on the hide for almost an hour, scraping the inside clean. Then she put the frame flat on the workbench, the fur side of the pelt facing down. She poured some of the brain mixture onto the skin and rubbed it in with her hands.

I shuddered. She must have seen me, because she said, "It's not bad. Feels a little oily. Like mayonnaise, sort of."

I couldn't let a girl show me up, especially not Darla, so I reached over and rubbed the hide as well. She was right; the brain mixture didn't feel as gross I'd imagined it would. We rubbed it for ten minutes or so, trying to work the brain into every bit of the skin. It wasn't a big pelt; our hands were constantly touching, sliding against and over each other, slick with rabbit brain.

Finally, Darla pronounced it done. We rinsed off our hands, pouring water for each other. Darla propped the frame against the wall and extinguished the torch, plunging us into darkness. I stood still, trying to let my eyes adjust, until I felt Darla's hand in mine. She gave my hand a squeeze and then tugged on it, leading me out of the barn.

The warmth of her hand sent an ironic shiver racing up my arm. I knew that she didn't like me much, that she saw me as a freeloader. I knew I should stay cool and detached. But I couldn't help myself. No matter how much I told myself to chill out, it didn't help. I wished we'd met before the eruption, when things were normal. Maybe then she would have seen me as something more than a helpless kid.

Darla dropped my hand, and I opened the kitchen door for her. It smelled intoxicating inside. Mrs. Edmunds ladled huge bowls of soup—she called it rabbit corn chowder—out of a pot bubbling on the stove. Darla began shoveling the soup into her mouth the moment the bowl touched the table in front of her.

"Darla!" Mrs. Edmunds exclaimed. "Manners."

"Hurmm," Darla replied, her mouth full of soup. But she quit eating.

Mrs. Edmunds put a cloth napkin and a glass of water at each place setting and took her seat at the head of the table. "Let us pray." She laced her hands in her lap and looked down. "Lord, bless this food and those who eat it. Hold us safe in your loving hands as we struggle to meet the test you put before us. And remember especially those less fortunate than us, who don't have enough to eat or the support of family and friends in this time of trial. Amen."

Finally, I could eat. I'd never had rabbit, and before I had walked into the kitchen, I wasn't sure how I felt about eating an animal that had been squirming in my hands only two hours before. But the heady aroma drifting out of the bowl drove all doubt from my mind. I dug in. It tasted even better than it smelled—a bit like chicken.

I wolfed down two huge bowls of stew. After dinner, we sat around the table talking for a while—mainly about plans for the next few days. I stifled the first few yawns that pushed up from my exhausted body, but eventually one escaped. Mrs. Edmunds shooed me off to my bed on the living room couch.

I was exhausted from the day's work, my side hurt, and I'd overstuffed myself on chowder. I fell asleep almost before my head touched the pillow. I vaguely remembered someone checking my bandages that night, but that may have been a dream.

Chapter 22

The next two weeks passed in much the same way: work, work, and more work. I was anxious to get moving, to continue my quest to find my family. But I was still weak—it wouldn't do me any good to start out again before I'd completely recovered. I knew I'd regret leaving Darla, but my family mattered more than some girl I'd just met and barely knew. And anyway, she seemed anxious for me to leave, too.

At least the work varied a little. Some things had to be done every day, like pumping water. We filled three five-gallon buckets each morning: one for the rabbits, one for the kitchen, and one for the bathroom. Darla told me the pump for the well had quit when the electricity went out, before the ashfall had even reached their farm. She'd rigged up a bamboo pole that protruded from the pump hole. I had to grab the pole and push it up and down fast to get water to flow out of a PVC pipe.

Wood had to be hauled to the living room fireplace every day as well, from a huge rick behind the house. We spent one day cutting more with a bow saw and ax. Well, mostly Darla cut and hauled the wood while I stacked it—my side was still too weak to do much of the heavy work. There was plenty of timber nearby: immediately around the house a bunch of trees grew, and there were more along a creek in the valley. Darla checked each tree before we cut it, bending a few twigs. If they were green and springy, we left the tree alone. But most of the trees were dead.

We spent the lion's share of our time digging corn. We worked our way along the ridge where the ash was thinnest, pulling bag after bag of corn down the hill. Even then the work wasn't done. The corn had to be shucked, scraped off the cob, and ground to meal. Darla had built a bicycle-powered grinder that I'd seen in action when I first arrived at the farm. Now I ground corn, endlessly it seemed, either pumping away on the bicycle or pouring the corn into the mill. I was starting to feel stronger, but Darla could drive the grinder at least twice as long as I could.

On my twelfth day on the farm, Darla cut the stitches out of my side. Droplets of blood welled up here and there when she pulled the threads from my flesh. Overall, the wound didn't look too bad. But it was going to leave a heck of a scar.

The rabbits got sicker. We killed and skinned eight more—the ones Darla thought were so sick they wouldn't survive much longer. That was too much meat to eat right away, so I helped Darla build a smokehouse. Helping Darla meant holding tools for her, scavenging nails, and cutting boards where she told me to, not to mention enduring abuse when I didn't know which tool she meant or couldn't cut a board straight enough to suit her razor-sharp eye.

We ripped up a chunk of the floor in the hayloft to get boards for the smokehouse. Darla said it didn't matter since there wouldn't be any more hay for years. It took the better part of a day for us to knock together a ramshackle structure about the size of a short outhouse, which seemed like a long time until I considered that we'd had to salvage all the materials and do the work without power tools. From then on, we had two fires to tend: one in the living room that we relied on for heat and a smaller one in the smokehouse.

We hung the rabbit meat on crossbars at the top of the structure where the smoke would pool. While we were building the first fire at the base of the smokehouse, I asked Darla, "So how long do we have to keep this fire going?"

"I don't know exactly. Never done this before."

"Like, a few hours?"

"No, days at least, a week maybe? I'll probably leave the meat out here until we eat it—it's cold enough that it shouldn't spoil, even without the smoke."

"How'd you know how to build this thing if you've never smoked meat before?"

"I saw a smokehouse once. Guy was using it to cure hams. And how hard can it be? Fire in the bottom, meat up top where all the smoke collects."

"I guess."

"I don't know how it's going to work for rabbit. Not much fat on them. Probably going to be pretty dry and tough when we get done smoking them."

"Better than nothing."

"Yep, it'll beat not eating."

Since I'd spent two days on the way here not eating, I had to agree with her. Almost anything beats starvation.

Chapter 23

The next day at breakfast, Darla proposed digging more corn. Mrs. Edmunds flatly refused. "Have either of you looked at the dirty clothes? If we throw one more thing on the pile, it'll collapse the floor, and we'll have to move to the barn."

After Darla and I took care of the rabbits and fed the fires in the smokehouse and living room, we hauled water. Endless buckets of water, to fill the bathroom tub. Once we had it mostly full, Mrs. Edmunds tossed in the clothing, and we started scrubbing. Our clothes were so filthy, they quickly turned the water into a grayish sludge thick enough that Darla worried about it clogging the drainpipe.

We then had to wring out the clothing, rinse the tub, and refill it. Each refill required pumping six buckets of water, hauling the heavy pails across the yard, through the kitchen, and into the bathroom, and pouring them into the bathtub. We refilled that stupid tub five times before Mrs. Edmunds was satisfied that the clothes were "clean enough." Then, of course, we had to wring the water out of the clothing and hang it on makeshift lines strung through the living room in front of the fireplace—the living room I'd been sleeping in. The damp clothes dripped onto the couch—my bed. I hoped it would dry before I turned in that evening.

After lunch, Mrs. Edmunds declared an afternoon of rest. She planned to read for a bit and maybe take a nap, she said. Darla frowned but didn't reply. The nap bit sounded good to me.

It was not to be. As soon as Mrs. Edmunds settled into the easy chair with her paperback, Darla said, "Come give me a hand. I've got a project that's perfect for this afternoon." I sighed and followed her into the farmyard.

As usual, helping Darla mostly meant handing her tools. And, like when we built the smokehouse, I got yelled at whenever I didn't know exactly what she was asking for or I couldn't find it, which totally spoiled the good part of this project: watching her bend over the engine of the old F250 pickup parked beside the barn. The pickup was half-buried in drifted ash.

"Are we fixing it?" I asked.

Her voice came back muffled by the hood. "No, I don't

think I can. I drove it a bunch before the ash got too deep. The air filter is completely clogged, and I don't have a spare. The ash probably tore up the engine, too. Might need a valve job."

I didn't know what a valve job was and wasn't about to ask. Odds were, the answer wouldn't make sense to me, anyway. "So why are we working on it?"

"I need the alternator. Gimme a medium ratchet with a half-inch hex head."

I found the ratchet but couldn't read the socket sizes in the crappy light. I put one that looked right on the ratchet and handed it to her.

She glanced at it. "That's 15/32nds. Christ. Put on the next size bigger."

I replaced the socket and handed it to her. "How can you even read the sizes?"

"Don't need to. Honestly, any idiot could've seen that wasn't a half inch."

"Well, I couldn't." I raised my voice a bit and shot clipped words at her. "And I'm not an idiot. And this is getting old. I know you've probably got ash in your panties, but do you have to take it out on me?"

She pushed herself out from under the hood. "Huh? What did you—"

"Ash in your—well, you seem so irritated at me all the time."

"Ash in my—" She laughed. "Yeah, I do. And it *is* irritating. And what are you doing thinking about my panties, anyway?"

I blushed, hoping the inevitable layer of ash on my face hid it. "Uh, sorry. But seriously, it's not my fault I wound up here. And I'll be moving on soon. I feel tons better already."

"Good. Maybe I have been bitchy, but having you around hasn't exactly been easy for me. Mom thinks we can take in all the world's strays, but who knows how long this will last? We might still be eating cornmeal a year from now—or three."

"Yeah, I understand. I won't hang around. I need to find my own family."

"And when you go, don't take all our supplies. I know Mom, she'll try to convince you to stay, and failing that, she'll load you down with more of our food than you can possibly carry."

"I won't."

"I guess you're entitled to some of it . . . . You've been working pretty hard, considering that hole in your side." Darla buried her head back under the truck's hood. "Gimme a big flathead screwdriver."

I found one and slapped it in her outstretched hand. Maybe it was my imagination, but it seemed as though her fingers lingered against mine a bit longer than necessary to take the screwdriver. Could the frozen shell she kept between us be thawing just a little?

We pulled the alternator out of the truck and carried it to the barn. Darla bolted it to a workbench. Then she welded a bicycle gear onto the disc on the side of the alternator. She had a welding setup that ran off two metal cylinders that looked like helium tanks. When that was finished, she disconnected the bicycle we'd been using to drive the grain grinder and connected it to the alternator with a long chain. She attached the alternator wires to a battery charger, the kind that held eight D-cells.

Meanwhile, I'd been doing nothing useful. Handing her a tool now and then, but mostly watching her work. She checked the tension on the chain, made an adjustment, and said, "Your turn to work. Get on your bike and ride." Darla grinned. "I think I just quoted some band Mom likes."

I climbed on the bike and started to pedal. It was easier than driving the gristmill—there was a lot less resistance. As I got the bike up to speed, a red light began glowing on the battery charger, lurid in the dimness of the barn.

"When that light changes to green, we're done," Darla said.

I pedaled away in silence, listening to the sound of my breathing grow louder and more labored as I rode. Each time I slowed a little, Darla snapped, "Faster!" or "Pedal harder!" I kept it up for a long time, maybe an hour or so, before she finally offered to relieve me. I might have gotten annoyed at her bossiness, but I was too tired to care.

I collapsed onto the dirty straw on the barn floor, utterly spent, as Darla mounted the bike and pumped the pedals. We traded off twice more, riding the bike at least three hours before that stupid light finally winked green.

By then, I was exhausted and hungry, and Darla wasn't looking too perky, either. She pulled the batteries out of the charger and put them in her jacket pockets. We

trudged to the house to wash up for dinner. I was surprised at how sweaty I'd gotten despite the cold air.

After dinner, all three of us sat around the fire in the
living room while Darla fiddled with an old radio. Mostly
we listened to static. My legs had paid dearly for that
static: They ached. I reached down to rub my calves—it
felt like rubbing tires, they were so tight.

Low on the AM dial, Darla finally got something. A
couple of stations drifted in and out, frequencies changing
slightly, as if the vagaries of the ash-laden atmosphere
were somehow distorting them. One of them was playing
music, of all the useless things they could do. Peppy,
annoying, big band music, the kind my great-grandmother
might have listened to on the radio. It baffled me why they
were playing it now.

Another station was more helpful. They read nonstop
news—all of it related to the eruption. The maddening bit
was that we could only make out little snatches of news
over the static as Darla chased the station around the dial.
She caught it the first time at 590 AM, but it would drift
as high as 640 and as low as 570 at times.

The first snatch of news was, ". . . In addition, the
Admiral announced that a U.S. Navy relief convoy will
dock at Port Hueneme in Oxnard, California, sometime
tomorrow. While most supplies are designated for federal
refugee camps in northeastern California, some food,
medical supplies, and tents will be available to citizens
through their local interim authority.

"Admiral McThune went on to say that a third Chinese
humanitarian mission has been granted permission to land

in Coos Bay, Oregon, joining the previous two in Newport and . . ."

"Damn. Lost it," Darla said.

"Watch your mouth, young lady," Mrs. Edmunds scolded.

Darla fiddled with the radio, looking for a signal.

"How big is this thing?" I asked. "If Oregon and California are as bad off as Iowa . . . how long will it take to get any help here?"

"Let's see." Mrs. Edmunds pulled an old Rand McNally road atlas off the shelf. Near the front there was a yellow map of the U.S. cross-hatched by blue interstates. Judging by the map, Oregon and Northern California were both closer to Yellowstone than we were.

The room was quiet except for the hiss and crackle of the radio and an occasional pop from the wood burning in the fireplace. I thought about all the people facing this disaster—the millions between me and the Oregon coast. Millions of them must have already died. I'd been incredibly lucky to survive this long. Darla and her mom were doing okay, digging and grinding corn, but most people wouldn't have access to fields of buried corn or know how to improvise a grinding machine. Millions more people would die unless some kind of help arrived soon.

Darla found the station again. "Responding to critics," he said, "the suspension of civil liberties contained in the Federal Emergency Recovery and Restoration of Order Act is temporary and will be lifted as soon as the crisis has passed, perhaps as early as late next year.'

"The vice president concluded his remarks with strong words for 'those nations whose hoarding and profiteering

caused the collapse of the international grain markets.' He
pledged to use the full force of the United States to insure
an equitable . . ."

None of us were sure what to make of that. It didn't
sound good, but it also didn't seem to affect us much. The
only functioning government I'd seen since the disaster
was Mr. Kloptsky's at Cedar Falls High. And our grain
market consisted of the corn we could dig up in a day.

We listened to the radio until the batteries died late that
evening, but we only caught one more intelligible fragment:
". . . announced earlier today that, using the emergency
powers granted it under FERROA, the Department of
Homeland Security has appropriated a large tract of land
near Barlow, Kentucky, to control the influx of refugees
from southern Missouri. Construction will begin . . ."

This was more interesting. We found Barlow on the
Kentucky page of the atlas. It took some searching—it
was a tiny black speck of a town near the Mississippi
River. Nowhere near us, but at least on the same side of
the country.

"Maybe there's help east of us," I said.

"Sounds like there must be," Mrs. Edmunds said.

"I need to leave soon." I said it with some regret. I
would miss Mrs. Edmunds. And I'd miss Darla.

"You're welcome to stay. You've worked so hard—
more than earned your keep."

"Thanks. I . . ." A thought seized my brain: I'd be dead
if not for them. I fought back tears. "I don't know how to
thank—"

"Shush," Mrs. Edmunds said. "Anyone would have taken you in. Why, you were half-dead when you fell into our barn."

Actually, anyone wouldn't have taken me in. I'd met people who wouldn't. The faceless person who'd pointed a rifle at me as I skied toward his farmhouse, for one. Target, for another. I shuddered at that memory. "I wish we'd heard more about what's going on in Illinois."

"Your family is there, right?" Mrs. Edmunds asked.

"Yeah . . . at least, that's where they were headed."

"Maybe someone in town would know more."

"I've been thinking about going to town, anyway," Darla said. "I need to ask Doc Smith about my rabbits. I'd feel better if I could save a few of them to breed."

"What town? How far is it?" I asked.

"Worthington," Darla replied. "About five miles. It's an easy walk—I've done it before."

"In this mess? Ten miles there and back? We might not be able to make it in a day."

"Who said anything about 'we'? I'll go, find out what's wrong with my rabbits, ask about Illinois, and come back."

"You should both go," Mrs. Edmunds said. "It'll be safer. I'll stay here, watch the rabbits, and catch up on my cleaning. If it gets too late, stay overnight with Loretta Smith or Pam Jacobs. They won't mind. But don't stay more than one night. I'll be worried enough as it is."

"I'll be okay, Mom."

"I know you will, dear. But I'll still worry."

Moms. They were all alike in that way.

Chapter 24

The next morning we fed and watered the rabbits by torchlight before dawn. I found my ski boots and skis in a corner of the barn. The right boot had dried stiff. I beat it with a fist and turned it over. Flakes of rusty stuff fell out and floated to the barn floor: my dried blood mixed with ash.

Mrs. Edmunds gave us each a huge stack of corn pone wrapped in old newspaper. Darla added two rabbit haunches fresh from the smoker. She cut a slit in one of them—it was still a bit raw, but they didn't smell spoiled. I packed my water bottles, tarp, and knife, just in case. I left my hiking boots behind;

I figured the ski boots would be okay for a day trip. I planned to carry the bö staff and ski pole.

Darla added a couple bags of cornmeal to her pack—to barter, if we found anything we needed, she said. Mrs. Edmunds pressed a wad of paper money into Darla's hand, and I hid a smile. I doubted that anyone would have much use for twenty-dollar bills now, except perhaps as fire starter. Darla took the money anyway, jamming it into her jeans pocket.

Mrs. Edmunds hugged Darla, kissed her on the cheek, and admonished her to be careful and look after me. Darla endured it all a bit impatiently.

I was surprised when Mrs. Edmunds hugged me. At first, I let my arms flap around at my side. But she didn't let go, so I hugged her back. Then I thought about my mom and had a hard time unhugging Mrs. Edmunds. Yes, my mom was a pain in the butt, and we fought a lot, but I missed her. I would have given anything to have her in my embrace now, instead of this wonderful ersatz mother who had adopted me.

So we set out, me on my skis, Darla trudging through the ash beside me. We followed the road that passed in front of Darla's farmstead, traveling on the crown where wind had blown away some of the ash. In some places, the ash had formed a crust Darla could walk on. But in most areas, loose ash still lay on the road, and Darla sank to her ankles with every step.

Skiing was hard work—my muscles seemed to have forgotten the movements over the last few weeks.

Nonetheless, I quickly got way ahead of Darla. I heard her
faintly behind me, calling, "Hey, wait up," as I topped a low
rise. I turned and looked—she was at least forty yards
back. I grinned at her and pushed off as hard as I could.

The hill wasn't very steep, but by pushing all the way
down I caught a little speed—enough to give me time to
flop at the bottom and rest there with a smirk on my face
as she struggled down the backside of the hill.

When she finally caught up, Darla silently stomped past
me. I felt a little bad watching her rip each foot free of the
ash, working for every step—but not bad enough to stop
me from sliding past her when I started moving again.

I rested for a bit at the bottom of the next rise, and
then began poling my way up. Partway up the hill, it got
steep enough that I couldn't push straight up it anymore.
So I had to duck walk. Well, I called it duck walking—I
wasn't sure if that was the right name for it or not.
Anyway, if I spread the tips of my skis way out, I could
walk uphill without sliding backward—it was hard work,
but faster than taking the skis off.

So I was duck walking up the slope, when Darla burned
by me. Her legs were pumping, thrusting her feet in and out
of the ash. She looked like an athlete doing a stair run. I
picked up speed and tried to catch her, but it was impossible.
By the time I reached her at the top of the rise, I was gasping for breath and my side hurt. Darla smiled triumphantly.

"Yeah," I said between gasps, "let's see how you do on
the downhill." I pushed off as hard as I could, pointing my
skis down the back side of the rise.

As I passed Darla, I felt a weight on the back of my skis, throwing me off balance. I whipped my head around: Darla was perched on my skis, clutching my backpack. I dug in with both poles, pushing hard. I thought a burst of speed might throw her off.

No such luck. She clung to me as I pushed, but I did get us moving. Soon we were flying down the hill.

I yelled over my shoulder, "Hey, this works pretty well. We—" Turning threw my balance off, and the inside edge of my left ski caught in the ash. We spun sideways and fell. The ash sort of cushioned my fall, but it did nothing to protect me from Darla's knee, which dug painfully into my thigh as she landed on top of me.

Darla pushed herself up. "You okay? Did I land on your side?" She extended a hand to help me up.

I took her hand. "Yeah, I'm fine." I grinned and gave her arm a vicious yank, pulling her down into the ash next to me.

"You butthead!" Darla grabbed a handful of ash and hurled it at me. I retaliated in kind.

It wasn't quite like a snowball fight. The ash wouldn't adhere into a ball, for one thing. It exploded into a gently floating mass of dust when I tried to throw it. But since we were lying next to each other, we could cover each other in dusty clouds of the stuff.

Pretty soon we were laughing and choking on ash at the same time. I called, "Truce!"

Darla said, "Done," and stood up again. This time I let her help me up. We were both filthy with ash. We looked sort of like those Africans I used to see on the Discovery Channel who painted their bodies with white mud. Maybe they still do, but there isn't a Discovery Channel to film it now.

"That worked pretty well. We should try it again," I said.

"What?"

"You riding on the back of my skis."

"Oh, yeah." She climbed onto my skis, and I pushed off, carefully this time.

We must have been quite a sight. Two gray-white ghosts, sailing down the rest of the hill on one pair of skis, cackling maniacally and trailing a plume of ash in our wake.

The rest of the way into Worthington, Darla rode on the back of my skis whenever there was a downhill slope steep enough, which wasn't often. It was more than nice, feeling her back there, her hands clinging to my chest, although it made the skis harder to control. I hoped for more steep slopes, but most of the way was flat or gently sloped. I kept my pace slow on the flat parts, so we could travel side by side and talk. We chatted about nothing in particular, mostly life before the volcano. I wished this, or something like it, could go on forever: Darla at my side talking about nothing much and—occasionally—hugging me as we sailed down a hill.

Chapter 25

I first caught sight of Worthington later that morning, just as my stomach started to tell me it was lunchtime. Three huge gray cylinders loomed in the dimness ahead: grain silos, much bigger than the ones on nearly every farm around there.

As we got closer to Worthington, I could make out a few other buildings, vague shapes beyond the silos. Between us and the town, a row of people worked in a field alongside the road. They were stretched in a long line, digging. Some of them had shovels, some had hoes, and some wielded only pointed sticks. There were men, women, and quite a few kids. Some of the kids looked younger than my little sister.

When we got close, a man carrying a rifle detached himself from the diggers. He held it casually in front of himself, pointed at the ground between us. "You have business in Worthington?"

"Since when do I have to have business to visit Worthington, Earl?" Darla replied.

"That you, Darla? Didn't recognize you under all that ash. What've you been doing, rolling in it?"

"Yeah, pretty much."

"How's your ma? I've been meaning to get out and check on you folks, but things have been a mite busy."

"Good as can be, I guess. We're getting by, anyway."

"Glad to hear it. You can head on into town if you want. Guess I've got corn to dig."

"What, you don't care what my business is now?"

"Now, I'm sorry about all that, but there's been folks coming down off Highway 20, thinking there's corn in those silos—"

"There's not—" I shut up midsentence when Darla gave me a withering look.

"Not right before harvest, there's not. It's all been sold and shipped out," Earl said.

"We'd better get about our *business*," Darla said. "See you later, Earl."

We passed the granary and then a couple of large metal commercial buildings that had been squashed by the ash. A block farther the houses started, small ranch-style homes on big lots on either side of the road. The second one we came to had a sign out front: Smith Veterinary.

From a distance, the house looked fine. The roof was mostly clear of ash. The metal barn beside the house was a different story. It looked as though an angry giant had smashed down his fist, punching the roof into the building. All four walls were standing, but the sliding metal doors had come off their tracks and hung cattywampus in the opening.

Darla turned, and I followed her across the front lawn—well, the front ash field. When we got closer to the house, we could see that the lock was broken off the front door. It stood slightly ajar, and a breeze carried ash inside.

Darla pushed on the door with her fingertips. It swung slowly open. The front hall was coated in a blanket of ash, smooth except for a raised rectangle that concealed the entry rug. Farther inside it was too dark to see anything.

"Hello? Anybody home?" Darla called.

"This doesn't feel right," I said, thinking it was downright creepy and wanting to move on.

"No." Darla pulled the door closed. It wouldn't latch, but it was good enough to look shut from the street. She looked right and left, studying the neighboring houses. There was a curl of white smoke twisting out of a standpipe on the roof of the house to the left. We walked toward it across the ash field.

The front door to this house was closed, and the lock looked intact. A piece of particleboard had been nailed over the upper part of the door, where perhaps there originally had been a window. Darla knocked.

A rotund woman with a ruddy face answered the door. Two things caught my attention. First, she carried a rifle, but she was holding it by the barrel, so it dangled from her left hand. In no way was she ready to use it. Second, she was clean, shockingly clean—not a spot of ash on her face, hands, or apron. I hadn't seen anyone that clean since I'd left the Barslow place over three weeks ago.

"Can I help you?" she said.

"Sorry to disturb you, ma'am," Darla replied. "We were looking for Doc Smith—"

"And you are?"

"Darla Edmunds. My mother's Gloria."

"Oh, yes, your mother knows Mrs. Peterson?"

"Yes ma'am, they used to play euchre together."

"I'm Jean. Jean Matthews." She put down the rifle, leaning it in a corner.

"Pleased to meet you," Darla replied.

"I'd invite you in but—"

"We're a bit dirty," Darla said. "Sorry."

"Come around back, to the deck. You can help me get lunch out to the harvest crew."

"We were just looking for . . ." Darla said, but the woman had already turned away and closed the door.

At the back of the house there was a big white propane tank beside their modest deck. A sliding glass door opened onto the kitchen. All four burners on the stove were in use. My mouth watered at the smell: bacon and corn.

"It smells delicious," I said.

Mrs. Matthews smiled. "It's only hasty pudding. I'd have been embarrassed to serve it before all this, you know. But now . . . well, it will keep a belly full."

Darla said, "About Doc Smith—"

"I'll tell you all about it on the way to the field," Mrs. Matthews said. "We've got to get everyone fed." Somehow it had become our job to help her feed everyone. I looked at Darla, and she shrugged.

Mrs. Matthews bustled around the kitchen, packing a couple of big canvas bags with a mismatched assortment of spoons and ceramic mugs. She shut off the stove and handed the pots out the back door to us. There were four of them: big, heavy Dutch ovens. I wasn't sure if I could carry them on skis, so I unclipped my boots and left my skis, ski pole, and staff on the deck.

The three of us walked back out of town to the field where we'd met Earl. On the way, Darla asked. "So is Doc Smith working in the field? We stopped by his place, but the front door's broken and nobody's home."

"No, dear, Doc Smith passed on."

"Dead? Wha—how?"

"He fell off his shed roof trying to shovel off the ash."

"Oh, God."

"Lottie, she moved into the school. There's a bunch of folks staying there now. But she doesn't say much these days. Took Doc's passing hard, poor thing."

"Hmm," Darla said. "My rabbits are sick. I was hoping to ask Doc what's wrong with them."

"The closest thing we have left to a doctor or vet is the paramedic down at the fire station. I hear he's pretty good at setting bones and whatnot, but I don't know if he'd be any help on rabbit sickness."

"Probably not."

"A lot of folks used to see a doctor up in Manchester, but I don't know if he's still there or not. We aren't getting any news from them these days."

"Is the library open?" Darla asked.

"Rita Mae's library? Just try to shut it down. Mayor took her assistant to work in the fields, and the front porch of her house collapsed, but she still opens that library every day. I hear she's living on a cot in the back now. Her ghost will probably be in there lending books fifty years after she's passed."

"We'll see what we can find out there, thanks."

Darla and I helped serve lunch to the crew digging corn in the field. Hasty pudding turned out to be a sort of cornmeal mush flavored with bits of pork. After we'd served everyone else, Mrs. Matthews scooped a couple mugs of it for Darla and me.

I didn't recall volunteering, but somehow we wound up helping Mrs. Matthews haul all the dirty dishes back to her house. When we got to her back deck, she reached inside the sliding glass door for a broom. She handed it to Darla, telling her, "Beat the dust off that boy and then have him try to clean you off."

Darla took the instructions to heart. I felt like an old threadbare rug by the time she finished thwacking me with that broom, avoiding none of my parts except my side and my manhood—what was left of it, so to speak. I endured it without complaint by reminding myself that my turn to use the broom on her would come next. Mrs.

Matthews was using a whiskbroom on herself, not that she needed to. Despite the hike to the field, everything but her pants legs was mostly clean. I couldn't figure out how she did it—dust just didn't stick to her.

By the time I'd beaten most of the ash off Darla, Mrs. Matthews was already inside. When we stepped into the kitchen, she was carefully scraping out the remnants of hasty pudding from the Dutch ovens into a plastic leftover container. She finished the Dutch ovens and started on the mugs people had eaten out of. Most of them were already licked clean, but when she found even a speck of food, into the leftover container it went.

But what really shocked me was when she put a stopper in the kitchen sink and began filling it. With water. From the faucet. I must have been staring, because she gave me a funny look and said, "You look like you've never seen indoor plumbing before, child."

"No, ma'am," I said. "I mean, yes, of course I have, but not since the eruption."

"Mayor's responsible for it. Got a crew to go around after the noise stopped. Made everyone promise to use less than five gallons a day. Anyone uses more, their water gets shut off. They say the water in the tower might last a year."

"Smart guy, your mayor."

"Gal. Yep, she's done all right. Helped organize the shelter at St. Paul's school and the crews out there digging for corn. There's folks that complain, of course, about the government rationing everything, telling them what to do and whatnot, but most see the sense of it and try to help."

The Dutch oven in the sink was full of water now. I grabbed a scrubby out of the plastic basket hanging in the sink and went to work on it. There was a bottle of Dawn beside the sink, but when I reached for it Mrs. Matthews knocked my hand away, saying something about how I'd ruin the finish on her good iron pans. I didn't know; it seemed to me that a little soap would help get everything cleaner. Whatever.

So I scrubbed while Darla rinsed and dried. It took us about a half hour to finish. By unspoken agreement, we hustled out of there as fast as we could just to keep Mrs. Matthews from volunteering us for any more jobs.

Chapter 26

The library occupied a third of a long metal building across from the town park. The rest of the building was shared by the city hall and fire department. A fire truck sat outside the big overhead door on one side of the building. It was halfway in the street and buried to its rims in ash, hopelessly stuck.

Darla hiked toward the library door, and I slid along beside her. There were huge drifts of ash surrounding the building except in front of the doors, which had been shoveled clear. I glanced up and figured out why. Someone had cleared the ash off the roof, throwing it down in piles below the eaves.

Darla tried the metal door labeled Worthington Public Library. "Weird, it's locked. Supposed to be open." She rapped on the door.

I heard a click—the lock turning in the door. A muffled voice came from inside, "Come in." I unclipped my boots from the skis and followed Darla through the door.

The first thing that caught my eye was the huge double-barreled shotgun pointed at us. It gleamed in the light of an oil lamp. My eyes followed the barrel of the gun back to where it was planted against its owner's shoulder. She was a tiny old woman; she looked smaller than the gun she was wielding. Her hair bloomed in a crazed white tangle above her eyes, which peered suspiciously along the barrel at us.

"Christ!" Darla said. "What is wrong with Worthington? Does everyone here have to point a gun at me?"

I didn't say anything—just held up my hands and shuffled backward toward the door. Antagonizing a little old lady holding a shotgun seemed like a very bad idea.

"Darla?" The woman behind the gun said. "Darla Edmunds?"

"Yeah, it's me, Rita Mae. Now would you put that goddamn gun down?"

She leaned the shotgun against the circulation desk. "Now there's no call to be cussing and using the Lord's name in vain, young miss."

"Maybe not but sh—, I mean, that's the third time in two hours someone's pointed a gun at me. That's not at all like people around here."

"Maybe not, but there's good reason."

"What, the pheasants have flown up out of the ash to exact revenge for years of hunting? Worthington's got to be the safest place in Iowa."

"Now don't get all impertinent. Why, you know the Fredericks' place, outside town? Someone broke in there and murdered them all. Horrible." Rita Mae glared at Darla.

I decided to interrupt before the argument got out of hand. "We came to see if you had any information about rabbit diseases."

Rita Mae swung her glare onto me. "And you are?"

"That's Alex," Darla said. "He's a . . . uh, friend."

"Well, son, I believe in free public libraries. But considering the situation we're in, it's become customary to offer something for the maintenance of the library in order to use our services. We're in dire need of candles, batteries, lamp oil, and the like."

"I don't have anything like that," Darla said.

"I might have a candle stub and a few matches," I said.

"What about food?" Darla asked. "That help?"

"Certainly," Rita Mae said. "A librarian can't live by books alone, and I wouldn't eat them if I could. Feel too much like cannibalism." She shuddered.

Darla dug through her pack and found one of the bags of cornmeal. "So, my rabbits. They're running a temperature, and they keep climbing into their—"

"Water bowls, right?" Rita Mae said. "You feel any funny bumps or growths on their bones, especially legs? Labored breathing, panting, or signs of respiratory distress?"

"I haven't noticed anything weird about their bones,

but I haven't checked that carefully."

Rita Mae pulled a book off the shelf behind her desk. "This is about the dig at Ashfall Beds. You know it?"

"No," I said.

"It's a paleontology site in Nebraska. They're digging up hundreds of animal skeletons there—ancient rhinos, deer, birds—"

"Okay, but what does this have to do with my rabbits?" Darla asked.

"I'm getting to that. About twelve million years ago, an enormous volcano erupted in what's now southern Idaho. It's the same volcano as Yellowstone, but the tectonic plate has moved above the volcanic hot spot, shifting it from southern Idaho to northwestern Wyoming.

"The eruption dumped more than a foot of ash in northeast Nebraska, about a thousand miles from the volcano. The animals living there breathed in the ash and got sick with silicosis, a lung disease. Symptoms include high fever, respiratory distress, and unusual porous deposits on bones.

"Since the animals were running a fever, they crowded into a watering hole to cool off. They died there and then were buried by drifting ash."

"So it's breathing the ash that's making my rabbits sick?"

"Yes."

"How do I treat it?"

"You can't. Clean air will keep it from getting worse, but there's no cure."

"Crap," Darla said. "Sure hate to lose all of them—if I could keep five or six to breed I could—"

"What about us?" I said. "Can we get this . . . silicosis, too?"

"Yep. Don't go outside without a mask, or at least a damp cloth over your mouth and nose. Stay in clean air, and try not to stir up the ash."

I remembered our ash-throwing fight on the way to Worthington. Brilliant. My thoughts were turning positively grim, so I changed the subject. "We got a bit of a radio broadcast at the farm, but nothing about what's going on east of here. You heard anything here?"

"Everyone with a working radio's been listening for news. Mayor organized info sharing at City Hall next door. If anyone hears anything, they write it down and post it on the wall over there."

"Anything about Illinois? Warren? It's not far from Galena."

"There's a refugee camp outside Galena. Government says they're focusing triage efforts on Illinois and setting up camps there for any Iowans who can make it across the Mississippi. Fools in Washington think Iowa's a lost cause. Guess we'll show them." Rita Mae looked like she was sucking on a sourball.

I didn't say anything, but I was relieved to find out people were getting help in Illinois. Maybe my family would be okay.

"You know anyone in town who might have an extra set of cross-country skis for sale?" Darla asked.

"Might be. I've got a pair gathering dust in the basement. What are you offering?"

Rita Mae haggled with Darla over those skis for more than half an hour. Darla wound up giving her both rabbit haunches and another bag of cornmeal on top of the bag we'd already given her as a "donation" to support her "free" public library. I had to throw in my candle stub and matches to seal the deal.

Rita Mae snuffed out the oil lamp and hung a Back Soon sign on the library door. The three of us walked to her house to pick up the skis—apparently the rumor that she was sleeping on a cot in the library was unfounded.

Along the way, we passed St. Paul's school. Rita Mae said, "You know, if things get tight out on your farm, you can come stay at the school. Mrs. Nance, the principal, is taking in anyone from the area who needs a place to stay. Everyone has to work if they're able, but that's only fair."

"Thanks," Darla said. "Looks like we'll be fine on the farm, though."

The ski boots didn't fit Darla very well—too tight. Darla said they'd stretch out, but I doubted it; Gore-Tex and plastic don't stretch much.

We said goodbye to Rita Mae as quickly as we could. I was getting worried about making it back to the farm before nightfall.

We made a lot better time with both of us on skis. Not long after we left Worthington, I felt a vibration under my feet. It picked up force, and in a few seconds the ground was rolling and heaving.

"More of this crap?" Darla said.

I shrugged and spread my skis wider, trying to stay upright.

The earthquake passed in less than a minute. It wasn't strong enough to knock us over, but it did raise a fine haze of ash that clung to the ground like early-morning fog.

Almost two hours later, a series of low booms rumbled out of the West. It was nothing like the explosions—Darla and I could, and did, talk over it, even though it continued for more than five minutes. I hoped it was the volcano's dying gasp and not a harbinger of more trouble to come.

Chapter 27

When we got back to the farm, the yellow daylight was just starting to fade to gray. The barn door was partway open. I pointed it out to Darla, and she said maybe her mom was feeding the rabbits. We headed for the house regardless. We both wanted to get washed up and rest a little. Skiing through the ash had been hard work.

I froze as I stepped into the kitchen, shocked to immobility by the scene within. My right foot hovered over the threshold. My face felt suddenly cold.

Darla's mom wasn't in the barn. She was lying halfway on the kitchen table, face down. A small,

wiry guy, filthy with ash, bent over her. He had a baseball
bat pressed against the back of her neck, holding her
down. Her face was turned toward us. Both her eyes were
blackened, and a thin trail of blood leaked from her nose
onto the table. His legs were between her knees.

Darla screamed. The guy took a step backward and
pulled his sweatpants up.

I didn't think, couldn't think. There was nothing in my
head but searing white rage. No room for anything else.
My icy immobility shattered. I charged the guy.

He lifted the baseball bat, but I was on him before he
could swing it. Left knife-hand to the wrist holding the bat.
I didn't feel the edge of my hand connect, but I heard something pop and then the clatter as the bat hit the floor.

His fist hit my right ear. A glancing blow I barely
noticed. I cocked my right hand up by my ear and let it
loose, spinning into the strike, my hips, shoulders, and arm
all turning for maximum power. My knife-hand crunched
into the side of his neck.

He slumped to the floor, twisting bonelessly on his
way down. I'd hit him perfectly.

Darla quit screaming and ran to the table. "Mom?"

"Uh," she moaned, as I pulled her skirt down. Darla
took one of her hands and leaned close over her.

It occurred to me to check on the guy to make sure he
wasn't going to get back up. He lay on the floor, unmoving. There was a large, crude tattoo on the inside of his
forearm—a rat or weasel or something. I bent and put my
finger against the left side of his neck. A huge red welt

marred his neck. Nothing. No pulse. I yanked my hand back in shock. I checked again, feeling his wrist this time. Same result: nothing. The room swam around me as I turned to Darla. "I think I killed this guy."

"Good," Darla pretty much spat the word. "Mom? Can I get you some water?"

"I . . . I didn't mean to kill him. I wasn't thinking." The spinning room made my stomach heave uncertainly. My hand shook as I drew it back from the guy's wrist.

Someone else spoke then, from the direction of the kitchen door. "Aren't you that little snitchface from the campfire? Alex?"

I glanced up. Target filled the doorway. A filthy gray rag was wrapped around his head, covering his left eye. Part of his face and one arm were crosshatched with ropy scabs and partly healed burns. He held a double-barreled shotgun in one hand and a rabbit in the other. The rabbit's head and shoulders looked like he'd started it through a meat grinder. He dropped the rabbit and lifted the shotgun to his shoulder, sighting down the barrels at me.

I thought about charging him, but he was ten or twelve feet away. He'd kill me before I got close. So I just stood there, staring at him. I felt numb, whipsawed by adrenaline and shock.

"Oh, this is rich—better than getting bunked with a fresh punk. I've been looking for you, you know. So you killed Ferret, huh? I knew you had potential."

I glanced at the dead guy by my feet and shrugged. "Guess so."

"I owe you big time. My goddamn eye isn't healing right. I've been dreaming about you—dreaming about digging your eyes out of your skull with a knife and—"

"Whatever."

"I don't want to shoot you. Too fast—"

"Fine. Let Darla and her mom go. Then you can take your time with me." I shrugged, trying to suppress the trembling in my shoulders.

"Darla, is it?" He smiled, a twisted thing that crawled across the bottom of his face. Then he swiveled the shotgun toward Darla, who was cradling her mother's head in her arms.

"Darla!" I screamed and jumped. I hit her at about shoulder height in a flying tackle. I heard the boom of the shotgun and felt a sudden pain stab my ankle.

When I turned my head to look up, Target was standing over me, pointing the shotgun at my back. I swallowed bile and struggled to keep Darla underneath me, hoping my body would block the blast. My stomach was a leaden ball, weighting me down. Darla squirmed beneath me.

Target pulled the trigger. There was a soft metallic click.

I opened my eyes. I hadn't remembered closing them. I'd never heard any noise quite so welcome as the click that shotgun made when it *wasn't* killing me.

Target pulled the trigger three more times. Click, click, click.

I guessed what had happened. Target, the dumbass, had killed a rabbit by shooting it and hadn't reloaded, so one of his barrels was empty. Why he didn't wring the rabbit's neck was beyond me. Criminals are stupid as a general rule, I figured.

I reached up and grabbed the gun barrel. It felt warm. Target tried to yank it away from me. I took advantage of his motion, letting him pull me to my feet. I launched a sidekick, using the gun for leverage and balance. I kicked him perfectly, right in the kidney. He grunted and sagged away from my foot—but only a little. Damn, but he was big and strong. That kick should have laid out a horse.

He held onto the gunstock with his left hand and stepped toward me. His right fist crashed into my side, hitting the spot where he'd cut me almost three weeks ago. I screamed and danced away, still holding onto the barrel with my right hand. I was afraid if I let go he'd use the gun to club me to death.

He tried to follow up with an uppercut. I swept it aside with my forearm and connected on a quick jab to his chest. He threw another punch. I blocked again and got in another solid body shot that seemed to have no effect whatsoever. He reached for the hatchet at his belt, so I threw a punch at his face, forcing him to block.

We traded blows this way four or five times. I blocked or dodged everything he threw my way, got in solid counterattacks to his body—and accomplished nothing. Neither of us would let go of the shotgun, and he couldn't get at the hatchet on his belt without leaving his head open.

In a flash, it came to me what I was doing wrong. I was sparring with this gorilla. Hundreds of hours of training had taught me too well—don't hit below the belt, no eye gouges, no groin strikes. . . .

Darla reared up behind him with Ferret's baseball bat. Target moved, and she missed his head. There was a meaty thwack as she clubbed his shoulder. He barely staggered. I lunged forward, trying to drive a spear-hand strike into his good eye. He spun, and my fingers hit his temple instead.

Darla wound up for another strike, but this time Target stepped toward her and grabbed the bat in his right hand as she started to swing. So now he was holding the bat in his right hand and the shotgun in his left, stretched between Darla and me.

That left him wide open for a round kick. I unloaded on him: one of those perfect, sweeping kicks that, on a punching bag at Cedar Falls Taekwondo, would have produced an echoing slap. But I wasn't kicking a punching bag—I was kicking Target in the nuts.

He screamed and doubled over, dropping the gun and bat. Darla and I both began clubbing him. He spun and ran for the door with his hands up around his head, trying to protect himself from our murderous blows.

Outside, Darla started to chase him through the ash.

"Darla!" I yelled. "Your mom."

She turned, ran back to the doorway, and pushed past me into the kitchen.

Target got fifty or sixty feet away and turned to stare at me. "You've got to sleep sometime. I'll be back. I'll slit your throat—and your girl's."

I stood silently and watched him. My breathing slowed, and my body started to hurt in a dozen places. Eventually Target got tired of shouting threats and disappeared into the ashy haze. I went back to the kitchen to check on Darla and her mom. Still shaking with the adrenaline aftereffects of one fight, I went to face another—one I couldn't hope to win.

Mrs. Edmunds was still breathing, but that may not have been a good thing. The shotgun blast had hit her head. Her face looked like fresh hamburger. Her breath burbled in and out of her mouth, blowing little bubbles in the blood welling around her shattered teeth. Her eyes were ruined—she'd never see again.

Darla was kneeling beside her mom in the cold room, wearing nothing but jeans and a bra. She'd stripped off her filthy outer shirt. Her undershirt was wadded up in her hand, pressed against her mother's neck. It wasn't doing much good; the pool of blood from Mrs. Edmunds's throat grew bigger as I watched. Already it surrounded Darla's knees, soaking into her jeans.

I doubled over, hands on my knees. Spasms wracked my body as if I were sobbing, but no tears came.

Mrs. Edmunds said something, one word so low and distorted I could barely understand. It sounded like "love."

Darla whispered, "I know, Mom. I love you, too."

I stood nearby and watched them, feeling utterly helpless. All my fury washed away in a wave of despair. What could I do or say? Less than a month ago I might have dialed 911 on my cell phone, asked Mom or Dad for help,

or run to Darren and Joe's house. Now none of those
options were available. Darla and I were alone with her
dying mother and the corpse of some guy called Ferret.
Alone on a vast plain of unforgiving gray ash.

Chapter 28

I stood there with my hands on my knees for a while. Ten minutes? Maybe longer. The burbling sounds coming from Mrs. Edmunds had long since ceased. My ankle hurt. I checked it; shotgun pellets had pierced my boot in a couple places, but there was no blood.

I looked at Mrs. Edmunds. There were no more bubbles at her mouth. The pool of blood around her head had stopped spreading. I bent down and put my fingertips against her wrist. No pulse. I felt wooden, like a numb marionette that the real Alex could only observe from a distance.

"Darla?" I whispered. "She's dead."

"Mom? Mom, wake up. You're going to be okay." Darla
pulled her blood-soaked undershirt away from her mother's neck. No new blood welled out of her wounds. She'd
bled out.

Darla put her fingertips alongside her mother's perfo-
rated throat. She bent down so her cheek touched her
mother's ragged lips. She moaned, "No. No. No—"

"She's dead. I'm sorry."

Darla leapt up, a motion so sudden it startled me. She
yelled, "This is all your fault!" She lashed out, swinging her
clenched fist against my chest like a hammer. "You led him
here." Thump, she hit me again. "We were fine until you
showed up." Thump. "He said he knew you." Thump. "Said
he was happy to find you again." Thump. "It's your fault!"

I was bruised, sore, and tired beyond words. Hot blood
trickled down my side where Target had punched me,
reopening the gash in my side. But I let her hit me. Made
no move at all to defend myself. What if she was right?

"I hate you." Thump. "I hate you! I hate you!" Thump
thump.

She was crying now. I reached out and wrapped my
arms around her shoulders. She kept beating her fists
against my chest within the circle of my arms.

Eventually her energy ran down. She quit hitting me,
which was a good thing, not only because of my bruised
ribs. I'd begun to worry whether Target might have
already circled back.

Darla looked about ready to fall over. I took hold of

her shoulders and guided her into a chair. I picked up her overshirt and draped it across her shoulders.

I wanted nothing more than to collapse into a chair beside her, to surrender to the despair, to let the world go to hell without me for a while. So what if Target circled back and killed me? Maybe I deserved it.

But Darla didn't. I walked to the door and peered out, looking for Target.

The sun must have been setting. I couldn't see it, hadn't seen it since the eruption, but the western sky glowed a dull, angry red. There wasn't enough light left to see much. Target could have been standing fifty feet off, and I'd have missed him in the gloom.

I returned to the kitchen and dug a candle out of a drawer. Darla sat where I'd left her, staring at her hands. The shotgun lay beside her on the floor. We didn't have any shells for it, so I tossed it onto the upper bank of kitchen cabinets where it'd be hidden.

"We've got to hide," I told Darla. "Hole up somewhere overnight."

No response.

"Come on, Darla. Where's the best place to hide? Just for tonight."

Nothing.

Great, like I didn't have enough problems, now Darla had gone catatonic on me. Not that I blamed her. Much. I wanted to curl up and give in to the tears finally welling behind my eyelids. But Target had said he would come back. I believed him.

I racked my brain, trying to think of someplace safe, hidden, and defendable . . . the hayloft in the barn where we'd gotten boards for the smokehouse. We'd only ripped up part of the floor. There was still plenty of room to hide. I suggested it to Darla.

She said nothing. She didn't follow me when I left the kitchen, either. I had to go back and take her hand, leading her outside like a three-year-old. It took some coaxing to get Darla, still silent, into her skis. It might have been easier to walk the short distance to the barn, but I was so tired and sore I wasn't confident I'd be able to pull my feet free once they'd sunk into the ash.

The aluminum ladder to the hayloft was still where I'd remembered it. We had to squeeze past Darla's bicycle-powered corn-grinding machine, which gave me an idea. After I'd convinced Darla to climb the ladder, I returned to the machine. I disconnected the drive belt and lifted the heavy runner stone. It weighed a ton, but I ducked and rolled it off the base stone onto my shoulder.

I made my way slowly up to the hayloft with one arm wrapped around the quern on my shoulder and one hand on the ladder. As soon as I could, I dropped the grindstone. It landed with an alarming thunk that shook the floor of the hayloft. I pulled up the ladder behind me and left it resting at the edge of the loft.

I checked the wound on my right side. Target's punch had reopened a corner of it, but it was already starting to scab over. I'd live—if Target didn't find me again.

It hurt to take off my boots. I shook out my right sock, and two pellets fell out. The right side of my ankle and foot were blotched with green-and-purple bruises where the edge of the shotgun blast had caught me, but it would heal.

I realized I'd forgotten the baseball bat, left it sitting on the floor in the kitchen. I was too tired to do anything about that now.

Darla sat on a hay bale, staring at her hands. I said goodnight and collapsed into a pile of loose hay.

Chapter 29

In my dreams, I was trapped again in my bedroom in Cedar Falls. The desk pressed down on my chest, suffocating me. The wall by my head was hot to the touch. And everything was smoky—my eyes burned with smoke, my nostrils swelled with its stench.

I woke, twitchy with remembered fear, but the smell of smoke hadn't faded with my dream. If anything, it was stronger now. A lurid orange light shone into the loft from the room below. Darla was still asleep, curled into a fetal position, almost touching my back. I shook her awake and stalked as quietly as I could to the edge of the loft.

There were two separate fires blazing in the room below. Target was there, trying to ignite the workbench with a torch.

I picked up the grindstone. It had seemed impossibly heavy when I'd lugged it up the ladder. Now, charged with adrenaline, I could move it as if it were Styrofoam.

I shuffled sideways along the edge of the loft. One of the boards under my feet creaked—a groan that seemed loud enough to be heard in Worthington. I held my breath, watching Target. He didn't look up.

I got into position more or less above him. He was wearing a big backpack, one of the old-school kind with an external frame. I stared down at the tattoo inked on the back of his head for a couple seconds, and then I dropped the grindstone, aiming for the center of the target.

There was a soft thunk. Target fell, catching his chin on the edge of the workbench. He landed on the barn floor on his side. The torch fell near his face. Even from ten feet above him, I could see the deep valley the rock had smashed into the back of his skull. He didn't move, despite the flames licking his nose.

I didn't feel much of anything. No gladiator's thrill of victory. Not even relief. Just a numb horror at all the senseless death Target had left in his wake.

Flames were already spreading in the dry hay and shooting up the barn walls. I glanced around for Darla and found her standing at the edge of the loft, staring down at Target. I grabbed the aluminum ladder and threw it into place. Darla just looked at it.

"Hurry up! Go, go, go!" I screamed.

Darla climbed onto the ladder and started down, so slowly she might have been on the way to her own funeral, not trying to escape a burning barn. I jumped on behind her. I wanted to kick her in the head, her pace was so frustrating. Instead, I kept screaming at her. When we finally got down, I grabbed her arm and yanked her out of the barn.

I froze and stared in shock. Target had obviously started with the house. It was completely engulfed in flames. The fire at my house in Cedar Falls was a weenie roast in comparison.

I clenched my fists and screamed. All our food, our water bottles, tarps, clothing—everything was in that house. I thought about trying to save something by running into that inferno. But as I watched, part of the roof collapsed. It was hopeless. Without any supplies, we'd die for sure. The only question was what would kill us first: silicosis, cold, thirst, or starvation.

I ran back into the barn. The heat and smoke seemed to suck all the oxygen from my lungs. I grabbed our skis, poles, and Mrs. Parker's bö staff and ran outside, dumping them in a pile at Darla's feet.

As I gasped cleaner air, I tried to think. There had to be a way to salvage something from this fiasco. Then it hit me: Target's backpack. Surely he'd scavenged supplies from the house—supplies that might keep us alive.

I dove back into the barn. Target's torch had started a fire by his face, but the backpack looked okay. I grabbed it and yanked. Nothing. The backpack wouldn't budge.

Target was on his side, his back toward me. One arm was under him, and the other one was flopped into the fire. The heat was so intense I could barely grab the backpack, let alone Target.

I tugged on the backpack, trying to drag Target away from the fire so I could get the pack off him. My feet slipped in the straw, and I screamed in frustration.

The hatchet on Target's hip caught my eye. I yanked it out of his belt loop and hacked at the backpack straps. I missed once and buried the hatchet in his side, ironically in about the same spot where he'd gouged me three weeks before. Blood dripped from the hatchet's blade. I chopped at the straps a couple more times before the backpack came free. I ran outside.

I dropped the backpack and hatchet and collapsed in the ash. Darla mumbled something I couldn't understand. I rested my head in my hands and gulped fresher air. Darla mumbled again.

"What was that?"

"My rabbits . . ." she murmured.

Crap. I'd totally forgotten them. I struggled back to my feet and ran into the blazing barn.

It was impossible to breathe, hotter than the inside of an oven and full of smoke. I held my breath and stumbled into the rabbits' room. Somehow I found the row of cages. I opened two, and got a rabbit under each arm. They were limp: dead or passed out from the smoke, I couldn't guess.

I ran outside and passed the rabbits to Darla. I tried to go back, but it was impossible. My skin already felt burnt, like a bad sunburn. I couldn't get within five feet of the barn door now, the heat had grown that intense.

I turned back to Darla. "It's too hot. I can't . . . sorry." She was sitting in the ash, cradling the rabbits in her lap and petting them. They weren't moving at all.

I inventoried the contents of Target's pack. It was a jackpot. A big plastic tarp and two heavy blankets were rolled up on top. Under those I found a dozen full water bottles, six bags of cornmeal, a frying pan, what looked to be our entire supply of smoked rabbit meat, a coil of rope, all the matches and candles from Mrs. Edmunds' kitchen drawer, and the five-inch chef's knife I'd carried from Cedar Falls. There was some clothing, too. Probably way too big for me or Darla. Anyway, the supplies would be enough to keep us alive and fed for a week, maybe longer with a little luck.

I used a bit of the rope to repair the backpack straps where I'd hacked through them. Darla was still petting the rabbits. One of them was moving a little. The other was clearly dead. I took the limp rabbit from her and got the chef's knife.

"Will you help me?" I asked. I wasn't sure I could butcher the rabbit by myself.

Darla didn't look up, just kept petting the rabbit squirming in her lap.

Fine. I'd do it myself. I put the tip of the knife against the rabbit's throat and started a downward cut. There were only a couple droplets of blood, but somehow it reminded me of the blood bubbling out of Mrs. Edmunds' mouth . . . and Ferret's body, his head lolling at an odd angle on the kitchen floor . . . and the soft thump as the grindstone crushed Target's skull.

I retched, bringing up nothing but scalding stomach acid. When I was done trying to vomit, I dug a crude hole with my staff and buried the dead rabbit.

Darla watched.

"We should go," I said as I finished kicking ash over the tiny grave.

Darla stared at the blackened husk of her home. The roof had collapsed completely. The walls and chimney still stood, but all the windows had burst from the heat. There were flames gnawing on the skeleton of the house here and there. Darla whispered something: "Mom," maybe.

"It's okay," I said. What a stupid thing to say. It definitely was not okay.

Darla just stared. Maybe she was looking at the roiling brown smoke rising from the fire, searching for her mother's face in the ever-shifting doppelganger cloud.

I took one of her hands in mine, pulling it away from the rabbit. I led her closer to the house, until we could feel the heat from the fire on our faces.

I stopped and tried to pull my hand away from hers, but she held on. "We should have buried her," Darla whispered.

One of the walls crashed inward, and sparks flew into the sky. "Some people get cremated when they die," I said. "And she's at home. I don't think she would have minded."

We held hands in silence for a while. The rabbit squirmed in Darla's other arm, and she gripped it tighter.

"You want . . . should we say a prayer or something?"
I said. "Like a funeral?"

She nodded.

I wished I hadn't said anything. I'd only been to one
funeral, for my grandfather almost ten years ago. At that
moment, I couldn't remember a bit of it, only the waxy pallor of his skin in the casket during the viewing and the way
his dead hand felt—cold and plastic, nothing like real skin.

But I had to try. "Dear God, um . . ." Not such a good
start. I had no idea what to say. I stood silently, holding
Darla's hand, searching my brain for something, anything,
to talk about. I thought about the first time I had seen
Mrs. Edmunds pouring corn into the gristmill, right
before I passed out on the barn floor. So I began there:

"When I met Mrs. Edmunds, I was almost dead. I'd
been running—skiing, I guess—away from trouble for
days. I was bleeding, dizzy with pain, struggling to keep
pushing one foot in front of the other. I was hoping for
nothing more than a quiet barn to hide in, a place where I
could heal or die.

"Instead, I met Mrs. Edmunds and Darla. They took
me in, fed me, and sewed up my side. I'm alive because of
the kindness they showed to me, a complete stranger.

"God, I don't know if I caused Mrs. Edmunds' death."
I tried to drop Darla's hand, but she held on. "Maybe I led
Target to her, or maybe it was just horrible luck. I wish . . .
I wish Target had killed me instead of Mrs. Edmunds. I
would have been dead anyway if not for her help.

"But I can't change that. And I guess You have some

plan." (A crappy plan, one that had transformed Iowa into an ashen hell, that had left Darla an orphan and me unable to discover whether I was an orphan or not. But saying all that wouldn't help her.) "So I'm thankful that I met Mrs. Edmunds. She welcomed me, made me feel . . . loved, I guess. Wherever she is now, please welcome her the way she welcomed me, a bleeding stranger at her barn door. Amen."

"Amen," Darla said. "I miss you already, Mom," she added, whispering.

I hugged her. We stood there a long time, warmed by the dying embers of Mrs. Edmunds' funeral pyre, the rabbit squirming between us. Three fading sparks of life on an endless, burnt field of ash.

Chapter 30

I snapped my boots into my skis and shouldered Target's pack. Darla hadn't moved.

"We've got to go," I said.

Darla stroked the rabbit.

"Put your skis on and get your poles."

Nothing.

"Damn it, Darla, we've got to go. There's no shelter here now." It was probably midmorning by now, and I was feeling antsy. I didn't know why. The burnt buildings, Target's body—I wanted to get away from the farm as fast as possible.

But Darla wasn't budging.

I wanted to scream in frustration, but instead I said as gently as I could, "Put your skis on, now, please."

Finally, she moved. She transferred the rabbit to one arm and slowly clipped her boots into the skis.

"Pick up your poles." I tried to take the rabbit from her, but she shied away, clutching it with both hands. I gave up and handed the ski poles to her. She took both of them in one hand, the other still clutching the rabbit tightly against her chest.

I sighed and pushed off powerfully with my pole and staff, heading for the road in front of Darla's farm. About thirty feet off, I stopped and turned. She hadn't inched forward at all.

"Come on, Darla. Get moving!" I yelled.

She shuffled out to meet me.

It was excruciatingly slow. Darla held the poles as dead-weight in one hand. Twice, the rabbit got unruly, and Darla dropped her poles to cuddle him. The second time, I stopped and strapped her ski poles to the back of my pack.

We made better time then. At least the rabbit wasn't holding us up—with both hands free, Darla could keep him under control. Better time didn't mean we made good time, though. Without poles, Darla couldn't balance as well or push herself along. I had to stop again and again to wait for her to catch up.

I couldn't keep going this way. I felt terrible for Darla. She'd lost her home, her mother, everything she'd built, and almost all her rabbits. I thought I partly understood how she felt—at that moment I wanted to stop, curl up into a ball, and let someone take care of me again. But even more than I wanted to check out and give my emotional wounds time to scab over, I wanted to live. Neither Darla nor I were likely to survive if we kept heading for Warren at a snail's pace. So when we reached the intersection where I'd planned to turn east, I turned south toward Worthington instead. Darla followed me.

A couple miles farther on, we skied down a steep hill into a small valley. A creek burbled merrily under the bridge at the bottom of the hill. It had washed away some of the ash from each bank, revealing a few tendrils of sickly yellow vegetation.

I stopped, shrugged off my pack, and sat on the guardrail along the edge of the bridge. As I dug through the backpack, hunting for lunch, I talked to Darla.

"We can leave the rabbit here. There's water. There are some plants to eat. It'll be okay." I didn't really believe this. That rabbit was dead either way. If it stayed with Darla, she'd probably eat it when she got hungry enough. The plants by the creek looked dead—and there weren't enough of them to sustain a mouse, let alone a rabbit. I was just hoping she'd give it up, so we could move at a reasonable pace.

"No," Darla replied.

Okay then, that was progress, I guessed. It was the first word she'd said since we'd left the farm over two hours before. I handed her a strip of smoked rabbit. Lunch.

She held the strip of meat in one hand and the rabbit in the other and sat beside me on the guardrail to eat. The rabbit sniffed the meat and wrinkled its nose—in disgust, perhaps.

When she finished eating, Darla rummaged through the backpack one handed. She came up with a handful of cornmeal and started feeding the stupid rabbit out of her hand.

"What are you doing?" I shouted. "We need that food!"

Darla gave no sign that she'd heard me. I yelled some more, but I might as well have screamed at the ash for all the good it was doing. I thought the rabbits wouldn't eat corn, but it seemed to be nibbling on it now. Maybe it had gotten so hungry it couldn't afford to be picky anymore. Anyway, I closed up the backpack and took off, skiing along the road to Worthington.

I got about a half mile ahead of Darla before I felt guilty and stopped to wait. I thought about our other trip to Worthington, just the day before. In places where the road was sheltered from the wind, I could see our tracks in the ash: one set of ski tracks going, with Darla's deep boot prints running alongside. Two sets of ski tracks returning.

How different that trip had been: Darla riding on my skis down the hills, pressed up against my back, rolling around together in the ash, and playfully hurling handfuls of it at each other.

Eventually, Darla caught up. I never let myself get more than thirty feet ahead of her the rest of the way to Worthington.

The putrid yellow haze in the sky was slowly being replaced by gray twilight as we skied into Worthington. Incredibly, we'd made better time yesterday with Darla walking than we had today with both of us on skis.

I led Darla through town to the school I'd seen yesterday, St. Paul's. There were ramparts of ash around it where someone had shoveled off the roof. A cleared path led to the front door, but it was locked and dark inside. I banged on the door, but no one answered. Surely this was the right place? Several people had mentioned yesterday that this school was serving as a shelter.

I slogged to the side door next to the gym, with Darla following. These doors were unlocked. I brushed as much ash off my clothes as I could, unsnapped my skis, and stepped inside.

The gym here wasn't nearly as large as the one at Cedar Falls High, but the scene inside was similar, if a little more chaotic. An elderly woman sat at a desk inside the gym doors, working by the light of a battery-powered lantern. The gym floor was covered with every type of bed imaginable laid out in a grid. There were leather couches, sleeper sofas, futons, cots, a bunch of twin beds, and even a heart-shaped monstrosity—a honeymooner's red nightmare bed. Some of the beds were surrounded with makeshift enclosures, drapes hanging on rough frames made of two-by-fours, curtain rods, and rope. Most of the drapes were pulled back at the moment, I assumed to allow light into the sleeping areas.

There must have been eighty beds in there, but there weren't many people in the gym, only the woman at the desk, a couple of adults napping on couches, and a group of very small kids playing Chutes & Ladders on the floor.

I stepped up to the desk. Nobody noticed me. The woman was completely engrossed in a piece of paper that had Duty Schedule printed in block letters across the top.

"Uh, hi," I said.

The woman jumped halfway out of her chair. She whipped open one of the desk's drawers and thrust her hand inside. I heard a metallic click, but her hand didn't emerge from the drawer. I held my hands up by my shoulders, palms open.

"Sorry I startled you," I said.

"You certainly did, young man. I'm going to strangle Larry."

That didn't make sense, but I let it pass. "Darla and I don't have a place to stay, and we heard this was a shelter. . . ."

The woman removed her hand from the desk drawer and looked at Darla standing beside me. "Darla Edmunds? I heard you were in town yesterday. Heard you and your mother were doing well, all things considered."

Darla looked away.

"Yes ma'am," I said. "They were. Doing well, I mean. Yesterday. But Darla's mom is dead now, and she has no place to stay. I wondered if she could stay here for a while."

"Gloria's dead? I'm so sorry. How?"

"Bandits. They're dead now. Darla and I killed them. But they burned—"

A beefy guy emerged from the locker room and ran to the desk. "Sorry, Mrs. Nance. I think it's all this corn. Gives me constipation—"

She cut him off with a glare and struck through a name under "Security" on her duty roster. She wrote "Larry Boyle" in a column labeled "K.P." Larry slunk off toward the gym doors. Mrs. Nance turned back to me, "Of course you can both stay here. You'll need to work—everyone's expected to do something. I've heard Darla's a wizard with machines. There's a crew trying to rig some of the old farm windmills to recharge batteries. That suit you, Darla?"

Darla didn't reply.

"Yes, that sounds fine," I said.

Mrs. Nance frowned but made a note on her roster. "And your name, young man?"

"Alex."

"Are you particularly good at anything?"

"Not really."

"Field duty then, digging corn. You look strong enough."

"If it's okay, I'd been planning to move on tomorrow. My family, they're in Warren, Illinois. At least I hope they are."

Darla turned her head and stared at me then. She had an expression on her face that I found impossible to interpret.

"Lot of lawless country between here and there," Mrs. Nance replied. "And where are you planning to cross the Mississippi? I hear there've been riots in Dubuque."

"Yes, ma'am. I'd noticed—about the lawless country, that is. And I hadn't thought ahead about crossing the river."

"Where did you come from?"

She teased the whole story out of me. I didn't really want to talk about it. I tried giving her one-word answers, but she kept asking me questions, and gradually I gave her the whole story. My room collapsing in Cedar Falls. The three guys trying to invade Darren and Joe's place. My lonely trek across northeast Iowa. When I finished, Mrs. Nance shook her head. "That's quite a story, young man. I can offer you dinner tonight and one night's lodging. I wish I had supplies to spare to help you along, but we have our hands full here."

"I understand. And thank you," I said.

"I hear FEMA is in Illinois. Maybe you can find some help there. There are no relief supplies for this side of the Mississippi yet, although I understand the politicians in Washington have figured out that this is a disaster area and declared it so." Mrs. Nance laughed, a short sharp sound halfway between a bark and a sob.

* * *

Dinner that night was thin corn porridge. Everyone filed into the school cafeteria shortly after nightfall. About seventy people were staying at the school. Most of them arrived for dinner covered with ash; they'd been digging corn all day.

Darla carried the stupid rabbit into the cafeteria with her. She got a few strange looks, but mostly people seemed too tired to care. I saw her sneak two spoonsful of porridge to the rabbit. I don't think anyone else noticed. There might have been trouble if they had. The portions were small enough without sharing food with a rabbit that would itself have made a nice meal.

The good beds were all claimed, of course. I'd been hoping for the leather couch or maybe that enormous heart-shaped bed, tacky as it was. An old, wiry guy stretched out on the couch, and a mother shared the heart

bed with her three young kids. Darla and I got twin mattresses on the floor near the gym door.

Darla flopped fully clothed onto her mattress, on top
of the blanket. She held the rabbit against her chest. I
hoped it would wander off in the night.

I stripped off my outer shirt, boots, and jeans and crawled
under the blanket. A little girl flickered through my memory—the girl who had tried to steal crackers from me
while I slept at Cedar Falls High. I pulled my backpack up
onto the mattress next to me and flung one arm over it.

"Goodnight, Darla."

Nothing.

Chapter 31

Someone moving nearby woke me. I looked around—about half the people in the gym were up, preparing for the new day. Darla still slept. The rabbit lay snuggled against her side.

I got dressed as quietly as I could. My right ankle was bruised and swollen. I had to grit my teeth and strain to force my boot over it. I stood carefully and shouldered my backpack. Mrs. Nance was up already, working at her desk.

"Thanks for letting me sack out here," I told her.

"You're welcome," she replied. "Breakfast will be served in the cafeteria in about ten minutes. You may join us if you wish."

"I'd better get going. I've imposed on your hospitality enough. Thanks again."

"Take care, young man."

I paused to look back at Darla. She looked small, alone on the mattress in the big gym. It felt wrong, somehow, to leave her there. I knew I'd miss her terribly. But my mind insisted it was right—she'd be safer here with people she knew, people she'd grown up with, than she would be with me, risking whatever dangers awaited on the road to Warren. And unless . . . until she recovered from the trauma of her mother's death, she couldn't move fast enough to travel, anyway. I turned away.

The temperature had dropped further overnight. My breath left clouds in the air, and I shivered as I snapped into my skis. I wasn't dressed warmly enough for the weather. I figured I'd be okay so long as I kept moving, but if I had to sleep in the open, it would be a problem.

I skied two blocks north and turned right on First Avenue, heading east. First Avenue became East Worthington Road. I set a fast pace, thrusting my feet forward and pushing off strongly with my poles. Outside town, there was a long, gentle upward slope. I took the whole thing without having to duck walk or side step. Moving felt good—I put everything I had into it, trying to keep my mind on the skiing. It beat thinking about Target, or Mrs. Edmunds, or my family . . . or Darla.

At the top of the hill I stretched and looked around. There was no wind, and the day seemed clearer than any since the eruption. It was still dim, like a very dark and overcast day, but there was a bilious tinge to the sky.

Ahead of me the road ran straight down a long, gentle slope. Along either side, a few lonely cornstalks poked through the ash. I looked backward. My passage had left a trail of ash hanging in the quiet air that led back to the edge of Worthington, barely visible in the distance.

There was another puff of ash there. A tiny figure on skis had left Worthington, moving east toward me. There was only one other person I'd seen skiing since I left Cedar Falls. I flopped sideways, sitting in the ash to wait. I wasn't sure whether to groan or cheer as I watched her slow progress up the hill toward me.

It took Darla almost a half hour to reach me. She was carrying the stupid rabbit under one arm. Her ski poles were dangling from her other hand, utterly useless.

"What the hell are you doing?" I asked as she skied up to me.

She didn't reply.

"You don't have any supplies; you're not dressed for the cold. . . . What if I hadn't seen you following me? You could die out here!"

Nothing.

"Go back to Worthington. You'll be safer there. Those people know you. They like you. I'm headed for God knows what. I'll probably be dead in a week."

She didn't move.

"Will you at least let that stupid rabbit go?"

She clutched it tighter against her chest.

"At least we'll have something to eat when we run out of food."

She eyed me sullenly, scratching behind the rabbit's ears.

"Crap." I thought about the problem for a minute. I could easily outdistance her, leaving her in the dust. But if she followed me east, she'd die for sure. She had no food, water, or bedding. And truth be told, there was a small lonely voice inside me—a voice I'd been trying to suppress—that was mighty glad to see her. I shoved violently off the ridge top, skiing back toward Worthington.

I made great time going back down the slope. I pushed with both poles and shifted my weight from ski to ski, hurling myself forward with a skating motion. When I got to the outskirts of Worthington, I looked back. Darla was less than a quarter of the way back to town, following me. I skied down First Avenue and took a left on Third, returning to St. Paul's gym.

Mrs. Nance was working at her desk. "You're back? I didn't expect to see you again."

"Yeah, I didn't expect to be back. Look, do you know anyone who has an extra backpack I could trade for?"

"We've got a few here—I can't spare any of the big ones, but I could part with one of the book bags."

She lit a candle and led me down the hall to a classroom. It had been converted into a giant supply closet. There was an amazing assortment of junk stacked in the room: six old mattresses, two red children's wagons, a stack of two-by-fours of various lengths, and piles of clothing, among other things.

We stopped at a table, one end of which held about a dozen small backpacks. I sorted through them and checked their zippers. Most of them had those cheap plastic zippers that always break halfway through the school year. I figured anything that couldn't make it through a school year wouldn't be good for a week out there in the ash. I chose the larger of the two that had metal zippers and asked Mrs. Nance what she'd take in trade for it.

Yipes, but she was a nasty bargainer. What was it with Worthington women, anyway? Maybe there was a Negotiate Like a Shark Club in town and Mrs. Nance and Rita Mae were founding members. I wound up giving her two smoked rabbit loins, a haunch, and a bag of cornmeal for that dumb backpack. By the time I got back outside, Darla was there, waiting for me.

I got a blanket out of my pack and jammed it into the bottom of the school bag. Then, thinking about my plan, I packed the plastic tarp over the blanket. Rabbit poop protection. That filled about half the small pack.

I grabbed the rabbit. Darla pulled it to her chest. "Let go. I won't hurt it," I said.

She released the rabbit. It began squirming, but I managed to jam it into the backpack on top of the tarp. I closed the zipper on it, leaving a two-inch gap so the stupid thing could breathe. Not that I cared much if it suffocated.

"Here." I held the backpack up so Darla could slip it over her shoulders. "Try to keep up, okay?"

She didn't reply, so I set off, following the four sets of ski tracks we'd already made that morning. The light outside had dimmed while I was inside St. Paul's. I glanced up. Gray tendrils crawled across the yellow sky, clouds presaging a storm, perhaps. But they looked like no clouds I'd ever seen.

My thoughts were as confused as the sky. Leaving Worthington the first time, I'd already started to feel Darla's absence, a dull ache as inescapable as a broken tooth I just couldn't quit poking with my tongue. So I should have been happy now, right? Only I wasn't. As I pushed my skis forward—shh, shh, shh over the ash—the gray-and-yellow sky settled on my shoulders like a heavy blanket.

I spent several minutes thinking about it before I figured out the source of my grim mood: fear. Right or wrong, I already felt somewhat responsible for her mother's death. What if following me got Darla killed, too?

Chapter 32

It got colder throughout the day. When we stopped for lunch, I was surprised to find that the water bottles I'd packed in the outside pockets of my backpack were partially frozen. After we ate (cold strips of smoked rabbit meat), I repacked everything so that the water was inside the pack, against my back. Hopefully that would keep it liquid.

Now that she didn't have to hold the rabbit, Darla kept up easily. She probably could have passed me—she was in way better shape than I was—but she skied behind, matching my pace.

I started searching for a place to spend the night about midafternoon. There were farmhouses along the road every half mile or so. The first three we passed had tracks in the ash between the outbuildings and the houses. Probably the people in them would have been friendly and let Darla and me hole up in one of their barns overnight, but I was tired of people and their stupid guns. I skied on.

The fourth place we came to was obviously uninhabited, obvious because the house, barn, and garage had all collapsed. The only intact buildings were two concrete grain silos. I slid twice around both the cylindrical silos, looking to see if we could get inside, but there was no visible entrance. There must have been some way to get in—they'd be useless if the farmers couldn't load them with grain. Maybe Darla knew how they worked, but she still wasn't talking.

The barn had stood next to the silos, but it was hopeless. The ash had flattened it completely—panels of wood siding and rafters jutted randomly from the heaped wreckage.

The front part of the farmhouse was standing, sort of. The whole back section and roof had collapsed, pulling the front wall backward so it leaned precariously at about a sixty-degree angle. I didn't want to get near it for fear it would fall on us.

A big metal garage had stood not far from the house. The roof and walls were down, but something was supporting the wreckage in the middle. I crawled under a bent wall panel to check it out but couldn't see anything inside. I had to duck out, fish a candle out of my pack, and try again.

There was a huge John Deere tractor inside, a combine, I guessed. It supported the wrecked roof, creating a triangular area big enough to walk around in. It seemed

safe enough; certainly the tractor wasn't going anywhere.
And finding a sheltered spot to spend the night was a huge
relief. At least we wouldn't freeze to death—not tonight,
anyway.

I led Darla in and built a fire beside the combine, using
scraps of wood from the fallen barn. It's a lot harder to
cook over a fire than you'd think. I made corn pone. Some
of it was a bit burnt, but Darla ate it, and she hates corn
pone, so maybe it wasn't too bad. Either that or she was
starving. She got some cornmeal from my pack and tried
to feed her rabbit. It didn't eat much.

We laid our blankets next to one of the tractor's huge
rear wheels. The concrete-slab floor was cold, but at least
we were out of the wind. "Goodnight," I said, as Darla lay
down beside me. She didn't reply, just rolled over to face
the oversized tire. I pulled my backpack close to use as a
pillow and rolled onto my left side, facing away from her.

* * *

When I woke up, Darla was pressed against my back, one
arm flung over my hip. It made me feel warm being
spooned together. Her body heat was almost enough to
counteract the chill radiating up from the cement floor. I
lay as still as I could, trying to enjoy the quiet morning
and the comfortable weight of her arm on my side.

The first sign I had that Darla might be waking up was
when she pulled her arm tighter around me, snuggling
closer. Maybe she came fully awake then, because a few seconds later, she yanked her arm back and rolled away.

We ate a cold breakfast and packed in silence.

* * *

It started to snow later that morning. Fat flakes drifted lazily down and clung to our clothes for a while before melting. At first it was great. As the snow began to accumulate on the road, our skis slid more easily. Pretty soon we were moving faster than I had since leaving Cedar Falls.

But the wind picked up and the snowfall got heavier. It got steadily more difficult to see. The wind snapped at the left side of my face, whipping icy particles into my eyes. I wished I still had Dad's ski goggles, but I'd lost those when Darla's house burned. Darla and I weren't dressed for this kind of weather. When we stopped for lunch, I started shivering uncontrollably.

Darla's lips and nose were tinged blue. Her hands were jammed into the pockets of her jeans, but I saw her shoulders quivering. I had a hard time repacking our lunch stuff because my hands shook so badly.

I set a fast pace, trying to warm up. The blizzard got worse. I skied by the edge of the road, looking for mailboxes or any sign of a place to stop and find shelter. Twice I veered off the road accidentally and had to sidestep laboriously out of the ditch.

We'd been skiing up a gradual incline for a while. Suddenly the slope changed, and I picked up speed, heading downhill. I assumed we had climbed a ridge and were starting down the backside now, but I couldn't see it. I could barely see the tips of my skis.

I accelerated dangerously. The wind and snow whipped at my face, turning the world blindingly white. I tipped the backs of my skis outward, forcing them into a down-ward-facing vee, trying desperately to slow my descent. I hoped Darla wouldn't run into me. For that matter, I hoped she was still behind me. I couldn't hear anything over the howling wind, and I was so focused on trying to stay on the road that I couldn't risk a backward glance.

I leaned forward and squinted, trying to see the road ahead. Tears leaked from my wind-burnt eyes and froze on my cheeks. We had to find a place to stop, but I couldn't spare the attention to look—it took everything I had just to stay upright and on the road.

The edge of an aluminum guardrail appeared sud-denly in front of my skis. I screamed and threw my weight to the right, trying to avoid a collision. My left ski clipped the guardrail. I slid down an embankment, totally out of control now, flailing my arms in an effort to stay upright.

Branches clawed at my arms and legs, breaking as I crashed through. A tree limb slapped my face, leaving a stinging line across my frozen cheek. My ski tips caught on something, and I pitched forward as my boots popped free of the ski bindings. I fell into darkness.

Chapter 33

I landed in water. It was so cold, the shock of it was electric—like getting zapped on every part of my body at once. I thrashed in panic, trying to get my head above water. A violent gray-and-white haze filled my eyes: rushing water and wind-beaten snow, indistinguishable from each other and equally frigid. Something brushed against my left hand, and I grabbed for it—a clump of dead grass or reeds, maybe. I pulled my face free of the water and drew a desperate breath.

The current sucked at my legs, trying to drag me back under. I screamed and strained my left arm, hoping to lift myself out of the stream, but the grass—or whatever it was—began to pull away from the bank. I flailed around with my right hand, reaching for something more substantial to grab. That motion ripped the clump of grass free. I slid back under the water.

I slipped deeper underwater this time, and the light faded to a dead winter twilight. My left foot tangled in some rocks, keeping me from being swept downstream. It was strangely silent, the water muffling every sound except my blood rushing at the back of my ears. Was this it, then, the way my life would end? Not with the searing flame of a fire or the boom of a shotgun, but trapped in the frigid embrace of this riverbed, dark and silent?

I kept thrashing, struggling to grab something or swim upward, but I couldn't even free my left foot from the rocks trapping me. I wondered if my mother would ever find out what had happened to me, or if Darla would turn around and go back to Worthington once she knew I was dead. I hoped she would. Maybe she'd be safe there.

A hand searched through the water above me. I grabbed for it but missed. The hand withdrew. The current twisted me partially sideways, and I tilted my head, trying to watch the spot where the hand had appeared.

Something yanked my hair, hard. I felt the rock trapping my foot lift as I was pulled out of the stream by my hair. When my head broke the surface, I didn't have enough breath for anything but a soggy cough. Darla stood there, holding onto a sapling and leaning out over the stream. I reached up and caught hold of her wrist.

God, but that girl was strong. She lifted me out of the stream with one arm and dropped me gasping on the bank. I turned my head and retched, bringing up creek water and the corn pone I'd eaten for breakfast. I took a grateful breath of icy air, but it triggered a convulsive fit of coughing. Darla rolled me onto my stomach and pounded on my back. When the coughs subsided, I lifted one of my hands to my face and noticed it was shaking. I tried to still it and found I couldn't. Within a few seconds, the rest of my body started shivering uncontrollably as well.

Darla grabbed me under my arm and half led, half dragged me along the bank, heading upstream. I kept stumbling, tripping over my own feet. Every time I started to fall, Darla yanked hard on my arm, pulling me upright and dragging me forward.

I tried to ask Darla where she was taking me, but I was shivering so badly that the words came out garbled. It took every ounce of concentration I had to keep moving forward without falling, and I wasn't even doing that well.

We pushed through thick underbrush, stripped of its leaves by the ashfall and the cold. Darla led me back to the bridge I'd missed. Underneath there was a dirt area between the foundation and the stream—shelter from the blizzard above.

When Darla released my arm, I fell in the dirt. I lay there, shaking so violently that I couldn't stand back up. I'd lost track of my arms and legs. I assumed they were still attached to my body, but I couldn't feel them at all. Darla rolled me onto my stomach and pulled the pack off my back.

I was vaguely aware of her going through the backpack, tossing stuff aside. A sopping-wet blanket made a
splat on the dirt nearby. She tossed out a wet undershirt
and then a pair of pants that seemed a little drier. I lay
with my face in the dirt, shaking incessantly.

She found a mostly dry change of clothes buried deep
enough in the backpack that water hadn't seeped into it
while I'd been submerged. She set the clothing beside me
and rolled me onto my back. I tried to help, but the arms
and legs that I couldn't even feel wouldn't respond to my
mental commands. The motion of rolling over provoked
an intense wave of nausea. I retched again, but there was
nothing left in my stomach.

Darla fumbled at my shirt buttons. She couldn't undo
them; her hands were shaking too much. After three failed
attempts, she grabbed the placket of my shirt and jerked
on it. The buttons popped free, one of them pinging off
the concrete bridge abutment.

Darla pulled off my ski boots and the rest of my wet
clothes. Mostly she had to rip everything off by force. I
was no help at all. The thought occurred to me as I lay
there naked that I should hide. At that moment it seemed
like a very good idea to dig a hole in the dirt and curl up
inside, where I'd be safe and warm. This was nuts, of
course. The ground under the bridge was almost as cold
as the snow above it. But to my frozen mind, it seemed like
a good idea.

Darla pulled a pair of underwear over my legs. They
were backward. I thought about protesting, but couldn't

summon the energy. When she seized my arms to push a T-shirt over them, I saw I'd been scratching in the dirt. Trying to dig a hole, I guessed.

She got a pair of jeans and an overshirt on me but didn't bother trying to button them. She draped the dry blanket from her pack over me. Then she disappeared into the blinding white blizzard beyond the bridge.

I felt a wonderful heat flood over my body. I stopped shivering. My arms and legs were hot—too hot, so I sat up, shrugged off the blanket, and tried to pull off my overshirt. Something still wasn't working right. I grabbed for the cuff and missed. I tried again, but my fingers wouldn't grip the fabric. On the third try, I got one arm of the shirt off. I gave up on the other arm. I smiled, enjoying the heat flooding my body. Everything slowed down; I watched individual snowflakes drift downward at the edge of the bridge, each one appearing to take several minutes to meander to the ground.

Darla returned carrying an armload of dead wood. She may have said something to me—it sounded hollow and far off, so maybe I imagined it. Something like, "Keep your goddamn clothes on, Alex!" She dropped the wood, stuffed my arm back into my shirt, and wrapped the blanket over my shoulders. I was way too hot. I tried to tell her so. What came out made perfect sense to me at the time, but later she told me I'd said, "Green hills wash sunlight blue."

Darla dug in the pack and came up with a candle and book of paper matches. She rubbed a match on the striker. Nothing. She tossed the wet matches aside and fished deeper in the pack. She found a box of wood matches that had stayed dry and used one to light the candle. She fed wet twigs into the candle flame. They hissed and popped as they dried, but eventually she got a fire going.

She left the candle at the center of the fire. I thought about protesting—we had only a few candles left—but the words wouldn't come out right. She added more wood, building up a roaring blaze that quickly made a black smudge on the concrete underside of the bridge above us.

Darla pushed me onto my side, facing the fire. She slid under the blanket behind me and threw an arm over my side, hugging me against her body. Her arm was still damp, but it felt warm against my flank. Her hand peeked out from under the blankets—even in the orange firelight, it looked blue and puffy. Something brushed my hair and I looked up; the rabbit was sitting on its haunches beside my head.

Ironically, as the fire warmed my body, I began shivering again. Darla had never stopped. I grabbed her arm and wrapped both my hands around it, clutching it to my chest.

We lay under the blanket trembling together, the way I had imagined lovers might hold each other in the afterglow of sex. But I wouldn't have known. I'm not sure why my mind went there, at that moment, to think about sex and the fact that I was still a virgin. Maybe it had something to do with death, with how closely I'd come to the end. The awareness of it sat in my chest like a knife, making me short of breath. The Grim Reaper had visited me again, had even poked me with his scythe, but Darla had dragged me by the hair from his dark kingdom.

I crushed her arm tighter to my chest and savored the feeling a tear made as it slowly ran along the bridge of my nose. The instant I quit shivering, I fell asleep.

Chapter 34

When I awoke, I was cold but not unbearably so. The fire had burned to embers. Darla was gone.

I noticed both sets of skis and Darla's poles stacked near the fire. There was no sign of my ski pole or staff. I was glad to see that my skis, at least, hadn't been lost. Maybe I'd hit a root, ripped my boots out of the bindings, and left the skis on the bank when I fell in. I felt bad about losing Mrs. Parker's bö staff, though.

I sat up, buttoned my shirt and pants, and pulled the blanket over my shoulders. The blizzard continued to vent its fury on the world outside our bridge.

As I watched, Darla materialized amid the white flakes, carrying an armload of wet wood.

I helped her feed the fire. We started with twigs, adding them slowly so that the ice and snow clinging to the branches wouldn't extinguish the embers. As we worked, I said, "You saved my life. Again."

She shrugged.

"Thanks."

Soon we had the fire roaring, and I'd warmed up. I wrapped myself in the blanket and stepped out into the blizzard. Every few steps, I looked back. The scene under the bridge grew dimmer and dimmer as I walked away. After twenty steps, all I could make out was the hazy orange glow of the fire. I decided not to go any farther. It would be too easy to lose my way in the snowstorm and wind up lost or in the river again.

I peed against a tree. It was freezing cold out. I felt bad for Darla, who had to expose a lot more of herself to accomplish the same thing. I looked around and found two long, Y-shaped tree limbs. Back at the campfire, I used the branches, some rocks, and our rope to rig up a clothesline. I had to rotate the wet clothing several times because the stuff hanging nearest the fire steamed and dried, but everything at the far ends of the clothesline froze solid.

Darla and I both gathered wood. There were a lot of dead trees, bushes, and driftwood near the bridge. By lunchtime, we'd amassed a huge stash against the bridge abutment—far more than we'd need to feed the fire for another day.

That afternoon, the wind changed. It had been out of the northwest, so the bridge abutment had protected us from the worst of the weather. Now it howled straight from the north, driving down the river and through our little camp. I had to hurriedly take the clothes off my makeshift line so they wouldn't blow away.

Darla threw more wood on the fire. We sat huddled with our backs to the wind. Still, we were freezing. I worried about surviving the night, exposed like this. We waited more than an hour, hoping the wind would shift. Instead, it got steadily worse.

Something had to change. I thought about it for a while, trying to figure out what to do. Then I got up, wrapped myself in a blanket, and walked out from under the bridge into the icy teeth of the wind.

I bent and formed a snowball with my hands. The snow was too cold and fine to pack well, but with a little force I got it to ball up. I rolled my snowball around on the ground as if I were making a snowman. It was difficult at first, but as the ball got heavier, the snow stuck better.

When I got about as big a snowball as I wanted, two feet in diameter or so, I rolled it back to the bridge. I jammed it into the corner where the bridge abutment met the ground at the north side of the bridge.

My hands were icy. I walked to the fire to warm them. Darla was watching me with a puzzled expression on her face, but she didn't say anything, so I didn't bother to explain.

As soon as I could feel my hands again, I went back out into the blizzard and made another big snowball. I jammed it in next to the first one. Pretty soon Darla caught on and started helping me. Using snowballs, we built a wall stretching about eight feet out from the bridge abutment toward the stream. It took all afternoon because we had to stop constantly to warm up, but when we were finished, we had a corner between the abutment and our wall that was sheltered from the wind.

Darla dragged a couple of branches from our fire to start a new one inside the shelter. We gnawed on frozen strips of rabbit meat for dinner.

When I lay down to sleep, Darla's rabbit nestled against the top of my head. For some reason, it seemed to like that spot. Darla curled against my back, so we were spooned together for warmth. We slept with our faces toward the fire.

* * *

The blizzard still raged the next day. It was easily the worst snowstorm I'd ever experienced. I wondered how much longer it would blow. Our food wouldn't last forever. At some point, we would have to leave to find more. If the blizzard abated. If the snow wasn't too deep to move through.

The new shelter was okay—it had kept us alive over-night, but gusts of wind occasionally swirled under the bridge, blowing cold snow into our fire and our faces. Darla and I spent all day improving it. We built two more walls, so we had a roughly square igloo under the bridge, about six by six inside. I left a small hole at the top of one of the walls to let the smoke out and used our plastic tarp to cover the entrance. I worried that the fire would melt the walls, and it did, a little, but the melted snow quickly formed a hard ice layer that seemed to want to stay frozen.

It was warm inside the igloo. Short-sleeve-shirt warm. Wonderfully, heavenly warm. I slept great that night, although there was one disadvantage to the shelter: Darla didn't need to cuddle against me. She laid her blanket on the other side of the fire.

* * *

The blizzard hadn't slacked at all the next morning—it was into its third full day. We ate breakfast and gathered a little more wood in the morning, but then there was nothing to do.

We sat in the igloo. I tried to start a conversation, but Darla only stared at the walls. The silence slowly grew oppressive between us. Eventually, I just started talking. I'm not normally a talkative guy, but something about that day, holed up with nothing to do, got me started.

I told Darla about my bratty little sister, Rebecca. How she'd always run screaming to Mom whenever I did anything even slightly questionable. What was wrong with putting Tabasco sauce in her tube of toothpaste, anyway? It added flavor, right?

I told Darla about overhearing my mom when she scolded Rebecca for losing so many pencils at school. Later that week, I saw an eighth-grader, Johnny Edgars, going through her book bag in the hall before school, while it was still on her back. He took out a pencil, broke it in front of her face, and dropped the jagged ends on the floor. Then he laughed while she picked up the pieces, crying.

They were standing at the far end of the hallway. By the time I got to them, Johnny was gone. At recess, I hid when my class was called in and waited for the eighth-graders to come out. When I saw Johnny, I walked up to him and kicked him in the face. Blackened his eye, too.

I got in *so* much trouble. Suspended from school for a day. Even my dad lectured me—and that never happened. Mom called Mrs. Parker at taekwondo. She demoted me a belt and suspended me from the dojang for a month.

But it worked. As far as I know, Johnny never bothered my sister again. He turned his tender mercies to torment-ing me instead. That was the year of the bully. I had never told anyone about it before Darla. I think my sister knew. But as far as Mom, Dad, and Mrs. Parker were concerned, that vicious kick was just a random act of violence in my otherwise boring elementary-school career.

I talked to Darla all day. I told her about my dad, the way his face would glaze over when I tried to talk to him. Oh, he'd nod and make the right noises, but I could tell nobody was home.

I told her about Mom. How she was always pushing: "Why'd you get a B+ in French?" or "Why don't you vol-unteer for the school play, Alex?"

I told Darla how much I missed them all.

After a while, it occurred to me that I was being cruel. Darla's mother and father were dead. She was an orphan, an only child. If she had any living relatives at all, she hadn't told me about them.

She didn't say anything, hadn't said anything in days. She stroked the rabbit in her lap, staring at nothing in particular.

I dug through my pack and found a bag of cornmeal. I got a handful of it and crawled around the fire to Darla. I held out my palm to her rabbit. He nipped me while he was eating the cornmeal, but it was only a little pinch, so I ignored it.

"What's his name?" I asked.

"Jack."

I was so startled to hear her respond that I almost dropped the cornmeal. "You named a rabbit Jack? Like jackrabbit?"

"Yeah. Stupid, huh?"

"And you had one named Buck? Did you have male rabbits named Bull? Or Gander?"

Darla laughed. It sounded musical after the days of silence. "Yeah, I had one named Bull. And Rooster. Didn't think of Gander. Good idea, though."

"It's good to hear your voice again."

She was silent for so long, I was afraid I'd said something wrong, somehow screwed things up. ". . . I've been a bitch, haven't I?" she said finally.

"No—"

"I know it wasn't your fault. Bad things are happening all over. Mom . . . We were unlucky. . . . I'm sorry."

"It's okay."

"It might have been worse if you hadn't been there. I

might be dead, too. You killed that Ferret guy. You killed
them both. Maybe I'd be dead if not for you."

I shrugged.

"I'm sorry. It's just . . . I miss Mom so much." A low
moan built deep in her throat, releasing into a full-fledged
sob. "I miss her so much, Alex," she said through her tears,
shoulders heaving.

I wrapped my arms around her and held her as she cried.
I might have cried a little, too, her sadness was so deep.

That night we moved the fire to one side of our igloo,
closer to the smoke hole in the wall. We slept on the other
side. It wasn't cold in the shelter anymore. But we still
curled up together to sleep.

Chapter 35

When we emerged from our igloo in the morning, it was bitterly cold. No snow was falling, and there was very little wind. The morning light reflected off the snow, making it the brightest day I'd seen since the eruption.

Darla made breakfast while I scouted around. The snow was deep—I sank to the top of my thighs in it. The north wall of our shelter was completely hidden by a huge snowdrift that sloped gently upward, reaching all the way to the top of the bridge.

I found two strong branches and hacked them off their tree with the hatchet I'd taken from Target.

One branch was the perfect length for a ski pole. The other was about six feet long, so I planned to use it as a makeshift bö staff.

We ate corn pone for breakfast and refilled all our water bottles. At least the snow had solved our water problems. Now we simply filled the frying pan with snow, held it over the fire for a few minutes, and poured the fresh water into our bottles. We packed up everything, clipped into our skis, and set out.

Sidestepping up the embankment to the bridge was difficult. We started at the north side, but the drifts were too deep. Even with the skis, we sank so far into the snow that we couldn't lift our legs high enough to make any upward progress. We gave up and skied to the south side.

We made it up that embankment. I sidestepped to the crown of the road, pointed my skis across the bridge, and pushed off.

What followed was utter fail on two levels: First, my improvised ski poles just poked holes in the snow. They never hit anything solid, so I couldn't push off. Second, when I tried shuffling forward without pushing off, my skis dug troughs five or six inches deep in the soft snow. The tips of my skis promptly dove under the snow ahead of me and caught, pitching me forward onto my face.

I lifted my head out of the snow and looked back. Darla was smiling, trying somewhat unsuccessfully to suppress outright laughter. "Fine. You try it," I grumbled.

Darla pushed off with her poles and glided smoothly over the surface of the snow. She looked back at me and shrugged.

I tried again. My ski tips pushed under the snow, nearly causing another fall.

I glared at my skis. That was when I noticed they were different from Darla's. For one thing, her poles had big baskets a few inches from the end that caught in the snow and let her push off, even in the deep stuff we were trying to cope with. For another, her skis were a lot wider than mine and a little shorter. They were slightly concave on each edge, too. My best guess was that the librarian had sold us a pretty good pair of off-trail skis, while my dad's old skis were designed for groomed snow. I shared this theory with Darla.

"I don't know anything about skis, but I think you're right," she said. "I've got an idea—I think I can make some baskets for the ends of your poles if we can find some twine somewhere. I can't think of any way to fix your skis, though."

"Me, either."

"Try skiing in my tracks."

That worked okay. So long as I stayed behind Darla and kept my weight centered on my skis, I could shuffle along in the grooves her skis cut in the new snow. I was a lot slower than she was. Being able to use her poles more than compensated for the extra effort she had to put in to break the trail. Every forty or fifty feet she'd stop and wait for me to catch up. I thought fondly back to our first trip to Worthington, when I'd been on skis and she'd been on foot. We had been a strange team, even back then.

* * *

We broke into a farmhouse that night. It looked deserted—
no tracks in the snow, no smoke from the chimney—and it
was, sort of.

Darla found a window ajar at the back of the house. We
unclipped from our skis and stuck them upright in the snow.
I shoved the window fully open and climbed through.

It was late and too dark to see much in the room.
There was a vaguely unpleasant smell, a hint of something putrid lingering on the knife-edge of the frozen air.
Darla stepped behind me and dug a candle and matches
out of my backpack.

By the candlelight we discovered we were in a bedroom. A queen bed, sheets pulled tight with military preci-
sion, filled the center of the room. A man wearing a black
suit lay in the center of the bed, his skin frozen to a blue-
white pallor. He looked almost normal—peaceful, even—
except for the gun clutched in his right hand and the huge
black stain wreathing his head in a sanguinary halo.

Darla jumped and let out a yelp. Maybe I should have
been startled, as well. Finding myself in a room with a corpse
would have scared the bejeezus out of me only five weeks
ago. But I'd seen a lot of corpses since I'd left home; this fel-
low wasn't the worst—and probably wouldn't be the last.

Darla turned away from the bed. She stared at a
cracked mirror mounted above the dresser. The mirror
was so coated in dust that it didn't reflect anything. She
dragged her splayed fingers across its surface, and our
reflections appeared, fractured into five narrow lines by
the paths she'd drawn.

I held the candle over the bed. Flecks of blood spotted the guy's lips, gleaming black in the candlelight.

"What do you think happened?" Darla asked.

"He shot himself. Put the gun in his mouth."

"He put on his best suit, too. His funeral suit. . . . Why?"

I wasn't sure if she was asking why he had killed himself, or why he had dressed up to do it, but either way the answer was the same. "I dunno." I reached out and touched the guy's hand. It felt cold and hard as marble.

"What are you doing?" Darla asked.

"Getting the gun." I had to bust his finger to get it out of the trigger guard. It cracked, like ice breaking. "You know anything about pistols?"

"Not much."

I handed the gun to her anyway. "Not much" beat what I knew, which was absolutely nothing. Darla found a latch on the left side of the gun that released the cylinder. There was one spent casing in there—no bullets. Darla picked the casing out with her fingernail and closed the cylinder. She put the gun in one of the exterior pockets of my backpack.

We looked through the rest of the house. It was small: two bedrooms, one bath, a kitchen, and a living room with a fireplace. Nobody else was there, alive or dead.

I unlocked the front door and opened it. Snow was piled so high against the storm door that I couldn't get out, so we trooped in and out through the bedroom window and around the dead guy's bed carrying firewood. We could have burnt a kitchen chair or the coffee table instead, but there were plenty of trees around the house. Besides, burning the furniture seemed rude somehow, since we were guests, albeit uninvited ones.

At first, walking by the dead guy creeped me out a little. But after hauling three armloads of wood and a couple of frying pans full of snow past him, I got used to it. I even said "hi" the last time I walked through that night.

I made corn porridge with bits of rabbit meat for dinner. Darla fed some of it to Jack. We'd make a cannibal out of that poor rabbit yet. He seemed to be doing better. One nice thing about all the snow was that it covered the ash, keeping it from blowing around. We were breathing the cleanest air we'd had since the eruption—maybe that was helping Jack, too.

I shook out a blanket and laid it between the fireplace and the couch. The spare bedroom held a nice bed, but it was frigid in there. We'd sleep warmly in front of the fire.

"You can have the couch if you want," I said.

"I think there's room for both of us."

There was *not* room for both of us on that couch. But Darla moved all our blankets onto it and got me to help her drag it closer to the fireplace. She efficiently stripped off her overshirt, boots, and jeans. I tried not to watch. She was wearing a T-shirt that read Rabbits Bite! in huge letters across her boobs and Dubuque County 4H below that. Her panties were cute girlie things with yellow stripes and pink hearts—not like her at all. The effect was ruined somewhat by the gray streaks of ash staining them. I'd seen them before, of course. I had no idea why I was noticing them again at that moment.

Darla sat on the edge of the couch and rubbed her feet.

"You okay?" I asked.

"It's just my feet—the ski boots are too tight."

"I'll help if you want."

"Sure." She stretched out her feet toward me.

I sat on the floor and massaged her feet. They were crosshatched with red welts. They didn't smell bad at all, which surprised me—my feet probably stank.

"Oh," Darla sighed, "that feels so good." She pulled her feet away from my lap, climbed under the blankets, and stretched out on her side with her face toward the fire. I sat on the edge of the couch beside her and pulled my boots off.

Suddenly I felt funny about getting undressed. It made no sense—I'd been completely naked in front of Darla repeatedly over the last few weeks. I sent strict orders to my body to chill out. Concentrating on my breathing helped. Two quick breaths in through the nose, two quick breaths out through the mouth, just like I'd use during a sparring match. I peeled off my jeans and overshirt and crawled under the blankets with her.

I spooned against her, my back against her stomach. Well, honestly, what I noticed were her breasts against my back. They formed two puddles of warmth beneath my shoulder blades, although maybe my overactive imagination was at work. I didn't think I was pressed that tightly against her.

I probably smelled rank in my sweaty underclothes. I had probably smelled rank for days, but it hadn't bothered me until then.

"Goodnight," Darla said.

"Goodnight."

My knees and arms hung over the edge of the couch. The room was bright—we'd built the fire up before we turned in. I stared into the flames for a while.

"You awake?" I asked, my voice pitched low.

"Yeah."

"Can I ask you something?"

"You just did."

"What?"

"Obviously, you can ask me something. You just did. You asked if you could ask me something."

"Do you know you're annoying?" I punctuated this comment by elbowing her in the side.

"Yeah, sorry. What did you want to ask me?"

"Nothing."

"No, really, what was it?"

I sighed. "It was . . . I was wondering. Why'd you follow me out of Worthington?"

"I dunno."

"No, I'm serious. You would have been safer there. They're organized. They've got water and food. The people there know you and like you. But I'm . . . with me, your chances aren't so good. I've almost died three or four times already. We've got food for what? Four or five more days, maybe? Maybe we can make it to Warren by then, but I don't know what's waiting for us, if anything. I mean, I hope my parents are there with my uncle and his family, but I don't know. I don't know anything, really."

She was silent.

"I mean, I'm glad you did follow me," I said. "I'd have been dead in that river without you. But I'm not sure it was so smart."

"I'm not exactly sure why myself." Her voice was so soft that the whisper of the flames in the fireplace threatened to drown it. "I . . . look, it's not logical, but I feel safe with you. I should be freaked out by the dead guy in the room behind us, but I'm not. I know I'd be safer in Worthington, but I didn't *feel* that way when I woke up that morning and you weren't there."

I reached back, caught her left hand in mine, dragged it to my chest, and held it there.

"I guess I never bothered to ask whether you wanted me with you," Darla continued. "Maybe you could make better time without me. And I know I was a real drag to have around—"

"Want you? Of course I do, Darla. I'd be dead twice over now except for you. And you're an amazing girl. I've never met anyone who works as hard as you do. Or knows as much about machines. When I first saw you in your barn, I thought you were an angel. If I didn't know you were already in love with Jack, I might seriously let myself—"

"Roll over."

I did. Darla's lips were on mine before I'd completely turned over. We kissed. I felt like I was falling, plunging headlong down a warm, moist tunnel.

My eyes were closed. My right arm was wrapped around her shoulder; my hand gently cupped the back of her head, as if it were some wondrous glass sculpture, fragile in my palm.

Darla started crying.

No, that's wrong. She wasn't crying; she was sobbing, in full-throated wails. I pulled away, shocked. What had I done wrong?

Darla wrapped her arms around me, pulling my body back to hers as she cried. She held on as if she were trying to crush my body in her arms. I returned her embrace a little weakly—I was having trouble breathing.

When she'd finally run out of tears, her arms relaxed, and I sucked in a deep breath.

"I'm sorry," she said. "That kiss. It was . . . how can we feel so good when so many people are dying? I started thinking about Mom, Dad . . ."

She was quiet. I held her tighter.

We lay like that for a long time, but eventually it got uncomfortable. Our knees knocked together. Darla rolled over again, and I snuggled against her back.

Her breathing calmed as she drifted to sleep. I watched the firelight play with her hair, watched it until the fire had burned so low that I couldn't see her anymore. Then, at last, I slept too.

Chapter 36

After breakfast the next morning, we thoroughly searched the house. We both thought there must be more bullets somewhere—what use is a gun with only one bullet, anyway? But we couldn't find any.

We did find clothing: hats, gloves, scarves, heavy flannel shirts, and even an insulated pair of overalls. By mixing and matching the new stuff with what we already had, we managed to put together two decent sets of winter gear.

There was no food at all in the house. The refrigerator stood open and empty except for a box of baking soda. We found two candles in the kitchen, fat pillars of the sort that would be annoying to carry in our pack. Darla borrowed my knife and gave them impromptu liposuction, whittling the excess wax off the sides.

I found a ball of string in one of the kitchen drawers, but Darla said it wasn't heavy enough. She wanted something tougher to fix my ski poles, so we explored the barn.

A snowdrift had covered the long side of the barn, reaching upward almost to the eaves, which made it something like fifteen feet deep. We skied around, looking for a way in.

There were no doors on the right side or back of the barn. When we got to the left side, we found a big square hatch set on the inside of the jamb so it would open inward. Darla said it was for unloading manure, but I didn't know how she could tell. There was no sign or smell of manure there.

I tried the hatch; it was locked. But it had a little wiggle to it on the right side, like it was loose. I took off my skis and kicked the door with a simple front kick. I got my hips behind the kick, thrusting forward for extra power, like I would for a board break in taekwondo. The door rattled, but the latch didn't break. I tried again. On the third try it finally gave, and the door flew open with a bang.

I stepped into the barn. The door had been secured from the inside with a simple hook and eye. My kick had ripped the hook out of the doorframe.

"Damn," Darla said appreciatively, looking at the splintered spot in the wood.

I shrugged. We broke boards all the time at the dojang. It was no big deal.

In the barn's loft, we found fifty or sixty bales of hay—the small, rectangular kind.

"Perfect," Darla declared.

"We need hay?"

"No, silly, the baling twine—I can make ski pole baskets with that."

So I cut twine off the hay bales while Darla searched for some wood. We carried everything back to the living room and built up the fire.

Darla whittled a shallow groove into both my poles about five inches from the bottoms, using my mother's mini-chef's knife. She cleaned off the bark from two sticks and cut them about eight inches long. Then she lashed the sticks to one of the poles in an X shape, wrapping twine in the groove so the sticks couldn't slide up or down.

I handed her stuff and cut twine for her. She talked while she worked. "This reminds me of working with my dad. He used to let me do everything—well, everything I was strong enough for. He'd hand me tools and tell me what to do with them. I'd usually screw it up, at least the first time, but he'd just tell me what I was doing wrong and let me try again."

"What'd you guys work on?"

"All kinds of stuff. We built a hydraulic tree-digger when I was ten or eleven. Big thing with four blades on it that you could hook up to the tractor and use to move live trees around. That's when he taught me how to weld."

"You learned to weld when you were ten?"

"Yeah. Why?"

"I don't think I was allowed to touch the stove when I was ten, let alone use a welder."

"Yeah, well. With your amazing mechanical aptitude, I wouldn't have let you touch a stove, either."

I might have taken offense, but she was smiling at me in a way that made it impossible to be mad. "Why'd you want to learn all that stuff?"

"I dunno. I've always been interested in machines. And Dad was a great teacher. He'd smile when I got to the barn after school. He had the most amazing smile—it lit up his whole face. Then he'd turn everything over to me, show me where the project was at. It was probably a lot slower than doing it himself, but he never once complained. We did everything together—fixed the tractor, mended fences, built stuff . . ."

"It must have been hard when he died." The moment I said it I realized how stupid it sounded. Duh. But Darla didn't seem to mind.

"Yeah. I tried to keep the farm going. At first the neighbors came by all the time to help. But that didn't last long."

"The farm? I thought you only had the rabbits."

"You didn't think all that corn we were digging up planted itself, did you?"

"You did all that?"

"Yeah. Got crappy grades at school. Kept falling asleep in class. Almost had to repeat sophomore year." Darla frowned. "It got better junior year. Mom and I sold off the cows and leased out some of our land, so it wasn't as hard to keep up."

"Junior year . . . how old are you?"

"I'll be eighteen in February. You?"

"Um, I dunno."

"What do you mean, you don't know?"

"What's the date today?"

Darla thought for a few seconds. "It's the fourth of October."

"I guess I'm sixteen then. My birthday was two days ago."

"Wow, missed your own birthday."

I shrugged. "So . . . I've fallen for an older woman? You going to take me to prom?"

"Yeah, right. Even if there was a prom, I probably wouldn't be going. Probably be too busy."

"So much for the benefits of dating an older woman."

"Happy birthday." She leaned over and kissed me, a quick peck on the lips. I hoped we'd keep kissing, but Darla returned to working on my ski poles. She tied a series of strings connecting the crossbars so that when she was finished they looked like diamond-shaped dream catchers.

When Darla finished she said, "Ta-da! New ski poles. For your birthday. Not much of a present, I know, but it's all I've got."

"When you followed me out of Worthington, that was my real birthday present."

* * *

The poles worked great. The combination of crossbars and string grabbed in the snow, so my poles only sank a few inches. It didn't do anything for my skis, of course. They still had an annoying tendency to dive under the powder instead of gliding on top of it, but if I stayed in Darla's tracks, we made progress.

Early that afternoon we came to an intersection. A wide road crossed our path. A sign poked about a foot above the snow. Darla knocked the ice off it: U.S. 151.

That startled me a little. The snow on 151 was completely undisturbed—no one had used it since the blizzard had ended. Shouldn't a major highway have had some kind of traffic? People walking along it, at least? Was everyone dead? The east-west road we'd been on for a while, Simon Road, had been deserted as well, but it was a minor county lane, probably not even paved.

"Highway 151 goes to Dubuque," Darla said. "We should head north."

"I dunno. Didn't Mrs. Nance say there'd been riots in Dubuque?"

"The only bridges across the Mississippi within thirty miles of here are in Dubuque."

"Crap. Okay." We turned north.

* * *

Two hours later, we still hadn't seen signs of anyone on the road. We passed two farmsteads that had tracks in their yards, and two more that appeared to be deserted, but it was too early to stop for the night.

Every now and then we passed a big rectangular shape covered in snow. I asked Darla what she thought they were.

"Abandoned cars," she replied. "Buried in ash and snow." That made sense—why hadn't I thought of that?

We hurled ourselves up a ridge, duck walking. At the top, a glorious downhill slope stretched out below us. Darla grinned and pushed off. I carefully fitted my skis into her tracks and shoved hard with my poles, racing to catch up. We flew down the slope, wind burning our cheeks, freezing air filling our nostrils. Darla laughed, and I let out a whoop.

About halfway down, Darla stood up on her skis and quit pushing with her poles. I started to yell, to ask what was wrong, but she held up a hand, motioning for quiet. That didn't make sense until I caught a glimpse of what lay ahead of her.

Someone was coming up the road toward us.

Chapter 37

Neither of us was much of an expert in cross-country skiing. I didn't think I could stop myself on the downhill slope without falling over. Anyway, Darla was in the lead and had a better view of the approaching people, so I left it up to her. She kept going, and I followed.

As we got closer, I could see them better. A woman plodded toward us through the deep snow. She was bent almost double, straining against a rope looped around her waist. The rope led to a toboggan. There was a suitcase at the front—a big black one with wheels on it, the type that people used to drag through airports. Three kids sat behind it.

The two kids near the front of the toboggan were tiny, maybe two and four years old. They were bundled up tightly in hats, gloves, and warm-looking snowsuits. A larger girl, maybe six or seven, rode at the back. She had on a good snowsuit, too, but no hat and only one glove. Her head lolled to one side, long blonde hair whipped by the wind. Her gloveless right hand dragged in the snow beside the toboggan.

I didn't think the woman had seen us. She was making a heroic effort to move up the hill in snow that deep, let alone pull a sled loaded with kids. Darla was fifty or sixty feet from them when the woman finally looked up.

She screamed—a wordless yell of surprise and fear.

Darla kept skiing toward her as slowly as the hill allowed.

"Stay away from me!" the woman yelled. She turned away from the crown of the road, pulling the toboggan toward the ditch. Somehow she managed a burst of speed. "They're my babies! Mine! You can't have them!"

The snow had drifted deep in the ditch. The woman fell into it, floundering in snow over her head. The toboggan tilted and came to rest at a steep angle, halfway in the ditch. The girl at the back of the toboggan toppled sideways.

I expected to hear crying, but it was eerily silent. The woman thrashed in the snow, trying to right herself. The two little kids stared as Darla and I approached, their eyes shining with fear. The older girl still hadn't moved.

Darla got to where the woman had left the center of the road. She kept going, skiing past the woman and her children.

I looked at the toboggan. I couldn't see the older girl's face, only her pink snowsuit and a lock of her hair, brilliant yellow against the stark white snow.

I turned toward the ditch. My skis instantly caught in the fresh powder, and I fell in a ten-point face-plant. When I dug my way out of the snow, two women were screaming at me.

Darla: "What are you doing, Alex? Christ!"

The woman: "Get away. Get away, devil man!"

I ignored them both, of course. Nobody ever claimed I was smart. I reached down, unclipped my skis, and forced my way through the snow toward the girl in pink. I called out in the softest, calmest voice I could muster, "I won't hurt you. I want to help."

Darla had snowplowed to a stop twenty or thirty feet on down the hill and was sidestepping laboriously back toward me. The woman yanked on the rope, pulling her toboggan close. It slid smoothly out from under the girl, leaving her sprawled alone in the snow.

The girl's face was porcelain white, her lips pale blue. I put my fingers against her mouth. She was breathing, but unconscious. Her ungloved hand felt hard and cold. The tips of her fingers were black.

The woman had been digging through her suitcase. I saw a flash, a glint of light on metal. She'd pulled out a meat cleaver. She waved it frantically, slashing the air above the two little kids' heads. She was still yelling, variations on the theme of demon from Hell, leave my children alone.

"I won't hurt her," I said. "I want to help. She needs help." I picked up the little snow-suited body in my arms. She weighed nothing. I looked around—there were scraggly looking stands of leafless trees on either side of the road. No evergreens or anything else that looked like easy shelter.

Darla huffed up to me, out of breath from sidestepping fast. "This is crazy, Alex. Warren. Your family. If we try to help everybody who's suffering, we'll never get close."

"I don't want to help everyone. I want to help this little girl."

Darla looked away.

"Can we build a shelter in those trees? We need a place to warm her up and spend the night."

Darla sighed. "I saw a car down the hill a ways. It might work." She picked up my skis and poles, bundling them with her own poles. She turned and slid back down the hill.

I looked at the crazy woman. She was holding the cleaver above her head. Her other arm was wrapped protectively over the other two kids. She'd quit yelling, but now she was growling—a low, gravelly noise that would have made a pit bull cower.

I backed up a few steps and then turned to follow Darla. Trudging through the deep snow was hard work. Darla quickly got fifty or sixty feet ahead of me.

The girl's right arm flopped away from her body. The dull black of her frostbitten fingertips looked unnatural against the backdrop of snow. I unzipped my coat and jammed her hand inside against my chest. Even through two layers of shirts, it felt icy.

Darla had stopped by a large rectangular hump in the snow. By the time I caught up, she'd dug a trench about two feet deep along one of the short sides of the hump.

"How can I help?" I said.

"Try to keep that girl warm. And keep an eye on Crazy Mommy over there."

I looked back the way I'd come. The crazy lady hadn't moved; she was still hovering over her other two kids in the ditch. I couldn't see the cleaver.

I unzipped my coat completely. The little girl hadn't moved or even made a sound, but tiny puffs of frosty air emerged from her lips. I hugged her to my chest and tried to zip up my coat around both of us; it wouldn't fit, so I had to settle for holding it around her.

Darla was digging in the ash layer by then. She used the front of a ski, stabbing it into the ash and scraping it out of the hole. I remembered the ash as being mostly white, but against the snow it looked dirty gray.

A bit of the vehicle emerged as Darla continued her assault on the ash. First, a strip of maroon paint—part of the car's roof, maybe. Then, as she dug deeper, she exposed a section of black-tinted auto glass. It was vertical, so I figured she was digging out the back end of a van or SUV.

It was going to take forever. She'd barely cleared a two-square-foot section of one back window. Getting the whole back end of the vehicle unburied might take hours, and even then, wouldn't it be locked?

"Done," Darla said. I looked questioningly at her. She smiled and said, "Here goes nothing." She took a spear grip on one of the skis and rammed the butt end through the window. The glass shattered into a thousand tiny pebbles that rained into the interior of the vehicle. Darla scraped the ski along the edges of the hole, clearing away the remnants of the window. Then she slid through it, feet first. I heard her voice, muffled by the car, "It's good. Pass the girl in."

I crouched in the hole and handed the girl to her. "I'll try to warm her up," Darla said. "Get some wood. We need a fire."

"Okay." I passed our skis, poles, and packs through to her and then slogged toward the scraggly copse near the road.

Every tree was dead—their few remaining lower branches snapped off easily. That was a relief, since any fallen wood was buried under deep snow. But would anything grow again in the spring? Would there even be a spring?

I crawled through the broken window with an armload of firewood. Inside there was a shadowy space, maybe six feet square, between the window and the first bench seat. The ceiling was low; I couldn't stand, only crouch. Darla and the girl lay against the back of the seat, wrapped in both our blankets. Darla's backpack was beside her on the floor; Jack peeked out the top.

I built a small fire on the floor to one side of the entry hole. The fire gave off an acrid, chemical reek at first. I figured the fire was burning the carpet. Some of the plastic door trim melted, too. Most of the fumes rose through the hole in the window, so it wasn't too hard to breathe, so long as I kept my head low.

The nasty smell got me thinking. "Isn't it dangerous to build a fire inside a car? What if there's gas in the tank?"

"This is a big SUV, an Expedition I think. The gas tank will be up here, under me. It'd have to heat up to four- or five-hundred degrees to explode without a spark. We'll be okay."

I kept the fire very small, despite her reassurance. Even so, the inside of the truck got toasty-warm in no time. I stripped off my coat and overshirt. Darla still lay with the girl, both wrapped in blankets. Sweat glistened on her forehead.

I was tending the fire a bit later when the woman's face appeared outside the hole. Her eyes blinked from the smoke. The meat cleaver followed, held in front of her mouth like a shield. I scrambled back a couple feet. "Where's my Katie?" the woman said. "You fixing to roast her? Give her back, you damned-to-Satan filthy cannibals."

"Cannibals?" I didn't know what else to say. The accusation, the mere idea of it, shocked me into silence. I held up both my hands, hoping to calm her.

"Give her back, so I can bury her proper."

"Bury her?" Darla said. "She's not dead. I'm trying to warm her up."

"Poor baby was dead ten miles up the road. Fever and the runs got her. She was cold as a rock."

"Well, this rock is doing an awfully good job breathing, lady." Darla pulled the blanket down, exposing Katie's head. She held the back of her hand to the little girl's mouth.

"She was dead. I was trying to find a safe place to bury her."

"We're trying to warm her up," I said. "She's got hypothermia and frostbite. You can come in and check on her if you want. But you've got to leave that cleaver outside. We're unarmed." My empty hands were still up. The unarmed bit was a lie—I had the chef's knife and hatchet on my hip, turned away from her. Plus, the gun from the guy who'd killed himself was in my backpack, but without bullets, that hardly counted as a weapon.

The woman's eyes swiveled from me to Darla. She stared, and I realized it wasn't Darla she was looking at but Katie, nestled in Darla's arms. The cleaver disappeared and the woman slithered through the window headfirst. She fell with a thunk on the floor next to the fire. Darla unwrapped the blankets from herself and Katie and handed the girl to her mother. The woman clutched Katie to her chest and backed into the corner where the rear seat met the wall. Darla wrapped both of them in our blankets.

I heard a faint mewling noise outside and crawled to the smoke hole to stick my head out. The toboggan was about ten feet away. The youngest kid, really only a baby, was crying softly while the older one, who couldn't have been more than four himself, tried to quiet her. "Shh. Mommy said shh," he whispered over and over.

I looked at the woman. "Your kids are cold and scared. They can come in here with you, if you want."

She stared at me for a long time. Finally she nodded.

"I'll hand them in to you," I told Darla. She shook her head no, but I figured she was expressing her general disgust at the whole project, rather than refusing to catch the kids.

I crawled out of the truck and pushed through the snow to the toboggan. "Your mom's inside. It's warm in there. Will you come with me?"

The older kid went dead silent and rigid as a board. The little one started screaming. So much for my way with kids. I hope I'm never a dad. I'd probably suck at it.

I picked up the bigger kid. He reeked of urine. He stayed stiff while I passed him through the window, which helped; I don't know if we could have got him through the little hole if he'd been windmilling his arms.

The little one did fight and scream. I had to clamp her arms to her sides to shove her through the hole.

I dragged the toboggan closer to our shelter. On impulse, I opened the suitcase resting at the front of the toboggan. It held mostly clothing. There was no food, no way to start a fire, no water or water bottles, and no pans. At the bottom, I found three framed pictures. One showed the entire family: the woman, three kids, and a tall, kind of geeky-looking guy. The other two were wedding photos. The woman looked young and so happy, I got the impression that she might float away in her billowy white dress. The guy looked younger and even more geeky in his rented tux, but he had this smug smile, as if he were saying he'd found the best woman, and the rest of us would have to settle for leftovers. I gently repacked all three pictures amid the clothing. I added the woman's cleaver to the top of the suitcase and zipped it shut.

Inside, all three kids were pressed against their mom. The back of the SUV was crowded with six people and a fire. I rummaged through our pack.

"What are you doing?" Darla whispered.

"Making some dinner."

"Alex, we should move on. Find another camp for tonight. We've helped them enough."

"I went through their suitcase." I was whispering, but

the woman no doubt could hear me in the tiny space. "They don't have any food or water bottles. Who knows how long it's been since they've eaten."

"And who knows how long 'til we'll eat again if you give away all our food."

"I won't give it all away."

"Where are we going to get more when we run out?"

"I don't know."

I made corn pone for everyone. Darla insisted that we give our guests only one pancake each—any more and they might vomit, she said. Then I melted snow to refill all the water bottles and passed those around.

The woman had gone silent. She took the food and water without comment, but her suspicious eyes glared at me, and she kept her back firmly against the wall. Katie was still unconscious, but the other two kids gobbled up everything I offered them.

* * *

That night, I spread our blankets on the bench seat. When I asked Darla to join me, she refused. "I'm going to keep watch half the night," she said. "I'll wake you up when it's my turn to sleep." I wasn't sure how she'd figure out when half the night had passed, but knowing Darla, she had a way to do it. I lay down alone and let sleep claim me.

Chapter 38

Katie died during the night.

It happened after Darla shook me awake and took my place on the makeshift bed. Katie was alive then, but hot to the touch. Too hot, as if a fire were spreading under her skin. She lay in her mother's arms, both of them mercifully asleep.

I watched her breathe by the firelight. She'd gasp and suck in a dozen breaths quickly, panting almost. Then she'd stop breathing for so long I'd wonder if she'd died—a minute, maybe longer. I laid my fingers gently on her neck the first few times she quit breathing—her pulse was fast and erratic.

I wished—no, wanted, needed—to do something for her. But I couldn't even get her to take a sip of water. If we'd had any medicine, I didn't know how we could have gotten her to take it without a syringe. But all that—medicine, doctors, and syringes—belonged to the pre-eruption world, the world that had died almost six weeks before.

A few hours later, Katie trembled for a moment. Her eyes snapped open and glanced left, then right. They were a rich blue, like the last August sky before the volcano. She drew a breath—a long, shuddering gasp—and then lay still.

I thought about doing something. Pulling her out of her mother's arms and trying CPR, maybe. I knew how. I had taken a class Mrs. Parker had organized at the dojang. Maybe I should have tried to revive her. But it felt wrong. Instead, I found her hand, still hot with fever, and held it. Her blackened fingertips felt stiff and lifeless against my palm. After five minutes or so with no breathing and no pulse, I knew she was dead.

Everyone else—her mother, her brother, her sister, and Darla—slept through it. But I watched Katie die.

* * *

Hours later, after sunrise, her mom woke. She pulled her arm tighter around Katie and glanced down. Katie's eyes were still open, staring at nothing and everything.

"She's dead, isn't she?" the woman asked.

I tried to reply. Something was stuck in my throat. No words would exit. Instead, I cried.

I felt a hand grip mine. I looked up. The woman was staring into my eyes.

"The troubles of this world can't hurt my Katie now."

"I wish I could have done . . . I'm sorry."

The woman nodded. A moment later, a change came over her face, and her stare took on a suspicious cast. "You won't eat her, will you?"

"Katie? God, no . . . who would do something like that?"

"There's them that will. My Roger, he . . ." She fell silent for a long time. I held her hand and waited. "We ran out of food a week ago. Couldn't get more. Katie was already sick. We decided to walk across the bridge in Dubuque: Roger, the kids, and me. Heard there's a camp on the other side, near Galena. FEMA camp with food and medicine."

"What happened?" I asked softly.

"Oh, we'd been told there were gangs in Dubuque, a couple of them, fighting over food and turf. Roger figured we could slip past them on side streets, get across the bridge. It didn't work. Three guys found us. Roger fought them, and that gave me time to run off with the kids."

She was quiet again for a while. Catching her breath or deciding whether to tell me the rest of her story, maybe. "I snuck back later, to see if I could help Roger. There was a whole group of them, at least a dozen. Right in the middle of Jones Street. They'd built a bonfire . . . . Above it, spitted like a pig, there was my Roger." Her face was contorted with fury; she spat her words out. "They were roasting my Roger. Roasting him like a pig."

I heard a groan from the front of the SUV.

"Darla? You okay?" I asked.

"Yeah. No." Her head poked up above the bench seat. "What a story to wake up to. Christ."

"I don't think we'd better go through Dubuque. Maybe we can find another bridge or build a raft."

"Okay. We'll figure something out."

"Every night since then I've had the same dream—nightmare, I mean. I see those men crowded around that fire. But they're not cooking my Roger. Instead, it's Katie over that fire. And she's screaming. She's screaming—" The woman broke down into quiet, choked little sobs. She let my hand go and clutched her daughter's corpse to her chest. The other two kids slept through it all.

Darla volunteered to cook breakfast, so I went outside to try to dig a grave. I found a likely looking flat spot on the far side of the ditch. I cleared away the snow, mostly using my hands and arms. The ash layer underneath was frozen, but it was only a thin crust of ice. I broke it up with my staff and then scraped the ash up out of the hole using the butt end of a ski. Under the ash, the ground was rock hard. Little white tendrils of dead grass lay in clumps atop the frozen earth, bleached remainders of a dead world. I poked the ground with my ski. It was hopeless. Without a sharp spade or pickax, I couldn't dig any deeper.

After breakfast, we carried Katie's body out to the shallow grave. Darla suggested we take off her pink jumpsuit, in case one of the other kids needed it. The woman glared at her, and Darla shrugged. I mounded the ash up over the body, but it was a very shallow grave—twelve inches deep at best.

"I'm sorry I couldn't dig any deeper. The ground is frozen solid."

"It's okay," the woman said, "the ashfall claimed my Katie's life, now it can have her body, too."

I said a prayer over the grave. I'd been getting way too much practice at leading impromptu funerals. I hoped this would be the last one.

When we got back to the SUV, I saw Darla had repacked our gear. Jack was poking his nose out of the top of her knapsack. I opened my pack. We had five bags of cornmeal left. I pulled out three of them.

"What are you doing?" Darla's eyes narrowed.

"I'm leaving them some food. They've got nothing to eat."

"What the hell? And exactly what are we going to eat? That's probably not enough to make it to Warren, even *before* you give most of it away."

I didn't answer. I didn't know the answer. She was right. There wasn't enough there for two of us to make it to Warren. I thought about Mrs. Barslow, who'd fed me steak and stayed up late to wash my clothes. She should have let Elroy run me off. Darla's mom should have rolled me back out into the ash outside their barn. If all we did was what we should to survive, how were we any better than Target? I took out three water bottles and the frying pan.

"You can't, absolutely cannot leave the pan here, Alex."

"How are they going to melt snow for water? They don't have one."

"I don't know, and it's not my problem. Why didn't they bring their own damn pot and water bottles?"

The woman had dropped through the hole into the SUV as we argued. "Roger had them in his pack: the water bottles and pans."

"Christ." Darla grabbed the knife, hatchet, and my staff and threw herself out of the SUV. "Just wait here!" she yelled back through the broken window.

"She's right, you know," the woman said. "You don't owe us anything. You should keep your supplies. Keep your wife alive."

"She's not my wife." Somehow, that made the situation feel even worse, the fact that she agreed with Darla. I took another bag of cornmeal out of the pack and set it with the pile of supplies I was leaving behind.

Darla was gone quite awhile. After forty minutes or so, we heard banging and screeching sounds coming from the front of the SUV. She returned a bit later, carrying a con-cave chunk of the truck's front quarter-panel. Two edges were roughly sawn, as if Darla had used the hatchet or knife to cut the sheet metal. I'd had no idea that was even possible.

"You can melt snow with this. But watch the sharp edges around the kids." Darla tossed down the improvised pan and jammed our skillet back into my pack.

"Thank you," the woman said. "And . . . I'm sorry."

Darla grabbed the woman's coat and got right in her face. "We might die because of all the stuff my stupid, softhearted boyfriend is leaving you. So don't you die, too.

You take this stuff, and you keep yourself and your kids alive. You hear?"

"I hear."

I didn't care much for being called stupid and soft-hearted. The boyfriend bit I could live with.

Darla grabbed her pack and dove through the hole, going back outside. I grabbed the woman's hand, gave it a goodbye squeeze, and followed Darla.

Chapter 39

Despite our late start, the day was still dim and overcast, adding to the now-normal haze of high-atmosphere dust and sulfur dioxide hiding the sun.

Darla set off at a furious pace. She stomped up the hill in a duck walk so fast I could barely keep up. We headed south on 151, following the tracks we'd made the day before.

About two miles on, we hit a crossroads. We turned left and set off across virgin snow.

Lunch was a sullen affair. We stopped and sat on a snow-covered guardrail. I dug out a strip of dry rabbit—our last meat, unless we ate Jack—and two cornmeal pancakes left over from breakfast. Darla got out a handful of cornmeal and fed Jack. Somehow, I didn't think we'd be eating him any time soon. As we ate, I tried several times to start a conversation and got nothing but grunts in return.

The land had changed around us. The hills were steeper here and more wooded. Instead of the gunshot-straight roads we'd followed earlier in the journey, this road meandered, following hillsides, creeks, or ridgetops. There were fewer farms, too. We spent large parts of the day with nothing but a partly evergreen forest on either side of the road. Then, occasionally, we'd pop out into huge open areas surrounding a farmstead. All the houses appeared to be occupied, so we avoided them.

Late that afternoon, when I started looking for shelter, we were skiing through one of the wooded areas. I carefully watched the forest on either side for almost an hour, looking for a large pine broken near its base.

I found a tree that might work and yelled for Darla to stop. It was one of the biggest pines I'd seen here, with a trunk almost two feet in diameter. It had broken six or seven feet off the ground. Behind the stump there was a huge hump that looked like a snowdrift extending for sixty or seventy feet. I figured that had been the rest of the tree, now submerged in ash and snow.

Using my hands, I dug a small tunnel alongside the stump. The fallen tree had created a protected space underneath it. I took the hatchet from my belt and chopped off some of the downward-pointing limbs. That created a nearly ideal spot to spend the night: dry, warm, and hard to see from the outside. The pine branches would make for a soft bed, too.

I yelled out, "Come on in. It's nice in here."

Darla crawled through the hole and glanced around in the meager light. "Great idea. It even smells good."

"Yeah, I spent one night under a tree like this a few days after I left Cedar Falls. It was okay. It might be a bit cold, but we'd probably better not light a fire in here. Too many dead pine needles."

"It'll be warm enough with two of us."

We built a small fire in the snow outside and cooked corn pone. We used all of our cornmeal except for a few handfuls Darla saved for Jack. We wound up with enough pancakes for two more meals, maybe three if we rationed them.

After dinner, I made a bed in our shelter by laying out the tarp and both blankets. We snuggled together under the blankets. I'd taken off my coat, overshirt, and boots, but otherwise we were sleeping fully clothed—it was warmer that way. I probably smelled pretty foul, but Darla didn't seem to mind. I could smell her sweat, too, but somehow it made me want to pull her closer, not push her away.

We lay there a long time. I couldn't sleep, and I could tell from her breathing that she wasn't sleeping either.

"I'm sorry," I said, "about giving away most of our food, I mean."

Darla rolled over. I couldn't see her, but I felt her lips press against mine. We kissed—a long, wet smooch. "It was dumb."

"I wouldn't have survived if nobody had helped me. Mrs. Barslow, your mom . . . Anyway, you could have stopped me. It was your food, not mine."

"It was our food. And I said it was dumb, not wrong." She kissed me again. "I know I've been bitchy today—"

"No, you've—"

"I'm scared."

I didn't know what to say, so I didn't say anything.

"It's just . . . when I was on the farm, I knew we'd be okay. I knew where to get food. I knew where I'd sleep at night. Mom was . . . well, I knew I could get help. Now who knows where we'll get anything to eat. Who knows what crazy crap we'll run into tomorrow."

"I won't let anything happen to you, Darla. I promise." Even as I said it, I knew it was stupid. All kinds of bad stuff could happen that would be totally out of my control. Still, it felt right.

We kissed again. I planted little kisses on the corner of her mouth, her cheek, along the line of her neck. When I kissed her ear, she giggled and pulled away. "That tickles."

"The first time I saw you, I thought you were a funny-looking angel. They're not supposed to wear overalls or ride bicycles, you know."

Darla kissed me again. When we broke the kiss, she whispered, "I love you."

"I love you, too." The words tumbled from my lips without thought. I realized I was only giving voice to what I'd felt for a long while: I'd been in love from almost the moment we'd met.

"Do you think we'll live through this?"

"We will."

"How do you know?"

I shrugged. There was no way she could have seen the gesture, but we were pressed so tightly together, I was sure she felt it. "I believe we will."

"I believe it, too."

We fumbled with each other's shirts. I felt the slick fabric of her bra pressed against my chest. Her fingertips traced the scar at my side, bumping over the ridges her stitches had left in my flesh. When her hand grabbed the tongue of my belt, I stopped her.

"What?" she asked.

"It's um . . . I don't think we should—"

"You're not ready? Isn't that the girl's line?"

"Um, no, I want to—I want you. But what if you get pregnant?"

Darla let my belt slide out of her hand. "I dunno—I can't worry about stuff that might happen nine months from now. I'm not totally convinced we'll survive the next week."

"We will." I tried to sound confident, but I wasn't totally convinced, either.

She wrapped her arms around me, and we held each other in the quiet darkness for a while.

"So, have you ever done it?" she asked.

I was glad for the darkness then; it hid my blush. "No. I only had one real girlfriend. Selene Carter. We, uh, messed around some, kind of like you and I are now."

"That's a pretty name, Selene. Is she still in Cedar Falls?"

"I don't know. I guess so. We broke up last spring."

"She didn't want to?"

"I dunno if I was ready. She wasn't, or didn't like me enough, or something. It wasn't a big deal, really. I didn't mind. Well, until she dumped me. I minded that."

"I would . . . I mean, I feel like I'm ready, with you, anyway. But you're right; it would suck to get pregnant. Maybe we could find some condoms or something."

"Yeah." Condoms instantly shot to the number-one position on my mental list of must-find survival supplies—far ahead of food, water, and a way across the Mississippi.

Darla was quiet for a while.

To break the silence, I asked, "What about you?"

"Sex, you mean? No. I was going to let Robbie McAllister do it. I mean, I was thinking about doing it with him or whatever. We'd gotten pretty hot and heavy, but then he got all pissy about how I was always working on the farm and would never go to the movies in Dubuque with him. So I dumped him."

"Pretty tough to keep up that farm and have a social life."

"Yeah."

Darla was silent for so long, I wondered if she'd fallen asleep. When I was sure she had, she whispered, "You know, there's plenty of stuff we can do without any chance I'll get pregnant."

"Like what?"

"I'll show you."

When she reached for my belt this time, I didn't stop her.

Chapter 40

About an hour after we set out the next day, the road left the ridgetop wood. Below us lay a huge valley blanketed in brilliant snow. On the right side of the valley, high on a hillside, a massive church stood alone. It looked old and imposing, its dark brick bell towers glowering over the snow below it.

On our left, high on the opposing hillside, a second church stared across the valley at the first one. This church was white, limestone or marble maybe, and if possible, even more ornate and imposing than the first. A small town nestled below the second church.

We skied down to where the road we were on teed into
a highway. There were two road signs there: Highway 52
and Welcome to St. Donatus. Even from a distance, we
could see footprints everywhere in the town's snow-covered streets. A few of the sidewalks had even been shoveled. Darla and I skirted around the edge of the town. It
seemed unlikely that anyone would want to share food
with a couple of strangers. And if they couldn't help us,
there was no reason to run the risk that they might try to
hurt us.

On the far side of St. Donatus we caught a small,
unmarked road that continued east, passing near the white
church. As I skied between the two churches, I had the
feeling they were looking down on us, blessing our journey. Maybe it was an aftereffect of the night before, but I
felt more hopeful than I had since we'd left Worthington.

* * *

By that afternoon, the hopeful feeling had left me. The road,
which had been heading steadily east, began twisting unpre-
dictably. Sometime after lunch, I completely lost track of
which way we were going. Darla thought we were still heading east, but she also said we should have hit the Mississippi
by then. We had only passed two farms, but both were obviously occupied, so we hadn't found any food.

A bit before dark, Darla spotted a low structure near
the road. She skied around it and found an open doorway
at the far side.

It was too low to stand up inside the building. The
ceiling was about three feet high at one side of the shed

and five feet or so at the other. We had plenty of room though: the building was seven or eight feet wide and at least thirty feet long. It reeked of pig crap.

"Sleeping in a pigsty. That's a new low," I said.

"It's a pig barn, not a sty. Pigsties are outdoor corrals. Anyway, it beats sleeping in the snow."

"I guess. Where are the pigs?"

"I dunno. Dead or in a barn closer to the farmhouse, maybe."

We ate our last two pancakes. Darla fed Jack from our dwindling supply of cornmeal.

We laid out our bedding in the cleanest-looking corner. I was hoping to fool around some more, but Darla just gave me a quick kiss and rolled over. Maybe she was tired, or maybe eau de pig crap didn't turn her on. Couldn't say I blamed her—much.

* * *

Only Jack got breakfast the next morning. I thought about suggesting we cook the last bit of cornmeal instead of saving it for the rabbit, but that would've made only one pancake.

The road ended in a T not far from where we'd spent the night. I wasn't sure which way to turn. I asked Darla, but she was as lost as I was. Her mechanical skills didn't include directional aptitude, apparently. We turned right, figuring that if we'd generally been heading east, that would turn us south, away from Dubuque.

By lunchtime, we'd been forced to make two more turns. We'd had to guess which way to go each time. The roads were getting narrower and the ditches at the side shallower. Where the road ran through trees, it was easy to follow. Where it ran through open fields, we had trouble. We'd seen no sign of the Mississippi, although Darla said the steep hills here meant we were close.

Lunch was a short rest break and some water. I struggled to think of anything other than food. But my mind returned over and over to corn pone, to the bags of cornmeal I'd left with Katie's mom. I wondered what Darla was thinking. Giving our food to Katie's mom seemed more boneheaded by the minute. I remembered desperately scrounging for Skittles in the gas station on Highway 20. How hungry and weak I had been. We needed to find food soon.

Less than an hour later, we came across another farmhouse. It was hidden at the back end of some twisty, no-name road. There was a small, ranch-style house and four big, low sheds, maybe ten feet wide by fifty feet long. Arrayed along the outside of the sheds was a series of big metal silos and tanks connected to the sheds by a system of pipes.

"Pig farm," Darla said.

I sniffed. The air was cold and clean, with a hint of pinesap from the nearby woods. "How can you tell?"

"Low sheds with silos and water tanks connected to them by an automatic feeder system—it's a pig farm."

"No tracks I can see. Check it out?"

"Yeah."

We skied up to the house. Everything was quiet and still—too quiet. It made me nervous. Darla popped the bindings on her skis. She tried the storm door—it was unlocked, but it wouldn't open because too much snow had drifted up against it.

I helped her dig out the snow until the storm door would open enough for us to slip through. Darla tried the main door. It was also unlocked, opening with a creak as if it hadn't been used in a while.

"Who leaves their front door unlocked?" I whispered.

"Lots of folks do. Or maybe whoever lived here wasn't planning on being gone long."

We stepped into a small entryway. Beyond, I saw a living room plainly furnished with a battered oak coffee table and a sofa upholstered in worn, striped cloth. A huge limestone fireplace dominated one side of the room.

"Should we call out?" Darla whispered.

"Might as well."

"Anyone home?" she yelled.

No one answered. I thought I heard a distant thump from outside, but I might have imagined it.

We tiptoed through the living room into the kitchen. A dirty bowl rested in the sink. White fuzz covered it, like the stuff that grows on food left too long in the freezer. Neither the water nor the electric stove worked, of course.

We searched the refrigerator and cabinets. Our whole haul was a box of cream of wheat with about two inches left in the bottom, a three-quarter empty can of Crisco, and four packets of Sweet'N Low. Not much of a meal.

"Where'd the people go?" Darla said softly.

"Dunno. Out to get food? They didn't have much, that's for sure."

"Let's check the sheds."

We left the house the same way we'd come in and skied to the closest pig barn. Darla found the entrance: a door so short we'd have to duck to get through. A yellow handle, leaning against the metal wall, protruded from the snow. I pulled it free—it was a full-sized ax with a fiberglass handle and rusted iron head. I looked a question at Darla. She shrugged, and I put the ax down.

I pushed down the lever-style doorknob. I'd only opened the door five or six inches when I heard a grunt, and the door was shoved closed violently from inside. I leapt back, holding my staff at the ready.

Everything was still for a minute. It was quiet, other than the blood rushing in my ears and my heart thumping in my chest. I yelled, "Hello? Who's there?"

Nothing.

I tapped the metal door a few times with my staff.

No response.

I started to open the door again, cracking it a few inches. A bit of snow fell past the bottom of the door into the space inside. It was too dark inside to see through the narrow opening. I stood and listened for four or five seconds. I heard a grunt and the door slammed again.

"This is weird, let's move on," Darla said.

I agreed with her, it was strange. But my hunger was stronger than my fear. "We need food."

"Maybe we'll find another place farther on."

I lowered my voice to a whisper. "Look, whoever's in there, if it comes to a fight, I need to be able to see."

"What is it with you and fighting, anyway? Let's just move on. We'll find food someplace else."

"There might not be anyplace else. And we need the food. Look, just give me a hand here."

Darla gave me the evil eye for a few seconds. "Humph." Then she dug a candle out of the pack on my back and lit it.

I unlatched the door, opening it a half inch, then stepped back and kicked it as hard as I could. It flew open about a quarter of the way and hit something solid. I heard a squealing noise and a series of thunks like wood hitting concrete, and then the door swung fully open. I ducked my head and charged in, holding my staff in front of me. Darla followed me with the candle.

Inside, the candlelight revealed an abattoir. There were partially chewed hog carcasses everywhere. The floor was slick with frozen blood. Two live pigs were in full flight away from the door, their hooves striking the concrete floor, their heads streaked with fresh blood.

Darla pointed. "Oh. My. God. What's that?"

I looked. To one side of the room there was a row of pens built with metal pipes. They were all empty. Beside one of them, I saw what Darla was pointing to. A man, or what was left of him, lay alongside the fence. One of his legs was obviously broken: a large yellow-white bone stuck out of his torn jeans, pointing almost directly at us. Half his face and most of his torso had been chewed way. The gnawed white ends of his ribs protruded like skeletal fingers from his chest. "That's disgusting," I said, turning away.

"Yeah," Darla replied. The two live pigs had moved around us, back to the door, while we looked at the corpse. They were lapping at the snow that had fallen into the barn, grunting and slamming into the door and each other in their haste to get fresh water.

"What do you think happened?" I asked.

"This guy ran out of food, came out here with his ax to butcher a pig, I guess. Usually people send their pigs to a processor for slaughter, even if they're going to eat the meat themselves, so he might not have known what he was doing. Somehow he broke his leg. Maybe the pigs were starving, thirsty, or whatever and crushed him against that fence. Once he bled out, well, pigs will eat anything."

"Gross," I said. "Too bad there's no food in here."

"Hello? There's enough food here for both of us to live on for weeks."

"You want to eat—you can't be serious."

Darla kicked one of the pig carcasses. It was frozen solid. "The dead ones would probably be okay to eat. But I was thinking we should butcher one of those." She pointed at the two pigs licking snow by the door.

"I don't know—"

"What, you don't like pork?"

"I like bacon, although it feels kind of slimy getting it out of the package."

One side of her mouth wrinkled. "City people. Let me see your knife."

I handed it to her. "You ever butcher a pig?"

"No. But how much worse can it be than cutting up a rabbit?"

It was way, way worse. Darla handed me the candle and retrieved the ax from where I'd left it outside the door. "Any idea what the best way to kill a pig is?"

"What, you don't know?"

"Um, no. Maybe a whack on the back of the head? Like some people use for rabbits?"

"Gonna need to be a heck of a whack." These pigs were huge—two hundred pounds or more. "I dunno if that will do it. Hitting a person on the back of the head doesn't usually kill them—it knocks them out or stuns them."

"Hmm, okay."

Holding the ax in a two-handed grip, Darla got alongside one of the pigs. She reversed the ax so the blunt end aimed down and raised it high above her head. The pig kept lapping at the snow, oblivious to the doom poised above it.

The ax fell, thunking onto the back of the pig's head. The pig went limp and slumped to the ground. The other pig let out a squeal and galloped away, seeking refuge at the far side of the shed.

Darla dropped the ax and grabbed the knife. She plunged it into the underside of the pig's neck, just above its chest, and pulled the knife upward toward its snout. It woke and thrashed, all four legs churning the air as if it were trying to run away. One of its forelegs caught Darla on her shin and she yelled, "Ow! Crap!" and jumped back, pulling the knife out of the pig's neck.

Blood fountained out, spraying her arm. The blood gleamed black in the candlelight. A few drops spotted Darla's face. I felt suddenly ill and turned away. The pig began squealing nonstop, a sound that resembled nothing so much as a kid throwing a full-throated tantrum. We were forced to listen to that awful noise for at least five minutes before the pig finally bled out.

I hadn't had anything to eat since the day before. Still, when I saw the carnage in the pig shed, I'd lost my appetite. Now I felt so sick, I wasn't sure whether I ever wanted to eat again. "If we live through this, I'm going to become a vegetarian."

"Not if I'm cooking for you," Darla said.

"That's okay, I'll do the cooking. Hope you like tofu."

"Tofu? Now that's disgusting," said the girl whose arm dripped with pig blood. "Give me a hand with this."

Darla and I each grabbed one of the dead pig's back legs and dragged the carcass outside. It left a wide, red smear in the snow.

I volunteered to build a fire, hoping to avoid butcher duty. By the time I got the fire done, Darla had gutted the pig and was trying to hack the hams free with the hatchet. Her arms and chest dripped with pig blood. I looked down for a moment, trying to get my stomach under control.

"That's a lot of meat. Won't it spoil?" I said.

"If we had time, we could smoke it. But I'm guessing you'd rather not hang around here."

"Right."

"So I figured we'd try to cook it all and freeze it. If the weather stays cold, it should be fine in our backpacks."

"Okay. I'm afraid you'll say yes, but is there anything I can help with?"

Of course there was. So I wound up getting almost as bloody as Darla. It seemed like we wasted a lot of that pig—I left tons of meat clinging to its bones and skin. Darla just shrugged. "Yeah, we're wasting a ton. But we can't possibly carry it all, anyway. And this is a lot different than butchering a rabbit. I'm doing the best I can."

I was wrong about never eating again. The smell of roasting meat brought hunger surging back to my stomach. We ate a late lunch of very thick-cut bacon fried in our skillet over the open fire. Well, Darla said it wasn't really bacon since it hadn't been cured, but it tasted similar: juicier and much less salty.

As I reached for my third slice, a thought occurred to me that stopped my hand in midair and brought my nausea back. "Um, so we're eating this pig . . ."

"Yeah?" Darla replied around a mouthful of pork.

"And this pig ate part of that farmer. Doesn't that make us cannibals?"

Darla quit chewing. "Gross." She thought a moment and then swallowed. "No. If a cow eats grass, and we eat the cow, then we aren't grass eaters. In fact, we can't eat grass. Cows have a special digestive system for that."

"Yeah, I guess you're right." I thought about it for another second or so, then served myself another slab of side pork.

It took all afternoon and part of the evening to finish roasting the meat. We spitted all the different cuts over the fire, which worked okay. Some of the meat was a bit burnt, and some was tough and hard to eat, but it would keep us alive.

We buried the meat in a snow bank to freeze it. Darla worried about wild animals getting into it. I didn't think that would be an issue because all the wild animals had probably died of silicosis. But it couldn't hurt to be careful, so I spread the plastic tarp over our cache and weighed it down with three logs.

After a late dinner, I built a fire in the farmhouse's living-room hearth. I poked around in one of the bedrooms and found two clean flannel shirts. We discarded the overshirts we'd been wearing, as they were both drenched in pig blood.

There were two bedrooms in the house, both with queen beds. They looked pretty inviting to me: plenty of room to spread out and, uh, do whatever. Darla said it was too cold in the bedrooms. She was right. We did just fine on the ratty old couch in front of the fire.

Chapter 41

Not long after we left the pig farm the next morning, we came back to Highway 52. I groaned. We'd spent two days skiing in a circle, damn it. At least we'd found the pigs—even though it had been disgusting, I felt a lot better with a full stomach and a heavy pack stuffed with pork on my back.

We weren't at the same place where we'd crossed 52 before. There was no sign of St. Donatus or the two sentinel churches. "You think we're north or south of where we hit 52 the first time?" I asked.

"South, probably. We were heading east, and we mostly turned right."

"Those roads were pretty twisty, though."

"Either way, if we turn right, we'll eventually hit Dubuque. I'm not sure where 52 goes if we turn left, but I think it follows the Mississippi River."

I thought about Katie's mom and her failed attempt to cross the Mississippi. "I don't want to go to Dubuque."

"Me, either. Left it is."

The highway ran along a ridgetop for a few miles and then veered left and began a long decline. We picked up speed as the slope grew steeper—I raced along behind Darla, trying to stay in her ski tracks. The wind felt icy on my face, but still it was fun; soon we were laughing and screaming as we shot down the hill.

We flew past a green road sign: Welcome to Bellevue, Population 2337. Then the road flattened out, and we were coasting through a quaint riverside town. Or rather, the buildings were quaint with lots of dark-brown brick and an old-fashioned main street. The town itself was weirdly deserted. There were no tracks in the snow, no signs of people. We skied past Hammond's Drive In, Horizon Lanes, and a Subway. The storefronts gaped like monstrous maws, shards of glass in their smashed windows forming transparent teeth.

Darla and I had fallen into an uncomfortable silence, mirroring the eerie quiet of the town. To break it, I asked, "Where are all the people?"

"I dunno. Crossed the river to get help from FEMA, maybe?"

I saw a drugstore, Bellevue Pharmacy. Its windows were smashed, too. "Let's go in there and look around."

"You think they have some food? We've got plenty of pork, but I wouldn't mind some variety."

"Well, um . . ." I felt the blood rush to my face and looked down.

"Condoms." Darla shook her head, but to my relief, she was smiling. "Okay. Look for sanitary supplies, too. I'd kill for something better than rags."

The drugstore had been thoroughly picked over. We searched for over an hour, even pushing two fallen shelving units upright to look underneath. We found nothing. Well, not exactly nothing. If we'd wanted to know what the latest celebrity gossip had been in August, there were plenty of magazines in the rack to inform us. The small electronics aisle was pretty much untouched. Hair dryers, curling irons, electric shavers, and electric toothbrushes were there for the taking. But everything useful—food, condoms, sanitary supplies, and drugs—was long gone.

"That blows," I said as we gave up the search.

Darla squeezed my hand. "We'll figure something out."

We skied down a hill to the river. The Mississippi itself had changed. A few years ago, my family had taken a three-hour riverboat cruise in Dubuque. Back then, the river had been wide and powerful, filling its banks from tree line to tree line. Now it was a narrow silver thread winding through a gray plain of ashy sludge. Upriver, I could see two barges, both partially grounded in the ash.

The area at the bottom of the hill was fenced-off. A sign on the chain link read: Mississippi Lock and Dam Number 12.

"Maybe we can cross here," Darla said.

"How? If the lock's closed, sure, but—"

"Let's check it out."

That made sense—it couldn't hurt to take a look. I climbed the fence. Darla tossed our skis over and followed me. The dam started at the far bank of the river and extended about three-quarters of the way across. Between us and the dam there was a lock, a huge channel over a one hundred feet wide and six hundred feet long, defined by massive steel and concrete walls at each side and a set of metal gates at either end. The upstream gate had been left wide open. The downstream gate was open, too, forced ajar by a barge stuck within its jaws. Atop both the gates and the walls ran wide metal catwalks. Dead fish lolled belly up in the water below us. It smelled atrocious, like the time Dad had brought home a bunch of bass from a fishing trip, gutted them, then left the trash in the garage for three weeks. (Actually, I was supposed to take the trash out. Whatever.)

"How are we going to cross that?" I said.

"We've got rope. We'll climb down onto that barge."

"The drop looks like twenty-five or thirty feet. How will we get up the other side of the lock?" From where I stood, it looked like a long drop onto the barge's hard, metal deck.

"I'll improvise something."

We climbed over another chain-link fence. That put us on the open-gridded metal walkway alongside the lock. We stepped along the catwalk, lugging our skis, and made a forty-five-degree turn as we followed it over the top of the lock gate. The ash and snow had fallen through the grid of the catwalk, but it was still slick with ice. I felt uneasy; there was nothing but a low, metal fence between me and a very long drop to the water below.

When we reached the end of the gate, directly above the stuck barge, Darla dug the rope out of my backpack. She bundled the skis and lowered them to the barge's deck, where they landed with a clang. Then she looped the other end of the rope around the top bar of the railing and lowered herself down hand over hand, clutching both strands of rope.

Darla yelled "Come on down!" just like a game show host.

I wasn't too sure. It looked like a long way down. And I wasn't very comfortable with heights. When I was in fourth grade, Dad had taken me to a huge sporting-goods store that had a climbing wall. He had needed new ski goggles, or something like that. Anyway, I bugged him 'til he let me try the climbing wall. It was easy and fun—I scampered up in no time. But when I stood at the top and peered over the edge, ready to turn around and rappel down, I just . . . couldn't. Couldn't turn around. Couldn't step backward over the edge. Couldn't even pull my eyes away from the drop. One of the store's employees had to climb up and pretty much drag me off the edge so another guy could lower my rigid body. I spun on the way down, slamming my ankles into the wall, but I couldn't move—I was frozen in terror. As far as I knew, Dad never told Mom or Rebecca about that incident. But he'd never offered to take me back to that sporting goods store, either.

I climbed slowly over the railing and got a good grip, holding the ropes with both hands. I didn't want to step off the metal platform. A little voice in my head screamed at me: Don't do it! You're going to fall! You're going to die!

But I couldn't let Darla show me up. And this was the best way across the river. Plus, I wasn't in fourth grade anymore. I'd faced far more dangerous situations over the last six weeks: the looters at Joe and Darren's house, Target, the plunge into the icy stream. I could do this. I would do this.

Darla yelled, "Any day now."

I scrunched my eyes closed and stepped off, slowly lowering myself hand over hand.

I let out a sigh when my feet touched the deck. Darla said, "You're afraid of heights, aren't you?"

"Uh, not really."

"It's okay."

"Just a little, I guess."

"You did good, Alex." She kissed me. If she'd asked me to join a Mt. Everest climbing expedition at that moment, I might have agreed.

Darla pulled on one end of the rope so it snaked free of the railing above us. On the far side of the barge, the other half of the lock gate loomed above us. "Hand me the hatchet, would you?"

Puzzled, I pulled it off my belt and passed it to her.

She tied the free end of the rope around the handle. "Watch out." She backed up a couple steps and threw the hatchet, aiming for the rail above our heads. The hatchet glanced off and fell back onto the deck with a clang. Darla tossed it again. This time the hatchet went over the top rail, but when she pulled on the rope it came free and clanged back down to the barge. "This may take a while."

I wandered away, both to avoid the tumbling hatchet and to check out the barge. It was really nine barges connected by chains with a tugboat at the back. I saw a large hatch in a nearby deck and tried it—it was heavy, but I could lift it.

I expected to find coal or iron ore, something like that. Instead, it was full to the brim with golden-brown grain. I scooped up a handful and let the hatch crash shut. I wasn't sure what it was, but it looked edible—and there was a lot of it.

Darla yelled, "Hey, I got it!"

I hurried back to her, clutching the grain in my hand. She'd thrown the hatchet up over the railing so that its head had caught on the middle rail and the rope looped up over the top rail. It didn't look very safe to me: if the knot came loose, or the hatchet broke, or the haft disconnected from the head, or it slipped off the rail, then the rope would come loose, pulling the hatchet down with it.

"What's this?" I asked, holding out the handful of grain.

"Wheat. You get it out of that hatch?"

"Yeah. This barge is packed full of it."

"Nice—if we had a way to grind it, we could make bread. Or tortillas, at least."

"You think Jack would eat it?"

"I dunno, wouldn't hurt to try. I'm pretty much out of cornmeal to feed him."

We walked back to the hatch, and Darla held it open while I scooped out kernels of wheat. My backpack was full of pork, but I fit in some wheat by dumping it over the top and letting it fill the cracks around our other supplies. I dumped some wheat into Darla's pack, too, right along-side Jack, but he didn't seem interested in it.

"Maybe we should stay here for a while," Darla said.

"I want to find my family. Besides, there will be food at my uncle's farm. They have ducks and goats and stuff."

"There's literally tons of food here, enough to last until it spoils—a few years, at least. Plus, it's hard to get down here—probably nobody will bug us. We could shack up in the tugboat's wheelhouse, build a grinder for the wheat, and we're golden."

My chest felt suddenly heavy. I didn't want to choose between my family and Darla. "I need to find my family. Maybe we can come back here and get more wheat after we find them. And I bet there will be other people after this grain soon enough. Surely there're a lot of hungry people out there who need it worse than we do."

Darla shrugged. "I guess so." We walked back to the precarious-looking rope Darla had rigged.

"You're going to climb that?" I asked.

"Yeah. If the rope comes free, catch me and dodge the hatchet, okay?"

"Um, right."

"Kidding." Darla climbed the rope slowly and steadily. She used only her arms, pulling herself up hand over hand to disturb the setup as little as possible. Damn, but she was strong. Maybe it was all the farm work. I couldn't have climbed the rope like that without using my legs.

When she reached the top, Darla untied the hatchet and fastened the rope to the railing. I tied the skis onto the other end of the rope, and Darla hauled them up. Then we repeated the process with my backpack. When we finished that, I grabbed the rope and started laboriously climbing.

"Want me to pull you up?"

"No, no—I got it." No way was I going to ask for help after watching her slink up the rope so easily. I made it, too, even though I had to wrap my legs around the rope to climb. I was glad I hadn't needed to go first—all my thrashing probably would have caused the hatchet to come loose.

Now we stood on a narrow metal walkway atop the other half of the lock gate. We followed the walkway until it dead-ended against the dam. There was yet another catwalk atop the dam about twenty feet above us. An ordinary metal door was set into the wall of the dam. I tried the knob; it was locked.

"I think I can use the hatchet trick again to climb to the top of the dam," Darla said.

"I've got another idea." I took the hatchet and reversed it, so I could use it as a hammer. I whaled on the doorknob, raising the hatchet high above my head in a two-handed grip and bringing it down hard. It took ten or eleven blows, but then there was a ping and the knob finally broke. It bounced on the metal walkway and fell into the river, leaving a round hole in the door where the knob had

been. I stuck my finger in the hole and pulled. Nothing—
the door was still locked.

"Let me try something." Darla took the knife off my
belt, knelt in front of the door, and jammed the blade into
the hole. She dragged the knife to her left. There was a
click, and the door swung smoothly open toward us. "You
broke the lock, but there's a slide in there you have to
operate." She never stopped amazing me.

A metal staircase inside led upward to another door—
fortunately unlocked, at least from the inside. It opened onto
the top of the dam. From there, crossing the Mississippi
required only a short hike along the last catwalk.

We had to climb an eight-foot, chain-link fence to get
off the dam. When I looked back toward the lock, I saw a
sign on the fence: Hazardous, Keep Out! U.S. Army Corps
of Engineers. On this side of the fence, there was an
earthen dike with a narrow, snow-covered road running
atop it.

We put on our skis and followed the road roughly east
for a couple of miles until we'd left the river completely
behind. Nobody had been here for at least five days—no
tracks marred the snow.

We came to another fence. The gate across the road
was chained and padlocked, but it was easy to climb. The
sign on the far side read: Keep Out! Hazard! Superfund
Site, U.S. Environmental Protection Agency. That seemed
a little confusing—was it an army site or an EPA site? At
least everyone agreed it was hazardous, although we'd
come through it fine.

The road continued past the gate and over a railway embankment. At the far side of the embankment, the road teed into a highway. We stopped and stared: the highway had been plowed.

Chapter 42

Before the eruption, a plowed road would have been no big deal. But this was the first clear road I'd seen since I left Cedar Falls, the first real sign of civilization. And it wasn't only the snow; the ash also had been scraped up. We could see honest-to-God blacktop here and there. Tall berms of snow and ash flanked the highway.

"Which way?" Darla asked.

"Left, I guess. Warren should be northeast of here. It's near the Illinois/Wisconsin state line, east of Galena."

The road presented a problem. We couldn't ski on the blacktop, so we tried the side of the road, but between the huge piles of plowed snow and ash and the underbrush beyond, there was no good place to ski. Finally, we unclipped our skis and carried them, walking north on the road.

We'd been walking a little more than an hour when we heard an unfamiliar noise: a faint whine coming from around the bend in the road. It took us a minute to figure out what it was . . . a car or truck, racing along the highway toward us.

"Let's get off the road," I said. Darla nodded, and we stumbled across a pile of ash and snow almost as tall as I was. Even if we'd wanted to, there was no good place to hide. The brush beside the road was leafless, and we'd left all kinds of tracks crossing the snow berm.

A truck roared into view ahead of us. It was a six-wheeled army dually with a cloth cover over its load bed, like a modern version of the Conestoga wagon.

The driver slowed as he approached the spot where we'd left the road. I saw printing in huge letters on the side of the truck: F.E.M.A. Below that, in smaller print, it read: Black Lake LLC, Division of HB Industries.

"Finally, some help." I thrashed back across the snow berm, waving my arms to attract the driver's attention. The truck stopped a little bit past us. Two guys in camo fatigues rode in the back. One of them was huge, the other almost as small as me. They both had black guns dangling from straps around their necks: Uzis, maybe.

The small guy jumped down. The big one stood on the back fender and trained his gun on us.

I swallowed hard and glanced at the gun above me. It looked like a toy in the guy's massive hands. "Um, hi," I said. "We're trying to get to Warren. I've—"

"Where are you from?" the little guy said.

"Cedar Falls."

"Serious? Damn, we don't get many from that far into the red zone."

"Any way I could get a ride to Warren? I've got family—"

"Hop in, we'll take you to the camp."

"Okay," I said. The big guy stepped aside and let his gun hang loose from its strap. Darla and I tossed our skis and poles into the truck bed and climbed in after them.

There were two people huddled inside already, a woman and a young boy. They looked dirty and tired, travel-worn. I said hi, but neither of them responded. Darla and I sat on a bench about halfway between them and the guards.

The truck had been roaring along for fifteen or twenty minutes when Darla whispered, "We're going the wrong way. The truck's going south."

"What? They said they were taking us to the camp."

"Well, we're going south. And we need to get to Warren, not some camp, anyway."

"I figured we could walk to my uncle's place from the camp—if it's the one we heard about near Galena, it's close."

"Maybe. But we're getting farther away right now," Darla whispered.

"Where are we going?" I yelled in the direction of the small guard.

He looked my way but didn't say anything.

"We're trying to get to Warren—it's near Galena."

He shrugged. "We're on a sweep. We'll loop around to the camp and drop you there. It's outside Galena."

"O-kaaay," I said doubtfully, but he had already looked away.

The truck stopped six or seven more times. Each time, one of the guards hopped out and one stayed in the truck with us. We never saw the driver, although we heard him over the guards' radios. Twice, they picked up more passengers: a guy by himself, then a family of four.

It was late afternoon by the time we finally arrived at the camp. The truck stopped for a bit, then rolled forward. We heard a clang and, out the back of the truck, caught a glimpse of a big chain-link gate. It looked to be at least twelve feet high, not counting the coils of razor wire at the top. I shivered: Was that fence designed to keep us in or someone else out?

The guys from the truck herded us into a huge white tent. Two new guards took charge of us there. They looked nearly identical to the others: young guys in camo fatigues with submachine guns. I tried to talk to them, to find out what was going on or whether we could get a ride to Warren. The only answer they'd give me was to wait and ask the captain. Every few minutes, the guards led a group of refugees through a flap in the tent—to the processing area, they said. There was nothing to sit on, and the plastic floor was filthy with mud, so we stood beside one of the canvas walls.

Eventually, a guard told us to follow him. He led us down a short, canvas-walled hallway to a large room—either the tent was subdivided into rooms, or we were in a new tent. There was a small metal desk in the center of the room. A gray-haired guy sat at it, typing on a laptop. Otherwise, the desk was bare. Two more guys in fatigues stood behind him, slouching as if bored. Freestanding shelves hid most of one of the walls and held a wide assortment of stuff: a dozen knives, two handguns, a shotgun, two rifles, some canned food, and a bunch of unidentifiable bundles and bags.

"Welcome to Camp Galena," the guy behind the desk said in a monotone. When I got close, I could read his nametag: Jameson. "Under the terms of the Federal Emergency Relief and Restoration of Order Act, you are subject to military rules of incarceration and must obey all orders given by camp personnel. In addition, you must read and follow all rules posted at the camp mess. Failure to—"

"Excuse me," I said, "we're trying to get to Warren. It's not far."

"You're from Iowa, right?"

"Yeah, Cedar Falls."

"Refugees from red zone states are specifically forbidden from travel in the yellow or green zones for the duration of the emergency."

I shook my head, feeling stunned. Forbidden to travel? I'd just traveled over one hundred miles on skis. I bit back an even snarkier comment and said instead, "If you'll drop me off in Warren, I won't be a refugee."

"Do you have any contraband to declare?"

"No—and what about a ride to Warren?"

"You evidently have confused Camp Galena for a taxi stand."

What an asshole. I swallowed that thought and said, "I'm happy to walk."

"As I've already told you, it's illegal for you to travel within the state of Illinois. This will go a lot smoother if you restrict yourself to answering my questions, son. Remove your backpacks."

The two guards looked much more alert now. They'd taken a couple steps toward us. I glanced at them and took a half step back, dropping into a sparring stance. I kept my hands at my sides, though. "Could you get word to my uncle in Warren? I'm sure he'd pick us up."

"Your name will be published in the camp roster. If your uncle exists and can show proof of relation and means of support, you'll be released to him."

"What about Darla?"

"Son, we've got forty-seven thousand inmates here. I do not have the time or the patience for this. Remove your backpacks. That will be the last time I ask."

"You didn't ask the first—"

"I'm not from Iowa," Darla said. "I'm from Chicago. I was in Cedar Falls, visiting family. Alex and I met on the road."

I looked at Darla, puzzled. She scowled back. I took the hint and kept my mouth shut.

"I'll need to see proof of residence. Driver's license, utility bill, or similar."

"My, um, a house we were staying in on the way here caught fire. My I.D. burned."

"I do *not* have time for this. Corporal, remove their backpacks."

"Captain." One of the guards moved behind me, grabbing my pack. The other one stood to one side of us, fingering his gun. I was tense and furious, but fighting would have been pointless. There were three of them in the room, armed and ready, and I had no idea how many more guards might be within earshot. I shrugged out of my pack.

The guard behind me set the pack aside and yanked the knife and hatchet off my belt. He put them on the shelves with the other knives. Then he patted me down from behind, feeling under my arms, my sides, the insides of my thighs, and down to my ankles. He repeated the process on Darla. Then he picked up one of our skis. "What do you want me to do with these, sir?"

"Put them on a shelf."

So our skis, poles, and my makeshift staff went on one of the empty shelves. Next he opened the top of my backpack. It was stuffed with packages of meat wrapped in newspaper. The corporal picked one up and sniffed it. "Pork," he said. The meat all went on the shelves, too. Then he got a plastic bin off a shelf and poured the loose wheat kernels into it. He found the bulletless revolver in a side pocket and placed it with the other handguns.

The only things left in my backpack when he was done were the frying pan, a blanket, and some clothing. "That's our food. And my dad's skis. I need that stuff—how are we supposed to survive without even a knife?"

"Weapons and personal caches of food are prohibited at Camp Galena," Captain Jameson said.

"I don't even want to be here. Why don't you give me back my stuff, and I'll go?"

The captain ignored me. In the meantime, the corporal had opened Darla's pack. He pulled out Jack. "Got a live one."

"Deal with it," the captain ordered.

The corporal stepped through a flap in the wall of the tent, carrying Jack.

"Wait!" Darla yelled. "What are you doing?"

I heard the crack of a gunshot. Darla ran toward the flap, and the other guard grabbed for her, but missed. I followed Darla.

Outside the tent, the snow had been trodden into a packed, icy mess. There was blood in the snow, some fresh, some old and frozen. The corporal holstered his pistol. Darla bent over a large wooden bin.

I looked into the bin. Jack lay there, twitching and bleeding from the huge, ragged hole a bullet had punched in his head. Beside him lay a golden retriever and a German shepherd, their frozen limbs tangled together. They'd been shot in the head, also.

"What did you do that for?" Darla screamed.

"Orders. No pets allowed."

"Murderers!" Darla ran at him, her fists flailing wildly. I took a half step forward, ready to unload a number-two round kick on the guard's face. But out of the corner of my eye I saw three more guards rushing toward us. Plus, the whole area was fenced—there was no way to escape. Fighting was useless, so I checked my kick.

The corporal hit the side of Darla's face with a vicious backhand, knocking her down. He bent over her, cocking his fist for another strike. I dove on top of Darla. The guy hit my back, but since I'd blocked his punch short of its intended target, it didn't have much force.

Darla struggled under me. I tried to hold her still and keep her head and body protected. Someone caught my right hand and wrenched my arm behind my back. I felt a plastic loop around my wrist, cutting into it as he cinched it tight. Then my left wrist was forced to join the right and locked into the other half of the handcuffs.

Someone grabbed me under my arm and dragged me off Darla, setting me upright. They cuffed her as well and marched us back into the tent.

The captain still sat at his desk. Darla strained against the guy holding her and yelled, "What the—"

"Quiet!" Captain Jameson roared. "I'll overlook this behavior since you're new here, but one more word and you'll start your stay at Camp Galena in a punishment hut."

I watched Darla. She screwed up her face to start yelling at the guy again. I kicked her ankle. She glowered at me, her face twisted into a ferocious scowl. I shook my head.

It worked, because Darla didn't say anything else, and we didn't learn what a punishment hut was. At least not right at that moment. The guards marched us to a gate in the fence and cut off the handcuffs. Then they thrust our backpacks into our arms and shoved us through the gate.

Chapter 43

The guards weren't the least bit gentle when they tossed us through the gate. I fell on my face in the packed snow. I pushed myself upright on arms that still trembled from the fight, wiped the ice off my cheeks, and looked around.

The first thing I noticed was how many people were there. This place was crowded. Old, young, families, individuals, white, Hispanic, black—the only thing everyone had in common was that they were all dressed in dirty, ragged clothing. I hadn't seen so many people in one place since the eruption; in fact, I hadn't seen a crowd like this even before the volcano.

The second thing I noticed was the camp's size. We were on a relatively flat ridgetop. The fence stretched three hundred or four hundred yards in each direction before it reached a corner. It was chain link, like all the fences we'd seen here, twelve feet high and topped by a coil of razor wire.

A thin guy with a dirty gray beard reached for my backpack. I shoved his hand away and grabbed our packs. He slunk off into the crowd.

Inside the fence, the snow had been churned to a dirty, frozen slush by thousands of feet. Outside, a smaller fenced area contained four large white canvas tents—the admissions area we'd come through. Beyond that, I saw the highway.

There were green canvas tents in ragged rows inside the camp. A few of them were erected on raised wooden platforms, but most were pitched directly on the cold ground. Almost all of them were closed, flaps tied tightly against the wind. The tents that weren't closed were full, each packed with a dozen or more people.

A loudspeaker mounted on a nearby fence post crackled to life. The sound was distorted and overly loud: "Mabel Hawkins, report to Gate C immediately. Mabel Hawkins, Gate C."

A narrow strip about five feet wide just inside the fence was clear of people. Darla walked into the clear area and I asked her, "You sure it's safe? What if that fence is electric?"

"It's fine," she replied. "You can't electrify chain link directly—it'd just ground out. If this were electric there'd be insulators and extra wires. She slapped the fence to prove her point. Then she squatted and reached into my pack, inventorying the contents.

They'd taken almost everything. Our skis, food, rope, knife, and hatchet were all gone. All we had left was our clothing, blankets, plastic tarp, water bottles, frying pan, and a few matches.

Darla snatched the frying pan and hurled it at the base of the fence. It hit with a dull clank and came to rest a few feet away. "Christ!" she yelled. "They took goddamn everything."

A nasty purple bruise was spreading across the side of Darla's face. I touched it as gently as I could, trying to figure out if the guards had broken any of her bones. "That hurt?" I asked.

"The pork, the wheat, our knife, and the hand-ax—what the hell do the guards need with that crap, anyway?"

"I don't know." I kept probing her cheekbone. It didn't seem broken, but I wasn't sure.

Darla slapped my hand away. "Quit messing with my face. It's fine. And Jack, what was the point of killing him? He survived silicosis, a burning barn, the blizzard, and a long trip in a backpack just to be shot by some asshole guard? Why? I just don't get it."

"I don't know." I tried to give her a hug, but she pushed me away and started ramming stuff back into my pack. At least our backpacks had plenty of extra room now. Darla stuffed her pack inside mine.

I squatted on my ankles, resting my back against the fence, and Darla squatted beside me. Her hands were on one of the backpack straps, crinkling it into a ball and releasing it, over and over, in barely restrained fury.

"We'll get out of here somehow," I said. "What's a twelve-foot fence and coil of razor wire to us, after everything we've been through?"

"Why pen us in at all? I feel like a pig on the way to the slaughterhouse."

"I don't know," I repeated. "We'll find a way out."

"Yeah, they're going to regret the day they locked us in here." Darla's eyes had narrowed to a hard squint, and she was scowling.

A pair of guards patrolling along the outside of the fence walked toward us. As they approached, one of them yelled, "Hey, you! No leaning on the fence."

I ignored him. When he got close enough, he kicked at my back through the chain link. I saw it coming and scrambled away, but not quite fast enough. His toe caught me in the small of my back.

"Asshole," Darla said aloud.

The guards laughed.

It was getting late, and neither of us had any idea where we'd sleep. But more urgently, we hadn't used the bathroom since we'd been picked up on the road hours ago. Darla stopped a kid who was hurrying by and asked him where the restrooms were. He pointed, then twisted free of her grasp and ran off.

We walked for a long time in the direction the kid had pointed without seeing anything resembling a latrine. It was slow going, picking our way around knots of people.

Some were huddled in groups, talking or just shivering together. Others lay on the ground, wrapped in blankets and pressed against their family or friends for warmth. Every now and then we passed someone who was alone. Most of the loners looked dead, frozen to the ground where they lay, but when I got too close to one of them, his eyes popped open and he glared, warning me away.

We smelled the latrine before we saw it—although calling it a latrine was far too generous. Beside the far fence, a long ditch had been dug, about twenty-four inches wide and eighteen inches deep. Ten or eleven people squatted along its length, doing their business in front of God and everyone.

The other problem, besides the complete lack of privacy, was the lack of toilet paper, sinks, or soap. Sure, Darla and I hadn't been too particular about those things as we traveled, but this was different: Thousands of people were using this ditch as a public restroom. I glanced up and down the line. Two people had brought their own toilet paper, but others were using newspaper or handsful of snow to clean themselves. Darla turned away and put her hands on her knees.

"You okay?" I asked her.

"Yeah. A little nauseous. I'll be okay."

I shrugged and stepped up to the ditch. I don't like going in public—even the rows of urinals without dividers at school used to bug me. So it took me awhile. But when I zipped up and left the stench of the ditch, Darla hadn't moved.

"You sure you're okay?"

"No, I need to pee."

"Well?" I shrugged.

"I can't squat over that thing without taking my jeans off. And there's nothing to lean against."

I understood what she meant. When she had needed to pee on the road, she'd find a tree to lean her back against and pull her jeans just partway down. I'd never, um, watched the whole process of course; I'm not that pervy. But I'd seen enough to get the general idea of how it was done. "Come on. I'll be your tree."

So I stood on one side of the ditch, and Darla stood on the other. She leaned her back against me and pulled her pants down just enough to do her business. I tried not to watch, but there was no point. Hundreds of people were within eyesight, and Darla wasn't the only woman squatting over that ditch.

"Well, that was humiliating . . . and disgusting," Darla said as she pulled up her pants.

"Nobody was really looking."

"You're not helping."

"And you're not the one who got splashed."

"Oh. Sorry."

"No worries. It's only a little bit on my boot. Goes with the territory when you volunteer to be a tree."

It was getting dark. I was hungry, but we hadn't seen any sign of food since we'd been thrown into the camp. I was more worried about finding a safe place to sleep. It would be a cold night if we couldn't find shelter of some sort.

At first, we wandered from tent to tent. But every tent was full, and just touching the flaps often brought shouted curses and threats from within. Some of the tents even had people posted outside guarding them. Other refugees clustered on the lee sides of the tents where they'd be protected from the wind. We might have done that, too, but all the good spots had been taken already.

"I've got an idea," Darla said. "Follow me."

She led us directly into the teeth of the wind, which had picked up as darkness fell, making it harder and harder to see. It started snowing—hard, icy pellets that stung as the wind whipped them against my skin. I shivered, remembering almost freezing to death under the bridge just a week before. Several times we stumbled over people lying on the ground, made invisible by the snow and darkness.

Darla led us all the way across the camp. The wind was fiercer here with nothing but a chain-link fence to block it. A few tents were scattered on this side of the camp, all of them full, of course. Darla trudged toward one that was built on a low wooden platform. The lee side of the tent was packed—people lay pretty much on top of each other in a long V shape, trying to escape the wind's nip and howl.

We walked to the windward side of the tent. For the first time since we'd arrived, we were alone. Everyone was avoiding this, the most exposed spot in the whole camp. I didn't see any reasonable place to sleep—hopefully Darla knew what she was doing.

Snow had drifted against the tent platform. Darla dug a trough in the snow against the tent. It was less than two feet wide and a foot deep, but it would hold us both. She lined the snow-ditch with our plastic tarp and blankets. Then we lay down and wrapped the tarp and blankets over ourselves.

At first, it was terribly cold. But as we lay there shivering and hugging each other for warmth, the snow began to blow up over us, covering our tarp. After an hour or so, we were completely buried and toasty warm. I drifted off to sleep.

I woke up once in the night, feeling sweaty and claustrophobic. I stretched my arm out over my head and poked a hole in the snowdrift. The icy air smelled sharp and relieved my sense of confinement. Darla murmured something in her sleep and pressed herself even tighter against me.

The next time I awoke, it was to the gentle pressure of Darla's lips against mine. I returned her kiss, getting more and more into it until it occurred to me that I probably had terrible morning breath. Still, Darla tasted fine, and she wasn't complaining. . . . I broke off the kiss, anyway.

"We should get up," she said. "I heard voices a while ago."

"Is it morning?"

Darla reached out and reopened the hole I'd made during the night. A spot of light hit my face. "Guess so."

We unburied ourselves from the snowdrift. It would have been a beautiful day if there'd been any sun. The snow and wind had died down during the night, leaving behind a thin white blanket that temporarily hid the camp's ugliness.

We packed our bedding and scouted the area. Nobody was around; the tents were empty, and the dog piles of people sleeping at the lee side of each tent were gone. Paths beaten in the snow led away from every tent. Strangely, all the trails ran parallel. Every single person had gotten up and walked, zombie-like, in the exact same direction. We'd slept through it all.

Curious, we followed one of the paths. It was almost perfectly straight, except for an occasional swerve around a tent. After a quarter mile or so, the paths started to blend into each other so that all the snow was pocked with foot-prints. There was no longer a discernable trail to follow, but we kept walking in the same direction.

We'd seen only one person along our route, a woman about my mother's age in the snow beside one of the tents, curled into a fetal position, unmoving. Her hands and feet were bare and tinged blue. I walked over to her, ignoring Darla's glare, and put my hand against her neck. It was cold and lifeless.

I stood and took a deep breath. The icy air entering my lungs brought something else with it: a wave of sadness so intense I had to close my eyes and fight to hold back tears. That woman could have been my mother. I felt Darla's arms around me. "You okay?" she said.

"Yeah . . . no." My sorrow dissolved in a wave of pure fury. What kind of place was this, where tens of thou-sands of people were herded together without adequate shelter, without decent latrines? A cattle pen, not fit for humans. And the guards, Captain Jameson, they were people just like me. For the first time ever, I felt ashamed of my species. The volcano had taken our homes, our food, our automobiles, and our airplanes, but it hadn't taken our humanity. No, we'd given that up on our own.

A little farther on, I heard a dull roar that slowly increased in volume as we walked. We rounded a tent and found the source of the noise—a huge crowd, thousands upon thousands of people pressed together in a mob that stretched as far as I could see to both my left and my right.

We stepped to the back of the crowd. It sounded worse than the high-school cafeteria used to at that moment when everyone had finished eating and a few hundred shouted conversations were going on simultaneously.

Darla tapped some guy on the back and yelled, "What's going on?"

He turned and shouted back, "New here?"

"Yeah."

"Chow line."

"Slop line, more like it," someone else yelled.

Slop mob would have been an even better description. There was no organization that remotely resembled a line. But we hadn't eaten anything since lunchtime yesterday, so we settled into the back of the crowd to wait.

After a while, we saw people forcing their way out of the mob. They had a terrible time of it—everyone else was pressing forward into any open space. But the folks trying to leave shoved and jammed their elbows into others, eventually managing to worm their way out of the crush. I noticed something odd: all the people leaving had a blotch of blue paint on their left hands. A few of them were carrying Dixie cups, but nobody had any food.

We waited in the mob for more than two hours before I got close enough to see. The crowd pressed forward toward a fence. Beyond the fence stood a series of field kitchens, something like what the Lion's Club used to set up every year at the Black Hawk County Fair. Dozens of small hatches had been cut in the fence at about chest height. Guys in fatigues were manning each hatch. I watched a refugee fight his way up to the fence. When he got there, he held out both hands. The guard spray-painted a blob of blue on the back of his left hand and put a Dixie cup in his right. The refugee wolfed down the contents of the Dixie cup before he'd taken more than two steps from the hatch, eating with his fingers. I couldn't see what he was eating.

It turned out to be rice. Bland, white rice—and not much of it. The paper cups held maybe eight ounces, and they weren't full. I squeezed the rice into my mouth. When I finished, I tore the cup in half and licked the inside. I was still hungry; we'd waited most of the morning for barely enough food to satisfy a robin.

As we walked away, I saw a kid, maybe eight or nine years old, sitting on the ground, furiously scrubbing his left hand with snow. It was raw and red, but the blue paint clung to it in stubborn patches. As I watched, he scrubbed too hard, and a trickle of blood seeped out of the back of his hand, staining the snow red.

"What're you doing?" I asked.

"Trying to get seconds," the kid said. "It's useless, they won't feed you if your hand's bleeding." He looked as if he might cry.

"When is lunch?"

"Lunch? Are you crazy?"

"Dinner?"

"You could try the yellow coats. But you're probably too tall."

"Too tall?" Darla said. "What do you mean?"

The kid jumped to his feet. Darla tried to grab his arm but missed. He ran off.

Chapter 44

We spent what little remained of the morning exploring the camp. The main area, where we and all the thousands of other refugees were fenced in, was about a half-mile square. At the south side, between the camp and the highway, were three separately fenced areas: First, the admissions area where we'd entered the camp, which also contained tents for barracks and administration. Second, a vehicle depot that held three bulldozers, a front-end loader, a bus, and a whole bunch of trucks and Humvees. And third, a small area dotted with little sheds that looked like doghouses.

The latrine ditch we'd used the night before was in the northeast corner of the camp, as far as possible from the admin area. Along the west edge of the camp, we found a row of five water spigots attached to wood posts. People were filling every kind of container imaginable. Ice coated the ground around the spigots.

The kitchens were also at the west end of the camp. They were closed and quiet now, except for one. About a dozen people in yellow parkas worked there.

Darla and I walked along the north edge of the camp. There was nothing beyond the fence here except the path the guards patrolled, an open space, and then the woods that began at the edge of the ridge.

"I don't think it'd take long to run to those woods from here," I said.

"Yeah. That coil of razor wire on top of the fence is a little bit of a problem, though."

"The captain said our names would be published in the roster—if my folks see it, they'll come."

"Yeah. I'd rather have a good pair of wire cutters than a promise from that captain."

"Did he even take down our names?" I asked.

"You know, I don't think he did," Darla said. "Bastard."

"I wonder if there's any way to call my uncle or send him a letter? Or if the captain would let us, even if there were?"

"Doubt it. For now let's go back to where those guys in the yellow coats were cooking. At least it smelled good there."

By the time we got back across the camp, there was a line in front of the yellow coats' kitchen. It was very different from the mob that morning—this was a fairly straight, orderly line with a few hundred people in it. Strangely, almost all of them were kids. There were a few mothers with babies up front and some kids with parents, but the line was mostly little kids by themselves. They weren't playing or fighting the way kids did at restaurants when their parents weren't paying attention. Some of them hung their heads, and some were sitting in the snow—on the whole, they looked miserable.

Two of the yellow coats were inside the fence with us. They moved along the line, talking to a kid here and there. When they got close to where Darla and I stood, I could read the writing on their coats: Southern Baptist Conference.

One of them approached us, a woman a few years older than my mom, with long, auburn hair. "You two can move up, you know."

"I don't want to cut," I said.

"It's not cutting. The line's organized by age. Well, that was the original idea, but it didn't work out, so we changed it to height. Come on."

We followed her to a spot about fifty places farther up. It was the first time I could remember being glad I wasn't very tall. Darla could have moved another twenty or thirty places forward, but she wanted to stay with me. The woman in the yellow coat moved on, chatting and organizing the line.

About fifteen minutes later the line began to jerk forward. Closer to the front, I saw a crowd of kids eating stew: black beans and ham served in Styrofoam bowls with plastic spoons. The acme of luxury—well, compared to breakfast.

The same two yellow coats were inside the fence, watching the crowd. Outside the fence, the rest of the yellow coats were serving the soup or cleaning up. Two guards in fatigues stood out there, too, looking bored.

We were about fifty feet from the front when everyone lurched to a halt. A low chorus of sighs floated down the line and then it dissolved—all the kids wandered away at once.

I found the auburn-haired woman I'd talked to earlier. "What's going on?"

"I'm sorry," she said.

"Why'd everyone leave?"

"We're out of food. Well, actually, we have food, but we're rationing it, trying to make it last until the next shipment comes in. Even with as little as we're serving, we'll run out completely by next week if the truck doesn't come."

"Oh."

"I trust—I have faith that God will provide. But everyone's saying this winter may last for years. Food prices have skyrocketed. Everyone's hoarding. The Baptists are one of the only churches still doing disaster relief, because we've been doing it for years. We were better prepared."

"So when is dinner?"

"You *are* new."

"Got here yesterday."

"The camp quit serving dinner almost two weeks ago. They don't have enough food, either."

"We're supposed to live on one measly cup of rice a day?" Darla said.

"For now. Our pastor is doing everything he can to find donations and to pressure FEMA to bring in more supplies."

We'd gone from a backpack stuffed with pork to this? I clenched my fists. Sure, some people might think we'd stolen the pork, but we'd worked hard butchering and roasting that pig. I'd never imagined that FEMA would make our food situation *worse*. But it obviously wasn't this lady's fault. I muttered, "Okay. Thanks," and turned to leave.

The woman caught me with a hand at the waist of my coat. "Trust in the Lord. You never know what He might put in your pocket." She met my eyes briefly then walked away.

Darla wanted to check out the vehicle depot again, so we meandered in that direction. We'd gotten just inside the first line of tents when someone bumped into my side, almost knocking me over.

Darla yelled, "Alex!" but I was already side-stepping to regain my balance. I glanced to my right—a tall, wiry guy was trying to thrust his hand into my coat pocket. I grabbed him by the hand and spun, twisting his wrist and arm as I went. The move ended perfectly, with me behind him and to his left, controlling his outstretched arm. I kept pressure on his wrist with one hand and launched a knife-hand strike at his neck with the other.

I didn't know why I chose that strike. I could have kicked his knee, broken his elbow or wrist, or done any number of less lethal moves. The guy was yammering something and trying to pull away. I checked my strike at the last possible moment and only tapped his neck.

"Ah! Crap, man. I was only looking for some food!" the guy yelled.

I let go of his arm, and he ran, rubbing his wrist.

We hadn't gone twenty feet before another guy planted himself in my path. "Got a proposition for you," he said.

"I don't have any food." What the hell was it with this place? Couldn't I take a walk without people bugging me at every other step?

"I saw you handle that guy."

"I didn't hurt him."

"Yeah, but you could have."

I shrugged.

"We've got a place in our tent. Eight inches. You stand guard for three hours each night, you can sleep there."

"Eight inches?"

He gave me a condescending look and started talking more slowly. "A safe place to sleep. Eight inches wide by six feet long. In a platform tent. The best kind. All you have to do is help guard it at night."

"I need two spots. She's with me." I gestured at Darla.

"Can't do it. I just have one. Only have that 'cause Greeley died last night."

"Forget it then." I turned my back to him.

"Wait a second," Darla said. "We'll take the one spot. Alex will stand guard half the night, and I'll watch the other half. If another spot opens up in the tent, we get it, and we switch to the three-hour guard shifts you proposed."

"You know kung fu, too?" the guy asked.

"It's taekwondo," I said.

"Yeah, I know it," Darla said. "I only know one move, though. Anything happens, I wake him up, and he beats the crap out of whoever's messing with your tent. Okay?"

"Works for me." The guy showed us the tent and told us to be back at dusk.

* * *

We spent the rest of the afternoon watching the vehicle depot through the fence. I already knew Darla was weird, but this clinched it. She could spend an entire hour staring at a parked bulldozer. Every now and then she'd ask me a nonsensical question, something like, "Do you think that's an auxiliary hydraulic system under those lifters?" Or "What kind of tool do you suppose they use to disengage the keyed link in that track?" The only response I could figure out was to shrug and grunt.

It wasn't all bad, though. I could spend an entire hour staring at Darla. Not that there was anything all that thrilling about either of us right then. We were tired, hungry, and wrapped in multiple layers of filthy winter clothing. None of that mattered to me; I was in love. I thought Darla was, too—but maybe with the bulldozer.

We'd been standing there awhile when I jammed my hands into my coat pockets to warm them. Something was in my right pocket—I took off my glove to investigate and found a handful of almonds.

"Check that out." I held my hand open against my chest so only Darla could see.

"Those were in your pocket?"

"Yeah."

"So that's what that lady was talking about—God will fill your pockets and all."

"Guess so. Nice of her to sneak us some dinner." I split them up and handed Darla her share: six almonds.

"Some dinner. More of a snack. Beats not eating, though."

"Yeah," I replied, munching surreptitiously on my almonds.

* * *

That night I asked Darla to take the first guard shift. I figured she'd do a better job than I could deciding when to wake me up. I've never been very good at judging time, and without the moon or stars, I'd be hopeless.

I stretched out in my eight inches of floor beside the door. I was nestled against an old woman—Greeley's wife, I thought. I used my backpack as a pillow so that nobody could take it without waking me.

It wasn't too bad, being packed into the tent like that. Sure, it was uncomfortable; I couldn't roll over without knocking knees and elbows with my neighbor. And it smelled bad, since nobody had showered in weeks. But the tent kept the wind out, and sleeping packed together kept us all warm. The worst part was lying there with nothing to do but think about the emptiness of my stomach. I was starving, but I'd only been without real food for two days. The other people in the tent were much worse off. Nobody talked about it much, but I could see the hunger in their hollow cheeks, hear it in their moans and sighs.

I was finally starting to drift off when Darla kicked me. "Alex," she whispered. "Get up."

I rolled under the tent flap and jumped to my feet. Darla led me to the far side of the tent at a run. I saw three guys there, kids really; they were probably younger than I. One of them was pulling up the side of the tent, while another knelt and jammed his hands under the canvas. The third was standing guard.

I struck a pose, double outer knife-hand block. "Get out of our tent." I tried to growl and sound like Clint Eastwood, but my voice cracked, and it came out more like Mike Tyson.

The guy standing guard punched one of the others on the shoulder. "Let's get out of here."

The other guy pulled his arms out of the tent and looked at me casually. "There ain't nothing in this tent nohow." He stood and the three of them backed away, watching me as they went.

"Thanks," Darla said. "That's the third time tonight. The other two were alone, so I chased them off."

"Maybe I should take the first watch—it might quiet down later."

"Yeah, let's try that. Wake me up whenever you get tired. We can always nap during the day."

I gave Darla a goodnight kiss, and she wormed under the tent flap to settle down where I'd been sleeping.

I slowly paced the circumference of the tent, trying to keep my strides even and counting one-Mississippi, two-

Mississippi as I went. I thought a circuit of the tent was taking me about forty seconds. During my seventeenth trip, I saw a man and a woman walking up. I planted myself between them and the tent and glared until they moved on. During circuit fifty-eight, I found a guy already halfway under the side wall—only his butt and legs protruded. Someone inside woke up and yelled. I grabbed the guy's ankles, yanked him backward out of the tent, and watched him run off into the night.

Things were quiet after that. When my count reached 360, I woke Darla. The blankets were warm and smelled faintly of her. I fell asleep instantly.

Chapter 45

I was awakened by someone kicking me accidentally as they tried to leave the tent. I grabbed my backpack and rolled out into the snow. Darla told me nobody had bothered the tent after I'd gone to bed—evidently the first shift was the busy one.

Breakfast was the same as the day before: a mad crush and two-hour wait for six ounces of boiled rice each. The guards sprayed yellow blobs of paint on our left hands, partly covering the blue from the day before.

We lay down in the tent after breakfast and took a nap together. Darla wedged the backpack between us.

I woke to Darla shaking me. "Hey, sleepyhead. I think it's time for the Baptists' food line."

"Okay." I shook myself fully awake and packed our blankets.

This time we lined up separately. Darla was an inch shorter than I, so she could stand about forty feet ahead of me. The same two yellow coats were out chatting with kids and organizing things.

Our new strategy didn't help. There were still at least one hundred kids in front of Darla when the yellow coats ran out of food and the line dispersed.

We caught up with the same longhaired lady we'd talked to the day before.

"Thanks for the almonds yesterday," I told her.

She glanced around. "You might be mistaken—perhaps someone else gave you almonds. We're not allowed to share our personal rations. Most of us would like to, but it caused . . . problems."

I whispered, "Well, thank your twin sister for me then, would you?"

She smiled and whispered back, "Okay, I will."

"I was wondering, why don't you get the wheat off that barge?"

Darla elbowed me in the side. "Don't talk about that, we might need it later," she hissed.

"There are a lot of people here that need it worse than we do," I whispered back.

"Wait, what are you two talking about?" the woman said. "A barge?"

"Yeah, there's a barge stuck in Lock 12, not far from here. It's loaded with wheat. Must be hundreds of tons of it."

"Lock 12?"

"On the Mississippi, in Bellevue. The barge is stuck in the lock. It might be tough to unload, but there's plenty of manpower here."

Darla let out an exaggerated sigh. "The wheat would have to be ground. But I know how to make a mill. Or we could improvise a zillion mortars and pestles. Like Alex said, there's plenty of manpower here."

"And it's not far?"

"I don't know, exactly. Fifteen or twenty miles, tops."

"Sounds like the answer to one of my prayers. You can show us where it is?"

"Sure, no problem. But it's right there in the lock, easy to find."

"What are your names?"

"I'm Alex. Alex Halprin. This is Darla Edmunds."

"Georgia Martin." She held out her hand. I hesitated a moment since mine was filthy, but she clasped my hand in both of hers, then shook Darla's, too. "Good to meet you both. Let me talk to the mission director. I'll look for you here tomorrow and let you know if we need you to show us the barge."

* * *

It didn't take that long. The next morning, we'd been waiting in the breakfast mob for about an hour when the loudspeakers mounted on the fence posts crackled to life. "Alex

Halloran and Darla Edmunds, report to Gate C immediately. Alex Halloran and Darla Edmunds, Gate C."

"Guess that's us," I said.

"Guess so, Mr. Halloran."

I scowled at Darla. "Well, it sounds sort of like Halprin."

"Hope this doesn't mean we're going to miss breakfast."

We fought our way out of the mob and jogged diagonally across the camp to the same gate we'd come through
on our first day. As we approached, I saw Georgia standing on the other side of the fence with an older guy. His
face was a little droopy, as if he'd lost a lot of weight
recently, and he had a neatly trimmed fringe of hair
around his otherwise bald pate. Georgia said something to
the guards and they waved us through.

"Thanks for coming. This is Mission Director Evans—"

"Call me Jim, please," the bald guy said. "Very exciting
news you brought yesterday. How much wheat did you say
is on the barge?"

"I only looked into one of them, but it was packed. And
there were nine barges tied together and stuck in the lock.
If they all carried the same thing, I don't know. . ."

"Hundreds of tons," Darla said.

"Mysterious ways. . ." Director Evans muttered. Then
he added out loud, "We have an appointment to see Black
Lake's camp commander, Colonel Levitov. Shall we go?"

He led us into one of the large tents. It was a pavilion,
really, much bigger than even the tent my cousin Sarah
had had at her wedding reception two years before, but
subdivided inside. We followed Director Evans through a

maze of canvas corridors and rooms until we reached a small office. A guy in fatigues sat behind a metal desk, typing into a laptop.

"Morning, Sergeant," Director Evans said. "We've got an appointment with the colonel."

"He's running late. Have a seat."

That presented a problem. There were four of us and only two unoccupied chairs in the room. Darla and I stood to the side and looked at Director Evans and Georgia.

"Have a seat," Director Evans said.

"We can stand," I said.

"No, please. With how few calories you're eating, you need to be off your feet far more than we do."

I sank into a chair, and Darla took the one beside me. Evans was right. I was tired and hungry, or maybe tired because I was so hungry. I'd been hungry for three days now, but it was better *not* to think about it. Not that it was possible to not think about it. Just Evans' comment about calories was enough to bring my empty stomach to the top of my mind. Maybe because it was morning, I thought about breakfast food. Donuts. Bagels. Wheaties, for some reason, even though I *hated* Wheaties. I put my head on my knees and tried to think about something, anything else.

We'd been waiting fifteen minutes or so when someone shouted from the other side of the canvas wall behind the sergeant's desk: "Coffee!" The sergeant left the room for a few minutes and returned with a steaming ceramic mug. The smell rekindled my hunger so powerfully that I was almost nauseated. He carried the mug through a flap in the wall and then returned to his desk.

We waited another twenty or thirty minutes. I heard a shout, "Ready!"

"You can go in now," the sergeant said.

We entered another small office and saw another metal desk, another guy in fatigues, and another laptop. He picked up his mug and knocked back the last of the coffee. I caught myself staring at the mug and had to force my eyes away from it. There were no chairs except the one the guy occupied. He stood and stretched his hand out, "Director Evans. Good to see you."

"Thanks for seeing us, Colonel," Evans said, shaking his hand vigorously.

The colonel looked at me and wrinkled his nose. He didn't offer to shake. "The purpose of this meeting is?"

Evans gestured at me. "This young man found a large supply of wheat, maybe several hundred tons."

"Where?"

"Lock 12, in Bellevue, Iowa," Evans said. "On a barge stuck in the lock."

"I know the place."

"I'd like your support to retrieve it—we could set up teams of refugees to grind it to flour. It's a chance to get the camp's caloric intake up to something sustainable. Exactly what we've all been praying—"

"I'll kick it up to Black Lake admin in Washington. Thank you for the intel. Dismissed." The colonel sat down and turned his attention to his computer.

"What?" I said. "That's it? Enough food for the whole camp and—"

"Sergeant!" the colonel yelled, without looking up from his computer.

Evans wrapped his arm around my shoulder, and I allowed him to hustle me out of the office back to the camp's main enclosure.

Of course we'd missed breakfast.

We saw Georgia again at the yellow coat food line that afternoon. She apologized at length for making us miss breakfast and even smuggled another handful of almonds into my pocket. We ate them fast and furtively, huddled against the fence.

We spent the balance of that afternoon outside the vehicle depot, watching a guy work on a bulldozer. It was parked about thirty feet away on the far side of the fence.

We'd been watching him awhile when Darla yelled, "Hydraulic control valve's messed up?"

The guy looked up, wiped his oily hands on his trousers, and stared at Darla for a couple seconds.

"Yeah, how'd you know?"

"Just guessed. You disconnected the fluid reservoir and the control linkage, that thing between them just about has to be the control valve, right?"

"Yeah. It's shot."

"Ash gets in there and tears them up, I bet."

"It's worse on the dozers, 'cause they stir up the ash and come back covered in it. They've all gone bad—the garage tent is packed full of dozers with wrecked control valves."

"That's rough."

"This one's had it. I'm out of valves. Distributor we get 'em from is out, too. Major's going to have my ass. He's all hot to clear Highway 35 north of Dickeyville."

"I bet you could make a master cylinder out of a truck work. As a control valve, I mean."

"No way. The fittings wouldn't be the same size, for one thing."

"My dad and I built a hydraulic tree digger a few years ago. Used old master cylinders off junk pickup trucks as controllers. I dunno where he got the lifters, but they weren't that much different from the ones on that dozer."

"And that worked?"

"Worked great. We moved a bunch of trees from Small's Creek to the farmyard. Then we sold the rig. Dad said he got two grand for it."

"Not bad." The guy messed with the dozer awhile longer, draining hydraulic fluid into a bucket and wiping parts off with a rag. "What'd you say your name was?"

"Darla Edmunds."

"Nice to meet you. I'm Chet. See you around, maybe." He picked up his toolbox and the bucket of oil and walked away.

* * *

Guard duty was crazy that night. I'd only walked two circuits of the tent when I caught the first invader, a little boy trying to worm his way into the tent—probably only looking for a warm place to sleep. I'd already dragged him out by his ankles when I realized how small and skinny he was. I thought about waking the tent boss—surely we could find a corner to accommodate this waif, but before I'd made up my mind, the kid ran away.

That's the way it went all night—the moment I caught someone trying to sneak into the tent, they'd leave. Some of them backed away from me slowly, some sauntered off, but most ran. Nobody wanted a fight, thank goodness. Even the group of four adults I caught loitering by our tent flap about an hour after dark moved on without a peep of protest.

At first, I thought maybe they were giving up because of me. Maybe news had spread, and I'd acquired a reputation for my mad "kung fu" skills. I flattered myself with that idea for a minute before realizing it was total bull. First, something like fifty thousand people were penned in the camp. There was no way even a small fraction of them could have heard about the incident yesterday. Second, it hadn't been an impressive fight. I'd twisted a guy's arm, so what? Third, it was so dark that nobody would recognize me anyway, even if I did have a scary rep.

While I was thinking about it, I ran an old guy off. He was trying to sneak into the tent sideways, so I grabbed

him by the shoulders and pulled him out. He weighed next
to nothing. He must have been rail thin, although I
couldn't tell from looking at him, since he had at least two
blankets tied around himself with scraps of old rope.
Pulling him upright brought his face within a few inches
of mine. A dirty beard clung beneath his gaunt cheeks. I
let go of him, and he almost fell over before regaining his
balance and stumbling off into the night.

These people weren't afraid of me; they were starving.
All of us were starving. I felt weak, and this was only my
third day with so little to eat. The folks who'd been here
since the eruption must have been near collapse. That also
explained why so many of the would-be intruders were
kids—they'd been getting more food than everyone else.
Kids and newcomers were the only ones with enough
energy to try raiding the tents.

It didn't seem likely that Darla and I would be getting
any food from the Baptists except an occasional handful of
almonds. We were too tall and too old—unless something
changed, they'd always run out of food before we made it
to the front of the line. Already we were weakening. We
had to get more food—and soon.

Chapter 47

The next three days were infuriating. Every morning we fought our way to the front of the breakfast line to get paper cups of rice. After breakfast, we'd wander over to the vehicle depot. Twice we saw the mechanic, Chet. Once he came over to the fence and talked to Darla for a while, speaking in some foreign language that might best be named "Diesel Truckish" (or should it be "Diesel Truckian"? Whatever). Every afternoon we stood in the Baptists' food line, but they always ran out before we got to the front. We saw Georgia every day, and every day she had the same news for us: nothing. Colonel Levitov hadn't told Director Evans anything about the wheat, and the Baptists couldn't go get it without trucks and support from Black Lake. Keep praying, Georgia said.

Prayer is all well and good, but I wanted to *do* something. Darla looked thinner every day, and she'd been slender to start with. I felt as if we were being hollowed out from the inside, so our skin might soon collapse, leaving only a papery husk to mark our passing. I figured my backpack could hold enough wheat to keep us both alive for a month or more. If something didn't change soon, I planned to try climbing the fence, razor wire and guards notwithstanding.

The next day, our sixth in the camp, something did change. Not long after breakfast, the camp's loudspeakers came on with a hiss. At first I ignored them, but when I heard Darla's name I tuned in. "Edmunds report to Gate C immediately. Darla Edmunds, Gate C." I glanced at her and saw her shrug.

When we got there, the gate was closed. Chet was on the far side, chatting with the two guards.

"Did you call me?" Darla asked Chet.

"Yeah, that idea about using brake master cylinders as control valves on the dozers? You want to try it?"

"Try it?"

"Sure, I had road ops tow in four pickups yesterday. We can scavenge the cylinders off them. I've got all the tools we need and a full shop . . . so, you in?"

Darla was quiet a moment. Thinking, I figured. I said, "You should—"

"What's it pay?" Darla asked.

"Pay?" Chet said.

"Yeah, you want me to help fix your dozers; I ought to get paid, right?"

"I guess so, but getting a job at Black Lake is really hard. I'd have to go to the colonel, and I dunno if—"

"I don't need money. I want three square meals a day. For me and for Alex. And I'll fix as many dozers as you want me to."

"Um . . . I can feed you when you're working. Maybe two meals. But if I let you take food back into the camp, I could get fired. Couple a guys caused a riot that way two weeks ago, giving food to girls through the gate. And I only got authorization for one assistant."

Darla was quiet a moment. "No. If we can't both eat—"

"Do it!" I whispered. "We've got a lot better chance if one of us gets enough to eat."

"You sure? It doesn't seem—"

"I have to get back to work," Chet said.

"Okay. Two meals. One before work and one after, every day. And I start after the camp breakfast."

"Come on, then." Chet opened the gate.

Darla gave me a peck on the lips and trotted through the gate after Chet. I watched as they walked across the administration compound and through another gate into the vehicle depot. I kept watching until they disappeared inside a huge canvas tent that served as a garage.

It was strange, being alone. There wasn't much to do; Darla and I had already visited the latrine trench, refilled our water bottles, and gone through the breakfast line that morning. I'd spent almost every minute with Darla for the last five weeks; being separated was . . . uncomfortable. It felt a bit like being naked in a room full of clothed people. Not that I'd ever done that, but I imagined it'd feel like I did right then.

I found a spot out of the wind where I could crouch beside a tent and still see the vehicle depot. I spent the rest of the morning and the early afternoon there, watching. When it was time to line up for the yellow coats' dinner, Darla still hadn't emerged from the garage. I was getting a little worried, but there was nothing I could do, so I crossed the camp diagonally to try my luck with the food line.

My luck held: bad, same as always. The food line dispersed even quicker than usual. There were three hundred, maybe four hundred kids between me and the last one who had gotten anything to eat. The only kids short enough to get fed looked to be eight or nine. Obviously nobody had gotten any wheat off the barge yet. The Baptists' food supply was getting smaller, not bigger.

Georgia wasn't there, either. There were two yellow coats organizing the line, but one of them was new. I caught him as everyone was leaving and asked about Georgia.

"Don't know if I'm supposed to say anything about that."

"Come on. She's a friend." When I said it, I was only trying to get information, but then I realized it was true.

The guy shrugged. "Where's the harm? She went home."

"She didn't tell me she was leaving."

"It was a sudden thing. Some kind of dispute with Director Evans."

"About what?"

"That's all I'm going to say. I've got to go help clean up."

I trudged to the vehicle depot. There was no sign of Darla there, so I walked to Gate C, where she'd met Chet that morning. She was standing a few feet outside the gate, waiting for me. There were grease stains on her shirt-sleeves and a big splotch of oil on her jeans. I didn't care. I wrapped her up in a tight hug.

"Let's go to the tent," she said.

"Okay." I took her hand and we started walking. "How was it?"

"Not bad. Chet's not much of a mechanic. He didn't even know to open the bleeder valve when you're draining brake fluid. He didn't get the line clear, so when I pulled the first master cylinder, I got oil all over myself."

"I wouldn't have known any of that stuff, either."

"You're not getting paid to be a mechanic."

Nightfall was at least two hours off, but there were two people in our tent when we got there. They seemed to be asleep—resting, I guessed. We ignored them and shuffled to the back, where we knelt side by side, facing the corner. Darla reached down the front of her jeans. She didn't need to unbutton them to accomplish this, which reminded me how much weight she'd lost—weight she couldn't afford to drop. She pulled out a crumpled plastic package and surreptitiously passed it to me.

I glanced at the front of the package. Something was written there, but it was too dark in the tent to read it. I ripped off the top of the package. An intoxicating scent wafted to my nose: chocolate. Saliva filled my mouth, and

I felt a little dizzy. I hoped the other two people in the tent were sick; maybe stuffed-up noses would keep them from smelling that heavenly aroma. I ate a piece—the first chocolate I'd had in seven weeks. Somehow it tasted even better than I had remembered.

The bar had been crushed to crumbs in Darla's pants. I poured myself a handful of chocolate and threw it into my mouth. I ate like a starving beast, but then again, I *was* starving. I wasn't a beast, though. I stopped myself before I'd wolfed it all and offered some to Darla. She put her lips against my ear and whispered, "No. Eat it all. I had one already. I'd have smuggled them both to you, but Chet was watching me too closely. Sorry."

I snarfed the rest of the chocolate and licked the inside of the package. Then I licked off my hands, which gave the chocolate a gritty, sulfurous taste. I stuffed the wrapper into my pocket. I'd find a place to bury it later.

Chapter 48

The next morning, Darla insisted that I eat her cup of rice as well as my own. I tried to argue, but she was right. She'd gotten two full meals out of Chet yesterday—MREs, the prepackaged meals the military gives troops in the field. She was probably eating ten times as many calories as I was.

Four more days passed like that. I'd heard nothing about the wheat. The yellow coats didn't know anything about it. When I asked to see Director Evans, they told me he was busy. Clearly the yellow coats were running out of food; the line broke up faster and faster each afternoon. Darla kept forcing her ration of rice on me, but despite the extra food, it got harder to stay awake and march circles around the tent each night on guard duty.

Darla, on the other hand, got more energetic and cheerful. Two solid meals per day were doing wonders for her. I took the first guard shift as usual, but twice she woke and relieved me before I'd finished my 360 circuits of our tent.

Darla got in the habit of sleeping in her "clean" set of clothes and changing into the greasy ones right before she went to work. That way only one change of clothes got messier. Although, to be frank, the grease was probably cleaner than the dirt that covered us head to toe. There was nowhere to wash clothes in the camp, nowhere to bathe or take a shower. Everyone was filthy. My head itched terribly. I hoped I didn't have lice, but I was afraid to ask Darla to check.

I watched the vehicle depot while Darla was at work. Usually, I couldn't see anything. They did most of their work in the big tent they used as a garage, which made sense because it kept them out of the wind. Sometimes I'd see Chet moving a dozer or towing a pickup truck into the garage. Once I saw Darla driving a bulldozer. Chet was crammed into the seat beside her. I couldn't hear what they were saying, but she laughed about something. The blade on the front of the dozer lifted and dropped. It looked like Chet was teaching her to drive it. I should have been grateful to him for giving Darla a job and making sure she got enough to eat, but right then I wanted nothing more than to smack him silly.

Since I wasn't getting any answers from the yellow coats about the wheat barge, I pestered the guards. Every time I saw a new one on gate duty, I asked about it. None of them knew what I was talking about.

Finally, I thought to ask Chet. He picked up Darla at the gate every morning and brought her back at night, since she wasn't allowed to be outside the refugee enclosure unescorted. He hadn't heard of the wheat barge, either, but at least he listened. I told him the whole story: how we'd met with Director Evans and Colonel Levitov and told them about the bounty of wheat on the Mississippi. And how we'd heard zilch about it ever since.

"I don't know anything about it," Chet said. "But if you don't have anything else to do, you guys can wait here, and I'll go see what I can find out."

"Sure," I said. Of course we didn't have anything else to do. Duh.

We waited about twenty minutes. Then Chet emerged from one of the admin tents with Captain Jameson in tow—the guy we'd met the first day, the one who'd ordered Jack shot. I hoped he wouldn't recognize us. Maybe he did, because as he passed through the gate to where we stood, his lips thinned and hardened, forming a cruel sneer. "The maintenance man tells me you two know something about a wheat barge. How'd you learn about it?"

"We're the ones who found it," I said. "We told Colonel Levitov about it."

"Oh? I guess we owe you, then. But it's classified now. Don't talk about it anymore."

"Classified? What? Why—"

"We won't tell anyone," Darla said. "I've got a good job helping Chet. You can count on us."

"Good." Captain Jameson turned to go.

"But where's the food? Why are we eating rice when there's all that wheat nearby?" I said.

"Wheat's not ours. The colonel kicked it up to Washington. Turns out Cargill owns it."

"Cargill?" I asked.

"Huge grain distributor," Darla replied.

"Yeah," Captain Jameson said, "Black Lake got a nice contract to guard it until they can pick it up. Bonuses all around, I hear."

"People are starving!" I gestured with my clenched fists, which was better than what I really wanted to do with my fists.

"People are starving all over. There've been food riots in fifty-six countries."

"Countries?" I said. "What, did some other volcanoes erupt?"

Captain Jameson gave me a condescending smile. "Nope, the U.S. produced twenty percent of the world's grain. And even before the volcano, there was less than a two-month supply. All that's gone. Whole world's starving, except the people with the guns. We've got more security contracts than we can service, but I guess you wouldn't know anything about that, would you?"

"All I know is that people are starving right here, right now, and there's plenty of food close by."

"What, you think we should steal that food? That's private property, son. Plus, I'd get fired. Maybe we do owe you for bringing it to our attention—I'll see that Chet gets you a candy bar or something."

I didn't know what to say. I stood and stared at him in total disbelief.

He cast his eyes at Darla. "Look, if you're that desperate, your girl could get some extra food entertaining soldiers in the evenings. Lots of girls are doing it, some not as pretty as she is."

Something about the way he said "your girl"—as if I were her pimp, not her boyfriend—stoked my fury past the boiling point. I screeched like the wail of a roiling teakettle and lashed out, kicking Captain Jameson squarely in his nose. His head snapped back, and his nose erupted with blood. He fell backward into the snow. I stepped forward, intending to beat on him a bit more, but the gate guards closed on me from either side. I blocked the one on my left, but the guy on my right clubbed my temple with the butt of his gun. I went down. As he raised his gun again, Darla screamed, "Stop! Don't—" Then the gunstock dropped and the world went dark.

Chapter 49

I woke to the evil stepmother of all headaches. For a while, I lay curled up in a tight ball. When I finally tried to sit up, my head hit something, touching off a fresh wave of pain and nausea. I lay still and focused on my breathing, trying not to vomit.

When the nausea had subsided slightly, I opened my eyes. I was in a room barely big enough to hold my coiled body—one of the doghouse-like buildings just outside the main camp enclosure: a punishment hut, I figured. Thin horizontal lines of gray light filtered in through the boards that formed the walls. The lines danced as I watched, merging and doubling, doing a slow, repetitive minuet that told me I literally wasn't seeing straight.

I closed my eyes again and waited. Time doesn't pass in the same way when you're suffering from a headache that severe. While I lay there, it seemed as if I'd always been in that hut and always would be: There was nothing but the pain. It might have been thirty minutes or all evening for all I could tell.

Eventually the nausea and double vision passed, and the headache faded to the annoying little sister of all headaches. My face itched. I scratched, triggering a flaky rain of dried blood. My backpack was gone—I didn't care much about the backpack itself, but I was cold, so the blankets and plastic tarp would have been welcome.

The punishment hut's walls and ceiling were made of rough slats, like the ones used for wood pallets. Posts at each corner provided structure. The floor was ash, which was okay—it wouldn't be the first time I'd slept on a bed of ash. A hatch had been cut into one wall. The hatch had a little play in it, as though the padlock didn't hold it tightly closed. Maybe I could break one of the slats, force the door, or dig though the ash floor. But I didn't have the energy to try anything right then. Instead, I slept.

* * *

I woke with a horrible crick in my neck and pain in the small of my back. Before I remembered where I was, I tried to stretch out and cracked the knuckles of my hand against one of the corner posts.

There was daylight outside now. Of course, the inside of the hut was dark, but enough light filtered between the boards so that I could see a bit. I heard noises from the camp, the muted murmur of fifty thousand talking people. By squirming around, I managed to roll over, putting my other side against the ash floor. I noticed there was dry blood on my boot—Captain Jameson's, I figured, smiling.

I didn't want to try to break out during the daytime, so I waited. At first, I hoped that a guard would bring water, my rice ration, or maybe tell me how long they planned to keep me in the hut. But the day wore on and nobody came. I got thirstier and thirstier, but I didn't think I was totally dehydrated because I needed to pee.

I realized I couldn't count on anyone to bring me water or food. Maybe they'd let me sit out here for a few days. I thought about it for a while and figured out a solution to my two most immediate problems.

To deal with the thirst, I dug in the ash. The hut had been built after the ashfall, so I could excavate a small tunnel under the boards that formed the sidewalls. Once I got my hand outside, I reached up past the ash layer and grabbed handfuls of snow. The snow wasn't very clean once I'd pulled it through my ash tunnel, but I ate it anyway.

Peeing was the other problem. My captors had made no provision at all for hygiene. I dug a hole in the ash at one corner of the enclosure. I peed as carefully as I could into the hole—which wasn't easy, since I had to do it lying on my side—and covered it with ash.

Then there was nothing to do but wait. I listened to
the sounds of the camp, hoping I'd hear Darla. But either
she didn't try to yell to me, or I was too far away to hear
her. The concussion and lack of food had taken something
out of me; I found myself yawning and sleepy only a few
hours later. There was no point in fighting it—the nightmares that haunted my dreams would beat the waking
nightmare my life had become—so I let myself drift back
to sleep.

Chapter 50

I woke to a cracking sound and the scream of nails pulling free of wood. For a moment, I flashed back and thought I was in my bedroom in Cedar Falls, hurtling across the room as the house collapsed. I curled into a tighter ball and put my hands over the back of my neck.

A diesel engine growled from very close by. The hut suddenly began to lift around me. The concrete foundation of two of the posts came up with them, scraggly lumps of rock poised above my head. I desperately scrambled away, clawing in the snow to escape the doom above my head. Then the whole hut toppled backward, landing on its side in the snow behind me with a surprisingly soft thump.

There was a bulldozer blade above my head. I heard Darla scream, "Get up! Go!" I rolled over, out from under the blade, and pushed myself upright. She was sitting in the dozer's cab. I climbed up onto the track and from there into the cab. She wore different clothing—fatigues and combat boots, like the guards. Her shirtsleeves were rolled up at her wrists, and the boots looked like clown feet on her.

There was only one seat in the cab, so I climbed onto the armrest beside her. I bumped a joystick as I was getting situated, and the dozer lurched forward, crushing the punishment hut under its treads.

"Stay off the throttle!" Darla screamed.

She grabbed the joystick and slammed it over to one side, sending the dozer into a slow turn. She straightened it out and drove straight toward the camp.

"Um . . . where are we going?" I croaked.

"I've got a plan."

We rolled toward the fence around the refugee yard. Darla steered straight into one of the posts. It broke with a low, metallic pong.

Darla turned the dozer and drove directly over the fence line. She revved it to the max so that every second or so we were hitting another metal fencepost. Pong! Pong! Pong! The chain link and razor wire disappeared steadily under our treads as if the dozer were eating them. Within a few seconds, we'd left the punishment huts behind.

We weren't going very fast, but there was still a breeze on my face. I leaned into it, tasting freedom on my tongue. I was tired, sore, and starving, but despite my maladies, I laughed.

It was too dark to see much beyond the dozer's running lights. A few lights had popped on in the direction of the vehicle depot. I heard shouts over the roar of the diesel engine. The commotion was waking up the refugees. A few groups of them ran across the crushed fence behind us. Pretty soon the trickle of people increased to a flood—hundreds running in our wake to escape the camp. I finally clued in to Darla's plan: All the fleeing refugees would block anyone trying to chase us.

"Will it go any faster?" If I hadn't been so weak, I could have easily outrun the bulldozer.

"Not much, and only in reverse."

"Not good."

"Duck!" Darla yelled and slammed her hand onto a lever to her right. The dozer blade began to rise. I spotted two guards ahead of us, raising their submachine guns. They must have been patrolling the fence. I ducked then heard the chatter of gunfire and the whang of bullets hitting metal. Darla raised the blade so its top edge partially shielded us.

"Raise it some more!" I clutched the dozer's armrest in a death-grip. The vinyl under my hands was slick with sweat.

"That's as high as it goes!"

We peeked over the top of the blade. The two guards were circling, running to try to get a side angle on us. Darla turned the dozer toward them, keeping the blade between us and the guns. They kept circling and getting closer.

"Stay low!" Darla reversed her turn, slowly spinning the dozer away from the guards. They raised their guns; for a moment they had a clear shot at Darla's side through the cab window. She leaned all the way over in my lap, as close to flat as she could. I curled over her. Bullets slapped metal somewhere close by. Darla finished the turn. Now we were rumbling directly away from the guards. I hoped the metal at the back of the dozer's cab was thick enough to stop bullets. We crashed back through the fence and into the camp.

"Watch out!" I screamed. "Get away! Get away!" People scattered from the front of the bulldozer. There were refugees running everywhere—the ruckus had woken the entire camp.

I didn't hear any more gunshots. Maybe the guards weren't willing to fire into the crowd. I hoped not, anyway.

I looked around; I didn't see the guards now, only a never-ending flow of running people. Darla turned toward the eastern edge of camp. When we got there, she turned again, driving the bulldozer right over the fence, heading north and plowing the chain link under the treads. Crowds of refugees dashed through behind us, racing for freedom.

When we reached the corner of the camp, Darla kept going straight. She dropped the dozer blade a couple of feet so we could see better. The camp was built on a ridge top, so about fifty feet ahead of us the hillside yielded to a wooded ravine.

"Uh . . . you know there's a cliff up there, right?" I said.

"I'm hoping it's a steep slope, not a cliff. We've got to go somewhere it'll be hard to follow. This thing is slower than a roadkill turtle, if you haven't noticed."

The front of the dozer nosed over the edge of the hill. We crushed a few saplings at the edge of the ravine and picked up speed.

"Hold on!" Darla screamed.

The bulldozer crashed down the hill. Darla's hands twitched on the joystick, nudging us right and left, trying to avoid the biggest trees. We hit one of them despite her efforts. The shock threw me forward. The tree fell, and one of our tracks rolled up over it, so the dozer canted steeply to the right for a few terrifying seconds. Then we were free of it. The left tread thumped back to the ground, and we continued our headlong rush down the hillside.

Somehow Darla got us down the slope without running into anything that would stop the dozer. We plowed through a patch of soft ground and flattened some bushes. The front end of the dozer fell alarmingly, coming to rest halfway in a creek.

"Wow. What a ride." My hands were trembling, and my breath came in gasps.

"Yeah." Darla was looking ahead, trying to figure out where to go next, I thought.

I craned my head out the side of the cab, looking up the slope behind us. A Humvee was moving slowly about a quarter of the way down the hill. A second Humvee was just starting down the ridge.

"They're coming!" I yelled.

The blade was down in the creek. Darla raised it and goosed the throttle. The dozer ground forward, and its back end landed with a splash. Now we could see the far side of the creek: a vertical wall of dirt about three feet high. The blade hit the bank and the tracks spun in the mud and water. We couldn't climb out of the creek. There was no room to turn around, either.

We were stuck.

Chapter 51

Darla tapped the throttle, lightly this time, and the bulldozer inched forward. When the blade hit the bank, the tracks slipped, and the dozer rocked backward.

"We'd better get out and run," I said anxiously.

"No, I've got this." She tapped the throttle again and again, setting up a rocking motion. Dirt, ash, and snow fell from the creek bank where we were battering it.

I looked back. The lead Humvee was halfway down now. Two more followed behind it.

The bulldozer's motion got more and more violent. Darla was rocking in time with it, tapping the throttle as her body swayed back and forth against the seat. The dozer knocked big chunks of earth off the far bank each time it rocked forward, slowly battering its way out of the creek.

I glanced back again. The lead Humvee was now within shooting range. I jerked my head back inside the cab. "Keep your head down, they're close!" I yelled. Darla crouched lower in her seat and rocked the bulldozer forward—hard. It slammed into the bank, but this time the tracks bit. We tilted up at almost a forty-five-degree angle. When we crested the bank, the dozer fell with a crash that threw me forward on the armrest, right into the throttle. The bulldozer accelerated to its max, heading straight toward a huge sycamore. I scooted back, and Darla grabbed the throttle, slamming it to one side. We turned, narrowly missing the tree. I glanced behind us. The first Humvee was mired in the creek. Two more were lined up behind it, unable to pass. I realized I'd been holding my breath and let it out in a heavy sigh.

We rumbled over a flat area dotted with huge trees. Darla veered in an S-pattern around two more sycamores and started the bulldozer up a long, gentle ridge on the far side of the valley.

The ridge was deceptive. It lured us in with the promise of a gentle slope but got steeper and steeper as we ascended. Still, the bulldozer climbed easily, crushing underbrush and small trees beneath its blade and tracks. Near the top, the slope became completely vertical, ending in a line of broken rocks and cliffs. They were only seven or eight feet high— easy to climb on foot, but impossible for the bulldozer.

Darla raised the blade to maximum height and eased the bulldozer forward until it touched the cliff. We clambered out of the cab and onto one of the big metal arms that supported the dozer's blade. Darla took two steps up the sloped strut and grabbed the top edge of the blade. Then she pulled herself onto it and balanced there for a couple seconds before stepping forward to the top of the cliff.

I started to follow. The arm felt slick under my boots. I tried to walk up it, wobbled a bit, and thought better of it. I sat down and shimmied up on my butt. I grabbed the edge of the blade—it was sticky, coated with sap from the trees we'd mown down. I dragged myself slowly upright, standing on the arm and gripping the blade. Stepping up to the top of the blade looked easy when Darla had done it, but I had a terrible time getting even one foot up there. I straddled the blade instead, pulling myself slowly up and holding on with a death grip all the way.

Darla stepped back onto the blade beside me. She had one foot on the blade and one on the cliff. "Give me your hand."

"I don't know what's wrong with me. This should be easy." My face was hot despite the freezing weather.

"You've been on a starvation diet for almost two weeks, and you probably got a concussion when the guards clubbed you with their guns."

Darla pulled me to my feet. I tried to control my trembling knees as I perched atop the blade. I sucked down a deep breath and stepped across the gap, pushing my leg into the snow on top of the cliff while I held Darla's hand for support.

She stepped back across the gap. I took another step away from the cliff and put my hands on my knees, resting and trying not to collapse altogether.

Darla waited beside me for a couple of minutes, then we slogged on up the hill. The slope wasn't as steep here, but it was still tough going. The snow was almost three feet deep. We had to high-step, lifting our feet up and dragging them through the top layer of snow. We started out side by side, but I quickly fell behind and took to walking in Darla's footsteps. Also it was dark, and without the running lights of the bulldozer, bushes and trees suddenly loomed at us from out of the night, forcing Darla to detour often.

After a few minutes of this, my pants legs were soaked through. Darla's fatigues were damp all the way up to the small of her back—she was getting the worst of it since she was breaking the trail. I felt cold, but the effort required to move forward was keeping me from freezing. I imagined that if we stopped now, without a fire or shelter, both of us would be hypothermic in no time.

At the top of the slope, the woods ended, and we stepped into a field. Darla bent double to rest. "Which way?"

"Northeast, somewhere. I sort of remember how to get there. In a car, anyway. We'll have to find a road."

"I was planning to stay off the roads until we were farther away from the camp."

"Makes sense. How did you manage to steal a bulldozer, anyway? That was . . . wow."

Darla looked away. I couldn't see her cheek very well in the darkness, but she might have been blushing. "I just did, okay?"

"It was amazing. I was trying to figure out some way to escape, find you, and slip out of the camp, and then wham! You knocked the whole hut down."

"Do we have to talk about it?"

"No, I guess not. . . . What's wrong?"

Darla didn't answer right away. "You remember when Captain Jameson was telling you about the 'evening entertainment'—"

"Yeah, I hope I broke his nose."

"You did. Both his eyes were turning black by the time he dragged you into that hut. I followed and watched from inside the fence."

"So that's how you knew which hut I was in."

"Yep. So anyway, he should have called it a prostitution detail—"

"I knew that's what he was talking about. Something about the way he said it—I could hear the slime oozing off his voice."

"So, anyway . . . I volunteered for it."

"You what?"

"You heard me."

"But—"

"But nothing. How else was I supposed to get in the guards' enclosure? Chet always watched me during the day, and I figured we'd have a better chance to get away at night, anyway."

"But that's why I kicked the guy. Because what he was suggesting was so repulsive in the first place. Because I wanted to protect you."

"Then you did a crappy job of it. He was propositioning

me, not you, and *I* didn't try to beat him down. What were you thinking? If you'd kept your cool, I wouldn't have needed to offer to prostitute myself, wouldn't have needed to steal a bulldozer and break your ass out of that hut." Darla poked me in the chest with one finger, hard.

"I would have gotten—"

"You don't even know how bad off you were! I wheedled it out of Chet. They may call those doghouses 'punishment huts,' but they're not for punishment. Nobody comes out of them alive, Alex. They throw troublemakers in there to die, so there's no physical evidence to contradict the reports they file with FEMA. 'Died of exposure' doesn't call for an investigation. It's safer for them than putting a bullet in your fool head. Although a bullet in the brain might not kill *you*, because it'd sure miss all the organs you do your thinking with."

Darla whirled away, following the tree line to our right.

For about fifteen minutes I struggled to keep up with the furious pace she set. Then I stopped and called to her. "Darla," I said between gasps for air, "I'm sorry."

"I don't know that sorry cuts it." She strode back to me, kicking through the snow. "As it happened, I only *volunteered* to be a camp prostitute. I didn't have to go through with it. But so what if I had? So what if I'd screwed every motherless guard in that godforsaken camp?"

"I don't—"

"Would that have made me less of a woman in your mind? Less of a person? Just one of those girls, the easy ones, the ones the high-school cliques gossip about and

call sluts? Is that the kind of boy you are, Alex? Is that the
kind of man you want to be?"

"No, I . . ." I didn't know what to say. I'd been angry
when she began her rant, but it occurred to me that she
was right. I had reacted impulsively when I kicked Captain
Jameson. That had made things worse for both of us. A
thought hit me almost physically, like the sound wave of
the eruption eight weeks ago: I realized exactly how much
Darla had been willing to sacrifice on my behalf. I fought
back tears. There was only one thing I could say. "I love
you, Darla."

I held out my arms. She stumbled into them, whispering, "God, I was scared, Alex. I was so scared." She was
crying, and I lost the fight to hold back my own tears. We
stood in the icy snow and hugged for a while.

"So," Darla said, "I was filthy, like everyone else in the
camp. Captain Jameson had some grunt take me to the
showers. He stood guard outside the shower room door—
either to keep me from escaping or to stop anyone from
bothering me, I don't know."

"Your hands still feel greasy."

"I didn't shower. When I got in there, I noticed it was
built of temporary walls under a big canvas tent—no ceiling. So I flipped on the water and climbed over the back
wall into the next room."

"How'd you know what was on the other side of the
wall?"

"I didn't before I climbed up there. Turns out it was an
empty barracks room. I stole a uniform and ditched my

old clothes. I was hoping I could pass for a guard—at least at a distance."

"And that worked?"

"Yep. I walked out to the vehicle depot. Nobody was around that late at night, so I used a hammer to bash open the lockbox and grabbed the key to my favorite dozer."

"That was crazy. And brave. Thanks."

"They should call us the seven-mile-an-hour bandits."

"Huh?"

"Top speed for that bulldozer. Seven miles per hour. Well, eight in reverse."

I laughed. "Lot better time than we're making while we stand here and talk."

Darla nodded. "Let's go."

As the night wore on, I got slower and slower. Darla was breaking the trail, but she still had to stop every few minutes and wait for me to catch up. I tried to up my pace, to force myself to keep up with Darla by willpower alone, but I couldn't. It doesn't matter how hard you push down on the accelerator of a car, if there's no gas in the tank, it won't go.

On top of that, the edge of the woods was meandering, following the contour of the hillside. I had no idea if we were still going east—if we even had been in the first place.

"We've got to find a road," Darla said.

"Be a lot easier for Black Lake to find us."

"I don't think they'll be looking—"

"Of course they will. They chased us in those Humvees."

"Yeah, but that was a knee-jerk reaction. Chet said Black Lake gets paid by how many refugees they've got in the camp. It's worth a lot more money to round up some of the thousands of people who ran than to chase the two of us."

"Maybe. But it might be personal to them now."

"We've got to risk it," Darla said. "I don't think I can keep up this pace all night, pushing through deep snow like this."

What she really meant was that there was no way *I* could keep up. I hated the fact that I was holding us back. I hated that she had to break the trail for us. I even hated her a little for being so damned nice about it.

Darla turned away from the woods, cutting across the field. At the far side, we stumbled onto a berm of snow. After we'd struggled across it, we found a gift: there was the road. It was a two-lane county road, but someone had plowed it to a solid layer of packed snow.

"Which way?" Darla asked.

"I don't know. We've got to find Stagecoach Trail. It runs mostly east-west."

"Okay, so I think we were going north, or maybe east. If we were going north, then this is an east-west road, and it might be Stagecoach Trail, so we should turn right."

"I don't think it's big enough."

"If we were going east, then we should turn left, and we'll run into Stagecoach Trail."

"And what if we were going south or west?"

"Then we're screwed. So which way do you want to turn?"

"I don't know."

"I don't know this area. You do. You have to decide."

"Left," I said, just because I was tired of talking about it.

Chapter 52

We plodded along the road, walking next to the snow berm on the left. It was much easier—we were probably going three or four times faster than we had been through the snow. Despite the faster pace, I could almost keep up.

"If we hear a car or see headlights, dive over the snow berm and hide," Darla said.

"They'll see our tracks."

"Maybe not—it's dark, and hopefully they'll be moving fast."

I grunted.

We hadn't been walking long when we came to

an intersection. The road we'd been following teed into a highway. A road sign poked out of the snow on the far side of the intersection, but it was so dark we had to walk right up to it to read it: W. Heller Lane and Stagecoach Trail.

"Good call on the left turn back there," Darla said with a smile I could barely make out in the darkness.

"Lucky, for once."

We turned right on Stagecoach Trail. Maybe it had started as a trail years ago, but now it was a plowed highway. We followed the same strategy, walking on the left side of the highway along the berm, ready to dive over it if we heard anything coming.

The road was deserted all night. I dragged my feet along in a fugue state, not thinking anything, trying not to feel anything: right foot, left foot, right foot, left foot.

Not long after dawn we passed over a bridge. A sign that barely protruded from the snow berm read: West Fork Apple River. I told Darla we were close, although I couldn't remember exactly how much farther we had to go.

An hour or so later I woke to Darla shaking my shoulder. "Get up. Get up!" I looked around woozily—I was lying in the road. "Goddamn it, Alex, get up and walk!"

"What happened?"

"I looked behind me, and you were fifty feet back, taking a nap."

"Sorry." I struggled to my knees. Darla knelt beside me and tucked her head under my arm. Leaning on her, I found I could stand. After that, we hobbled down the road with my arm over her shoulders.

Sometime later, we heard the noise of an engine approaching behind us. Darla dragged me toward the berm. We were still trying to thrash our way over the snow pile when a car whizzed past.

The next time we heard a car engine, we didn't even bother trying to hide. There was no sign of Black Lake; if we were lucky, they were busy chasing refugees closer to the camp.

I found I could close my eyes and keep moving, stealing a sleepwalking nap with my arm draped across Darla's shoulders.

Ages later, I woke from one of those semiconscious snoozes. "Alex, hey, you in there?" Darla asked. "We're close, check it out." I cracked open my eyes and looked around. There was a graveyard on the left side of the road, with a sign: Elmwood Cemetery. I could see the buildings of Warren ahead.

"Canyon Park," I mumbled.

"What?"

"Think we went too far. Supposed to turn south on Canyon Park Road."

"We passed that an hour ago. I think you sleepwalked through it."

"Ugh. Turn around. Sorry." I was too tired even to feel upset with myself over the extra hour of walking.

Darla must have felt the same way, because she didn't say anything. She just wheeled us around, and we crossed the road, walking on the other side back in the direction we'd come. I fought to stay awake, to spot the turnoff we'd missed. "Left here," I said. "It's close. Less than five minutes in a car."

Canyon Park Road was plowed, which surprised me. I remembered it as a little-used dirt road. The prospect of ending my journey brought out some hidden reserve of energy within me. I leaned less on Darla and picked up the pace some. My mother, father, and sister might be only a few hundred yards down this remote lane.

We'd walked about a half-hour when I saw the front of my uncle's long driveway. It wasn't plowed, but someone had shoveled a path in the snow. The light wasn't bad; it was early afternoon, so when we got closer I could make out his house at the end of the driveway. The barn and duck coop were still standing, and there were two other structures, long half-cylinders constructed of wood and plastic sheeting. Greenhouses, I remembered. Darla and I turned up the driveway, walking in the shoveled path.

We'd traversed maybe half the driveway when we heard a faint noise from inside the house. A drape was thrown open, and I saw my uncle looking through the window, holding a long gun against his chest. Then I heard a high-pitched shout. The front door was flung open, and my sister tore down the driveway toward us.

"Alex! Alex!" she screamed. She ran pell-mell into my arms, knocking me backward into the snow. "You're alive! You're alive—"

"Good to see you, too, Sis." I didn't know if she was laughing or crying or some mixture of the two. I wanted to do both, but I couldn't summon the energy. So I just hugged her close and looked over her shoulder.

Uncle Paul, Aunt Caroline, and my cousins, Max and Anna, were all standing around us now. Everyone looked thinner and older than I remembered. I scanned the faces again, looking for my parents.

"Where's Mom and Dad?" I said.

My sister's laughter ended abruptly. She didn't reply.

"Where's Mom, Rebecca?"

"They're . . ."

"They're what?"

"They're gone, Alex. They're both gone."

Chapter 53

I woke in a bed, confused. It was sublimely soft, made up with old cotton sheets conditioned by hundreds of washings to near-perfect comfort. A heavy bedspread lay over the top. Despite my uncertainty about how I'd gotten there, I felt warm and safe for the first time since I'd left Cedar Falls.

Darla was slumped in a chair beside the bed, napping. Her head was completely bald.

"Darla . . ." I said. "You awake?" The question didn't really make sense. She was asleep—I was trying to wake her.

"Uh?"

"You in there?"

"Yeah." She stretched her arms and yawned. "You scared me. Just folded up right there in the snow."

"I don't remember."

"I don't know if it was starvation, exhaustion, or what, but you passed out. How are you feeling?"

"Okay. Hungry and thirsty. Sore. How long have I been out?"

"I dunno. Not sure how long I've been asleep." Darla walked to the window and pulled the curtain aside. "It's getting dark. Guess we've been asleep all afternoon."

"What happened to your hair?"

"Bald is beautiful, huh?" Her tone of voice didn't suggest she found it particularly beautiful.

I shrugged.

"Well, you look pretty odd without your hair, too."

I touched my head. Sure enough, my hair had all been shaved off. "What? Why?"

"Lice. We were lousy with them, ha ha." She didn't sound the least bit amused. "They don't have any pesticide shampoo, so . . ."

"It doesn't look so bad. And it'll grow back."

"I guess."

I put my hand out from under the covers and held hers. My hand was a shocking white—the layer of grime and ash had been scrubbed off. It was hard to believe I'd slept through being washed and having my head shaved; I must have been deeply unconscious. Darla and I sat in silence for a minute or so until I remembered what my sister had been saying before I passed out.

"My parents. Are they—"

"I'd better get your uncle to explain. He's been . . . weird." Darla dropped my hand and stood up. "I'll be right back," she said as she left the room.

Not sixty seconds later, my uncle came in with Darla following. He turned, looked at her, and cleared his throat. They stared at each other a moment.

"I'll be in the kitchen," Darla said, then left the room again.

"Who is she?" Uncle Paul asked.

"What happened to my parents?" I said.

"She said you met in Worthington? How well do you know her?"

I pushed myself up in the bed with some effort. The covers fell away from my torso. Blood rushed from my head, and I felt a bit woozy. "I wouldn't be here if it weren't for her. She saved my life. More than once." I stared into my uncle's eyes, making an effort not to blink. "I'd die for her."

Uncle Paul looked away. "Heck of a scar on your side."

"Darla stitched it."

"She didn't tell us about all that. I guess we can count on her, then."

"You can."

"I'm sorry. It's . . . there's all sorts of crazies out. Don't see much of them here, but we hear stories. Folks who live out on Highway 20 have had a rough time."

"Tell me about it. . . . Where are Mom and Dad? Are they dead?"

"Yes. That. I tried to talk them out of it, but they were determined."

"Out of what? And quit dodging the question. Are they dead?"

"I don't know. They left five weeks ago. They went back to Iowa."

My chest felt suddenly heavy. "Why? And why'd they leave Rebecca here?"

"They went to look for you."

"They what?"

"They went into the red zone to find you, Alex. We haven't heard any news of them since they left."

"Crap." I swung my legs out of the bed, realized I was naked, and pulled a corner of the covers over my lap. I'd spent the last eight weeks struggling to reach my uncle's farm, figuring that once I got here my quest would be complete. But it wasn't. Sure, I'd be safe here, but if I were only looking for a safe place to stay, I never would have left Mrs. Nance's school in Worthington. "I've got to go back. Try to find them." I looked around for my clothing but didn't see it.

"No. You're safe here—"

"But they're not safe in Iowa. They've got no idea what they're getting into."

"They had some idea before they left. Things have been rough here, too. I traded a pair of breeding goats for a shotgun and gave it to your dad."

"My dad? With a shotgun? No way. He's liable to hurt himself."

"People have changed. Your dad's not the same man he was. Heck, you're not the same either—I don't see any sign of the sullen kid who used to bury his nose in a computer game or book the moment he got here."

"Yeah, well." I didn't care much for being called a sullen kid. But maybe he was right. I *had* changed. "I should go back. I know what to expect in Iowa now. They might need help. I didn't even leave a note at the house, and my bedroom is completely collapsed. There was a fire, too. If they get there, they might think I'm dead. I guess Darren and Joe know I was alive when I left, but they might be dead or gone by now."

"If they can't find you, they'll come back here for Rebecca. If you go, how will you find them? You've already passed each other on the road. And this winter is only going to get worse. All the ash and sulfur dioxide in the air is going to wreck the weather for years. It's going to get colder and harder to travel—"

"With skis I can—"

"You might need skis just to travel next summer. The volcanic winter might last a decade, nobody knows for sure."

A decade of winter? That hit hard. How would anyone survive?

"Just wait, Alex. Maybe they'll come back. If they haven't shown up next summer, maybe conditions will be better so you can go look for them. Maybe by then FEMA will be in Iowa."

"Huh. That'd hurt more than it'd help."

"At least they clear the roads and maintain some order."

"You haven't done time in a FEMA camp." My face was tense, scowling.

"No. But there's another reason you shouldn't take off after your folks. You're needed here. I need your help. We could be looking at years without a reliable food source. We need to stockpile corn and wood, build more greenhouses, and figure out some way to keep feeding the goats and ducks. There's an immense amount of work to be done."

I nodded grudgingly. "Okay. I'll think about it. But if Mom and Dad haven't shown up by next spring, I'm going to go look for them. In the meantime, I'll help—although Darla will be way more helpful than me. She was running a farm practically alone when we met."

"Let's not make any decisions today. It may be summer before the weather improves—if it does at all. But okay. If we can get things on a solid footing here, I'll consider supplying you for an expedition back to Cedar Falls."

"Where's my clothing?"

"It was infested with lice. We hung it in a corner of the barn. I'm thinking the lice might die eventually if there's no one for them to feed on. I'm not sure."

"Yuck." I felt itchy all over.

"I'll get some of mine for you. Come to the kitchen when you're dressed; it's dinnertime."

Chapter 54

My cousins Max and Anna, my sister, and my uncle were sitting at the table in the kitchen. I saw Aunt Caroline and Darla through a window, cooking over a fire outside.

The table was already set. I sat down and drained the glass of water in front of me in a few gulps.

"Jugs on the counter are drinking water," Uncle Paul said. "Help yourself if you want more."

I got up and refilled my glass. While I was up, Darla came through the back door carrying a frying pan and a plate stacked high with omelets. Aunt Caroline followed, hefting a plate of cornbread.

It was an odd dinner, but by far the best meal I'd eaten in weeks. The cornbread was real—not corn pone. The omelet was delicious, but it didn't taste quite like any omelet I'd ever eaten. The stuffing was some purplish leaf I couldn't identify, and the eggs and cheese tasted weird— not bad, but different. I asked Aunt Caroline about it.

"It's a duck-egg, goat-cheese, and kale omelet," she replied.

"The ducks are mine," Anna said, grinning proudly.

"I don't know how long we'll be able to keep the ducks," Uncle Paul said. Anna glared at him, but he continued, "Or the goats, for that matter. We're going to run out of hay."

"How'd you keep them alive through the ashfall?" Darla asked.

"We didn't—not as well as I'd have liked, anyway. We lost four ducks and two goats to silicosis. But when we figured out what was going on, we started keeping them in the barn all the time and spreading wet straw to keep the dust down."

"Where'd the kale come from?" I asked.

"We planted a fall garden in our greenhouses, before the eruption. But it got cold so fast that only the kale survived. We've been feeding the dead cucumber vines, tomato plants, and so on to the goats, but we're out of those now. We've replanted—mostly kale, so I hope you like it."

"Tastes fine to me," I said.

"Your taste buds need tuning up," Max said grumpily, although he was eating his kale omelet, too.

"Tell us about your trip," Uncle Paul said. "From the little bit Darla's told us, you had a rough time."

"I don't really want to talk about it," I said. That wasn't exactly true. I didn't even want to think about it, much less talk.

"That bad, huh?"

"Yeah."

I hoped he'd drop it, change the subject or something, but he kept asking questions. So I slowly released the breath I'd been holding in and relented. For the rest of the dinner and a couple of hours afterward, I told them my story. Darla pitched in some after I got to the part where I had met her. I paused before I told them about Darla's mom being raped and murdered. I wasn't sure how much I should say with Anna, Max, and my sister there. Anna and Max were ten and twelve, or maybe eleven and thirteen—I wasn't sure. My sister would be fourteen next month. I asked Uncle Paul, "How much of this do you want me to talk about with your kids here? What happened when we got back from Worthington, it was . . . obscene. I'm not sure I even want my sister to hear this."

Paul and Caroline glanced at each other. He said, "Go on. They need to know about the world they live in now."

"Anna might get nightmares," Caroline said.

Paul turned to Anna, "Do you want to stay? You don't have to listen if you don't want to."

"I'll stay," she said.

So I told the whole story to everyone. Still, I tried to gloss over the worst parts of it. Darla certainly didn't need to relive that day. I took her hand and squeezed it, offering whatever meager support I could.

When I finished talking, Rebecca was staring at me, her head tilted at a slight angle.

"What?" I asked.

"I can't believe you did all that. I always knew that you were, like, tougher than you seemed, but—"

"I wouldn't have survived without Darla."

Rebecca turned her gaze on Darla. They looked at each other for a moment; then my sister nodded, and Darla smiled a little. I wasn't sure what to make of the exchange. Somehow during the last eight weeks my exuberant, chatty sister had been replaced by this thoughtful alien who could communicate with a look what would have taken the old Rebecca an hour's worth of words.

"We'd best get to bed," Uncle Paul said. "There's more corn to grind and wood to cut tomorrow."

"Where do you want us to sleep?" I asked.

"You can bunk with Max. Darla and Rebecca will have to share the guest room—the room you were in when you woke up."

Max and Anna erupted into simultaneous protests.

Max: "Why do I have to share my room? Why does Anna get her own?"

Anna: "How come I don't get a roommate? Why does Max always get everything?"

Aunt Caroline overrode them both. "Anna, I want you to find the air mattress. I think it's in the linen closet. Max, come with me. I'll help you shovel out some space for Alex in that pigsty you sleep in."

Darla grabbed my arm and whispered, "Alex, I'd rather if we slept—"

"I'll talk to him."

She nodded.

Uncle Paul got up from his chair. I looked at him. "Uh, can I talk to you?"

"Sure." He sat back down.

My sister was still at the table. I made a get-out-of-here gesture with my head. She didn't move. "In private?" I said. "Please?"

"Oh. Yeah." Rebecca and Darla left the kitchen.

"Um . . ." I thought furiously. How should I start? "Darla and I have been together for six weeks now."

"An eternity in the life cycle of the American teenager." Uncle Paul smiled, not unkindly.

"Darla's almost eighteen, and I don't really think of myself as a teenager anymore."

"You've been through stuff no teenager should ever have to face, that's true. But you're still a minor, Alex."

"I know, but . . ." This wasn't going the way I'd hoped. "Look, Darla and I have been sleeping together—"

"Exactly how should I take that? Is there a chance she's pregnant? Do you have any idea how risky that could be, how often women and their babies died in childbirth before we had modern medical care? Which we *don't* have right now."

My cheeks burned. I'd tried, unsuccessfully, to break in between each of those rapid-fire questions. Now he took a breath, and I said, "When I said sleeping together, that's exactly what I meant. There's no chance she's pregnant.

Even if it were perfectly safe, the last thing we want is to bring a baby into this mess."

"That's a relief."

"I feel safe with Darla. She's the reason I'm alive."

"And we're grateful—"

"Anna wants a roommate. Max doesn't. Why don't we move my sister in with Anna, and Darla and I will take the guest room?"

"What I was going to say was, we're grateful to Darla for getting you here in one piece. And I'm sure she'll be a big help. But you're both minors. Until your parents return, you have to live by the rules Caroline and I set."

"Which is why I'm asking—"

"You've only known each other six weeks. I know it seems intense to you now, and you're sure you'll love her forever, but things change when you're young. You're too young to be making permanent decisions—and too young to be sharing a room."

"But—"

"Final answer, sorry. When your folks get back you can revisit it with them."

A hot wave of anger washed through me. My muscles tensed. I sucked in a deep breath and fought down the anger. Several retorts occurred to me, but none of them would have helped my case. From his perspective, it made sense—maybe. He saw me as the quiet, angry kid who used to visit his farm under duress. The kid I'd left behind in Worthington—along with a couple quarts of my blood.

"Okay," I said.

Paul stared—his lips parted, and he tilted his head to the side.

"I don't like it, but you're right about one thing. It's your house and your rules. You see me as a kid—"

"I know you've changed."

"We'll live with it for now. But eighteen is only a number. The magic number could just as easily be—has been, for other societies and other times—thirteen or sixteen or twenty-one."

"True enough."

"You're going to need all of us to act like adults to get through this."

My uncle nodded. "It's one of the things that bothers Caroline and me most. What kind of childhood can the kids have in the midst of this chaos? A few chores, the responsibility of caring for the animals—those things have always been good for them. But now we're all working dusk to dawn, trying to prepare for the long winter."

"Darla's spent the last few years working every waking minute to keep her farm going. She turned out okay. The kids could do worse."

"Yes. But I still feel guilty. I should be sending them to school every morning, not into the fields to dig for corn."

I shrugged. "There'll be time for school when things get better."

"I hope so. I'm off to bed. Goodnight."

"Goodnight." I scowled at his back as he left. I'd done the best I could, stayed calm, and made a solid rational argument, but what good had it done me?

I walked to the guest room at one end of the first floor and knocked on the door. Darla opened it dressed in an oversized T-shirt—one of Caroline's, I figured.

"How'd it go?" she asked, closing the bedroom door behind her.

"Not so good. We're kids, we haven't known each other long enough, we'll fall out of love, we're both minors, oh my God don't get her pregnant, and it's my house and my rules."

"That bad, huh?"

"Yeah. The problem with adults is that they always see you in the crib you slept in as a baby. The one with the bars on the sides. I was hoping Uncle Paul might see things differently."

"He will."

"I've got half a mind to go back to Iowa to look for my parents."

"I'm not sure how we'd find them."

"I'd go back to Cedar Falls. Maybe they've been to the house." Then I thought about what she'd said. "We . . .?"

"You didn't think I'd let you go back to Iowa alone, did you?"

"Uh—"

"I'm not sure I trust you to walk from here to the barn without hurting yourself, let alone all the way to Cedar Falls."

It sounded mean, but Darla was smiling as she said it, so I forgave her. "You're right—we might not be able to find them. And the weather is probably going to get worse. The smart thing to do is to wait here."

"Doing nothing is tough, even when it's the right choice."

"It's more than that. During the trip, I was free. In Cedar Falls or here, I'm just somebody's kid. In between, I was Alex. I decided where I slept and when, who I talked to and who I avoided. Sure, the ash and psychotic killers weren't fun, but I've only been here one day, and already I miss that feeling of freedom, of being my own man."

"Your uncle will figure out that you're not a kid. Give him some time to stop remembering the old Alex and start seeing who you are now."

"I hope you're right. And thanks."

I wrapped an arm around her waist and kissed her. We stood in the hall and made out until Aunt Caroline's voice wafted down the stairs, telling me my bed was ready. Darla said goodnight, and I clomped up to Max's room.

Chapter 55

The air mattress was comfortable, but still I slept poorly. I woke sometime in the wee hours of the morning, my mind roiling with images of people: Darla, Target, Mrs. Nance, Colonel Levitov, Darren and Joe, my mother. . . .

I thrashed around in the bed for a while before giving up on further sleep. The clothing I'd worn at dinner yesterday was next to the mattress; I pulled it on, moving quietly so as not to wake Max. I slipped downstairs in my socks, thinking I'd get a glass of water.

Darla was in the living room adding a log to the fire. "Want a glass of water?" I asked.

"Sure. You couldn't sleep?"

"No."

"Me, either."

I fetched a glass of water from the kitchen to share. When we finished, I slouched into the corner of the couch, where the back met the arm. Darla leaned against me, and I wrapped an arm around her. We'd sat together comfortably for only a few minutes when I heard her breathing slow down and felt her body relax in my arms. Soon after, I followed her into sleep.

* * *

I woke to Darla shaking me. "I heard footsteps upstairs. You'd better get back to Max's room."

I stood up and stretched. "Okay, love you."

"Love you, too." She gave me a kiss. I kept my lips firmly sealed together; I was pretty sure I had vile morning breath. She didn't seem to notice, or maybe she didn't care.

I stole up the stairs to Max's bedroom as quietly as I could. He was still asleep. I slid on my boots and left the room again, this time stomping all the way.

Breakfast was corn pone and kale fried in duck fat. When Darla finally got to the kitchen, she made a big show of rubbing sleep from her eyes and announcing "Good morning, Alex" as if we hadn't just seen each other. I had to suppress the urge to laugh.

After breakfast, Aunt Caroline retrieved two crude mortars and pestles from the pantry. They were only slightly concave stones with a round rock for each to serve as the pestle. "Who's going to grind corn this morning?"

"I will, I guess," Rebecca said.

"Why do you grind it that way?" Darla asked.

Everyone looked at her a little funny, so I said, "Darla built a bicycle-powered grinder on her farm. It worked great."

"I've been thinking about trying something like that," Paul said. "But there hasn't been time."

"It didn't really work all that well," Darla said. "I made the grindstones out of concrete, so they threw a lot of dust and grit into the meal."

"Bet it saved a lot of time, though," Rebecca said wistfully.

"I think I could make a better one. I'd like to try making grindstones out of granite—that wouldn't throw grit the way concrete does. I'd need some decent-sized chunks of granite."

"I know where you can get some," Max said. "Most of the gravestones at the cemetery are granite."

"Max!" Aunt Caroline exclaimed. "That's terribly disrespectful."

"It's a good idea," Uncle Paul said. "I don't think the dead will mind. I know I wouldn't if it were my gravestone." Aunt Caroline glared at him, and he said, "We can make rubbings and replace the stones when things get better."

"It'd be a lot easier to cut gravestones than river rocks," Darla added. "All I'd have to do is cut the flour channels in the face, maybe rough it up a little, and chip it round. Oh, I'd have to drill a feed hole in the runner stone, too."

"It's disrespectful," Aunt Caroline repeated. "What would the neighbors think if they saw us robbing gravestones?"

"They'd probably forgive us in return for grinding their corn," Uncle Paul said. "If we could build a gristmill, maybe we could charge to use it. Ten or twenty percent of the grain we grind? What else would you need to build it?"

"Tools for working stone," Darla replied. "Cold-forged chisels, that sort of thing. A couple of bicycles. Parts off an old truck or car. A welding rig would help, but I can probably manage without it."

"Our closest neighbor, Bill Jacobs, used to moonlight as a mason. I'll ask if we can borrow his tools. A welding setup would be tougher to come by—try to make do. As for parts, there are four bikes in the garage. Use whatever you need. Car parts can come from the minivan—"

"The minivan?" Aunt Caroline protested. "It's almost brand new."

"It's not like we have any gas. And if we get some, we'll probably want to use it in the truck for hauling stuff."

"But the kids can't all ride in the truck."

"I don't think we'll be driving them anywhere soon, honey."

Aunt Caroline didn't look happy, but she quit objecting.

"Okay, Max," Uncle Paul said, "show Alex and Darla how to do your morning chores. After you've finished, take them down to the creek with the toboggan and a couple of pry-bars. If you can find any rocks in the creek bed that will work, great. Otherwise, take them to the cemetery and borrow two gravestones. If anyone's around, come home and get me before you take the gravestones."

"Okay, Dad."

"I want to go, too," Rebecca said.

"Get your morning chores done, and then you can help me build the third greenhouse," Uncle Paul told Rebecca. Then he looked at Darla. "Work on your gristmill in the mornings. Let's reserve the afternoon for other projects. There aren't enough hours in the day to do everything that's got to be done."

Darla nodded.

"Oh, and while you're at the creek, think about what it would take to build a scaled-up version of the mill. Maybe we could dam the creek and run it on water power."

"Will there be enough demand to justify it?" Darla said. "Eventually the buried corn will spoil. It might be years before we can plant more. Will we still need a big mill then?"

"I don't know. Think about it, anyway."

* * *

The rocks at the creek were hopeless. Either they were too small, the wrong shape, or stuck so thoroughly that all three of us straining on our pry bars couldn't budge them.

The cemetery was deserted. It turned out to be ridiculously easy, compared to our failed effort in the creek bed, to find two suitable gravestones and topple them onto the waiting toboggan. Darla rigged up a pair of wooden crosses. She carved the dead people's initials on each cross and pounded them into the ground where we'd taken the granite markers.

Dragging the loaded toboggan back to the farm was not so easy. It took all three of us straining at the rope to move the sled. Those gravestones were *heavy*.

By the time we got back, it was noon. After lunch, Uncle Paul sent me and Max back to the creek with the toboggan, this time to cut wood. They needed a lot of it. The only source of heat was the living room fireplace, which meant most of the house was freezing. Plus, they were doing all the cooking on a wood fire outside the kitchen door.

Uncle Paul assigned Darla to help him build the new greenhouse in the afternoon. They were building the frame out of leftover two-by-fours and tree branches. When they finished the frame, they would cover it in plastic and prepare the inside for planting. They only had enough plastic for one more greenhouse, although Uncle Paul said he was going to try to trade for more.

It all seemed a bit futile. There were hundreds of acres of fields surrounding their farm. All of it had been planted in corn and soybeans before the volcano erupted. No matter how much plastic we got, most of those fields would go fallow. A lot of people were going to starve. I hoped we wouldn't be among the victims.

Chapter 56

The next few weeks passed in much the same way. The first week or so was tough; I was weak from my starvation diet at the FEMA camp. But once I recovered my strength, I worked harder than I ever had before.

I'd spent most of my time digging corn, chopping wood, or carrying water. Some mornings I helped Darla build the gristmill, but usually she was carving the grindstones and couldn't use my help. She ruined one of the stones, cracking it as she tried to drill a hole through it, and we had to raid the cemetery for another grave marker.

Digging corn got tougher and tougher. It snowed twice more, so more than four feet covered the ground. The ash layer here was only a few inches thick, but getting through all that snow to the ash and the corn beneath it was a ton of work.

Sometimes I helped my uncle with the greenhouses. I learned that one of the tricks for a winter greenhouse was building a heat sink: an array of dark stones designed to soak up the sun's rays during the day and release the heat at night. It didn't seem to me that it would work since the sun was hidden, blocked by ash and sulfur high in the atmosphere. But my uncle thought enough UV light was getting through for the heat sink to be worth the effort.

He fiddled incessantly with the greenhouses: moving stones, watering the plants, and weeding. He was testing a plot of turnips and another of potatoes. He'd traded for the seeds and potato eyes in Warren, buying them with duck eggs and goat meat. So far, everything had failed to grow except for the kale.

Rebecca, Max, and Anna took care of the goats and ducks. After we'd been there a few days, the kids taught me and Darla how to do it so we could take turns. We fed the ducks corn and a little kale. The goats got mostly hay, although the hayloft was nearly empty. We also fed the goats everything else that humans wouldn't want to eat: cornstalks, weeds, failed plants from the greenhouses, pine needles, even green twigs—they ate it all. Still, they steadily lost weight and gave less milk.

So Uncle Paul decided to slaughter one duck and one goat, a kid. He offered to teach Darla and me how to

butcher them and seemed surprised when we agreed. He
patiently explained each step to us, but except for plucking
the feathers off the duck, it didn't seem that much different from what Darla had done with her rabbits. And it was
way easier than butchering a pig. Uncle Paul seemed
amazed at how fast we caught on.

I was surprised that Max and Anna didn't protest
when Uncle Paul decided to slaughter two of their animals. The kids had evidently put a lot of effort into caring
for them, so I assumed losing a goat and a duck would be
a big deal. Even Rebecca seemed attached to the ducks. I
asked my uncle about it while we were butchering the
goat. He didn't answer at first.

"I think we got through that with the dogs," he said
finally.

"The dogs?"

"You remember them? Denver and Gypsy?"

"Yeah."

"We ran out of dog food. We could have fed them
meat, but we didn't . . . don't have enough. They were
starving, suffering. I had to . . . I thought it was more
humane to kill them than let them starve to death. The
kids were pretty upset. We all were."

"Did you eat them?" Darla asked. I glanced at her,
thinking maybe she was telling some kind of sick joke, but
she was serious.

"No. We should have. I should have lied and told the
kids it was goat meat. But I couldn't make myself do it.
They're buried at the edge of the farmyard. You can ask
the kids to show you, if you want. I avoid that spot. . . It

was horrible; I didn't want to waste a shotgun shell. . . I used a knife. I don't want to think about it."

"I'm sorry," I said. The corners of his mouth and eyes drooped. Sorry didn't seem to cover it. I put my hand on his arm and squeezed.

Uncle Paul blinked and turned back to the goat carcass hanging in front of us.

Chapter 57

It took Darla two weeks to finish her gristmill. It worked so much faster than the mortars and pestles that it freed up a lot of time. Since it took two people to operate—one to feed grain into it and one to pedal the bike—I got nominated to help her run it. Not that I minded. It meant we got to spend more time together.

We ground the farm's entire stockpile of corn in one afternoon. The next day, Bill Jacobs, the guy my uncle had borrowed the stone-working tools from, brought six bags of corn to us. We ground it all as payment for the use of his tools.

The other time Darla and I saw each other was in the middle of the night. Most nights, like the first, I'd wake up, slip downstairs to the living room, and find Darla there napping on the couch. We'd sleep through the wee hours curled up together. Darla was a light sleeper, so she'd wake me when everyone else in the house started to stir, and we'd return to our separate rooms.

Before the volcano, I would have thought a secret rendezvous to make out with my girlfriend in the middle of the night would be thrilling. But most of the time it wasn't like that. Well, some nights it was, and yeah, that was fun, but usually we'd talk for a few minutes, snuggle up together, and drift back to sleep. For one thing, we were both tired; we worked crazy hours during the day—grueling physical labor that left us exhausted.

For another thing, the most important part of seeing Darla every night wasn't the fooling around. It was the few minutes we talked while holding each other, the feeling of security I got with her, the feeling of being understood and loved. Before the eruption, I wouldn't have believed that I could cuddle up every night with the girl who starred in my dreams and not be totally preoccupied with sex. But the trek across Iowa had changed something. I wanted, needed to see her so badly that it woke me up at night. But making out was incidental to my need—nice when it happened, but secondary to the simple pleasure of sleeping beside her.

We'd been in Warren a little more than a month when Uncle Paul discovered what was going on. I woke on the couch one morning, not to Darla shaking me but to my uncle clearing his throat. I was on my back with Darla halfway on top of me, also on her back. My right arm lay across her shoulder, and my hand cupped her left breast through her shirt. I snatched my hand away, waking her.

"How long has this been going on?" Uncle Paul said.

My heart was thudding, and I could feel the heat in my face, but I answered as calmly as I could, "Since we left Worthington." I stared my uncle in the eye.

"Hmm. Get ready for breakfast."

Darla got up and scurried toward the guest room. I plodded up the stairs to get my boots.

All day I waited for the hammer to fall. I could sense it hanging above my head, dangling from a thread like the sword of Damocles. But my uncle didn't say anything to me except instructions about where to stack the wood that Max and I had chopped. His silence on the subject persisted until we'd finished dinner.

"I've talked to everyone involved today," Uncle Paul said. "We're going to make some changes to the sleeping arrangements. Rebecca's moving upstairs into Anna's room, and Alex will be moving into the guest room."

"Dad found out you haven't been sleeping in my room much, anyway, huh?" Max whispered to me.

"Yeah, you knew?" I whispered back.

Max smiled.

"Thanks for keeping it quiet."

"Sure thing, cuz."

"Alex," Uncle Paul said, "I want to talk to you." I stayed behind at the kitchen table while everyone else left for the warmer living room. "Um—"

"Thanks for changing the sleeping arrangements," I said.

"Yes. Well, even I can see the obvious, sometimes. Caroline and I aren't totally convinced it's the right call. What if you or Darla change your mind?"

"I don't think that will happen, but if it does, I'll tell you, and you can change the bedrooms again."

"Okay. Look, there's a doctor in Warren, but without electricity and supplies, he's pretty much practicing 1800s-style medicine. If Darla got pregnant . . ."

Oh, God. Not this again. My face was burning. "We aren't doing . . . well, we'd like to. We talked about it before we even got out of Iowa. But I don't want to add a baby to this mess any more than you do. I mean, someday maybe we'll get married and maybe have kids, but—" I quit talking, shocked to silence by my uncle's face. *He* was blushing.

"That's, um, responsible. I know how I'd have felt about it at your age. I'm not sure I would have made the same— the right—choice. Here." He pressed something into my hand. I looked down: two foil-wrapped squares. Condoms.

"You shouldn't feel pressure to use them," he said. "Abstinence is perfectly fine, preferable actually, as young as you are. But if you should . . . you know, I wanted you to have—"

"Thanks."

"I can only spare two."

"Okay."

"And if you decide not to use them, I'd take them back."

"Okay." I wasn't trying to be terse. I just had abso- lutely no idea what to say. Uncle Paul apparently didn't know what to say, either, because he clapped me on my shoulder and fled the room.

I found Darla in the guest room, helping Rebecca move her stuff.

"Why are you blushing?" Darla asked me.

"Well I, um . . ." I looked at my sister.

"Mind giving us a minute?" Darla said.

"Sure." Rebecca left without a peep of protest. Boy, had she changed.

I pulled the condoms out of my pocket and opened my hand to show them to Darla.

"You got . . .? Wow, I didn't see that coming," she said.

"Yeah, me neither."

"Your uncle gave them to you?"

"Yeah."

"Only two?"

"He said it was all he could spare."

"Do you think they're reusable?"

"Gross!" I said. Darla cocked an eye at me. I thought about it a moment then added, "I'll ask."

Darla smiled. She stepped to the guest room door, closed it, and twisted the handle to lock it. Then she took my hand and led me to the bed.

* * *

So I thought I'd feel different afterward, after the invisible neon sign proclaiming "virgin" had blinked out on my forehead. I'd spent years obsessing about it, so it seemed like something should have changed. Maybe it would have if I'd still been at Cedar Falls High surrounded by the gossip and braggadocio of teenage boys.

But on my uncle's farm, nobody noticed, or at least nobody said anything. The next day, like every day, we dug corn, chopped wood, and carried water. And it didn't even really change much between me and Darla, either. Yes, making love was fun, but it wasn't really any more fun than anything we'd already been doing together. Just different.

I was glad nobody had noticed. I might have been offended if my uncle had punched my shoulder and said something inane like, "So you're a man now." Besides being unspeakably embarrassing, that would have missed the true date of my passage into adulthood by a month or more.

One thing did change. After Darla and I moved into the guest room, I slept better. It was colder than the living room, but I didn't have to wake up in the middle of the night anymore to move. She was never more than an arm's length away.

Chapter 58

A few weeks later, another winter storm blew through. The wind ripped a series of huge holes in one of the greenhouses. Uncle Paul and Max worked on patching the plastic skin of the damaged greenhouse. From the outside, they leaned an aluminum extension ladder against one of the rafters. Paul stood at the top of the ladder, trying to tape the tears from above, while Max steadied the ladder's base.

Most of the kale had frozen at least partially. Rebecca, Darla, and I spent the morning inside the greenhouse plucking mushy leaves off the plants. We hoped they'd survive if we excised the frozen parts.

"What a waste," Rebecca said, plucking off another ruined leaf and dropping it into a bucket.

"At least the goats will eat well today," Darla said.

"Yeah, but what are we going to eat?" Rebecca's face reddened, and her hands started to tremble. "What if the storms only get worse? We could lose all the greenhouses at once. And even if the storms don't wreck the greenhouses, it's only getting colder. Will the greenhouses keep working? What if there's no spring next year? What if—"

"Rebecca." I grabbed her shoulders and gripped them gently. "Don't think like that. We'll make it."

"You don't know that. You can't know that. I keep thinking Mom and Dad are going to come back. I look down the driveway all the time, expecting to see them walking up, but they never come. Maybe they'll never return. Maybe they're dead. Maybe we'll die, too. Starve to death or freeze in this never-ending winter." Tears rolled from her eyes.

I pulled my sister into a hug. "We won't starve to death. Or freeze. And if Mom and Dad haven't shown up by spring, I'll go find them. I promise."

Rebecca was sobbing now. Darla stepped up beside her and hugged us both.

Uncle Paul stopped his work and looked down at us through the clear plastic greenhouse roof. "You guys okay?" he shouted.

"Yeah, we're fine," I yelled back.

He nodded and returned to his work, stretching out to patch another hole. I heard him yell and glanced back up just in time to see his left foot slip, falling between the rungs of the ladder alongside the rafter. He overcorrected and fell, landing on the greenhouse roof with a whump and the pop of breaking plastic. The ladder twisted as he fell, violently wrenching free of Max's hands and hitting him in the side hard enough to knock him to the ground. Uncle Paul's left leg was trapped between the ladder and the rafter. I heard a nauseating crunch, like a bunch of celery stalks breaking at once, as Paul's leg snapped just below the knee. He was left dangling into the greenhouse between two rafters, held upside down by his broken leg.

Paul moaned, a sound that started low and pained but quickly grew into something approaching a scream. I shoved away from Rebecca and ran to him. Darla stood still for a second, taking in the ladder that had trapped Paul's leg and Max in the snow outside the greenhouse. Then she ran toward the greenhouse door.

The greenhouse roof was low enough that I could reach Paul. I grabbed his shoulders and tried to lift him to relieve the pressure on his snapped leg. It protruded from between the rafter and ladder at a sickening angle, as if he'd grown an extra knee in his shin, turned ninety degrees in the wrong direction. I couldn't see any blood on his jeans, so perhaps the bone hadn't come through his skin.

Darla reached Max just outside the greenhouse. He had jumped up and was wrestling with the ladder. Darla grabbed the ladder and helped, trying to force it sideways off the rafter to free Paul's leg.

Uncle Paul screamed as the ladder shifted. Sweat rolled off his face and splashed against my cheek below him. Darla and Max heaved on the ladder again, and Paul's leg popped free. He fell, and I tried to catch him. Rebecca was there, too, reaching up to grab him, but he fell through our arms and landed with a thud amid the kale.

I knelt by his head. He was sweating, panting, and shivering—all at the same time. "I think he's in shock!" I yelled. "Get a bunch of blankets. And two poles we can use to make a stretcher." Darla and Max ran toward the house. I noticed Max was holding his left side where the ladder had slammed into him. Rebecca looked at me, and I said, "I'll stay with him. Go get Aunt Caroline." She nodded and ran for the greenhouse door.

"Hang in there," I told Uncle Paul. "Help is coming." He moaned, and I squeezed his hand.

Less than a minute passed before Darla, Max, and Rebecca ran back into the greenhouse with Aunt Caroline and Anna in tow. They had armloads of blankets and two long poles left over from constructing the greenhouses. Aunt Caroline cringed when she saw the unnatural angle of her husband's leg, and Anna turned away, burying her face in her mother's side. Darla spread out the largest blanket and folded it over the poles, forming a makeshift stretcher.

"We should splint that leg before we move him," Darla said.

"Wouldn't we have to straighten it out first?" I said.

"Don't do that," Caroline said. "You might make it worse."

"We'll have to set the bone at some point," Darla said.

"No. I want Doc McCarthy to do it," Caroline insisted.

"He's in Warren?" Darla asked.

"Yes."

"Let's just get him inside for now." I moved down to Uncle Paul's broken leg and slid one hand under his knee and the other under his calf, just below the break. "I'll try to hold the break still. Everyone else grab on. We'll slide him over onto the stretcher."

When everyone was in position, I called out, "On three. One . . . two . . . three!" We slid Paul onto the stretcher. I tried my best to hold his leg steady, but I heard the bones grind against each other. He grabbed my arm, clutching so tightly it hurt.

We spread two blankets over the top of the stretcher and carried it slowly to the house. Uncle Paul moaned as we lowered him to the living room floor in front of the fireplace. Anna got a pillow off the couch and tucked it under his head.

"Put the pillow under his good leg," Darla said. "He's in shock, so we want to elevate his legs, but we probably shouldn't disturb the broken one until we get it splinted." Anna moved the pillow.

"I don't have any idea how to splint that," Aunt Caroline said, staring at the break.

"We're going to have to set and splint it to get him all the way to Warren," Darla said.

"No," Aunt Caroline said. "I'll go to town and get Doc McCarthy. I'm sure he'll come—he's been our family doctor forever."

Uncle Paul's hand shot out from beneath the blankets and seized her ankle. "No. Fix the greenhouse." His voice sounded thin and breathy.

"We can worry about that after we get your leg fixed, honey."

"No. The greenhouse is the top priority. We can't afford to lose the kale."

"Taking care of your leg is the top priority." Aunt Caroline's lips were pressed together in a determined line.

"I swear to God, if someone doesn't get out there and fix that greenhouse right now—" Uncle Paul let out an involuntary moan and scrunched his eyes closed, "I'll crawl out of here and do it myself."

"I'll get the doctor," I said. "I can probably run most of the way to Warren."

Aunt Caroline sighed. "Okay, take Max with you. He knows where the doctor's office is."

"Can you run?" I asked Max.

"Yeah," he said. "My side hurts, but I think it's just bruised."

"Take Darla, too," Aunt Caroline said. "It will be safer with three if you run into any problems. Anna, you take care of Dad. Build the fire higher in here—we want to keep him warm. And get him some water. Rebecca, you and I will try to fix the greenhouse."

"Work from inside, on a stepladder," Darla said. "It'll be safer."

I had already turned away, heading for the kitchen. I grabbed a backpack, a water bottle, a knife, some dried meat, and a half-full book of matches. In seconds, Darla, Max, and I were jogging down the road toward Warren.

FEMA hadn't cleared the road after the last storm, but only a few inches of snow had fallen, so it wasn't difficult to run along the road. Just a little slick. We ran for about ten minutes, then took a breather, walking fast for a few minutes before breaking into a run again.

We covered the distance to Warren in record time, less than an hour. Nobody was out on the streets, but it was cold enough that anyone sensible would stay inside. Max led us to a low building on the south side of town. The sign out front read: FAMILY HEALTH.

Inside the office, a line of people snaked through the waiting room, past the reception desk, and through the door that led to the exam rooms. Almost everyone in the line was either a kid or elderly, although some of the kids had parents with them. It was almost as cold inside the office as it had been outside; everyone was bundled in hats, gloves, and heavy coats. An oil lamp on a table in the middle of the waiting room provided what little light there was.

"Where's the doctor?" I asked the guy at the back of the line. He gestured toward the front. I hurried forward, pushing past the people standing in the door to the exam rooms.

"Hey, end of the line's back there!" someone yelled.

"Emergency, sorry," I said.

Past the door, the line broke into two, leading into adjacent exam rooms. I ducked into the closest one. Another oil lamp burned on the desk at one side of the room. The guy on the exam table had a face corrugated by age and was wearing an old-fashioned Elmer Fudd hat with earflaps. The guy standing in front of him was younger and bundled up tightly against the cold, but he had a miniature flashlight and was shining it into the first guy's mouth, so I assumed he was the doctor.

"My uncle broke his leg," I said. "We need help."

"Hold on, son," the doctor replied. "I'm almost done here." He peeled his patient's lower lip back. It was spotted with deep purple bruises and blood filled the spaces between the guy's teeth. The doctor reached into a drawer and pulled out what looked like a plastic bag of Froot Loops. "Take these and stop back next week."

"Thanks, Jim." The patient slid off the exam table, took the Froot Loops, and left.

"Okay. Now tell me about your uncle."

I rushed through the story of Uncle Paul's fall from the top of the greenhouse.

"Is it a compound fracture?" the doctor asked.

"What?"

"Is the bone sticking through his skin?"

"I don't think so, but we didn't take his pants off."

"Hmm. Okay, follow me." The doctor plucked the oil lamp off the desk and left the exam room. In the hall he yelled, "Belinda! I'm leaving for a trauma call."

A woman's voice came from the open door of the other exam room. "Crap, it's going to take me all night to finish this line by myself."

"It's just a fracture. I should be back in time to help you finish up." The doctor ducked through another door and started stuffing supplies into an old-fashioned, black leather doctor's bag.

When he finished, I turned to head back toward the waiting area.

"Car's in back." The doctor turned the other way.

"You have a car?" I asked as we followed him.

"It's not really mine, but yeah." The doctor opened the back door, letting daylight and a cold breeze into the hall. He blew out the lamp and left it on the floor just inside the door.

There was only one car in the parking lot—an antique sedan with a huge triangular front hood and big fenders humped up over its white-wall tires.

"Nice." Darla whistled appreciatively. "This is what you're driving?"

"Only car in town that runs decent," the doctor said. "Hop in."

There were no seatbelts in the car, but Dr. McCarthy drove so slowly that it didn't worry me much. Max gave him directions, and soon we were rolling down Stagecoach Trail back toward the farm.

"So what is this thing?" Darla asked. "It looks kinda like a '39 Ford I saw once."

"It's a Studebaker," Dr. McCarthy said. "'41 Champion."

"Beautiful car. But I thought all doctors drove Mercedes—" Darla said.

"No, Beamers," Dr. McCarthy snorted. "I had one. After the ashfall started, the ambulance couldn't make it here from Galena. So I used my BMW. Ash got in the air intakes and tore up the engine. Pretty much all the cars in town were wrecked by the ashfall. Gale Shipman kept this beauty in his garage under a tarp. Man, he was mad when the mayor told him he had to lend it to me. I don't know if he'll ever speak to either of us again."

"What in the world were you giving that guy at the clinic?" I said. "It looked like . . . Froot Loops?"

"Yep, Kellogg's Froot Loops," Dr. McCarthy said.

"Why?"

"We ran out of Special K."

"Never heard of a doctor prescribing breakfast cereal," I said.

"I work with what I have. All those people in the clinic have scurvy—it's caused by vitamin C deficiency. We're all going to get it if we can't find anything to eat other than pork. It simply manifests in children and seniors first."

"And breakfast cereal has vitamin C?"

"Yep, exactly. We found a whole truckload of it abandoned up on Highway 11. I'd have preferred a truckload of multivitamins, but I'll take what I can get. Don't know what we'll do when we run out, though."

"How is it that you've got pork to eat?" Darla asked.

"Factory hog farms. There were three of them near Warren. Had better than ten thousand head of hogs. Whole town pitched in to butcher them and preserve the meat. Still, most of it would have spoiled if we hadn't gotten this cold weather so early. Saved our bacon, so to speak."

Darla groaned. "At least you don't have to worry about getting enough to eat."

"You don't have to worry, either," Max said. "We've only run out of food twice, and that was before you got here and built the corn grinder."

"Yeah," Darla said, "But with your dad hurt, we won't be able to dig up as much corn. And losing that greenhouse—"

"It'll be okay," I said. I didn't want Max to worry about the food situation, although truthfully, I was a bit worried myself.

"Turn here," Max said, and Dr. McCarthy cranked the wheel over, turning down Canyon Park Road. A few minutes later we stopped in the road in front of the farm's driveway. We had only shoveled one path in the snow from the house to the road, nowhere near wide enough for the Studebaker. All four of us jogged down the driveway toward the house. Aunt Caroline and Rebecca left the damaged greenhouse and joined us.

Uncle Paul's skin was gray and sweaty. Anna had cut off his left pant leg. Livid bruises blotched his leg around the break, and it was grotesquely lumpy, but there was no blood. Dr. McCarthy knelt by his leg and examined it for a moment.

"How's it look, Jim?" Uncle Paul asked.

"Not bad. Wish I could X-ray the break, but I think it should set fine."

"Good, good." Uncle Paul exhaled heavily.

"I'll get to work, then. Now the good news is that I still have some fiberglass casting tape."

"What's the bad news?"

"We've been out of painkillers for weeks."

"I was afraid of that."

"I need a pail of water."

"I'll get it," Anna offered.

Dr. McCarthy took a thin stick wrapped in leather from his bag. The leather was dented and scarred with tooth marks. A deep frown creased Uncle Paul's face, but he reached up and took the stick from the doctor, put it in his mouth, and chomped down.

"Let's have the adults hold his arms and legs," Dr. McCarthy said. "The less he moves around, the better."

I wasn't sure who he meant at first. Aunt Caroline knelt and took hold of one of her husband's arms. Dr. McCarthy was looking at me, so I grabbed my uncle's other arm.

"Who's the strongest?" Dr. McCarthy asked.

"Alex," Darla said.

"Darla," I said.

"Well, one of you should hold his left leg above the break. I need it immobilized while I set the bone."

"You do it," I told Darla.

Darla held Uncle Paul's thigh, and Max grabbed his unbroken leg. Dr. McCarthy gently ran the fingers of his left hand along the break. With his right, he took a firm grip on Uncle Paul's ankle. A low moan escaped Uncle Paul's lips around the stick. Rebecca and Anna stood to one side, holding hands and watching.

"Everyone ready?"

I nodded.

Dr. McCarthy pulled back on the ankle, straining with the effort. Uncle Paul screamed, a trumpeting sound muffled by the leather-wrapped stick locked in his teeth. All his muscles clenched, and I had to lean forward, using both hands and all my weight to keep his arm forced against the floor. His face turned into a flaming rictus mask of pain. Even over his scream, I could hear the bones grind as Dr. McCarthy straightened his leg.

The scream ended abruptly and Uncle Paul's arm went slack in my hands. "Check his breathing! Make sure his airway is clear," Dr. McCarthy ordered.

I bent lower and put my cheek against his mouth. I felt a puff of breath against my skin. "He's breathing fine." I put my fingers against his neck. "Pulse feels strong."

"Okay, good." Dr. McCarthy had straightened the leg and was wrapping it in a cloth bandage.

Aunt Caroline swayed. I grabbed her upper arm. "You okay?" I asked.

"A little woozy," she said.

"You should lie down." I helped her stretch out on the couch.

Dr. McCarthy ripped open a foil packet and removed a bright purple strip of fiberglass tape. He dunked the tape in water and wrapped it around the break, over the cloth bandages. Darla helped, holding Uncle Paul's leg off the floor to make it easier to wrap. Dr. McCarthy wrapped three more strips of fiberglass tape over the bandages, completely immobilizing the leg and ankle.

"That should do it," Dr. McCarthy said as he repacked his bag. "If you see any red streaks or if the leg starts to smell bad, come get me again. Aspirin or willow bark tea would help with the swelling, if you can manage it."

"Thanks for coming," I said. "How do we pay you?"

"Pay me with whatever you can. I need medical supplies, gas, lamp oil, batteries, flashlights, candles, and the like. Vitamin C tablets are worth more than gold, on account of the scurvy. Food would be welcome also, so long as it's not pork. Only reason I've been able to keep practicing is that folks have been so generous. Some of them even bring supplies when they're not sick."

Uncle Paul was still unconscious, and Aunt Caroline's eyes were closed. "I'll get some supplies," I said.

I went to the kitchen and gathered a dozen duck eggs, two small goat cheeses, a bag of cornmeal, and some kale. "This is all we can spare right now," I said when I returned to the living room. "We'll bring more stuff later."

"That'll be fine." Dr. McCarthy pulled a purple leaf out of the bag. "Is this kale?"

"Yeah. The greenhouses are too cold to grow anything else."

"It's a member of the cabbage family, right?"

"I think so," Darla said.

"And none of you have scurvy?"

"I don't think so," I said.

Dr. McCarthy reached toward my mouth. "Mind if I look?"

"No, go ahead."

He peeled back my lower lip and looked at my teeth. Then he repeated the process with my upper lip. "No sign of scurvy at all. I bet that kale is loaded with vitamin C. How much of it do you have?"

"Not enough. That storm last night ripped up one of the greenhouses, and a bunch of it froze. It's all mushy—really only good for the goats."

"No, no, no. Mushy or not, it'll treat scurvy fine."

"I didn't feed the goats yet," Rebecca said. "I'll go get the buckets of frozen kale."

"Now look," Darla said, "we appreciate your help, and we'll give you all the kale we can spare, but we've got to eat, too. We don't have a lot of extra food—we need most of the kale ourselves."

"That's no problem," Dr. McCarthy said. "We've got plenty of pork in town. I'm sure the mayor will agree to give you all the pork you need in return for your kale."

"We'll trade," Darla said, "ten pounds of pork for one pound of kale."

"Darla," I whispered. "He said he'd keep us supplied with pork. And we should help out, anyway."

"What if the greenhouses fail?" she hissed back. "We need to have a supply of stored food in case something goes wrong."

I nodded. "Okay," I said out loud. "We'll give you all the kale we can now as payment for your help, and then as we harvest more, we'll trade it for pork."

"I'll have to confirm it with the mayor, but that sounds fine," Dr. McCarthy said. "Why don't you ride back to town with me, and I'll set you up with as much pork as you can carry. Call it a down payment for future kale harvests."

We gathered up all the kale we had: two five-gallon buckets of frozen leaves and four bags of good stuff. I got our three biggest backpacks, and Max, Darla, and I squeezed into the Studebaker for the ride back to town.

Dr. McCarthy drove us to a huge metal building north of town. The sign over the door read: WARREN MEAT PACKING. A wiry guy sat on a metal folding chair in front of a small fire just outside the main door. A shotgun rested on his knees.

"Hey, Stu," Dr. McCarthy called as we walked up. "Need to trade some pork for medical supplies. I'll go down to the mayor's office and get you the paperwork as soon as we're done."

"Aw, Jim, you know you're supposed to bring the paperwork first." The guard shrugged and handed Dr. McCarthy a key. "But you may as well go ahead. He always approves your trades, anyway."

"Thanks, Stu." Dr. McCarthy unlocked the door and ushered us inside.

Pork gleamed pink in the light filtering in through the open door. The plant was packed with hundreds, maybe thousands, of frozen hog carcasses hanging from the ceiling. Shelves lined the walls, filled to overflowing with pink hams, white loins, and huge slabs of uncut bacon.

"Take as much as you can carry," Dr. McCarthy said. "I'll weigh it for the paperwork, and you can pay in kale later."

My mouth hung open, watering as I imagined that bacon sizzling in a pan. The slaughterhouse held enough pork to feed the small town of Warren for years—enough to feed our family forever. And Dr. McCarthy hadn't hesitated when Darla proposed trading one pound of kale for ten of pork. All our work building and tending the greenhouses had paid off. Our kale, loaded with vitamin C, was more valuable than gold. Food represented wealth in the post-eruption world, as surely as a bank vault stuffed with one-hundred-dollar bills had represented wealth in the old world.

Darla must have been thinking something similar. She turned and hugged me, her face lit by a smile of the sort I'd rarely seen since we left Worthington—since her mother had died.

Thinking about Mrs. Edmunds turned my happiness bittersweet. I stretched to kiss Darla's forehead, then disentangled myself and stepped outside to clear my head.

The western sky glowed with a dim, yellow-gray light. I stared at the horizon as if I could see back to the start of my journey in Cedar Falls, 140 miles to the west. I thought about all the people I'd met who were worse off than we were, struggling just to survive: the refugees at Cedar Falls High, the people of Worthington, Katie's mom and her kids, the inmates at the FEMA camp. And wandering somewhere among them, my mom and dad.

Maybe one day my parents would trudge up the driveway to my uncle's farm. But if they didn't, Darla and I would go find them. With Uncle Paul injured, we couldn't leave anytime soon, because even more of the farm work would fall to us. But I'd made a promise to myself before I'd left Cedar Falls: not just to get to Warren, but to find my family. A promise I planned to honor.

Darla stepped beside me and wrapped an arm around my waist. Despite my worries about Mom and Dad, I felt strangely hopeful. Even in the icy wind, the warmth of Darla's body against mine felt like spring.

Author's Note

There is a colossal volcano under Yellowstone National Park. The volcano's caldera, or crater, is visible in some places as a ring of cliffs and measures roughly 34 by 45 miles. It has erupted three times in the last 2.1 million years, events so powerful they are usually classified as supervolcanoes. The largest of these eruptions released about 2,500 times as much magma as the 1980 Mount St. Helens eruption.

It's often said that the Yellowstone volcano is "due" for another eruption, since the last three were 640,000, 1.3 million, and 2.1 million years ago,

respectively. Actually, it's extremely unlikely that the volcano will explode in our lifetime. The eruption preceding
the last three was 4.2 million years ago, so the regularity
of the most recent events is deceptive.

The problem with writing a book set in the aftermath
of a volcanic supereruption is that no supervolcano has
exploded in recorded human history. So in describing it, I've
had to make do with scientific speculation and accounts of
survivors of normal, or Plinian, eruptions such as Mount
St. Helens in Washington State and Krakatoa in Indonesia.

For example, early in this book, Alex's house is hit
with a piece of rock thrown 900 miles by the volcano at
supersonic speed. Plinian volcanoes don't do this; all the
heavy material they eject falls near the volcano's vent, and
only the much lighter ash travels farther. Some scientists
believe supervolcanoes behave differently, blasting chunks
of rock on ballistic trajectories from deep pipes in the
lithosphere (the solid part of the earth consisting of the
crust and outer mantle), but this view is controversial.

The loudest sound in recorded history was probably
Krakatoa's eruption on August 27, 1883 in Indonesia.
That eruption was audible almost 3,000 miles away on the
island of Diego Garcia in the Indian Ocean. There, it
sounded like the roar of heavy artillery for several hours.
Yet the Yellowstone supereruption 2.1 million years ago
was about 120 times more forceful than Krakatoa's blast.

The ashfall I've depicted in the book is similar to what
Yellowstone released 2.1 million years ago. This amount
of ash would have darkened the skies for months, possibly
years, and caused a global volcanic winter lasting a

minimum of three years. Ash particles are tiny and electrically charged, so they are often associated with lightning storms. They can also cause odd weather effects, usually abnormally heavy precipitation in the short term, followed by years of drought.

No one knows exactly how much warning we'd get before an eruption at Yellowstone. It's possible it could happen suddenly, but more likely there would be years of earthquakes and topographical changes to warn us. Whether we'd prepare adequately, even if given enough warning, is another question, of course.

If you'd like to read more about the science behind *Ashfall*, the following books are a good start:

Supervolcano: The Ticking Time Bomb Beneath Yellowstone National Park by Greg Breining. MBI Publishing, 2007. Provides an excellent overview of the history and geology of Yellowstone. Includes an account of major volcanic events that have impacted humans and speculates about the possible consequences of a Yellowstone supereruption.

Supervolcano: The Catastrophic Event that Changed the Course of Human History by John Savino, Ph.D. and Marie D. Jones. Career Press, 2007. Contains information on supervolcanoes around the world, including Yellowstone (Wyoming), Long Valley (California), and Toba (Indonesia). Chapter 10 is an interesting fictional account of a future supereruption at the Long Valley volcano.

Krakatoa: The Day the World Exploded, August 27, 1883 by Simon Winchester. HarperCollins, 2003. An exhaustive and beautifully written account of the biggest modern Plinian eruption.

Catastrophe: An Investigation into the Origins of the Modern World by David Keys. Ballantine, 1999. Describes how a volcanic event in 535 A.C.E. changed civilizations across the globe. Very useful for considering the possible political, social, and epidemiological consequences of a supervolcano.

Acknowledgments

First and foremost, my thanks go to my mother and father, Shirley and Stan Mullin. Without their unwavering support, *Ashfall* would not exist. I'm also grateful to Helen-Louise Boling for her feedback on *Ashfall* and for being the good kind of mother-in-law.

Thank you to Ian Strickland, who showed me *Ashfall* through a teen's eyes and boosted my confidence, and to Dorothy Menosky, who showed me *Ashfall* through a teacher's eyes and boosted my humility. It is a better novel for their input.

To everyone at Critique Circle who gave feedback on pieces of this novel (Angela Ackerman,

Ardyth, Vicky Bates, Darla Davis, Liam Deihr, Karla Gomez, Gorse_wine, Greenguy, Molly Hart, Katy, Helen Kitson, Audrey Koudelka, Andrea Mack, Martha 2150, Memyselfi, Shannon O'Farrell, Quotelover, Sky, Tamamushi, and Elizabeth Taylor), thank you. I also appreciated the generous advice Jim McCarthy offered, if not the rejection that accompanied it. *Ashfall* improved dramatically due to his insight.

I'm grateful to Pete Matthews and Erin Stoesz, who volunteered their geology expertise to ferret out scientific errors in *Ashfall*. Any errors that remain are mine alone.

I owe my publisher and editor, Peggy Tierney, an unpayable debt for her steadfast belief in *Ashfall* and patience with me as we worked to make it the best book it could be. I came to dread her emails that read, "Could you rewrite the ending, just one more time?" But she knew exactly what the novel needed, and the blame falls on me for taking six tries to get it right.

Lisa Rojani Buccieri did a masterful job editing *Ashfall* . . . twice! I've placed the only exclamation point in these acknowledgments in her honor. She made my writing better than I believed it could be. Thanks to Dorothy Chambers for saving me from unspeakable embarrassment. To Ana Correal, who brought the emotional subtext of *Ashfall* to life through her cover art, thank you. I also appreciated the help Gabe Tierney offered in regard to the first chapter and cover.

Mrs. Parker and Mr. Wesson at Indianapolis ATA Black Belt Academy showed nearly superhuman patience and perseverance in teaching me the taekwondo that became such an important part of *Ashfall*. Thank you both.

Thank you to my brother, Paul Mullin, for his help with Darla's Macgyver moments. Also thank you to Paul, Caroline, Max and Anna for teaching me about goats, ducks, and greenhouse farming.

A huge thank you to Larry Endicott, who is such a brilliant photographer that even I look good in his camera lens. Thanks also to Mab Graves, who provided cheerleading and much needed help with artistic questions.

I've been thrilled and humbled by the support of the authors, booksellers, librarians, and teachers who read *Ashfall* and offered advance praise: Charles Benoit, Cinda Williams Chima, Carol Chittenden, Robert Michael Evans, Michael Grant, Carl Harvey, Kathy Hicks-Brooks, Christine Johnson, Saundra Mitchell, David Patneaude, Richard Peck, and Dave Richardson.

And most of all, thank you Margaret: my wife, first reader, best friend, and true love.

About the Author

Photo by Larry Endircott

Mike Mullin's first job was scraping the gum off the undersides of desks at his high school. From there, things went steadily downhill. He almost got fired by the owner of a bookstore due to his poor taste in earrings. He worked at a place that showed slides of poopy diapers during lunch (it did cut down on the cafeteria budget). The hazing process at the next company included eating live termites raised by the resident entomologist, so that didn't last long either. For a while Mike juggled

465

bottles at a wine shop, sometimes to disastrous effect. Oh, and then there was the job where swarms of wasps occasionally tried to chase him off ladders. So he's really hoping this writing thing works out.

Mike holds a black belt in Songahm Taekwondo. He lives in Indianapolis with his wife and her three cats. *Ashfall* is his first novel.

COMING IN OCTOBER 2012

sequel to *Ashfall*

Visit www.tanglewoodbooks.com
to read an excerpt.